SHOCKING TRUE STORY

GREGG OLSEN

TABLE OF CONTENTS

BONUS CHAPTERS

Empty Coffin Series

AUTHOR'S NOTE

BOOK IDEAS ARE BORN IN ANY NUMBER OF WAYS. Some come to authors in a burst of happenstance and, even, brilliance. Some come in the throes of a good dream. A few, I'm told, come from God. I have never been so lucky. My books have always been born of the truth. The one you are holding is one of those. I am a writer of true crime, a much-maligned genre, but one in which I felt I could stake a claim for a respectable career. It seemed that there were a million stories out there that—given some shaping and research—might make for interesting reading. The ideas come from television, prisoners who write to me, fans that show up at book signings (though I can't say I have enough of those to provide much of a stockpile) and, of course, newspapers and the internet.

Shocking True Story is different. This is a story hatched from my own experiences; my own life.

About a year ago my wife, Valerie, retrieved a carton under our bed amid rolls of Christmas wrapping paper and white and brown tufts of dog hair. She set the legal-size box with its ill-fitting, strapped-down lid next to the computer where I did most of my writing. She smiled reluctantly and said only three words.

"Honey, it's time."

I understood what she meant. I knew it even if she had said nothing. I had tried to avoid the idea of telling the story contained in the beat-up box. I had resisted it for all the right reasons, though deep down I knew it was beyond my ability to do so. Beyond my need. Beyond the necessity of supporting my family.

I had a dozen such boxes in various spots in my house. In the garage, too. Three that had been stacked and draped with a cheery chintz fabric passed as a bedside table in the guest room. Those contained Renata's story, one about a woman who had killed her husband for insurance money. They held her entire life in three boxes, including her video-store card, her purse (a blue and white nautical shoulder bag) and love letters to the man with whom she had conspired to commit the murder. I even had the convicted woman's Costco shopping lists (she loved salsa and chips) and a brush embedded with her Clairol Frivolous Fawn-dyed hair.

Each was a Pandora's Box of sorts, a repository in which I was the keeper, the curator of little murder boxes which held the remnants of the books I had written. Inside each were the unspeakable and the unbelievable. I had been writing true crime books for nearly a decade and the memorabilia I had collected was suitable for a murder museum, if such a place existed. I had Christmas cards from Pamela Smart; a signed page of sheet music from Charles Manson. I even had a sketch by John Wayne Gacy (he was a better killer than artist, for sure). Inside each box of source material were numerous memories. All had been tagged with the name of the book that I had regarded as a potential bestseller.

The carton my wife put near my desk was labeled with the name of a story I started to write, but was never destined to complete: *Love You to Death.*

I took an X-acto knife from Val's art bin and sliced the silver duct tape I had used to seal the box. Even the tape rekindled a recollection of a terrible night not so long ago. The glint of silver. The flash of steel. A kind of coldness and fear I had never known before seized me once more. Some things, I know all too well, are too powerful to forget.

I pushed the lid aside and drank some coffee before looking inside. The contents were remarkable, not only in their diversity, but in their very familiarity. The top was blanketed by a green leotard, a Halloween costume worn by one of my twin daughters. A small but unmistakable crescent of blood had stained the garment's neckline.

I drank more coffee and pushed the green fabric aside. At first, I used a pencil to do so. Almost instantly, I felt clinical and foolish. Embarrassed. I was the little girl's father. Her blood was mine. I had carried her and her twin from the delivery room like two peachy footballs, one in each arm. I was the Daddy who saved her spit-up cloth because I knew that the smell would always remind me of my baby.

I gently folded the leotard and peered deeper into the box. The contents had come so close to being the province of someone else's collection; some other writer who made his or her living from the anguish of others. It had been too damn close. The interview tapes, the photos of the hard-bitten players in a ridiculous drama, a photocopy of a lineup of fingerprints that resembled a black and white rendering of five small beehives. Everything was in there. Everything that had nearly cost me all I held precious in my life—the lives of every member of my family, my freedom.

And so I agreed with Valerie. It *was* time. I fiddled with the yarn-covered pencil holder that little Teddy Bundy had made for his mom for Mother's Day in 1964 (I purchased it along with other personal belongings from the Bundy family's garage sale in 1989, after Ted was electrocuted in Florida for the murder of a schoolgirl). I had re-glued the uncoiling rainbow yarn twice before, as if keeping it intact somehow mattered.

I have always been fascinated by crime. I have always wondered what brings a child like Teddy Bundy to seek the dark side of murder. How a child, born seemingly perfect, is transformed into the embodiment of evil. Before the events took place in the book you are now holding, I pondered the *why* of a crime from a distance. A safe distance.

I'll never forget that summer day when the wheels of homicide had been set in motion, when my own story would eclipse the crime I was chronicling.

This is my story.

In Memory of June Rose Parker

CAST OF CHARACTERS

Kevin Ryan — *True-crime writer, Port Gamble resident*

Valerie Ryan — *Kevin's wife*

Taylor and Hayley Ryan — *Kevin and Valerie's twin daughters*

Hedda — *The Ryan family's dachshund*

Jeanne Morgan — *Kevin's top fan, website master*

Rita Adams — *Host of tabloid TV talk show*

J. Jackson — *Ellison County Coroner employee*

Muriel Constantine — *Riverstone Women's Prison public relations*

Martin Raines — *Pierce County Sheriff's detective*

Monica Maleng — *Tabloid TV producer*

Adena King — *Tabloid TV producer*

Gina, Carlton and Cecile — *The Ryans' "up the hill" neighbors*

Wanda-Lou Webster — *Sleazy true-crime writer*

Fred Ross — *Sleazy true-crime writer*

Ashlee — *Jerry Springer Show producer*

Susan — *Sales rep for Kevin's publisher*

C.J. Cunningham — *Seattle-area author*

Misty Dawn — *Seattle-area author*

Darlene Fulton — *Riverstone corrections officer*

Vernon Hess — *Riverstone chaplain*

Davidson — *Pierce County sheriff's deputy*

Mona/Moans-a-Lot — *Pierce County sheriff's deputy*

April Raines — *Wife of Martin Raines*

Kate O'Brien — *Kitsap Regional Library researcher*

David R. — *Maplewood employee*

Lynette Watson — *Maplewood nurse's aide*

Austin — *Jett's late boyfriend*

TIMBERLAKE

Jett Carter — *Daughter of Connie Carter, sister of Janet Lee Kerr, convicted of attempted murder*

Connie Carter — *Jett's mother, imprisoned at Riverstone*

Janet Lee Kerr — *Jett's sister, imprisoned at Riverstone*

Deke "Sugarbutt" Cameron — *Janet's boyfriend, victim of murder attempt*

Danny "Sugarbutt" Parker — *Janet's stooge, Deke's shooter*

Paul Kerr — *Janet's ex-husband*

Anna Cameron — *Deke's mother*

June Parker — *Danny's mother*

Melba Warinski — *Cameron shooting witness*

Andy Lowery — *Cameron shooting witness*

Buzz Carter — *Jett's late father*

Davy Parker — *Danny's brother*

Dwight Parker — *Danny's father*

Brian Jackson — *Friend of Danny Parker*

Lindy Kerr — *Janet's daughter, Jett's niece*

Liz Kerr — *Paul's wife*

Michelle McMahon — *Teenage friend of Janet Lee*

Jim Winston — *Friend of Deke Cameron*

BOOK I

MURDER MOST PERSONAL

*"Kevin, you even thought
that serial killer from Lincoln City was nice.
Serial killers are always nice until they get what they want."*
—*VALERIE RYAN*

Chapter One
Friday, July 5

I GAVE MY SLIGHTLY BALDING head a repeated shake. A good one. Back and forth like the last A-Rod bobble-head—before Madonna, before performance-enhancing drugs ruined his run at the all-time home run record—at a sports memorabilia fair. *Again*. I thought I'd be able to reconnect the synapses in my brain that I was sure were misfiring. I just didn't get it. I looked at the words printed out in pristine neatness by my laser printer. They were printed in Times New Roman, a crisp typeface known for starchy little serifs that saluted each word with definite preciseness. And the *sequence* of those words—they were arranged in an order of drama and truth.

What was going on here?

I considered the proposed book once more while the voice on the phone rambled on.

It was the tale of Amanda Winfield, a woman of murderous charms. The setting was good—a small town in the fir-blanketed foothills of the Cascade Mountains east of Seattle. The lead characters were benign on the surface—Amanda was a part-time kindergarten teacher; her lover, a laid-off newspaper reporter in charge of the *Family Life* section (since lost to budget cuts) at a mid-size suburban daily. The crime—unbelievable. With promises of sex, insurance money and more sex, beguiling Amanda convinced her not-so-secret reporter lover, at loose ends after the loss of his job, to kill two of her husbands, six years apart. *Two*. Not one, but *two*.

I thought it had all the elements of a true crime opus, a runaway best-seller.

I, it now seemed, was alone in that regard.

The editor's words over the phone continued to stupefy.

"If only she killed with a little more originality, more over-the-top."

The very idea hit me like a Frisbee in the back of the head. *Come again? What was this guy saying?* I stared once more at my opening chapter, the teaser to my proposed book. What kind of meaning was I supposed to find in his suggestion that murderess Amanda Winfield might have been a better book subject if she had offed her old man with a bow and arrow or maybe sliced his jugular with the crinkly metal edge of a tuna can lid? The fact was in the days of maybe-baby killers from Florida, the infectious outrage of Nancy Grace and other headline-chasing cable wonks, the Investigation: Discovery network, and *CSI*-inspired TV shows, truth was no longer interesting.

I wondered if this is where we had sunk. Murders were so commonplace that a good story had to rise to a level of outrageousness faster than a two-day-old corpse in a pond before it would make the basis for a good book. Because of O.J. The Innocent, Eric and Lyle "We Are Orphans!" Menendez, Casey "Tot Mom" Anthony, Scottie "The Hottie" Peterson and Drew "Not Related to Scott and Not Particularly Hot but Still a Killer" Peterson, the next crazed killer had to do something really off the hook, totally off the wall, to get the notice of a publisher. A good story, a *meaningful* story, had been replaced by the likes of *Lobster Boy Murders* and *any* maniac who ate flesh or held his family captive for at least a decade.

"Market's a little tough now," the book editor droned on.

It was true, a sea of black and white and red covers stare out from the true crime section like a penguin massacre. But was that my fault? Was it the fault of women like Amanda Winfield? Were the killers running the art department of every mass market true crime book publisher in New York? I didn't think so.

What I did think was that Amanda wanted her husbands (numbers two and three) out of the way so that she could be with her ex-reporter lover, who claimed he wanted to get into true crime himself. Husband No. 2, a geologist, was bludgeoned to death with a chunk of granite and husband No. 3, a fireman, was shot and torched.

Torched! The fireman was *torched*, I had reminded the book editor.

"There is some irony there, but it would have been better if Amanda had been a little more devious about it."

I couldn't believe what I had heard. *A little more devious?*

"Devious isn't screwing your lover ten minutes before sending him to kill your husband, with the promise of a blow job when he returns?"

"It is and it isn't," the editor said.

All I could do was drum my fingers on my mouse pad as I thought it all over while the young man, who lived in one of the most crime-ridden cities in the world, rambled on over the phone. He didn't get it. He just didn't get crime. This guy failed to understand that America extended beyond Manhattan, and true crime readers were interested in the shocking kind of murder among people they can relate to. It didn't have to be a greedy Boston socialite or a love-struck astronaut in diapers to strike a chord of interest among readers. The occupation didn't necessarily define the crime. Yet a preacher's wife who enlists two boys from the choir to kill, or a kindergarten teacher, like Amanda Winfield, who manipulates her lover—they are the people next door.

Middle America loved those kinds of killers.

"With Inside Edition*and* Dateline*out there you really have to have something on the edge to compete,"* the editor concluded before hanging up to take a more important call.

And so I sat there, two months from financial ruin with the hope that I'd find the right story in time to get my twin daughters braces, pay the mortgage, have my wife's hair highlighted and keep the gas tank reasonably full.

I scanned the pages of *USA Today*. I flipped through back issues of *People*. I surfed through everything from CNN.com to TMZ.com. I Googled. I pawed through letters postmarked from San Quentin to Huntsville and every correctional facility in between. Envelopes were decorated with multicolored pen depictions of flowers and ferns, deer and tears. Prisoners spent as much time inking the outside of their envelopes as they did composing the contents held inside. Some weren't bad, at least insofar as their artwork was concerned. Most were, well, criminal.

I thought about putting the Amanda Winfield book out myself. Self-publishing was huge, now that a quarter of all books sold were electronic editions, now that Kindles and Nooks and Kobos and iPads could be found on every ferry and in every coffee shop. I let my mind run wild with it for a moment. I'd put it up on Amazon—the new center of the book universe—and make 70 percent on every sale! I'd design my own cover! I'd promote it on Facebook and Twitter and Goodreads! I'd do blog tours! I'd work my media contacts! The word-of-mouth would be huge! Editors like that little twerp in Manhattan would beg me to sign with them!

Then I thought about the cost of libel insurance. The *prohibitive* cost of libel insurance. Which every true crime writer had to have. Publishing true crime without legal cover—the kind publishers provided—was like going grocery shopping in the nude. You just couldn't get away with it.

Moving right along...

I'd sleep on it. I'd agonize over it. I just wanted a good crime. Was that too much to ask?

Something else was on my mind. *It*. I kept it under my desk blotter. I couldn't even call it a letter. Just *it*. I had read it only once, which seemed enough given that its content was fairly direct. I remember picking through the stack of bills and opening it at the post office, thinking it was a fan letter. Like I got that many. Instead, it was a single sheet of paper with letters cut from magazines and newspapers and pasted down like some kind of

18

ridiculous ransom note, the kind a deranged scrapbooker might fashion:

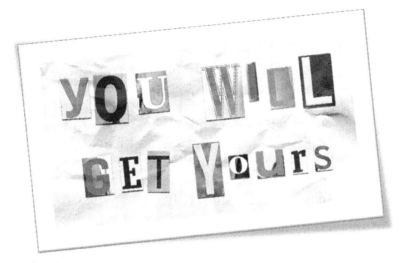

Although I put crafty nutcase's note away, the implied threat never really left my mind.

♦

SUNDAY AFTERNOON, JULY 7, WAS HOT and the girls were restless. Fireworks littered the roadway, and the acrid smell of gunpowder still hung in the air. From our kitchen window I watched an eagle return to a snag that he had wisely abandoned the day of the Fourth of July festivities. The cracked-mirror surface of Puget Sound reflected through the soft branches of fir and cedar trees like a store searchlight. Valerie had gone to work and I had to get our girls occupied with something so I could rifle through my old-school, battle-scarred Rolodex and get on with my work. But no DVD would satisfy. Nor a game of Scrabble, which they usually loved. No suggestion for an outside activity would pull eleven-year-olds Taylor and Hayley from my peripheral vision so that I could get busy. I broke down and let them watch MTV while I made an early lunch.

"Later, we'll have a discussion, girls, on why pole-dancing in a wet T-shirt is demeaning to women," I said.

19

Both rolled their eyes before turning full attention to the manic cut-with-a-shredder video flashing on the screen.

While the microwave resuscitated macaroni and cheese, the horn affixed to my front door sounded. The previous owner despised doorbells and instead installed a bicycle horn to announce the arrival of friends and family. It was a dumb idea, but in the years we lived in Port Gamble, Washington, I had grown used to the dumb and different. Especially when we bought House 19, the oldest and creakiest of the original nineteenth-century row houses built for mill management. The mill had died, however, and sometimes I was convinced our house wasn't far behind, with all its leaks, drafts, groans, and creaks. None of which I could afford to fix.

Before answering the horn, I went to the freezer and grabbed three Mr. Freeze pops, tossed two at my girls, and hid the other behind my back.

"Any other blues, Dad?" Taylor asked, lifting her head off the floor and away from the television for the first time since I had given in to MTV.

"No," I lied, as I shoved the blue frozen bar into my back pocket. "Only orange."

I hated orange. I also hated the idea that blue was called raspberry. I had never seen a blue raspberry in my entire life. Red, yes. Even gold once on an episode of the Food Network's *Barefoot Contessa*. Never blue. Blue raspberry, I was sure, was the malicious invention of a misguided chemist at the FDA.

Maybe there was a culinary true crime book somewhere in that?

I looked at my calendar for next day. Coffee with Jeanne Morgan was on tap.

Good old Jeanne.

♦

Forty miles away a woman logged on to the Prime Crime chat room, as she did nearly every day at that precise time. Chat rooms were becoming old school in the Facebook-is-the-center-of-the-universe era, but this one had a dedicated following and was still going strong. She sipped her diet Coke through a plastic straw and picked at some edamame, her favorite snack, in a white porcelain bowl. She scanned the roster to see who was online, and before she could finish reviewing the list, a window popped open on the screen of her Dell laptop.

Crimeguy: *Hi.*

KEVFAN: *Hi yourself.*

Crimeguy: *Tomorrow's the big day, right?*

KEVFAN: *Yes! Kevin and I are having coffee. I've sent him an e-mail telling him I have big news. That news is YOU, you know.*

Crimeguy: *No. Please don't tell him.*

KEVFAN: *Why not?*

Crimeguy: *I'm not ready. Please.*

KEVFAN: *I think he'd want to know. He's very caring.*

Crimeguy: *I know. But, please. I have more thinking to do.*

KEVFAN: *If U R sure.*

Crimeguy: *Yes. U R so nice. He is so lucky to have you supporting him.*

KEVFAN: *He's told me he can't live without me.*

Crimeguy: *Cool. Good to know.*

Chapter Two
Monday, July 8

Jeanne Morgan was my Number One fan, a designation that she arrived at with the assumption that there was actually some kind of ranking among my readership. I accepted it as a compliment and immediately embraced her as the archetypical true crime reader. Jeanne was in her sixties, had undergone a hip replacement, and wore her brassy, blonde-dyed hair in an updo that made her more Down and Out Librarian than Homecoming Queen.

Which, she had told me on at least a dozen occasions she actually *had been* some four decades ago.

Valerie thought Jeanne came from the *Misery* region of devoted reader territory, but I didn't mind. I liked her from the first moment she showed up at one of my "events," telling me all that I needed to know.

"I read your books."

Love it.

"You look younger in person."

Love it more.

She clinched the deal during an especially excruciating mall bookstore signing by telling me that her best friend Tobi-Shay had been murdered by a stranger. The case was still unsolved.

"I know you could do justice to the story, Mr. Ryan. You understand the pain and suffering of victims like no other true crime writer working today."

I wanted to tell her true pain came from the indignity of a mall signing, but I held my tongue.

"Maybe someday I will be able to tell your story." I stopped to correct my caring self. "I mean, *Tobi-Shay's* story. Do you mind getting me a latte?"

She didn't.

After that, there wasn't an event that Jeanne *didn't* attend. Latte in hand. Nodding at whatever I said. She created a Goodreads page for me, a Facebook group, and made sure that Oprah Winfrey's Next Chapter got an email whenever I had a new release.

"You never know," she said. "She might want something different."

I smiled at her. "Long shot, Jeanne. None of my books have an incest-survivor angle or push personal empowerment."

She smiled and titled her head. "You empower me."

If Valerie had been there her creep-meter would have clanked, but not mine. I liked Jeanne. I dedicated my last book to her:

For Jeanne Morgan, My Number One fan...

I write the wrongs because of readers like you.

Every few months, we'd have coffee. She'd tell me how great I was and I'd tell her how much I appreciated her support. We met ostensibly so she could show me what she was working on with her website promotions. But in reality, I just figured Jeanne was lonely. I'd looked at her websites every now and then, wondering how many "friends" I'd have if she hadn't been working the internet like a Liberian heir in search of a dim-bulb American with a bank account.

Jeanne was on the calendar for the next day for one of our get-togethers.

She e-mailed the night before: *I've got something BIG to tell you.*

AS SHE ALMOST ALWAYS DID, Jeanne Morgan posted a bulletin on Facebook: *Today I'm meeting with our favorite author. Will let you know more later.* Anyone who read the Jeanne's Kevin's Krime Blog knew that meant coffee at a Starbucks off Highway 16 in Gig Harbor, a town west of Tacoma, separated from the big city by the distinctive green-hued arching span of the Tacoma Narrows Bridge. Regular readers of Jeanne's blog knew that before schlepping over to Starbucks, Jeanne always bought a small houseplant for Valerie because "author's wives are people, too, and they deserve our support."

Valerie appreciated the gesture, of course. But frequently lamented the obvious.

"Jeanne thinks that I'm married to you as some kind of social work, Kevin. Like you need some—"

"Empowerment?" I asked.

Valerie shook her head. "More like a muse to inspire you to absorb the rhythm of blood spatter on a davenport or the lyrical way a knife slices a spinal cord."

I grinned. "I love it when you talk that way. You really get me."

Valerie made a face and threw her hands up into the air. "Yes, dear. This is art. Go to your real muse now."

That afternoon, I dropped off some shirts at the dry cleaner's, returned a few library books, and made my way to the Starbucks. I was late. I hate to be late for any "event" or meeting. It is so much easier to drink in the full dose of disappointment when one arrives early and can sit there for every agonizing minute. While the barista steamed and swirled, I searched the throng of hipsters and suburbanites for Jeanne, but she wasn't stuffed into one of the big brown velvet chairs that she usually commanded like a throne. She wasn't anywhere to be seen. A call to her cell phone went to voice mail.

The minutes ticked by. Then a half hour.

Jeanne, where are you? You're my Number One fan. I want to talk about Tobi-Shay. Really, really, I do!

24

I drove back home. No houseplant. No nothing.

♦

"How was Jeanne-O?" Val asked, using her irritating shorthand for Jeanne-the-Number-One, but it sounded like a brand of turkey. Val was propped up in bed reading a magazine, glasses halfway down the bridge of her nose. The magazine was some variety of home and garden porn with matching this and that, raffia here and there, lettuce in twenty colors. Our house and yard would never look anything like the images that coated the glossy stock.

"More like Jeanne No Show," I said.

Val flipped to the next page, an article about turning a wheelbarrow into an herb garden, and smiled at me. "You must be slipping. Maybe she's moved on to a vampire novelist?"

I dropped the rest of my clothes and slid next to her in bed. "Actually, I'm kind of worried. I thought she might have called or e-mailed, but nothing. I hope she's OK."

"Anyone who's stuck with you as long as Jeanne-O and I have is pretty tough, I'd say."

I nodded. She was right about that. Both were still waiting for that ship to come in. *Just when would it?*

Chapter Three

Tuesday, July 9

SHE STOOD IN THE DOORWAY. She looked to be fourteen. Her unkempt brunette hair was cut short and she wore little makeup, but her budding breasts indicated she was either a girl, or a boy in need of some kind of hormone therapy. Her wide-set eyes were dark brown, the size and shape of peach pits; her teeth were even and very white. She carried a DVD and a clear plastic purse. Inside the purse I could make out the following: two dollar bills, a Smashbox lip gloss (sheer raspberry), a wad of Kleenex, a set of car keys on a *Lord of the Rings* key chain, a pencil, and a tampon.

"Mr. Ryan?" she asked. "You don't know me. My name's Jett Carter. My mom has read all of your books. I'm starting one now. They're real good."

"How many has your mom read?" I inquired. I always asked, like some savvy telemarketer pre-qualifying a prospect. I always felt compelled to make sure it was me they had read and not another writer with the same last name, another writer far more successful than I.

"Four or five, I think," she answered without hesitation.

Good, I thought. I had published seven books and if she had said ten or some really outlandish number I knew she would have been knocking on the wrong door.

"What can I do for you?" I asked, a little guardedly.

"Mr. Ryan," she said, "my sister and my mother are in big trouble and they didn't do anything to deserve it."

I didn't invite her in. Valerie told me under no circumstances should I ever have someone in the house who had read any of my books or had the idea for a new one. "Could be a kook," she advised numerous times.

I told the girl that my carpets were just cleaned and she couldn't come inside. I walked out onto the step.

"Needs to dry. Some kind of chemical. Like dry cleaning," I said.

She nodded before she continued. "Well, like I was telling you, my sister and mother did not do what they're saying. And we think the only way justice is going to come out of this mess is if someone will write a book about it."

I studied her for a second. I asked if she had contacted other authors, perhaps the woman who is considered the Danielle Steel of true crime?

"Yeah, she was too busy with a miniseries or something. I talked with one of her assistants."

Assistants? My sole assistant was my dog, an utterly lazy dachshund that, when she felt like it, answered to Hedda. Hedda's winter job was to keep my feet warm while I typed on a Mac so old it was often mistaken for an early microwave oven. Her summer task was to eat whatever my girls dropped from their plates so that I didn't have to race the vacuum around five minutes before Val drove her "horizon gray" Honda Civic DX up the driveway.

"Passed on it, huh?" I asked, referring to the to the other author's lack of interest in the case.

"Yeah, I guess so."

I asked her to tell me more about the alleged crimes of her sister, Janet Lee Kerr and her mother Connie Carter.

The petite girl with the peach-pit eyes and sweet smile hedged. "You really ought to talk with them. They're at Riverstone. Watch this tape. It's from the *Rita* show."

Riverstone was the women's prison not far from my home. I considered it a convenience in the way some might consider a donut shop close to the office as handy. I had been to the prison many, many times. One woman I saw over the course of a six-month period had been convicted of molesting children in her day care. Lulu's Day Care was the name of her business. She was an attractive woman who had won me over with her charm. I decided that I couldn't write a book about Lulu's case because I had the feeling that she had been railroaded.

True crime books were seldom about the innocent.

I made sure I had Jett Louise Carter's telephone number and address, and promised if I was interested in the story, I'd call her for further information; otherwise I'd make arrangements to return her talk-show DVD.

"You won't be sorry for getting involved in this," she said over her shoulder as she walked to the driveway. "There's a real story here. Real injustice and stuff."

I smiled at her enthusiasm and waved as she drove off. As I made a mental note to ask her how she found our house, I felt something wet and cold against the back of my thigh. I had probably made a great impression: A Mr. Freeze that I had transferred to my back pocket melted and burst.

I patted my soggy blue butt with a paper towel and sat down at my computer, Googled my name, a ritual as entrenched as a morning latte (nonfat, one packet of Equal) and found the usual crap—people selling my books on eBay or Amazon for a penny (plus shipping) and 10,000 other references that didn't add up to much.

But this one was new. My name was mentioned in a true crime fan forum called House of Evil.

"I know where Kevin Ryan lives. I've even seen him in his yard. He'll get his. They all do. Hope he doesn't lurk here! LOL!"

It appeared I was as welcome in the House of Evil as Casey Anthony at a*Honey Boo Boo* taping.

28

I skipped the other stuff I usually searched for ad nauseum. At that moment, I didn't care one whit how many times my name popped up in China. The idea that someone hated me, knew where I lived was too much.

I couldn't wait to tell my family the news: *I finally had a stalker!*

♦

My joy was short-lived. The article on the screen of my laptop made my heart drop to my knees.

"Val! Come here!"

"What is it, Kev? Are the girls OK?"

I looked up from my computer as my wife hurried into the room. "Honey, they found a body in a wooded lot behind the Gig Harbor Safeway."

Valerie looked puzzled. "That's too bad. Does it say who it is?"

I started to read:

The body of a woman in her late fifties to early sixties was discovered behind the Safeway food store at 4831 Point Fosdick Dr. NW. by children picking blackberries....

Val leaned closer to the screen. "It can't be Jeanne."

"I know it is," I said.

...Store workers recovered identification that tied the woman to a van found in the parking lot overnight...

"You can't know for sure," Val said.

I clicked on the "enlarge photo" icon on the sole image that accompanied the article. It was a picture of a silver van.

A familiar one at that.

"It's Jeanne's all right," I said, touching my index finger to the spot on the screen that held all the little pixels that made up the back bumper of the van.

29

I PRAY FOR WHIRLED PEAS, read a bumper sticker.

Val compressed her brow. "I don't get it."

"Jeanne's a vegetarian. It's her van all right. I'd know it anywhere."

"I'm sorry. I wonder what happened to her?"

"Me, too," I said.

"You don't think she was murdered?"

I looked into Val's eyes. "I almost always think that of every death, so maybe. But really, the evidence always tells the truth."

Val put her hand on my shoulder. "I hope it isn't her, Kevin."

"I'll make some calls."

♦

The Ellison County Police were reasonably helpful. Cops usually are. They relayed the basics of their investigation and what they thought had happened. The dead body was found in a thicket of blackberries. She had no ID, no purse.

"She was picking berries when she passed out," he said. "She keeled over with Tupperware in hand. End of story."

"Meaning no investigation," I said.

The cop let out a sigh. "Look, I know you're a crime writer type and you'd like to embellish what happened to Ms. Morgan with a little drama, but there's nothing there. Tragedy. Case closed. Sorry about your friend, but if you want to do something for her go to the morgue and do the ID. She'll be cleaned up and ready around noon tomorrow."

I couldn't let it go.

"But what about her missing purse?"

"Someone probably took it after she dropped dead. Creeps like that everywhere, you ought to know considering the kind of books you write."

"OK, but why did you think the victim is Jeanne if there's no ID?"

"A barista at the Starbucks ID'd her van. She's a regular there. Trust me, nothing sinister here. Just another sad story."

I thanked the officer and hung up.

Tragedy. Nothing more. I felt sorry for Jeanne. I'm sure that given her true crime reading habits, she'd have wanted much, much more.

I Mapquested the morgue and set the printout on my desk. I'd watch Jett Carter's DVD first thing in the morning, then head down to see My Number One fan on a slab.

Full day I had planned.

♦

Before I went upstairs to crawl in bed with Val, I did a little Net surfing. I fought hard to make sure that I didn't get sucked into the search engine where one click becomes one thousand. Just enough to feed my sorry obsession and maybe to forget a little about Jeanne on ice at the morgue.

TODAY'S LIST

Google: Nothing new about me. Not even on the low rent turf of the internet — the blogosphere where everybody with a laptop and a pot of coffee is the next Drudge or Perez.

Crime case in the news with the most hits: Patty Ward, a former Miss STP motor oil pinup, was found murdered in her West Hollywood apartment. She'd been submerged in a bathtub of motor oil, her winnings from the pageant. Suspect in custody: her jealous ex-boyfriend.

Possible book title: *Slippery When Dead.*

Amazon ranking for backlist: No movement. Not up. Not down. My career was flatlining.

Shopping list: Extra interview tapes for the mini-cassette recorder. Flowers for Jeanne.

Chapter Four
Wednesday, July 9

LIKE MY COMPUTER, MY DUAL VCR/DVD PLAYER WAS A RELIC gasping its last breath. Our daughters had used it as an oven for frosted strawberry Pop-Tarts when they were four. And though it had been resuscitated at the repair shop, it was on its last legs. I could not afford a new one, nor afford to get TiVo or Slingbox or Netflix or Amazon Prime or whatever new digital convenience was flooding the market like the latest Justin Timberlake album. With the visitor gone and a DVD I wanted to play, I told Taylor and Hayley they could dehydrate some watermelon or make some turkey jerky in the food dehydrator I had ordered from QVC. I had ordered other things, too—a cleaning system for jewelry and silver my wife and I didn't own; a set of Ginsu knives that could slice a penny like a carrot; even a hand-knotted Persian-style rug for the entry to our home. I didn't buy often, but I did whenever something caught my eye and my Visa had a little breathing room. It had been a while.

My blonde-headed girls decided on watermelon fruit leathers and left for the kitchen.

I turned on the DVD and the familiar music that introduced cable's *Rita Adams Show* announced its arrival. The show's producers opened this edition with a jigsaw puzzle graphic made up of pictures of the players interlocking in freeform shapes. It was an obvious visual by nearly everyone's standards; yet for a television talk show, it was just short of clever. Yes, there was a puzzle here. The announcer's monologue was peppered with a crime writer's favorite words. *Bizarre. Shocking. Murder. Love. Love. Love.*

32

First was a photo of Janet Lee Kerr, her face framed by long straight hair, frozen in a mug-shot grimace. She looked hard, but so very young. She was not a *femme fatale* by anyone's standards.

"Janet was convicted of the attempted murder of her boyfriend...and the conspiracy to kill her ex-husband."

The next puzzle piece was identified as Deke Cameron, the ex. His was not a mug shot, but a color photo taken during a portrait special at an Olan Mills. He was full in the face, and had the kind of deer-in-the-headlights affect of a man none too bright.

"The victim of the shooting Janet had arranged... testified against her and sent her to prison... but now says he forgives her and—get this—wants to marry her."

A picture of a man identified as Danny Parker flipped onto the screen and interlocked with Janet's photo puzzle piece. He was heavy, blind in one eye, and looking to the right. Another mug shot.

"Danny says Janet told him that she would marry him in a Las Vegas wedding if he killed Deke for her. Danny shot Deke three times ... but Deke didn't die."

The music went louder then cut out all together. I guessed it was someone's idea to emphasize the drama of the story.

"There's more!"

A woman in her fifties with Malibu Barbie blonde hair and another mug shot smirk came into view. It was Connie Carter. She had the tough attitude and the been-around-the-block appearance of the kind of woman guys liked to say could suck-start a Harley.

"Janet's mother Connie is also in prison. She tried to hire a hit man to kill another of Janet's men, her ex-husband Paul Kerr."

Deke Cameron's photo reappeared.

"...It was Deke who told the police of Connie's plan!"

Janet and Connie of course, denied any wrongdoing via satellite from the Washington State Corrections Center for Women at Riverstone. Danny Parker, however, chose not to appear from his cell in Walla Walla. On stage was Paul Kerr, Janet's ex-husband, who had custody of Lindy, Janet and Paul's preschooler. Sitting next to Paul was Janet's boyfriend, Deke Cameron, who now claimed that he had been tricked by the prosecution and police into identifying Janet's involvement in the crime. He was in love with her.

"You say you are still in love with her, but she had you shot!" Rita barked at Deke.

Deke sat silent for a moment. He pulled open the front of a cheap blazer he had more than likely purchased to wear on the show. A camera close-up revealed four white stitches that held the tag in place.

"Well, Rita, love hurts, you know," he said, pointing to his T-shirt from classic rock band Nazareth's *"Love Hurts" World Tour.*

Rita Adams tried to pin the man down. "You've forgiven her?"

Again, Deke was slow to answer. "Yes. She is a good woman, she's had a hard life, and I'm going to marry her."

"Marry her? She tried to have you killed!"

"That's what they say, but they lie like a rug."

"You testified in court against her, correct?"

"Yes," he said, hesitating, "but I was tricked. I *lied*. She didn't set me up. The cops and prosecutor did."

Rita turned to the monitor showing Janet, now blowing her nose and sniveling into a tissue.

"Do you love this man?"

"Yes...I do. And Sugarbutt loves me."

Her mouth agape, Rita looked utterly dumbfounded. "I guess that's some kind of sweet talk. And you are going to marry him?"

"Yes, we are."

34

Rita exaggerated her disbelief and disgust by shaking her head to and fro.

"Will they let you marry in prison? He's technically the victim of your crime, er, *your crimes.*"

Janet Kerr had miraculously gained her composure. "It's been okayed by the prison counselor."

The camera zoomed in on a middle-aged woman in the third row of the audience. She identified herself as Anna Cameron, Deke's mother. She jumped up and grabbed for Rita's microphone.

"You stay away from my boy!" she yelled at Janet's face on the television monitor. "You almost killed him! Stay away! Stay out of his life. You and your mother are in prison."

The camera cut back to a bewildered Janet. Her eyes wandered as she tried to determine where to direct her response. Of course, she could hear Anna Cameron, but could not see her.

"Mrs. Cameron," she said, "you know I didn't shoot that gun. I love Deke. I only thought he and Danny were going to fight for me."

"If I won," Deke interrupted his mother, who continued her unintelligible rantings from the third row, "Janet and I were going to Vegas to get married. She is a victim of Parker's obsession."

Another lady, further back in the audience, stood up and Rita introduced her as June Parker, Danny's mother. She was a tall, plain woman. Her eyeglass frames were as large and round as bagels, and a silver pin of a horse decorated the right shoulder of a sweater in need of a shave.

She nearly whispered as she spoke.

"I'm so sorry for what my boy did, but it wasn't his fault. He was in love and he didn't mean to hurt anyone. I think Deke provoked him."

Anna Cameron plunged her way through the audience.

"You liar! Your son is a —*bleep!*— lovesick killer. I don't fall for none of that poor-us stuff! Your family is the biggest bunch of liars in Timberlake!"

Mrs. Cameron raised a fist and shook it at Mrs. Parker.

"I wish you people would cough up some blood and die!"

With a shudder at the commotion, Rita looked on as a commercial rolled.

I tried to write down all the names of the players when the program came back on with a close-up of the talk show hostess.

"Deke told me something interesting during the break," Rita announced. "We were talking about how it was that his testimony sent these two women to prison. Deke, what did you say?"

Deke Cameron looked at the camera as directly as an anchorman.

"I lied. I lied on the stand. I told them what the prosecutor told me to say. They wanted Janet and Connie to go down for the crimes and they needed me to lie."

"That's a pretty serious charge you're making. Moreover... aren't you admitting to perjury?"

A worried look flushed over his full face.

"I guess so. I guess I did lie under oath. But they made me. They really did."

Another commercial, a question from the audience, a commercial and Rita shook her head again. It was over.

I pushed the rewind button and allowed a smile at my good fortune. Maybe, just maybe, this is what my editor was seeking.

"Over-the-top" seemed as good a description as any for what I had just seen.

I looked over the notes I had made as I tried to keep track of who was who among the cast of characters.

Janet Lee Carter Kerr—a twenty-something, for whom the term *slacker* had been tailor-made. Hard-looking, not completely unattractive. Mother to Lindy. Jett's sister.

Deke Cameron—kind of Joe Palooka-looking fellow, not too bright. Loves Janet. Took a bunch of bullets in the gut because of her. Wants to marry her now. The idiot forgives her. At least thirty years old.

Danny Parker—fat, lazy-eye. The shooter. Another true crime dimwit. Think Joey Buttafuoco, but younger and dumber.

Connie Carter—former bottle blonde, hard-bitten as a tough steak. Conspired with daughter Janet to kill boyfriend Deke and ex-husband. Jett's mother.

Paul Kerr—blue flannel shirt, stubble on his somewhat craggy chin. Ex-husband of Janet. Target of murder plot conceived by Janet and Connie. Nice guy, just married into the wrong family.

If the crazy cast and the crime were any indication, the story Jett Carter brought to me was certainly worth some follow-up. I called the prison to set up an interview appointment with Connie Carter and Janet Kerr.

Mother and daughter agreed to see me the next afternoon. *Ca-ching.*

37

Chapter Five
Thursday, July 10

I stood at the entrance of the Ellison County Morgue wishing that I smoked so I'd have an excuse to delay my entrance into the Land of the Dead. When I'd phoned before leaving, a lab worker had confirmed that they were "99 percent sure" that it was Jeanne Morgan they had "on a slab," but an in-person ID at the morgue would still be helpful.

"You a relative?" the woman on the other end of the line asked.

"No. Just a friend. Do you know the cause of death yet?"

"She got overheated. Hot day, you know. Looks like she had a stroke. The doc is ruling later today. I'm sorry about your friend."

"Thanks."

"Does she have family in the area?"

I hated that I really didn't know. "I think they're all out of state."

"Can you come in? We'd like to get her out of the chiller and out the door as soon as we can. Bodies tend to pile up this time of year. You know, with everyone on vacation."

"Right. Yes, I know."

"Well? Can you come in?"

"Yes. I'll be there."

And there I was. I'd managed to call Jeanne's sister in Portland (Facebook friend, with phone number listed in the About section) with the tragic news. I explained how I was going to meet her sister for coffee and she likely arrived early for some berry picking behind the stores.

"That's when she must have been overcome by the heat and suffered the stroke," I said.

"She ate too much, vegetarian or not," the sister shot back. "And after her hip surgery she sat around all day watching TV and reading trash. No offense."

"None taken," I said, now knowing why Jeanne never mentioned her sister.

The sister said the family had a burial plot in South Tacoma and they'd hold a service near there as soon at they could. I promised to come.

"You better," the sister said. "She raved about you."

And there I was without a cigarette and an excuse. I stepped on the electronic panel that flipped open the doors to the morgue. The cool, stale air from the basement floor of the county building charged at me. I could smell formaldehyde and Caesar salad. It must be lunchtime. As instructed, I pressed a buzzer and waited. A beat later, the knob on a solid wood panel door turned and a middle-aged man in a white lab coat with J. Jackson nametag on the pocket let me inside.

"You Ryan? Here for the Morgan ID?"

I nodded.

"OK, this'll take a second."

"I don't have to peel back a sheet or anything, do I?"

"Nope. But I guess you know that. You're the crime writer, right?"

"That's right."

"That's just on TV. In real life no one's embarrassed about their bodies. You know, because, well they're dead. We use a roll of paper towels. Saves dough. No cleaning bill. Just toss 'em before we send the stiffs to—"

He stopped and looked at a clipboard, before continuing. "This one's going to Cleveland's Funeral Home on Western Avenue."

I followed him down the hall, past the employee break room where the Caesar salad had been leaking garlic and parmesan in the air.

J. Jackson flipped a switch and a blast of yellow light fell over a body on a gurney.

There she was.

My eyes started at the top of her head. Her perfect updo was now a ratty down-do. Her eyebrows so very, very faint. I hadn't realized until that moment the heavy hand Jeanne Morgan must have used to apply her makeup. She looked marshmallow white, almost powdered, so pale. My gaze was like that big roller at a car wash, passing over her slowly, then stopping before continuing on.

She had a scratch on her face and I asked about it.

"Blackberries can be a bitch. Scratches on her hands, too," J. Jackson said.

She was a smaller woman than her sister gave her credit for. She had tiny hands and tiny feet. I noticed the light tracings of a scar that had indicated where the surgeon had cut her for her hip surgery. Through the thin layer of paper toweling, I could also see the jagged lines of the coroner's knife, the fabled Y-incision—the cut with the alpha initial that always screamed to me "Yield, don't move that scalpel."

J. Jackson's eyes caught mine. "She was a friend?"

I nodded. "Yes."

"Yeah. They found a stash of your books in her van."

My head bobbed up and down. "She ran my website. She was super...."

I almost started to puff up who and what Jeanne was in life, the way people always seem to do when death comes suddenly.

As a writer, I hated that kind of reflex, to gloss over the scabs of a person's life. It usually obscured the true nature of someone's character. No one was perfect, except in tragic death. My eyes landed on her neck. It appeared that there were two slightly darker patches of skin, almost indentations.

"Are you sure this is heatstroke?" I asked.

"Of course, coroner's sure. She died of a stroke. Brain blew up."

For the first time I noticed why the updo had come undone. The coroner had plugged in a power saw and sliced her skull to examine her brain. That and the garlic turned my stomach.

"But what of those marks around her neck?" I asked.

J. Jackson nodded. "EMTs. Got to love those guys. They don't give up easily. Had a stiff here last week with two broken ribs from another failed resuscitation. Heart attack, that one."

I'd found out all I could.

"Do me a favor," I said.

"What's that?"

I could feel my emotions rise, but I kept my focus and hit J Jackson with both barrels.

"Cover her up with a sheet and if you need me to pay for it, bill me. And if you don't, I'll make sure you, your boss's boss, and his boss, are written up for abusing a person in death. Have some respect, Jackson. Would you treat your mother like this? Jeanne Morgan deserves better."

♦

Forty-eight hours later, Valerie and I were at a small gathering in a Gig Harbor Unitarian church to celebrate Jeanne's life. It wasn't exactly a church, but a banquet room at an Embassy Suites.

"Hi, Kevin Ryan," said a young man with a soul patch the shape and size of a guitar pick.

41

I gave him a quick once-over. With his black suit and white shirt, he seemed too well dressed, too young, and the wrong gender for a TC reader. He looked more graphic novel.

"Sorry," I said, brightening a little, "have we met?"

The young man shrugged. "No. I guessed it was you from all my Aunt Jeanne's photos on the Memory Board." He indicated a panel of tagboard with dozens of photos affixed. They were familiar photos, too. Most of them were pictures of me with Jeanne at various events. At the mall. At the library. At a school assembly. At all places, as they say, wherever books were sold.

Val took in the photos and leaned close to my ear. "A perfect ten on the creep-meter."

"Your aunt was a lovely woman," I said to the young man. "I thought a lot of her."

Soul Patch nodded. "Yeah. She was always bragging on you. I figured you were a better person than a writer."

I figured Soul Patch was a prick.

"Thanks, I appreciate that," I said, my face growing warm, and I was sure, quite red.

Val tugged at my sleeve. "Beating up a kid at a funeral would be at least an eleven."

I took a deep breath. "Nice turnout."

The kid looked around. "Thanks. I put up a Pinterest page for Jeanne. I think I got a few bites."

The memorial service was short and sweet. I learned for the first time that Jeanne had been a flight attendant and once competed in the Iditarod dog sled race in Alaska, her home state before moving to Washington in 1982. One of the first women to do so. She had five cats. Outside of that, she didn't have much in her life but a love of all things true crime. She liked forensics, courtroom dramas, and knowing that the bad guy usually gets caught in the end.

Tears came to my eyes and Val handed me a tissue. I was sorry Jeanne was gone, of course. But I was even sorrier that I hadn't paid more attention to her story. You never know who's going to end up dead at any given time.

"She was a nice person, Val."

"I know. A little strange though."

"How so?"

"Five cats? Kevin, that's creepy. Your biggest fan was a cat lady."

I didn't answer. I could forgive Jeanne for having five cats. She was, after all, my number one fan.

Chapter Six
Monday, July 15

IT TOOK ME ABOUT TEN MINUTES to be processed by the guards at Riverstone. That was a good thing because seeing Jeanne on the slab had cost me precious time. And shook me up hard. They ran my driver's license and verified my Social Security number. A female guard behind a counter that looked like a library reference desk told me to take off my shoes, put my things in a locker and pass through the metal detector. I could keep my notebook and a pencil. No pens.

"Community Relations is coming down to get you," the guard said, motioning me through with a rubber-gloved hand.

The buzzer sounded.

"Take off your belt!"

My face went hot. I started to protest.

"Scanner is reading your buckle, sir! New equipment, more sensitive than Rick."She motioned to Rick, a Pacific Islander with keys to a private room. He looked like he was itching to probe anyone who made fuss.

I removed my belt faster than a Chippendale and passed through without a sound.

The public relations flack at the prison was a good-looking petite woman with red hair, picture perfect teeth and a trim figure who answered to the name Muriel Constantine. Her blood-red nails had been glued and lacquered by a professional. I figured she probably made the ladies of the cell block wet with desire. Muriel apologized for keeping me waiting, but explained she had been delayed by a camera crew from *Nancy Grace* who was there to do an interview with a woman who claimed she had a sexual relationship with Satan's brother.

"I didn't know he had a brother," I said as I stuck my feet into my laced-up shoes and worked the heels inside. My socks bunched up, looking flaccid and droopy. I felt stupid as I struggled to put on my shoes to catch up with her.

"He apparently has *two*. She was involved with the younger one."

I clipped a visitor's pass to my shirt pocket and walked with Muriel through the gates that led from the reception area to a breezeway to the unit where mother and daughter were to meet me for our first interview. Coiled razor wire was a deadly slinky atop a twelve-foot fence. Muriel's heels clacked against the pavement and a couple of ladies pulling weeds looked up to watch her pass.

"Must like you," I said.

"Must like *you*," she shot back without a smile.

My mind raced to every *Chained Heat* type of prison movie I'd ever seen. I hated that I felt a little flattered and said nothing more while the red disappeared from my face.

I always liked the part of the true crime book-writing process where I came face-to-face with the person doing time. I knew that when they wrote back and said they were only "considering" talking to me that they were ready to spill their guts. Women and men in prison are lonelier than hell. They act as though they have ten thousand people visiting them, but the truth is unless they have had a TruTV or Lifetime movie produced about their story, or an ID channel episode, the list is usually quite short. As time goes by, it grows even tinier.

I followed Muriel's clacking heels to a little conference room where I was told to wait. The blind-date feeling always sets in during the minute or two it takes to retrieve the inmate from the holding cell for the interview. Outside the window, more women were weeding the flowerbeds and a few others were in small clutches of disharmony on various benches. Sometimes I wondered why these ladies had ended up where they did and why some just as tough as them were rolling back prices at a Walmart store. I felt a little queasy. I wondered if the women I was about to meet would like me. Will they trust me? *Should they trust me?*

And more importantly, was I their last shot?

Muriel clacked back into the conference room.

"Janet changed her mind. But Connie is on her way."

"Oh," I said, registering obvious disappointment. "I hope she's all right."

Muriel shrugged, stuck her pen in an empty Starbucks mug, and informed me that she'd be down the hall taking care of business.

Connie Carter and I would be alone.

Connie was in her late forties, a former NASCAR Barbie with bottle blonde hair, a penchant for swimming-pool-blue eye shadow, and tube tops at least one size too small. She had chipped teeth, puffy eyes and the kind of throaty laugh that spoke more to a two-pack-a-day habit than a terrific sense of humor. Now she was tired, worn out and dressed in jeans and a blouse. She was a woman who had literally gone back to her roots—no longer blonde, but now with brown hair was so unbelievably dark it boggled the mind that she even *thought* she could get away with a nearly platinum color.

When she entered, I stood up and extended my hand in courtesy.

"Mr. Ryan?" she asked.

Who else would be here? I thought.

"Mrs. Carter?" I answered back, though she had a Washington State Corrections Center for Women ID tag and it didn't say "staff" so there was no room for doubt that this social hour would be between the author and the inmate. That done, I waited for her to sit and we talked about the weather, the food, the fact that her daughter had become involved with a prisoner. In fact, Janet had been Connie's roommate until the week before when she requested a transfer and ended up with another cellie.

"Her name is Angela and I don't like the looks of her. She's scary. *Really* scary."

"I'm sorry," I said.

"Me, too. It's too late for me to change. Everyone tells me that I'll be a lesbian before I get out of here, but they're wrong about that. Too late for me to go that way."

Connie played with her file folder of briefs as we talked. She had carried them into the room like a shield; her proof that she was innocent of any wrongdoing. Every page within that folder verified the tragedy that had befallen her. She had been framed. She had been set up. She was the victim.

God, how I had heard that before. The woman in one of my books had put cyanide in headache capsules to kill her husband and in an effort to throw the authorities off the track, set more tainted bottles out in grocery stores. A young mother, an innocent bystander, took some tainted pills and died. The convicted tamperer told me in unblinking eyes that she had been framed.

Everyone said so.

Another woman I wrote about had been convicted of suffocating her son repeatedly in an effort to gain the sympathy and attention of others. She too, insisted quite convincingly that she had been a victim of a witch hunt. Was there anyone in prison who was supposed to be there? Or at least owned up to the possibility that she had done something to warrant the desolate accommodations of an eight-foot cell?

Connie Carter was not to be the one to stake that claim. As we neared the end of our allotted time, I asked her if Janet was as innocent as she.

"I've agonized over that one," she said carefully. "I'm not ashamed to tell you that I've even prayed over it since I got here."

I decided to push. "Well, what do you think? Could she be guilty?"

Connie bit her lower lip. Lipstick scraped off in the parallel lines left by her front upper teeth. Either she was a damn good actress or she was having a difficult time letting her words come.

"I am beginning to wonder. I... I... I think she might have led on Danny Parker so that he would shoot Deke."

I prodded her for evidence, something to back up her story. She didn't seem to have anything. She made me promise to keep her theories to myself and I gladly agreed.

"It... it's just a feeling, really. A feeling that she's lying. Now, don't tell her I said that. We have to have trust, you know."

Considering where she was and why she was there, trust would be hard to come by. I agreed again. I thanked her and told her I'd see her again soon.

♦

I DID NOT CONSIDER MARTIN RAINES a close friend, but I certainly knew him well enough to feel confident when I made that first call to his office at the Pierce County Sheriff's Office. He was the lead investigator for the county and we had met at a symposium in Portland three or four years before. Ostensibly, I was there to talk about crime writing and the responsibility writers shared with law enforcement. I was really there to sell books and provide a little sizzle for the two-day event.

Raines cornered me the first day to tell me he had considered writing a few books of his own.

"I've seen it all," he said over a beer in the hotel lobby bar. "From the boy next door who slaughters his parents to the woman who shoved a hot poker up her husband's ass when she

48

found out he was having a homosexual affair with the man who detailed their cars every Saturday."

I swallowed the last of a plate of deep-fried ravioli. "You really *have* seen it all," I said. Marinara dripped on the front of my shirt. I quickly moved my convention name badge to cover the stain.

Raines and I talked for two hours, and while I encouraged him to contact my agent, I doubted he could pull off a book, no matter how much firsthand knowledge he had. Outside of a parking ticket, most cops can't write. We exchanged phone numbers and actually talked once or twice a year, whenever an interesting case popped up in his jurisdiction.

Until the Carter women, there hadn't been any interesting enough to cross over from "interesting" to "book material."

"What do you think about Connie Carter and Janet Kerr's case?" I asked over the phone after my meeting with Connie at Riverstone prison.

His recognition was swift. "Piece of work, those two. A dumb crime."

"A book?" I asked.

"Not like any you've written or I've read."

"Good," I said. "That's just what I'm looking for. I've got to come up with something different or I'll be back at the Food King passing out samples."

"Could be the one," he said.

◆

OVER THE COURSE OF THE WEEKS and months that would consume me as I researched the story and listened to the players, the words of my editor would ring in my head like some insipid ditty I could never shake.

"We want a story that's bigger than life. More bizarre than bizarre! That's what we're after. That's what will pull you out of the midlist to compete with Jan Rule."

49

"Ann," I corrected him.

"Huh?"

"Ann. Not Jan."

"Yeah, right. Ann."

"Something over-the-top! Run-of-the mill cases just can't compete."

When I was ready, when it was all laid out, I would spring it on the pointy-nosed New Yorker whose yea or nay had hung my life out like a row of diapers on a saggy clothesline. I promised my wife, like a losing gambler who can't give up the craps table or the fat person who can't stop at one dish of ice cream, I would make one more stab at the genre.

"Valerie," I said, "this is our chance out of the middle class!"

My wife let out a sigh of exasperation. "When you used to say that I thought you meant *up* from the middle class," she said. "I didn't think we'd be dropping below it."

"Just one more, Val, and then I'll quit. Then I'll get a real job."

I had said that so often, even I thought the words were hollow. I was almost forty. *Four-oh.* I had held more part-time jobs than an alcoholic, yet drinking was never my problem. I had two beautiful and bright little girls who could do a crime scene analysis as good as any criminal science major—or at least I thought so. I had a wonderful wife who could no longer feign excitement over the free samples I brought home from my latest job. We still had a freezer full of chicken taquitos that I had been given in lieu of cash from my stint as a supermarket food-demo person. I had flipped burgers. I had sold RVs. I had done it all, and I only did so to get food on the table.

"When you said, 'Food on the table,'" I could hear Valerie saying, "'I thought you meant *groceries*, as in a variety of foodstuffs, not twenty-five *pounds* of taquitos.'"

"God, Val, how would I know old man Martinez was a scammer? His first name was *Jesus*!"

We had a lovely home in a wooded country setting with neighbors we cared about. We had fled the city for greener pastures because we wanted to and because we could. Just barely. Valerie commuted to call on clients for the artists she represented. Approaching twelve, our daughters, Taylor and Hayley, were making what every father considers the nightmarish but impossible-to-stop leap from girls to young women.

Even though I felt like I had not achieved much in the career I chose, I knew that as far as the Jetts of the world were concerned, I lived like a king. I had two vehicles, a computer, and a purebred dog that went to the groomer every single month. I even had a plasma TV. We went on vacations, though mostly to places where I could research a book. We lived a life that wasn't anybody's dream but our own.

Hedda underfoot, I took the last blue Mr. Freeze pop from its hiding place under a frozen pillow of tater tots and sat down at my Mac to type the title that would set the tone for the story that I would try to shape into a book. I tried several ideas, different titles and the subtitles that reminded the reader of what they were going to read, "Tell them and tell them what you told them," I heard over and over. I sucked the last bit of blue from the plastic tube and dropped it into the waste can. Hedda worked on a flea that was giving her grief at the base of her hot-dog-cropped tail.

It wasn't too bad. At least I felt it gave the editors what they were clamoring for:

Love You to Death:
The Positively Shocking True Story of Murder,
Obsession and a Wedding in Vegas.

By Kevin Ryan

I studied the title further, wondering if *Love You to Death* should be punctuated with an exclamation mark. Maybe the subtitle was a little off-the-wall, but I felt it truly fit the absurd nature of the story. It was ridiculous. Besides, if my editor didn't like it, he'd change the whole damn thing. He always did, anyway. I'd leave that decision in his hands. I just wanted to get on with it.

◆

I FOUGHT THE URGE TO TURN ON *The Rita Adams Show*. To start watching was to see an hour whirlpool into a black hole of wasted time. Instead, I made myself a pot of coffee and waited for the kitchen clock to hit three in the afternoon. I knew that Monica Maleng's masseuse finished working her over by 2:30 and Monica would be settled back into the sumptuous hunter green leather of her office chair at Green Light Pictures off Wilshire Boulevard in Beverly Hills.

Before I tackled any project, I talked with Monica. She was a TV producer and also my ears and eyes to what television networks and cable companies were optioning. Monica had worked for seven years as *Rita* executive producer when Rita, rich with a five-year multimillion-dollar contract, spun her off to

Green Light Pictures. I met Monica when I was on Rita's show promoting *Dead No More*, the true story of a Baltimore man who faked his own death so he and his wife could collect on life insurance benefits. The twist was that the wife had a lover and the two of them killed the supposedly already dead husband.

Green Light optioned the book as its first or second property. It looked good for *Dead No More.* I was certain it was going to be produced. I told Valerie to start picking out carpet samples (and upgrading the pad) for the living room. It went through four rewrites before it finally came together. Eddie Cibrian was slated to play the hapless husband; LeAnn Rimes, the murderous wife. Then rival Slash TV Network beat Green Light to the punch and did its own movie about a similar case that took place in Florida. Slash TV did the story without the rights to a book. Without paying a dime to the sources whose story they were telling.

They did it "public domain."

I loathed the very concept of public domain. Public domain meant that producers could send a screenwriter to the local library and courthouse, and cobble together a story based on what was in the public record—newspaper accounts, court documents, trial transcripts. It didn't matter how true it was, for they were always able to use the *Inspired by a True Story* tag line. *Inspired by* was a cannonball dive below *Based on*.

If TV people were the worst, than worst among them was Adena King. Years later, even typing her name gives me the creeps. She claimed to be a former series actress (actually, she appeared on *Law & Order SVU* in a courtroom scene and in *Home Improvement* as an audience member on *Tool Time*). She telephoned me out of the blue one afternoon to say she had read a copy of *Murder Cruise* before it had even been typeset.

"Kevin, don't get mad at me!" she said during the first call. "I love your work and I want *Murder Cruise*!"

"It isn't ready, and when it is my agent will send it to you."

"*Murder Cruise* is mine!"

"Not ready, sorry."

"Don't get angry, but I got a copy this morning!"

I thought I must have misheard her. The book wasn't available for months. "How?"

"It's done all the time, Kevin. It's called a 'slip it.' I had someone at your publisher's slip it to me."

"For money?"

"Guilty!" She laughed. It was an obnoxious, horsey laugh that sounded almost unearthly. I tried to imagine the face that went with the awful laugh.

I dialed my agent immediately after I hung up. She promised to look into it. The next day she called back with the bad news. Adena King had already shopped the book to everyone in town as if she already optioned it. I was stuck. I was ruined. No one wanted to work with Adena; no one wanted *Murder Cruise*.

54

I loathed the woman. She had burned my best chance for a TV movie before the book even hit grocery store racks. The topper was when a T-Mobile operator called to inform me that my "friend" Adena King had put me in her "calling circle" as a member of her Colleagues and Confidants Group.

"Take me out or I'm going to Verizon," I told the phone company solicitor. "I want out of her damn circle!"

Monica Maleng, on the other hand, had integrity. I trusted her. She was someone whose advice I sought when I considered taking on a new book project. She knew what the networks and cable companies were salivating for, and we had actually developed a couple of projects together.

At three on the dot, I called her.

It turned out there had been no time for a massage that afternoon. She had come back from a meeting at Lifetime that she said didn't go particularly well. The network that still reveled in true crime was feeling a bit of the backlash churned up by a family rights group calling for a kinder and gentler type of TV fare.

Monica was dejected. "Nobody wants any more stories on family members killing each other," she said. "It seems so unfair. The numbers for movies based on true stories are still solid. America is as bloodthirsty as ever. These network people go whichever way the wind blows."

"So I've heard," I stammered, before I launched into my pitch. "Two different guys plot murder for the love of a girl. She promises that she'll marry each one in Las Vegas. One guy shoots the other boyfriend, the boyfriend tells the police he was not only a victim but he was also an accomplice to the murder plot of the girl's ex-husband."

"Strong female characters?" Monica sounded very interested.

"Tougher than Charlize Theron in an ugly suit," I said. "The girl's mother is now in prison for plotting to kill her daughter's ex-husband. The daughter is in prison for attempted murder of her boyfriend and the conspiracy to kill her ex-husband."

"Good. Good. CAA is looking for something for Misty," Monica said.

I knew she was referring to Misty Wexler, the surgically augmented actress from *Texas Hold 'Em,* whose mega-producer father had helped turn her into a surprisingly formidable force in the crime-of-the-week television movie genre. She had played every side of the coin. She was a murderous cheerleader in *All for Sandi, Stand Up and Die!* She starred most recently as the victim of a stalker in *She's Being Watched* for Lifetime. She was arguably the worst actress in Hollywood. I couldn't stand her.

"She'd be perfect," I said. "She'd make a great Janet Lee Kerr."

"The mother? Who for the mother?"

"Megan Mullally," I suggested. "I read in *Entertainment Weekly* she's looking for a part where she can play bad."

"Never believe *EW.*"

"Right."

"You know what I like best about your story?" Monica didn't let a beat pass for an answer. "It has the quality to it like the Texas cheerleading murdering mom that HBO produced before it got hung up on overhyped prestige pictures. It is ridiculous like the cheerleader movie. Imagine, a fellow gets shot, testifies against his girlfriend, sends her to prison, sends her mother to prison, and then becomes engaged to the girl, and to top it all off, he recants."

Her quick-draw words wore me out. The woman never came up for air.

"Is it what they're looking for?" I asked, mentally catching her breath for her.

"Tailor-made. Kevin. I'm talking mini here."

Mini to me always meant *many*, as in *more* bucks.

56

"No kidding. A miniseries?"

"Sure. The fact that no one was killed could be a major plus. It falls right into the networks' new philosophy for television movies. They want bloodless murder or something approximating that. They want the unbelievable, the sublimely ridiculous. No more mothers killing babies! No more children killing their parents. No more families killing each other. It's a new approach and I like it. Keep me posted and if you get something, promise me the first look, all right?"

I promised. We planned to talk later after a few weeks or so of additional research.

In my mind, Monica's words rang like a symphony of musical cash registers. Sweet, melodic, rich.

"I'm talking mini here."

Chapter Seven
Monday, July 21

VALERIE WAS PAYING THE BILLS when I returned home from a meeting with Connie Carter and the Community Relations staff at the Riverstone prison. I asked for more time with Connie, and the Powers That Be didn't feel I should have any. I also wanted another interview request sent to Connie's daughter, Janet. It was clear that these prison people regarded me as small potatoes. I was an annoyance to them. I sunk even lower as I realized I had no bragging value like *Maury*.

Or even *Steve Wilkos*.

"You're not a real journalist," said the Community Relations director, a man with a nose the shape and size of a Chinese potsticker. "Those books you write aren't journalism," he said, turning up his potsticker nose, "they're entertainment."

"If *that*," remarked a snotty woman who wore glasses on a chain as a pretense to being an intellectual. She was the type who claimed to watch only PBS and read literary fiction. But I knew she either read my genre or, even lower on the bookshelf, romance.

I realized that most anyone I ever interviewed in prison was a liar, but I still found great value in meeting the incarcerated. I begged the woman. "Three more interviews with Connie and the same number with Janet if she comes around. I'll ask for no more."

She said they would think it over.

If I were Anderson Cooper, they would have kissed my toned butt.

"Get the interviews locked up?" Val asked.

"Like a cell on the Green Mile," I said.

I didn't want to bother Val with the small stuff. I'd get the interviews, because I had to.

♦

VALERIE HAD NUMBERED EACH PAYMENT ENVELOPE with the date it should be mailed in order to arrive at the last possible minute—and still on time. My wife was efficient with juggling what little we had and I loved her for it. She was thirty-five and as lovely as the day I met her working on ads for the university newspaper in Bellingham, north of Seattle. She was a graphic designer/artist's representative, and I had committed the cardinal sin of journalism school of leaving editorial for advertising to make some money. The other students shot me how-could-you! gapes, but I had plans that didn't include working at the *Podunk Weekly*. I wanted to get to know that brown-eyed girl, too.

And today, she wore her hair pulled up in a clip, revealing streaks of kitten gray from her temples. Yes, she wanted those highlights, and she deserved it.

"How'd it go?" she asked, barely looking up from her checkbook and bank-freebie calculator.

"Fine. Connie says she's innocent. Janet got cold feet."

"What else is new?"

"I don't know, Val, I guess I liked her."

"You always like them."

"Not always," I said defensively.

"Yeah, you do. You even thought that serial killer from Lincoln City was nice."

"I meant, *personable* in the way that serial killers often are."

"Uh-huh," Val answered, moving to the kitchen and pulling pans out of the cupboard. "Serial killers are always nice until they get what they want."

"These women aren't serial killers. They're just dumb."

Valerie turned on the tap to fill a pot. I guessed we were having spaghetti.

"Want to get Hayley and Taylor?" she asked. "They're up at Gina's. She took the girls across the Narrows Bridge for a picnic today."

Gina and her husband Carlton lived up the hill from us in a house they had literally built from the ground up. Board by board, bit by bit. Gina had even dug out the foundation with a garden shovel and a wheelbarrow. They were enterprising and sweet. Their family had been friendly with ours from the first day we moved to our ancient and impossibly creaky, company-town house in Port Gamble. The immediate bond, of course, had been our children. They had a daughter named Cecile and we had two new best friends for her. The Narrows Bridge picnic had taken place before school was out for summer break. No one expected me to go. I would never walk across that thousand-foot-high bridge whose predecessor was nicknamed Galloping Gertie before she fell to the seafloor with a car and hapless dog going down for the ride. Nevertheless, the bridge connected the peninsula, where we lived, to the mainland.

"Okay. But, you know, you would have liked Connie. Sure, she's a little on the rough side, but she is so pathetic that you've got to feel some sympathy for her."

Valerie stopped what she was doing. Her eyes narrowed. "Like Wanda-Lou?" she asked.

I didn't respond. *Wanda-Lou.* The very name sent chills down my spine. She was one of those people Val insisted I "collect" by the very nature of my work—the type of people you would never meet unless you're tracking the lives of killers and cops. *Wanda-Lou.* Good, God, she was something else. As I drove up the hill to pick up my girls, I recalled what Val always termed *The Wanda-Lou Incident.*

Wanda-Lou Webster was the forty-year-old cousin of a woman who killed her husband by throwing a running hair dryer into the bathtub when he was soaking and reading the newspaper. For years, Marianne Mason had been plotting the murder of her sleaze-bucket husband, a former-biker-turned-sand-candle-maker named Dick Mason.

I could still hear Wanda-Lou: *"At least the bastard's first name fit his personality."*

Dick had been cheating on Marianne since the day they married at the Little Chapel of Flowers, a wedding and latte shop outside Spokane. If that wasn't bad enough, he had a thing for young girls. And though it was never proven in court, he might have had a thing for Marianne's eight-year-old daughter.

Wanda-Lou provided enough details to lead me to believe that the *Die, Jerk, Die* story might make the basis for a mega-selling true crime book. It came with a hitch. She, of course, wanted to be the focus of the story.

"I'll be like the detective that pursues justice," she said over a coffee and French toast breakfast at our first meeting at a suburban Denny's Restaurant.

I couldn't help but like Wanda-Lou Webster and because of my affinity for her I came to feel a measure of sympathy for her imprisoned cousin Marianne. Her husband Dick was an animal. An undeniable creep; a veritable garbage pit of depravity. I detested him. I wanted so much to believe Wanda-Lou's version of what happened. But Marianne had left a trail, as most killers do. An Ace Hardware receipt dated the day of the murder was the new widow's greatest undoing. All she purchased was a twelve-foot extension cord. The cord was attached to the hair dryer, making it long enough to toss into the tub from the hallway. She cooked him like a lobster and called 911 when he was done.

Over the course of a four-week period, I saw Wanda-Lou about ten or eleven times at either her home or at the Denny's. We had enough contact that I began to feel that I really knew her and trusted her.

That was a mistake.

Wanda-Lou said she was headed out my way and had some letters Dick had written that she wanted to drop off. It was perfect "insight into the mind of an abuser" type stuff. I told her that I wouldn't be home, so she could just mail them to the Port Gamble P.O. box.

"I don't trust the damn post office," she said, insistently. "Could I just FedEx it to you?"

I gave her my street address.

Bigger mistake.

When we arrived home from a day of errands, a car was in our driveway. I recognized it immediately because of the by-then familiar bumper sticker: *Bitch On Board.* It was Wanda-Lou's car.

Valerie gave me a wary look as we all went inside.

Our iHome was playing some kind of country tune that at first I thought was the radio. Later I found out it was a CD that Wanda-Lou had brought from home.

That was not all she brought.

Laying on the sofa next to a pair of soft-sided luggage was Wanda-Lou. Her eyes were puffy. A snowdrift of crumpled facial tissue had dropped from her hands. She was crying. And the white couch we never should have purchased in the first place was staining anew.

"I'm sorry for letting myself in, but the window was open a bit and I hoped you wouldn't mind."

"What is it?" I asked while Valerie and the girls made a beeline for the kitchen.

"My old man threw me out. He said I care more about Marianne and your book than I do about him."

I sat next to her. "Oh, Wanda-Lou, I'm sorry. He just doesn't understand that you're trying to help your cousin."

"I have no place to go. No place. Marianne's in jail and my old man dumped me. Dumped me! I've never been dumped in all my life. *Never.*"

I doubted she was being completely truthful with that particular disclosure, but I didn't say so.

Wanda-Lou Webster stayed for fourteen days. Valerie often exaggerated the duration of the extended visit by stretching the time to "almost a month!" Val threatened to dump me if I didn't get rid of Wanda-Lou. She told me she didn't mind the books I wrote, but she didn't like the idea of our family having to live with the people I wrote about.

Wanda-Lou wasn't so bad. She helped around the house. We cleaned out the garage. She fancied herself an expert on talk shows so we did some mock run-throughs. She was the host and I was the guest. She even insisted I work on my signature. A real writer, she persisted, had a wonderful signature reserved for book signings. She said mine was not explosive enough, too legible. I needed more drama in my John Hancock.

"If you ever want someone to value a signed copy of one of your books," she told me straight-faced, "then you'll have to sign 'em like you mean it."

The only way to get out of the Wanda-Lou-as-permanent-guest scenario was to lie.

"I got some bad news today," I told her one afternoon. "My publisher wouldn't go for *Die, Jerk, Die.* Another publishing company has a book coming out about a woman who sets her house on fire with a curling iron to cover up the murder of her boyfriend.

"They said *Curled Up to Die* is too similar to our project. They don't think we can compete with another true crime book related to hair care."

Wanda-Lou's face registered shock, then disappointment.

"It's not all bad news," I continued. "My friend Fred Ross is looking for a new story to fulfill his contract at Toe Tag Books." I scribbled down his address and telephone number.

I told Fred that Wanda-Lou was the best source he could ever have and that I hated to give up her story, but I was overbooked and it would be wrong for me to hang on to such a powerful tale.

"It is the story that has to be told. I wouldn't give this story to anyone but you."

Wanda-Lou packed up her things and drove away. As her taillights disappeared into the night, I took her file and tossed it in the box I called DEAD DEAD BOOKS. Freedom never felt so good. I wasn't giving up a great story, I was saving my marriage. Besides, I never liked Fred Ross in the first place.

With Wanda-Lou finally gone, I tried to make it all up to Valerie. I promised her that when my television movie was made, we'd slipcover the sofa.

"Martha Stewart says slipcovers are back in," I said.

More than a year later, our sofa was still in need of a dozen throw pillows or that slipcover.

Thursday, July 25

THE DAY AFTER MY INTERVIEW WITH CONNIE CARTER at Riverstone, I drove my classic Chevy LUV a hundred miles south to Timberlake, the scene of the crime. The town, cruelly spliced in half by the Ocean River, was a logging center whose salad days had long since wilted. The Columbia Mall had drained what little commercial viability that had survived from the dwindling downtown shopping district. The frequently empty acreage of the mall parking lot was a testament to the developer's great ambition or absolute foolishness. The mall was the hub of the town. "The mall," as its marketing VP always said, "had it all."The Red Lobster in its southwest corner had been voted "best special occasion restaurant" by the readers of the local paper. Second place was Pizza Hut, which secured the lot to the east.

There were not enough votes for a third-place winner. There simply was not a third restaurant which could stretch the very concept of special occasion.

That was Timberlake.

And while there was a kind of sad desperation to the place, there was a sweetness to it, too. Some of the tiny homes that had been built by the mills were painted in lemony yellow and periwinkle blue. Grandma houses in grandma colors. Faded flamingos bobbed from borders of pie-plate sized dahlia blooms. The town's park was named for Sacagawea, the Indian guide who led Lewis and Clark across the Great Plains to the Oregon Territory. A bronze statue of the guide was frequently festooned with chains of dandelions and daisies.

I ran around most of the morning talking with the cops, looking at court files, just generally getting a feel for the place. In a way, it was odd. I had lived all my life in the Northwest and I couldn't begin to even guess about how many times I had driven the portion of the interstate between Seattle and Portland. How many times had I seen the exit to Timberlake and just kept going? Hundreds of times. And I never had a reason to stop. Not until *Love You to Death*.

My final stop before pulling into my driveway was our P.O. box at the Port Gamble Post Office. Bills. Newsweek. Country Living. Property taxes.

And a second gray envelope.

I opened it on the little counter set aside for patrons to read and toss junk mail.

How I wish it were junk mail.

But it wasn't. It was more magazine clipping letters. I recognized the "S" on the fourth word as the Safeway logo.

YOUR TURN TO SUFFER IS COMING.

I'm not even sure of the drive home. My mind was so far gone. I came inside as fast as I could, made a beeline for the bathroom, shut the door, and threw up. Oddly, I was proud of myself that I made it to the toilet and not all over the interior of the LUV truck.

"Honey, are you all right?"

It was Val from the other side of the door.

"Yeah, just had some bad fish," I said, the first thing that came to my mind.

"I have some Tums in the kitchen."

"Be out in a minute."

I splashed water on my face. I wasn't having a good day at all. I'd received a second letter and it scared me more than a too-small print run of my next book, or any of the things that I thought were important.

Chapter Eight
Friday, July 26

JETT CARTER SENT ME TO SEE Melba Warinski, the woman who had been a witness of the events the night of Deke Cameron's shooting. Mrs. Warinski was described as a "real nice lady" who lived in one of the fancier subdivisions of Timberlake. Fancy, I knew, is relative. To Jett, the concept of "fancy" probably meant anything other than the dented aluminum shell of a singlewide mobile home.

I looked for the address: 1422 Strawberry Lane. The housing development had a row of hot pink and electric purple flags stuck in the earth like Peter Max lollipops alerting mill workers or store clerks and others that they had arrived at their homes in Riverview Land. The garish proclamation made me grimace.

It was one of those housing developments in which its moniker recalled what the location had once been. Eagle's Nest Estates. Royal Woods. Or Windsor Meadows. In such neighborhoods there were never any eagles, meadows or woods. At least not since the developer took a dozer and cut in building sites. Riverview Land was that kind of place—no river and no view.

Instead, there were neat rows of houses that sported a kind of affected country look—a cement goose wearing a hat, a wide porch with a wicker rocker purchased at Home Depot, or a replica metal milk can used as an umbrella stand.

A hand-painted plaque next to Mrs. Warinski's door read:

FRIENDS ARE NICE, BUT CLEAN FLOORS ARE WONDERFUL!

The first chapter of most true crime books opens with blood and guts and a murder. Publishers almost require it. While *Love You to Death* lacked a murder per se, it had plenty of blood and guts. Even better, it had twists and turns. Jett had been helpful in setting up the interview with Mrs. Warinski, a part-time night clerk at the River's Edge Motel, next door to the Ruston Tavern where Deke Cameron went for help the night of the shooting. I appreciated Jett's help and knew from our first meeting on my doorstep that she would be the person that I could count on whenever I needed help around town. Though I couldn't use her to facilitate meetings and interviews with Danny's or Deke's families and friends, I knew she'd be a big help with her sister and mother's side of the story.

Mrs. Warinski's breasts were large and pendulous, and swung with such force when she greeted me that I thought she'd knock over her early—or very, very late season—scarecrow door decoration. And they undulated when she introduced herself and shook my hand.

"I made coffee, come on in!" she said.

Melba Warinski was a pleasant woman in her mid-forties. She had a ready smile and smelled of cinnamon.

"Making apple pie?" I asked, following implied orders by taking off my shoes and setting them by the door.

"Thank you, but it's my stove-top sachet you're getting a whiff of now."

I settled into a chair at the kitchen table. I told her about myself, my books, my wife, and my children. I was there to get information, but I was there to win her over. And I did. We talked about her life, her children, her husband, her interest in crafts and the night of the crime.

She was still shaken by what she had seen.

"When I think about that bloody young man and how he fought for his life...it just makes me wonder: what would have happened if I hadn't been there? He might have died. Good night, there was so much blood on his chest! And on the pavement. At first I thought the black pool was an oil puddle. But it wasn't. It was blood."

She took a deep breath and ate another store-bought cookie.

"Mr. Ryan, we're living in a very violent world," she said.

I nodded. I didn't want to say that violence kept police, doctors and true crime authors in business, but it fluttered through my mind. When it was time to go, Melba Warinski gave me two little angels made of rolls of Life-Savers as gifts for my daughters. The wings were fashioned of the silver foil of a gum wrapper.

"Doublemint," she said, proud of her handiwork. "For your twins!"

"I've never seen anything like these," I said as I waved from my truck. "My girls will love them. Thank you."

I had one more appointment. A man who rented one of the River's Edge Motel rooms as an apartment had been on the scene near the same time as Mrs. Warinski. Andy Lowery was a fry cook at the Green Grasshopper on Meriwether Avenue.

I introduced myself and sat down in a booth with a plate of waffle fries and ketchup.

"Good job on the fries," I told the cook, dumping pepper on the ketchup pool dammed by the fries.

Andy Lowery grinned, revealing a man in considerable need of serious dental work. The Green Grasshopper Cafe was not a leader in health care for its employees, though management had hung a sign in the men's room that reminded workers to *wash your hands after your business, so that we can do our business.*

Andy was thirty-two, thin as a wicket, and as excited as could be to tell me what he had seen the night the story began.

"My girlfriend woke me—we're getting married next year—at one-twenty in the morning, yelling that someone was in front of the motel screaming that he had been shot! *Shot*! I threw on some clothes and ran out there to see what was going on. My girlfriend's name is Amber."

"Pretty name," I offered.

"Melba, the night clerk, was out there and she had already called 9-1-1. I didn't know what I was getting myself into so I went over carefully. I didn't want to go right up to this individual, because he seemed so agitated, so husky and *big*. I don't mind telling you that I was a little bit afraid of what might happen. I told him to stay down, to lay still. There would be blood everywhere. I mean *everywhere*. The inside of the truck was red. I saw chunks of skin, and stuff, too. Melba and I kept telling the bleeding guy that he would be all right. We would stay with him until help arrived."

I picked at my ketchup-bloodied fries and made a few notes. If I needed anything else, Andy told me he was more than willing to help out. I thanked him and got up to leave.

"Can you leave Amber out of it?" he asked as we walked to the door of the cafe.

"Why?"

His face went red and he stammered out a reply. "Uh. Uh. She's married and I don't want to get her into trouble."

"You know, Andy, I'm writing a true story. If she's important, she's in. If she's not, she's out."

"All she did was wake me up. That's all."

"I'll do what I can."

I left Timberlake with enough information to begin the writing of the critical first chapter—the chapter that would hook my editor into another contract. I drove north on I-5 as fast as I could without the worry of the flashing blue light of a Washington State Patrol car. The house was quiet when I got home. No new letters from any haters, which was good. I slipped behind my computer to answer e-mail (nothing but spam) and do a quick Google search.

TODAY'S LIST

Google: Not much on the blogs ("Crimella" is still yammering about the corpse photo in one of my books. Not my idea!) Sympathy posts for Jeanne-O dropped off on Kevin's Krime Blog.

Crime case in the news with the most hits: Monica Dewars killed her preacher husband, Matthew Dewars, over an affair he was having with a church secretary.

Possible book titles: *"Unholy Matrimony"* or *"The Devil Made Her Do It"*

Amazon ranking for backlist: Stuck in the 400,000s.

Need from the store: Coffee, corn and a pint of Chunky Monkey ice cream.

Chapter Nine
Saturday, July 27

I GOT UP EARLY TO MAKE SOME CALLS TO THE EAST Coast before trying to write something. I made Valerie a pot of coffee and we watched a little bit of the morning news before embarking on the day. She was going to a seminar to learn to empower herself in the business world. Empowerment for me meant Taylor and Hayley sleeping in until almost ten.

"Shh!" Taylor instructed her sister when they converged into my office that morning. "Daddy's calling a bookstore in Atlanta to see if they have his book."

"He picked Georgia today?" Hayley asked, a towel wrapped around her head as proof that she had showered and washed her hair. "It was my turn to pick the state."

It was the one area to which I would admit I was somewhat obsessed—after Googling my own name. I wanted to know if my books were doing well and I used my girls' Wonderful United States flash cards to pick the state that I would call at random to check on a title's availability.

My first call went to a Barnes & Noble that had closed four months earlier—a store that had filled the space left behind by a Borders that had closed two years before that. My second call went to a mystery bookshop that was open only three days a week, and today wasn't one of them, according to the answering machine. But my third call was answered by a live human being.

"Hi," I said to a clerk at a Hastings. "Have you got any copies of *Murder Cruise*? I think the author's name is Ryan."

Though I felt silly, I thought it was clever that I was unsure of the author's name. *My name.*

"I'll check the computer," the girl said, coming back on the line after a few bars of Muzak tune I could not pin down.

"We do! Want us to hold a copy?

I thought of the box of a hundred copies I kept in my garage. Copies that would never see the light of day, never be taken to the bathtub or beach to be read. Never be sold at a garage sale.

"Oh, that would be great."

"Name?"

"Lyons," I said, wondering why I hadn't come up with a better book-buying name than one that so closely resembled my own.

"Mr. Lyons," the girl said, her voice radiating as much enthusiasm as a video store clerk, "we'll hold it for three days."

I thanked her and asked her how the book was selling. "It's based on a true story that happened in my home town," I said, instantly feeling like an idiot. *Murder Cruise* was a murder on the high seas case and there was no town. My embarrassment faded when I remembered that most chain bookstore clerks didn't read.

"Sounds cool. We have quite a few; they're not exactly flying out of the store. Bye."

I had wanted a title like *The End of Melinda*. Melinda Moser's husband, Dan Moser, and his lover (and Melinda's best friend) Maddie Andretti conspired to kill Melinda while vacationing together on their boat in Hawaii. While "Aunt" Maddie waited in a rental car with the Mosers' little boy, Dan took Melinda to a fern-shrouded canyon and bludgeoned her with the back end of a sugar cane machete. Two days later, Dan and Maddie came back to retrieve the already decomposing body because they were worried someone would find her, with Dan and Melinda's only child, an infant daughter, asleep in the back seat. Criminals were always doing things like that. It always made me laugh when someone would remark at how "diabolically clever" the subjects were in any of my books. Smart killers were those no one wrote about; the ones who never got caught. Not a single true crime book had ever been written about a clever criminal. I'd also thought of calling the book *Tropic Blunder: The True Story of Love, Madness and a Machete.*

The murderous duo dumped poor Melinda's body in the sea and claimed she had been attacked by sharks.

My editor remarked that he was certain the *Murder Cruise* title would appeal to boating enthusiasts.

"It seems kind of odd to me," I told him, "but you guys know better." I didn't argue because I didn't know how many of those boaters actually read books in the true crime genre.

Later, I found out there were about fifty such readers.

Murder Cruise sank like Paula Abdul's career after her firing from *American Idol.*

But I kept trying.

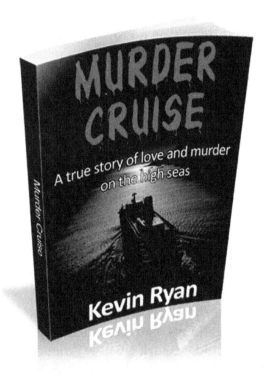

Monday, July 29

SEVENTEEN DAYS AFTER I MET with Connie Carter, the Community Relations specialist from the prison left a message on my answering machine.

"Kevin? This is Muriel Constantine from Riverstone. Janet has reconsidered your offer for an interview. I've scheduled you for four tomorrow afternoon. If you want to see her anytime soon, that's the best I can do. Bye."

I was elated. Of course, I knew she'd come around. I called it the true crime domino or TCD effect. One important source begets another important source. One side of the story leads to the other. No one wants anyone else to speak for them.

TCD was proof that no one ever wanted to be left out of a story.

Janet had undoubtedly talked with her mother and Connie probably mentioned I was out interviewing everyone who knew her daughter from the day she came home from the hospital to the day she was shipped off to serve her time in prison.

I could hear mother and daughter now:

"Jan, he's one of those investigating types...there's no telling what he might find. Best be on his side and cooperate. He can help us and you don't have to tell him anything you don't want him to know."

"Yeah, like the producer from the Rita Adams Show. *She wanted the true story. She said she'd look into things for us. She said she'd send us a goddamn transcript and an autographed picture of Rita! She promised to tell our side, too, and look where it got us?"*

"It got us to Kevin Ryan, that's where. Either we talk or we sit in here and rot until an appeal comes through or we die."

"Why do I even ask you? It's not like listening to you has done me any good."

"I'm your mother. That's why you listen to me."

Tuesday, July 30

PRISON FOOD HAD FATTENED HER UP. It did to so many. When I finally came face-to-face with Janet Lee Kerr in Riverstone's special visit room, I could see the pounds that months of double scoops of mashed potatoes with hamburger gravy and bowls of Riverstone Casserole had done to the young woman's figure since she had been on the *Rita Adams Show.* I estimated at least a twenty-pound weight gain. Maybe more. Her long brown hair had been cut short on the sides, a kind of modified Jane-Fonda-in-*Klute* shag. It looked a little—I hated to think—*butch.* It was not an especially attractive hairdo.

I hoped Angela, her cellmate, liked it. I assumed it had been styled for her.

"Pleased to meet ya," she said, extending her hand.

"Okay to shake?" I asked an enormous male guard who sat at the end of the table like some denim-clad Buddha.

"Yeah. No monkey business, though."

Monkey business? What was I going to do, pull something out of a body cavity and hand it over to her?

Janet rolled her eyes and we shared a little laugh.

Over the course of the hour, my recorder consumed a mini-tape as we talked about Janet's life and her cocksure insistence that she had been framed. She had been tricked. She had been hoodwinked.

I could see that she was likable enough, though, certainly not anyone I'd want to pal around with. She was more like someone I might ask how to change the oil on the LUV. I wondered what power she had over these men that would make them contemplate and attempt to kill on her behalf?

76

"Danny was in love with me. Still is," she said, tugging at the collar of a shirt that was too tight. "He wanted Deke out of the way so he could have me to himself."

"Were you in love with him?"

"You gotta be joking! He was a loser that I felt sorry for. I hung around him, but I never led him on."

"Lovers?"

Again, Janet let out a snicker of denial. "Have you seen him?" she asked skeptically.

"Just the photo on television. You know, the talk show."

"Let me tell you, they did him a favor by cutting Danny's puzzle piece smaller than the others. With as big as he is, he'd need a 500-piece jigsaw of his own."

"You were never boyfriend/girlfriend?" I asked one more time.

Her denial stayed firm. "Never. Never in a zillion years. I never even let him touch my hand."

"So this whole mess was caused by Danny? Misguided goofball Danny?"

She lowered her gaze. "And Deke. Deke's at fault here, too. He was weak and let those bastards in the DA's office pressure him into lying at my trial."

"What about you, Janet? Are you responsible for any of this?"

Like flipping a switch, Janet's eyes welled up with tears. She brushed aside her shaggy, brown hair with a finger accented by a coiled snake ring.

"Yeah, I am," she said, her chapped lip now quivering. "I made a mistake by loving the wrong man. That's my only crime."

I nodded as I thanked her and packed up my recorder, the time allotted by the prison over. There was always a little truth to that statement. Through my work, I knew that it was frequently the combination of people that led them to the

77

unthinkable. On their own, they'd have brewed in their contempt for their target. With some urging, however, plans were swung into action. Murder or violence was like an eBay auction or drinking game, with the sway of others pushing you to do more than you wanted.

Or should.

♦

Another letter came earlier that day. I recognized the envelope: gray, unremarkable. No return address. Simple lettering that looked more creepy than cursive. Inside, the single sheet wasn't a direct threat. Those are easy to handle. You know what to expect. But this was veiled in the most insidious manner possible.

Just four little words.

PRETTY WIFE PRETTY GIRLS.

It was like cancer, I supposed. If you felt all right, you could ignore it. It was there eating away at your body. But as long as there were no outward indicators, you were fine. Denial was so very powerful. But every now and then, as I typed I thought about the letters. It was like a dripping faucet mocking every click of my keyboard.

I finally had to tell Val about the letters. I found her upstairs buried in a stack of laundry. She set down Taylor's pink and purple swimsuit, regarded the letter and shrugged. She didn't seem to get the seriousness of what I was showing her.

"I'm concerned and a little creeped out," I said, coolly as I could.

Val handed the letter back and turned her attention to the laundry. "I thought you'd be happy to have a stalker," she said. "I mean, finally, about time, Kevin."

She was deadpan, but I knew it wasn't how she really felt.

Chapter Ten
Saturday, August 3

JETT CARTER CALLED MY OFFICE LINE SATURDAY MORNING with bad news. Her sister had taken ill at the prison the night before and had been shuttled off to the infirmary under the care of sadistic nurses who—according to Janet—enjoyed probing and poking and sticking their rubber-gloved fingers where they weren't supposed to. As Jett recounted it, Janet had choked on the rice pudding at dinner the night before. Another prisoner rushed to her aid and administered the Heimlich maneuver, but apparently had done so with such force it cracked two ribs.

"She's real upset because she won't be able to work in the sewing shop for at least a week. She needs the money to pay for her appeal."

The sewing shop offered the *creme de le creme* of prison jobs, paying almost five dollars an hour. The prison shop made sleeping bags, duffel bags and totes. Each was tagged *MADE BY THE LADIES ON THE INSIDE.* Years ago, MLI designs were highly coveted by college students for their prison cachet. A major Northwest sportswear company jumped on the idea and created a line of apparel and accessories called Jail House Frocks. The "prison-inspired" line sold like gangbusters at JC Penney's and Kohl's. In a matter of weeks, the Jail House Frocks success turned the MLI product line into has-been, hand-me-downs. No college or high school student wanted to wear or tote something that even *suggested* Penney's.

MLI never recovered their glory days, though they still did enough business to employ twenty-two of the prisoners, whose names were drawn by lottery. Janet was one of the lucky few to get one of the coveted positions.

"Janet is afraid she will lose her job doing zippers," Jett told me. "She needs the cash."

Jett was already working two jobs and sending whatever money she didn't absolutely need for her own food and shelter to the prison for her mother and sister's canteen expenses. The girl simply couldn't work harder.

"How long will it take for her to recover?" I asked.

"Doctors don't know. Hell, the doctors in there aren't worth a crap. They do as little as they can. Mom and Jan tell me that if you are going to prison, you better stay healthy. There is no such thing as medical care for the girls on the inside."

"So I've heard," I said as I switched on the speakerphone so I could neaten up the little piles of murdered lives that deluged my desktop.

"I'm getting ready to write the first chapter and if you're up for it, I have a couple of questions for you."

We talked another twenty minutes or so and I wondered why it was that the nicest people are trapped in families in which there is no hope. No chance even. Why is it that once the ball is rolling, it can never be stopped? Everyone wants to believe that they are in charge of their own destiny, but what of the baby born to a woman like Connie? Jett had barely escaped and the sad truth was that at any time she could be pulled back into the whirlpool like her sister. If the worst that could happen ever did, and Jett committed some airhead crime and was sent to prison, every day could be a family reunion for mother and daughters.

"Your name is unusual," I said, winding down the conversation.

There was a short silence. Then a gusher.

"My mother named me after her favorite singer, Joan Jett. Obviously, 'Joan' wouldn't work. For the longest time I wished she had named me Mariah or something else. Even Madonna would have been better. But she thought Jett was a strong, unique name. She had heard somewhere that strong names make for strong women. She already had a Janet and figured Jett would be better."

I told her I liked her name.

"I think it's kind of stupid," she said flatly.

I tried to convince her otherwise, but she would have none of it. She didn't take compliments well and she didn't know how to give them. She had been isolated from the good that people had to offer. Yet, she was so trusting of me. I liked her right away.

◆

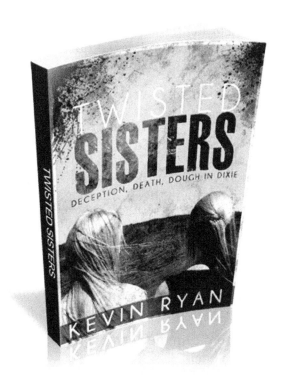

I SPREAD OUT MY NOTES AND TURNED ON my iPod. It was a ritual that had sustained me through my other books. I always typed to the sound of music. I tried to pick a performer whose music fit the milieu of the story I was telling. For *Twisted Sisters: Deception, Death, Dough in Dixie*, I typed to a Dolly Parton disc that I picked up at Silver Saucers by exchanging my girls' Raffi CDs. I felt country tunes would help me write the story of two sisters from Knoxville who murdered the husband of one because he was lazy, mean and wouldn't buy her a new car. I guess it worked. *Twisted Sisters* was optioned for a television movie to star post-*Clarissa*, pre-*Sabrina* Melissa Joan Hart. The movie, like all the others optioned by some hotshot producer with little money and a gigantic line, was never made.

For *Murder Cruise*, I typed to Jimmy Buffett, realizing that the Florida Keys was nothing like the Hawaiian Islands, save for the fact the islands—like any—were surrounded by water.

When I wised up and figured out that my books needed more intellectual appeal, I wrote to *Musical Jewels: A Golden CD Collection of Classical Composers' All-Time Favorites*. I played it on repeat for days on end, hoping the flow of the compositions would rub off on my phrasing.

My editor considered my work-in-progress *Fatal Killer* my masterpiece at the time.

"The rhythm of the murder scene is outstanding," he said, while I watched Hedda awkwardly dig into her back after a flea. "The way in which you have the girl find her mother with the blood still spurting out of her head was magical."

"Thanks," I said. "I'm trying to reach a different crowd. Don't you think we could do better than *'Fatal Killer'* for a title?"

"Marketing says *Fatal* works. Look at *Fatal Vision*."

I rolled my eyes at the never-ending list of *Fatal* titles. *Fatal Voyage, Fatal Mother, Fatal Wedding, Fatal* blah, blah, blah.

"I'm just trying to lift up the genre," I finally said. "I want it to be better than it has been."

"Better doesn't work," he said. "*Better* doesn't sell books!"

"I see."

"Besides, wait until you see the cover for *Fatal Killer*. I think you'll like what the art department is trying to do with it."

"Red and black?"

"No, a dark ebony and mahogany. Very different. Incredibly classy."

When I saw a jpeg rendition of the cover a few days later, it looked red and black to me. I dialed my editor right away.

"It's just your monitor," he said, somewhat impatiently. "It's more cherry than red and more of a warm black than anything. You'll see."

In the end, I counted my blessings. It was not the worst cover I had ever seen. I doubted *For the Love of a Baby* could ever be topped. It was, of course, red and black. But the art department at Death Penalty Books touted a unique die-cut, pop-up cover that they believed would set a new standard for the publishing world. They were right. It set a new low-water mark.

The cover depicted a tombstone with a child's date of birth and death cut into the cold gray of a granite slab. When the reader opened the book, a die-cut flap popped up like a gruesome jack-in-the-box. It was a little baby, eyes closed, wearing a pink sleeper.

Baby in the grave. Baby out of the grave. Open and close. Open and close.

Whenever I thought of it, I cringed and felt a sense of relief at the same time. It could always be worse.

I settled down and went to work, each day fading into the next as I soaked up the story and planned how I'd make this the best story ever.

♦

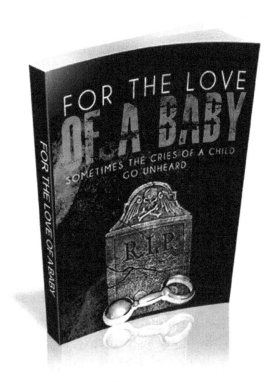

Thursday, August 8

THE SUN CAME OUT ON THURSDAY. The girls begged me to take them to the lake and I begrudgingly agreed. I didn't mind going to the beach, as it gave me time to do a little reading and it kept Taylor from killing Hayley and vice versa. We put Hedda on a leash and secured her in the back of the truck. Cecile, from up the hill, had been invited to go along because I knew that with three there would be one unhappy child. With two, there would be an unhappy adult and two unhappy children. Cecile was a good sport and I was glad for the diversion.

We had to be home by late afternoon because Jett was coming for dinner after her prison visit with her mother and sister. I wasn't about to try anything to impress company. I just wanted something good and easy to serve.

"No meat," Taylor advised while I dug through the refrigerator. "I can't have any meat even *touching* my food."

"Me neither," Hayley chimed in.

With the notable exception of McDonald's hamburgers and cheeseburgers, our girls had emphatically insisted that they were vegetarians. I failed to see how they could justify a burger when its starting place was an Argentine cow.

"Fine," I said, somewhat annoyed. "I'll put the shredded chicken on a separate plate. No meat will touch anything you don't want it to."

"Better not," snapped Hayley, the one who could make my blood boil faster than anyone. She was the daughter everyone said was most like me, though I didn't see it.

"Mom cooks us tofu for our tacos now, you know," Hayley added.

"No, I didn't," I said. "And no, before you ask, I'm not going to do that."

Valerie came home at seven, in time to share a glass of wine and witness a mess in the making. She was hot and miserable from her long commute from the city. The instant I saw her I felt the unmistakable pang of guilt. It had been my idea to pass on air conditioning for the new Honda.

"Who needs it in Seattle? It's an extra nine hundred that we don't really have to spend," I had told her, uttering the famous last words that I had to live with.

Val was dubious at the time, but she finally consented. The first day she drove it in eighty-degree weather she knew she had given in too soon. She'd have paid nine grand extra for the comfort of an air conditioner.

"It is like a little silver coffee can," she said of her car. "If I were a lizard you'd take a nail and hammer out a row of holes on the top so I could breathe."Pinkness slowly faded from her face.

Jett arrived five minutes after Val. She wore jeans and a cropped T-shirt. She was cool and refreshed. Her car, it seemed, had air conditioning. "This isn't what I had on in prison," she said. "No skin can be exposed—except arms, of course. I wore a sweatshirt for my visit with mom and sis."

Jett brought what she called her "Kids Kit," though she was quick to point out that she was not babysitting that night.

"I thought the girls and I could make some barrettes or charms before dinner."

I called Taylor and Hayley to pry themselves from the TV.

"Do you girls want to make hair bows?" I asked.

"Barrettes," Jett corrected.

The girls gathered around while Jett cut colorful strips of plastic and melted them with a hair dryer. When it was heated, the plastic could be bent, stretched and twisted. She made two fast friends that night. Taylor made a rainbow clip and Hayley made a cat pin. Val and I even played with the stuff before we all sat down to dinner. Taylor and Hayley gobbled their food, pretended to be bored by the adult conversation.

Val excused them and suggested they watch a movie.

"I brought home two new releases from the RedBox," she said.

I could tell Val liked our dinner guest. She was listening intently and even reached across the table to pat Jett's hand when I returned from getting the girls settled. It was a touching gesture. She had never done that for Wanda-Lou.

"Kevin never told me," Valerie said.

"Told you what?" I resumed my seat and pulled out my little tape recorder.

"About her father's suicide," Val said quietly, never moving her sympathetic eyes from the young woman seated at our table.

I was pleased Jett had opened up to my wife. Pleased and surprised. I thought *I* was the good listener, I thought I was the one who could draw out the most intimate of details.

"We've never really talked about it in detail. Could we now?" I asked.

Jett looked at Val and slowly nodded.

"I don't like talking about it, but if you need me to, I will," she said.

Chapter Eleven
Friday, August 9

CONNIE CARTER WAS WORKING NIGHTS at the Rusty Anchor serving drinks and "hostessing."She wore a short black skirt and a white sailor top trimmed in blue. Jett was seven and in her eyes her mother was a vision, as pretty and elegant as Vanna White in one of those gowns by Climax of Rodeo Drive. Her dad was a short man with hands like oven mitts and a belly that made the waistband on his Wranglers roll over. Two times. He was a hardworking and sometimes hard-drinking man who never hit the kids. Connie, however, was known to slap them around if she thought they needed it.

"One time," Jett recalled that night in our kitchen, "my mom came after my sister with the electric cord of her curling iron. She held the iron in her hand like a mini-baseball bat and beat Janet on the back of the legs until the welts erupted like tree roots under the asphalt."

Val put her hands to her lips and shook her head. I gently urged Jett to go on. I wanted to know more about life with Connie Carter.

She pushed a dark lock of hair behind her ear, though it was too short to stay in place. She poured milk into her coffee and told Val and me what we knew had to be the understatement of the year.

"We had no money," she said, "and we were fresh out of hope."

It was true, she explained, the Carter family lived paycheck to paycheck. Light bills were paid just moments before the power company turned off the electricity. A mattress and box spring set was divided into two sleeping platforms—"the softy" and "the hardy," as she and her sister dubbed them. Janet took the softy, leaving little sister Jett with the rigid box springs.

When she was about ten, Jett said her mother left her logger father, Buzz Carter, and took up residence in a second-floor room with a kitchenette at the Seahorse Motor Inn. Connie told her daughters things weren't working out with their father and they needed time apart. The distance would allow them the time and space to see if they still loved each other.

Connie left her girls in the room when she worked at the bar. When the motel manager complained that the Child Welfare people wouldn't take the idea of leaving little ones unattended all night, she took them to the Rusty Anchor and had them sleep in the car until after her shift ended. The girls liked the motel-room arrangement better. It had a television set and two real beds. The fact that it had moth-eaten bedspreads and a toilet that was ringed in a bloom of rust was lost on the girls. Anyone older would have called the Seahorse what it was—a flop house, a fleabag, a crash pad.

For four months, the Carter girls called it home.

According to Jett, her mom had a boyfriend by then and they saw less and less of Buzz. One afternoon Connie sat her girls down and announced that they would never see their daddy again.

"Mom told us he left a note saying he wasn't coming back," she recalled.

Jett remembered how Janet cried and blamed both her mother and sister, making Buzz mad at the whole family. They had been bad. Connie shouldn't have moved away and Jett shouldn't have been born.

"It was two years before I figured out what they were talking about," she said softly, her words growing fainter as she struggled to fight the emotions that she had kept locked away so well. So long.

Painful as it obviously was, I prodded her to continue. I didn't want to force her to reveal more than she was ready to tell. And yet I didn't want to be left hanging.

"What happened?" I asked once more. Val glared at me. Her eyes told me not to push. It was too late.

Tears came quickly, in such a rush that it startled me. Jett got up and took her plate to the sink, turning her back on us.

"Daddy *didn't* move away," she said. "He jumped off the River Bridge into the Ocean River. His note was a suicide note. This was no, 'I love you', no 'goodbye.' But I didn't know that. I thought he had moved to another town because he didn't love us. I didn't know that he jumped into the river because he knew Mom had a boyfriend. For two years my mom and sister let me think he was still out there."

Val moved closer. "Why on earth did they do that?" she asked, tears now filling her dark brown eyes.

Jett looked out the window, far off into the soft green boughs of the Douglas firs that fringed our property, as though the words she was seeking could somehow be found out there.

Finally, she spoke. "It was to spare me, I guess. That's what they told me. To *spare* me."

"How did they tell you?" I cut in, jumping back into the conversation.

"They didn't. My foster parents did. My *fourth* set of foster parents, to be exact. Written out on my junior high enrollment papers after my father's name was *'deceased'.*"

She studied our reactions before continuing.

"I asked the snippy woman, who told my caseworker she loved children—of course, what she really loved was the money from the state—what gives, and she looked at me and said, 'Didn't your mommy tell you?'"

Jett Carter had never thought of her mother as the mommy type, but she resisted the temptation to say so.

90

"'*Honey,*'" Jett recalled, mimicking the singsong voice of her foster mother, "'*your father's dead. He jumped off the bridge.*' God, I can still see him drunk, stumbling against that railing, throwing out his arms to stop himself—I mean, uh, that's how I always pictured it, you know, in my nightmares."She looked up at us, as if suddenly breaking out of a trance, or coming to the surface after swimming deep under water, and for just a second she looked so hateful that I took two steps back.

Val and I were breathless. The words shocked. This girl had been through a nightmare that was inconceivable. She was telling her story so calmly, so serenely, I knew she had told it before. She had talked it out; she had worked it out.

"I started to cry and the woman told me to let it all out. Instead I gave her the finger and ran up to the room I shared with another foster kid. In fifteen minutes, I was out of there. Mom and Janet had their own apartment then and by the time I got to their place, the foster mother had already called."

"I didn't think there was supposed to be any contact between parents and foster parents," I said.

"There isn't, but Timberlake is such a small place... that particular foster mother knew Mom from the Rusty Anchor. She and her husband used to come in to play pull tabs and drink beer. Anyway, Mom met me at the door and gave me the line about wanting to *spare me.* It took me years to forgive her for that."

◆

VALERIE AND I TALKED FOR ALMOST AN HOUR after Jett went home. We both hugged the petite little wisp of a girl. Val and I both knew that by doing so, we had crossed the line from book source to friend. It didn't matter. In the case of Jett Carter, it was the right thing to do. To be unmoved by her lot in life was to have a granite heart. Jett, who we now knew was a surprising twenty-one years old, was a fighter. She might have been on the wrong side of the tracks most of her life, but she still had the desire to better herself. She wasn't going to throw in the towel. Val and I wanted to help her, if we could.

"Think how strange, how tragic it is," Val said as we turned off the living room and kitchen lights and told the girls to go to sleep. "Jett is an outsider in her own family, and has been since she was a kid. Now her mother and her sister are together in prison of all places and she's *still* on the outside."

It was an astute observation. For Jett, it was just as it had been after Buzz Carter took the plunge off the bridge so many years ago in Timberlake. Valerie was so right. In a family of sour milk, Jett Carter was the sweetest cream. Against all odds, she had risen to the top.

Chapter Twelve

Friday, August 13

FUELED BY A KING-SIZE KIT KAT, A POT OF COFFEE, and this belief I actually had something to write about, I finished the first chapter of the true crime book that would put me back in the game. I left it next to the coffee maker for Val to read in the morning. I even set out the reading glasses she purchased from a drugstore rack—not to save money, but because she didn't want to admit that she needed "real" glasses. I added a postscript to the chapter because I know the way my wife thinks. She's been slogging through my stuff since I picked up my first zebra-bloodbath-covered tome and thought, *Wow! This author gets money for this?*

♦

Love You to Death

PART ONE

THOUGH EVERY ONE OF THEM ENDURED their lives under clouds so dark and low they could be poked with a sharp stick, none particularly liked the rain or paid it any mind. It just was. It came from the sky with such maddeningly regularity that most never carried umbrellas, never bought galoshes, and most certainly, would never be caught dead swirled in the protective plastic of a poncho. The town of Timberlake was a soggy reminder of what the Northwest's timber industry had once been. Smokestacks from the mills choked ash through the rain but half the time of the good old days. Worker shifts had been cut by almost two-thirds. Most of what had once been, however, was still in evidence. Taverns and pool halls still ran good businesses and college students from Portland, less than an hour south, came to buy Timberlake castoffs at the thrift shops. Fridays were "Two-fer" days, with the tattered row of shops offering half-price deals.

And while it rained, rivulets coursed through the gutters to the streets, then on to the Pacific Ocean. Tired workers lugged their sweaty bodies home, a video and a six-pack in tow. Mothers microwaved leftover Top Ramen and served up smiles for their babies.

Outside of town on the old Pacific Highway, young people pulled off the black sheen of asphalt and climbed the rutted logging roads tumbling down the mountainsides. Up the slope, through the mud, jacked up and juiced, they went. Little pockets of music could be heard throughout the fall of the evening. Though it was long since their prime, Deep Purple, Led Zeppelin and Jimi Hendrix still ruled. Most hadn't a clue Hendrix was dead and had been since the time they were born. The local record store had requests for a new Hendrix album so often it put up a sign behind the cashier: NO NEW JIMI.

The fact was that if any group was stuck in a rut it was the youth of Timberlake. Out of a class of 245, only twenty-one arranged for further education-and two of those were headed for Merilee's School of Beauty. Most planned on jobs at the mill or the mall. Career Day at the high school was such a flop that spring that only the recruiters for the U.S.

Army and a pimply-faced man from Buckle showed up with application forms. Four boys and one girl signed up for the service, and Buckle had a line out the door for its new teen lifestyle apparel outlet. There were seven openings for the thirty-five dreamers that had decided on careers in fashion merchandising.

And so at night the rain would fall, the mall would close, and bulked up young men and their bulls-eyed butt-tattooed girlfriends would head for the logging roads where they could guzzle beer from tepid cans, screw their brains out, and just plain forget they lived in Timberlake.

IT WAS JUST AFTER ONE in the morning, November 28. Cool and wet, the forecaster had promised, and he was right. Melba Warinski was sitting at the front desk of the River's Edge Motel working on a pinecone wreath that would be a Christmas present for her mother. She was a pleasant woman, with a round face and a nose so tiny it was a modern-day miracle that her glasses did not slide from her face. She was in her forties, a mother, and with her husband's hours being cut at work, she willingly took up the slack with a part-time job at the motel. She wanted a little extra money for craft supplies and she figured that the front desk job was as easy as any place to get it. Hardly anyone ever stayed there after the Holiday Inn Express went in alongside the interstate. The slick little upstart had a free continental breakfast and in-room movies. There were no honor bars. To compete, the River's Edge's owner picked up a dozen donuts for breakfast and bought a used VCR for what he called "Courtesy Cinema."

In the four weeks Melba worked there, only one man asked for the video player. He brought it back a half hour later.

"Thing isn't worth a damn. Movie won't track right."

"I'll let the manager know as soon as possible. I'm sorry for the inconvenience, sir. Would you like a copy of the paper?"

The man shuffled back to his room without another word and Melba went back to her hot glue gun. Her fingertips were burned and she was about ready to call it a night when the noise of a honking car turned her toward the window. The driver was laying on the horn, easing up only every ten seconds or so.

For a moment Melba Warinski wondered if it was another husband trying to find his wife or a drunk looking for a room.

She went to the front door and swung it open. Two beams of light stared at her from across the parking lot. The honking stopped and a car door opened. In an instant, there was a thud. A man fell onto the asphalt and it was quiet, save for the noise of a talk radio station.

"You okay?" She squinted her eyes at the headlights.

"Help. She set me up," a voice called from the darkness. "She set me up. I've been shot."

Melba hurried to the truck. The slippers her husband gave her the previous Christmas were not meant for the dampness of the weather. But Melba didn't even think about them when she went to the man, though later she would regret that she hadn't gone barefoot to save on the wear and tear. She loved those slippers.

"You all right?" She repeated as she bent over the body of a young man, maybe twenty-three or twenty-four. Red oozed from his chest

96

and the smell of beer and gunpowder came from the open cab of his pickup.

"She did this to me. She did it."

"Who? Who did this?"

"Janet did. Janet set me up."

"Son, we've got to get you a doctor."

Melba looked around for something to put under the young man's head. Blood and rain swirled toward a leaf-chocked storm drain. The man was mumbling and Melba's heart raced. She was scared. She took off her slippers and put them under the young man's glistening head.

Was it blood? Was it rain?

"Don't you go to sleep, now," she yelled as she ran back to the office phone to call 911. As she crossed the parking lot she nearly careened into Andy Lowery, a 32-year-old cook who had rented a room monthly for the past year.

"What's going on?" he asked.

"Can't talk," Melba said. "Kid's been shot. Calling 9-1-1. Keep talking to him!"

Andy Lowery made his way to the victim and Melba disappeared inside the motel office.

Her hands were shaking as she spun the 9 digit of the rotary dial. It seemed to take forever...then the two ones and an answer. Melba told the operator what she found, verified the location and promised to keep the victim talking while help arrived. She unplugged her smoldering glue gun and went out into the rain. In the time it took her to run back to the man in the parking lot she could already hear the sirens warning drivers to pull over.

Help was on its way.

97

"Can you hear them? They're coming to help you...what's your name?" Andy Lowery asked the man as Melba joined them.

The young man rolled his head to the side and vomited.

"Deke. Deke's my name. Deke Cameron. My name is Deke."

Andy noticed a twelve-pack of Bud. It seemed that Deke Cameron was not drunk. Of course, being shot could sober up anyone lickety-split.

"Can I turn off the radio?" Andy asked.

"Okay."

Andy fumbled with the radio for a bit and couldn't find the right button.

"Just push the knob in," Deke Cameron said between rekindled murmurs of utter agony. "Just push it in."

♦

Note to Val: *Yes, the phone was a rotary dial—this is not one of those "embellishments" that befall true crime writers as they seek to add "layers of detail" to make reality more "real" as my editor on* Murder Among Friends *once insisted I do. We're talking a town populated with people who still have microwave ovens the size and heft of a deep freeze. Don't ask me why. Keep reading. —K*

♦

PACIFIC OCEAN MEDICAL CENTER was a mile from the River's Edge Motel on Big Leaf Avenue. It had been opened amid a parade of grade-schoolers and bunting-bedecked fire trucks in 1952. It was the pride of the county, and indeed the region. In 1977, in celebration of its silver anniversary, Pac-O, as the locals called it, was remodeled top to bottom. Bulbous-shaped orange and lime green plastic molded chairs were installed in the waiting areas and a green and rust plaid carpet was laid wall to wall giving the rooms the flavor of a pumpkin patch in October. The decor was out of date ten years before it was put in place.

Deke Cameron was brought to the Pac-O emergency room at a few minutes past two in the morning. He was still conscious and continued to repeat his name and the name of the woman he blamed for the shooting. Melba Warinski, now wearing shoes, had followed the ambulance from the motel. She wanted to make sure the young man made it.

"Are you his mother?" a nurse asked as she breezed past, clipboard open, pen poised for a response.

"Oh, no."Melba answered, stepping away. "I just found him in the parking lot. I don't know him from Adam."

♦

MARTIN RAINES WAS AT HOME TRYING to sleep off his wife's shredded beef enchiladas and a bad sci-fi movie he had watched with his kids. The Pierce County Sheriff's detective was up twice in the hours after he went to bed. Each time he made it to the toilet he expected some kind of relief. But he sat there like a statue and nothing happened. He drank a couple of gulps of Pepto-Bismol and went back to bed.

Finally finding himself drifting off, the bedside telephone rang. It was his sergeant calling, telling him to get his tired butt down to the Pac-O.

"There's been a shooting," the sergeant monotoned into the phone. "A guy's in ICU and it looks like he won't make it. Been shot at least twice by his girlfriend."

The detective made one more pass at the toilet and dressed for work. He was ten minutes from the hospital, but given the ungodly hour, he knew he'd be there in five or six, tops. His sleeping wife didn't stir. The dog, a messy little black and white thing with an overbite, didn't move. No one ever bothered to say goodbye. Slipping into the night was a matter of routine in the Raines house.

Martin Raines was a round little man with sandy hair and blue eyes that suggested the color of bluebonnets. It was appropriate since he had, in fact, been born in Austin, Texas. He was just four when his mother and father split up from a marriage made in hell. His father had used his mother as a punching bag since before the two wed. His mother had stuck by her man because she was raised to believe in God and marriage for life. Deeply depressed, she sought solace in prayer and food. When the young woman finally reached her limit, she loaded Martin on a Greyhound bus for the Pacific Northwest to live with her mother. The hope, however, was short-lived.

Little Marty and his mama moved to Timberlake where his mom worked at her mother's hair shop until her death of a self-inflicted gunshot wound at thirty-two. No one had seen the signs of impending suicide. No one saw her as she sculpted daggers out of wet hair. No one watched as she held the scissors as a weapon against herself. No one knew anything was up until she failed to return from her half-hour lunch break. Martin came home from school to find his grandmother on her hands and knees scrubbing the pieces of her daughter from the floor.

"Mama's gone, hon. Your mama's gone to heaven to sleep with the angels," the old woman with the bicycle-pumped hairdo said, holding back tears.

The second-grader with the big ice blue eyes cried for the next ten days. In his heart, of course, he never stopped crying.

Martin was raised by his grandmother in an apartment she kept above the Clip Joint. When he was eighteen, he joined the Army, did a tour in Desert Storm, came back to odd jobs, and finally, a law enforcement career.

As he passed the old storefront of the Clip Joint, by then a pet grooming place called Love on a Leash, the memories of growing up in Timberlake came back to him as they always did. He let out a sigh. He had battled the depression that was an occupational hazard among many in his profession. He didn't want to end up like his mother. Iraq had not made it any easier. Thankfully, counseling and an understanding wife had. Detective Raines only wanted to make the world a better, safer place for his own children. He wanted to be a good cop.

And so he drove on to Pac-O.

♦

Note from Val: *Love on a Leash sounds like an S and M dive Rhianna would sing about. Are you sure it's a pet groomer? Anyway, reminds me that Hedda's due for a bath and haircut herself. If I make the appointment, will you drop him off at Shampooch? Like what I'm reading so far, but Marty might be unhappy being called a "round little man." Even though, he is. —V.*

Chapter Thirteen

Friday, August 16

I HAD FORTY-FIVE MINUTES TO KILL IN TIMBERLAKE, so like a spawning salmon, I followed the road along the river and made my way to the Columbia Mall. It was just opening and I followed the throng of semi-bargain hunters into the forty-four-store shopping center. Right by the door was the Food Circus with its white and blue Under the Big Top theme, a place where nations of food battled each other for dominance with the overreaching aroma of their cuisines.

The Swiss Hut Pretzel girl, a boomeranged-pigtailed Pippi Longstocking wannabe, offered a basket of cut-up pretzels.

I smiled at her and patted my stomach.

"Too early for me."

After finding the true crime section of the as-expected under-stocked Book World outlet, I pulled two copies of my books and placed them front cover facing out. I always did this. In the trade it was called "facing" a book, and for me, it was a compulsion. It might not be if I had ever taken a moment to figure out that if by the off-chance someone bought both copies, the sales would net me less than one dollar. For all the times I did it over the years, I would be lucky to have made enough to pay one month's phone bill.

After a driver for our local book and magazine distributor chewed me out for moving my book to Number Nine on the store best-seller list, I never did it in grocery stores again.

"Don't you ever mess with my racks!" said the man with the embroidered patch that proclaimed his name as Happy. He had short, brown scrub-brush hair. His eyes were dark, and I was sure, cold and unfeeling. He looked nothing like his name.

"Sorry... just trying to boost sales," I said sheepishly.

"I'm the one who decides which books get which boost. You touch my racks again and I'll leave your books on the truck until its time to rip off their covers to send back to your publisher."

"Hey, it's not like I made the book Number One or anything."

Wrong retort, I knew right away.

His eyes went a shade darker. "Listen, paperback writer, I'm the one who decides Number One. Got it? There's a mystery writer in Seattle that will never see Number One again, even if she earned it. She used to leave me little notes demanding to know why we were out of stock on her titles. And I fixed her, good. Her stuff stays on the truck."

I hoped I hadn't angered him for good. "Sorry, Happy. It won't happen again."

Perhaps Happy took pity on me. He never screwed me over and I stayed out of his way. The good Lord knew he had seen dozens of my kind circling the racks, facing the books, pretending to be interested in a book to lure other potential readers over.

"This story's unbelievable!" I said one time loud enough for a woman fifty feet from the book section to hear. I looked at her and pointed to my book. "Unbelievable."

"I only read romance," she replied as if they were based on some kind of reality.

"It's like romance," I persisted. "The woman kills her husband because she's so very much in love with another man."

It was one of those moments when you'd like to rewind the tape of what you said and start all over. The woman glared at me and moved on. I had lost another sale.

I had lost so many, yet I wasn't about to give up. Years later, I would say the feeling that I was *on the verge* was just as strong as it had been when I first started. I was going to make it. Yes, right out of middle class.

It was 10:45 a.m. I had fifteen minutes to catch up with my interview appointment. I gave into the charms of the Swiss Miss and grabbed some pretzel pieces before heading for my truck. They were greasy and good. I went back for another handful.

Thank God, I was tall. Sure, I was losing my hair. Sure, I swore each pint of Ben and Jerry's Chunky Monkey ice cream would be my last. I thanked God, and I would never embody the triumvirate of the attributes of the dumpy—short, fat and bald.

At least I would always be tall.

♦

I FOUND DEKE CAMERON'S MOTHER in the back of the Timberlake Dairy Queen. The smell of chocolate and French fries overwhelmed the cold, overly air-conditioned restaurant. Blizzard indeed. A group of kids in baseball uniforms crowded around the counter; their faces either glum because they lost their late-season playoff game, or the fact that the soft serve ice cream machine was sputtering alarmingly as it swirled. Mrs. Cameron stirred a paper cup of coffee with one of those plastic sticks, oblivious to the kids overtaking the place. Five little containers of cream had been dumped into her cup. A wadded napkin indicated nervousness, maybe apprehension. The television camera at the talk show had been kind to Deke Cameron's mother. She looked a lot older than she had on *The Rita Adams Show*.

"Mrs. Cameron?" I asked.

"Yes," she said, looking up from her cup. She did not smile. "Mr. Ryan?"

I nodded. "Kevin. I'm sorry if you've been waiting. I went to the mall to kill some time. If I had known you would have been early I'd have been here sooner."

Anna Cameron was a heavy woman with strong arms and broken blood vessels on her face. Her hair was too dark to be natural and she wore it in a style that reflected the tastes of the mid-1960s. A bit of a bubble added a couple of inches to her hair height. It was a look that had been with her since she was a teen. Anna, a bus driver for the school district, was named Driver of the Year five years prior. She wore earrings that reflected the honor: on her right lobe dangled a gold #1, on her left, a gold school bus.

"I don't have much to say to you," she said. "I am only meeting you because I don't want you to make a freak show out of my son. He's a victim, you know."

"I know," I said.

"He didn't do anything wrong but get involved with the wrong girl. That happens every day. I suppose you're going to believe those inbred idiot Parkers. My son taunted their precious Danny? That's a laugh. That's the biggest laugh in the county."

I told her I hadn't talked with the Parkers yet, though it was my intent to do so.

Mrs. Cameron gulped her coffee. She watched the baseball players as they carried their banana splits and curly-topped cones to an adjacent row of tables.

"You people just want to write a book and make money and move on to the next freak show. You don't care what happens to anyone."

I had heard that argument before. Many times. The woman was half right. True crime writers wanted to make money, but we seldom did. Sure we eked out a passable living, but the smartest of us held down a regular job and did their writing on the weekend or in the evenings.

"I do care about victims," I told her. "Have you read any of my books? I don't exploit the victim. I'm trying to shed a little light here and help people come to grips with what happened—and why it happened in the first place."

Anna Cameron stiffened her already unyielding posture.

"Listen," she said, "if you mess with me, my boy, or anyone in my family, I'll take you down so fast you won't know what happened to you."

"More coffee?" I asked, hoping my interruption would slow her tirade.

"If you mess with Deke, you mess with me."

"I don't intend to mess with anyone. I'm just trying to get the story right."

"You are a long way from getting it right," she said. "You're getting your facts from known liars."

"Who?"

"Connie and Janet, that's who. I know for a fact that you have been seeing them up at Riverstone. Plus that Parker bitch and her clan of dumbshit mountain men... she's always whining about her poor son, victim of love."

I stared hard at her. "I won't deny that I've interviewed Janet and Connie, but don't you see that it's my job to talk to both sides?"

Mrs. Cameron jumped up, shaking the tabletop with her palms planted firmly against its bright orange plastic surface. She was a curious blend of incredulity and anger.

"Job? I have a job driving a bus. I do four routes in the morning and three in the afternoon. I drive a ski bus on Saturdays to Crystal Mountain. It is a *job*. On Sundays, I cut lawns in the summer. In the winter, I clean apartments for move-ins. I don't see how you can call what you do a job of any kind."

"Mrs. Cameron!" I called after her as she stomped out of the Dairy Queen. "Sure you don't want another refill?"

Apparently she was certain. I reached down for my coffee and as I put it to my lips, I noticed it was nearly butterscotch color. She had left with my coffee and I had her cup. I loaded up her tray with her spent cream containers and cup and dumped the garbage into the swinging hatch of the Formica trash container. I

106

considered Anna Cameron to be a somewhat hostile source. Even so, I wouldn't give up on her. I was convinced she didn't agree to meet me just to threaten me. She met me because she didn't want her family dragged deeper into the mire. I planned on calling her later. She would talk.

They almost always did. The TCD effect never failed.

♦

MY NEXT STOP WAS THE FLYING J FAST FUEL just off the freeway for seven dollars' worth of gas. Just enough to get me home. When I arrived in Port Gamble, it was dark. I slowed as a mother raccoon and her babies looked at me as they skittered across the road. Their eyes were a string of garnets in my headlights.

A beam of light soared from our front window, turning tree branches into spider webs of light. I found Valerie sitting in her chair, her drugstore specs sliding down her nose, and once again fiddling with the checkbook and calculator.

"Can we make it through this month?" I asked, putting my briefcase away.

"This week's a little iffy," she said, taking off her glasses. "Kevin, we've stretched it to the limits. We've got to have this book be your greatest success or we've got to find another way to live."

I knew she was right, so I didn't argue. Genuine desperation filled her eyes. I knew I had used up my quota of arguments to justify this life that I chose.

"I'm willing to do my part. You know that, honey. Just tell me what to do, Kevin. Tell me how I can help you make this book a success. I'll do anything."

I kissed her gently on the cheek. It was a sweet kiss, brief and soft. It drank the moment in. Her skin was still flawless. Her hair accented by sandy streaks, was full and shiny. I imagined that I could send all the love from my heart to hers. If a choice were ever forced upon me, I would choose Valerie Ryan over a serial killer or an ax murderer any day. I just didn't want to be forced into making that choice.

"Just keep reading the chapters and keep your fingers crossed. It'll work out. I know it will. This one's the one."

"I know," she said as she had countless times before. Sometimes I detected a sad and knowing look on her face; the kind that troubled people had likely seen when their friends plotted a drug abuse intervention.

"By the way, Anna Cameron phoned about an hour ago."

I brightened. "Great, she's coming around. She probably changed her mind about an interview."

Valerie didn't think so. "Let's see... her words were, 'Mrs. Ryan, tell your bloodsucking husband to stay away from my family.'"

"I knew Mrs. Cameron would come around," I said, ignoring the reality of the words relayed by my wife.

Val gave me an annoyed look.

"Well, she called, didn't she?" I shrugged as I turned to make my way to my own private hell, my office and the blank screen of my computer.

"I'll leave the next chapter on the kitchen table," I said, knowing Val would fall asleep before I finished.

I started to type.

◆

Love You to Death

PART TWO

THE YOUNG MAN WAS IN AND OUT of consciousness. No one could get more out of him than his name and the name of the girlfriend he blamed for the shooting. At one

108

point, Deke Cameron muttered the name of Danny Parker as someone involved in the shooting. He didn't know who was holding the gun, Danny or his love, Janet. For the most part, his admittance form remained blank. What hospital staff did know was that he had been the victim of a terrible shooting, the kind no one likes to see. The kind that usually ends in death.

Deke Cameron was anesthetized and put under the knife twelve minutes after his arrival at Pac-O. With his clothing cut from his body and most of the blood swabbed away, it was easier to see the extent of his injuries. They were severe. He had been hit three times at close range-or so it was initially believed-with what the doctor who hunted guessed was a .20-gauge shotgun. Chunks of flesh had been blown from his chest and leg, and his left arm was shot halfway off. With his arm laid flat against his side, it was clear Deke had been shot once there. The blast damaged both arm and torso. Two shots total.

The dull clink of pellets hitting a stainless steel tray was the sound of the tedious collection of evidence.

An X-ray had revealed a spray of pellets spread throughout his lower torso like measles. It would not be medically necessary to remove each bit of metal from the victim, nor would it be necessary from a police perspective. The silvery tray was peppered black on the bottom.

"Looks like he'll make it, though he'll be setting off airport metal detectors for the rest of his life," an ER surgeon said as he exited the operating room.

"When can I talk to him?" Detective Raines asked.

"It'll be a while. Have some coffee."

Martin Raines passed on the coffee and cooled his heels outside in the waiting room as Deke Cameron was wheeled into recovery. A nurse told him that Deke might be able to make a brief statement, provided the anesthesia had worn off sufficiently.

Twenty minutes later, the detective was shown inside.

"Deke? I'm Detective Raines. I'm here to ask you a few questions."

The young man winced as he nodded. Though he was flat on his back, still feeling the effects of the drugs that had delayed the pain he would feel for weeks to come, Raines judged the victim to be at least six feet tall and 215 pounds. His hair was dark and wavy; his eyes were blue, dull and heavily lidded. Under the unforgiving fluorescent lights of the hospital, the lines underscoring his eyes and the subtle cracking around his mouth indicated he was a man close to thirty. Cut in an exaggerated mullet, his medium length hair was either too young for him or indicated he was stuck with the hairstyle he wore in high school-a common occurrence it seemed in Timberlake.

He was awake. *Weak*, but awake. There was no telling if he'd live long enough to give a statement. Some might have considered forcing him to do so at such a time bad taste. Poor judgment. Cruel.

Martin Raines called it a job.

He wasted no time. "What I'd like to know, is, where were you when you got shot? Do you know?"

110

"I think, the Edge Road there by Ruston, I'm not sure."

"The Edge Road by Ruston?"

"Uh-huh."

"You were in your car when you got shot?"

Deke shut his hooded eyes and nodded. The sharp smell of vomit wafted from his lips.

"The whole thing of it is," he said, as if a picture of what had happened snapped him back to attention, "I was with my girlfriend, we were driving along fine. She hops out, so I get out, and when I get out, I get shot. She takes off, I was screaming and hollering for her. She's nowhere to be found. I get hit twice. I didn't realize what happened."

"Do you know who shot you?"

"All I can say is, I think it was Danny Parker, because his car was there, too. I turned my car around... his car was there."

Raines asked what kind of car Parker was driving, and the man in the hospital bed said something about a Ford Escort hatchback.

"Hatchback?" the detective asked.

Deke Cameron's eyes rolled back for a second. "Yeah. Blue and white."

The investigator knew it was time to leave, time to let this guy get some rest before he died in the middle of a police interrogation. It wouldn't look good in the papers.

"I haven't got too much more time here," he said, "but is there anything else you can tell me, like why you were there?"

Deke tried to lift up his head, but seemed unable to gather the strength.

"I was set up, man, swear to God," he whispered. "We'd been drinking a little bit, and I was getting sick. I don't know why, I jumped out of the car for some reason. I should never

111

have got out, 'cause that's when I got... I think I got hit once in the car. I think so."

"You got out of the car and were hit?"

"I got hit *twice*, after I got out of the car."

"Do you know if Janet got hit?"

"No. I think she was in on it, 'cause she disappeared. I couldn't... I was screaming for her to take me to the hospital."

"Did you hear the car leave?"

"Uh-huh. Yeah."

"Okay. Do you know why they would shoot you?"

"Danny don't like me. I mean, he wants to be her boyfriend and whatnot, and they been friends for years."

"Okay. Janet was with you all evening? You picked her up at her house."

"Yeah... uh-huh."

"Is there anything else you can tell us? Where can we find them?"

"I don't know, if they're not in town, they're hiding out on a logging road somewhere."

"A logging road someplace?"

"Uh-huh. Back roads from here to uh, shit, where he is, it's near where his mom and dad live at."

"You probably better rest now. Be talking to you a little later. Okay, Deke?"

"Thank you, sir."

"You say you were at the old Edge Road?"

"I think so."

"By Ruston?"

"Uh-huh."

"Thank you very much, Deke. See you later. Good luck."

The man in the bed mumbled a thank-you as his eyelids dropped to a thin slit. In a second, the sound of snoring mixed with the beeps and tones of a hospital room.

Detective Raines felt his pockets for a roll of Tums. Looking at Deke Cameron and his gargantuan wounds turned his stomach even more so than the enchiladas. Blood oozed from the dressings. And the corrosive smell of vomit coated every word he uttered. It was too early in the morning for the sights, sounds and stomach-turning smells of a crime scene. Violence, he knew, did not punch a time clock.

"The clothes and personal effects from our guest," a pretty young nurse said as she and Raines walked toward the doorway out of the recovery room.

She handed the detective a Santa-sized bag, the kind with a yellow drawstring used in summer for hauling lawn clippings and in winter, soggy leaves. Inside were Levis, men's bikini briefs, a long-sleeved shirt with mother-of-pearl buttons, some work boots, socks, and a bloody pair of ladies' slippers. Everything had gone into clear plastic bags before being placed in the larger black bag. The procedure was in accordance with Pac-O and sheriff's procedure for the preservation of evidence.

Raines did a double-take on the last item.

"What gives with the fuzzy slippers?"

"Like I would know?" the nurse said with a half-laugh. "I only work here."

The next morning, I found my pages marked up, the coffee still hot, and a note from Val: *Like it. Glad you skipped starting with the Michener-style "Two million years ago, glacial ice carved the valleys of what would be Timberlake, Washington..." Also, thanks for mixing the words blood-oozed, corrosive smell of vomit AND enchiladas in the same paragraph. I'll never eat Mexican again. I'm sure you'll answer, but what's up with those slippers? —V*

Chapter Fourteen

Late Sunday, August 18

WHO KNEW JOAN JETT COULD BE SUCH AN INSPIRATION? Her greatest hits owned my iPod as I finished my latest chapter of *Love You to Death*. The rock anthem that made her name—"I Love Rock 'n Roll"—was probably the best tune I'd ever typed to. I downloaded the album from iTunes and must have hit replay ten times.

And as always, in my head, I changed the lyrics.

I love true crime books!
Write another chapter about some serial killer, baby!
I love true crime books!

I Googled a bit while I waited for the new chapter to roll off my printer, stopping once to shake the toner cartridge to eke out a few more pages. The last thing I needed was Val saying that the type was too faint to read—glasses or not.

TODAY'S LIST

Google: Crime case in the news with the most hits: Rick Rosen, an Ohio doctor, was arrested for the murder of his wife, Carlene. Carlene Rosen reportedly slipped on a layer of bath beads when getting into tub. She hit her head, slipped under the water, and drowned. Turns out the doc's first wife, Shannon, met a similar fate—she drowned during a boating accident on Lake Erie.

Possible book titles: "*The Depths of Evil*" or "*Slip 'n Die.*"

Amazon ranking for backlist: No change. But a two-star review on my first book made my blood boil. The reviewer "didn't like" the ending! Jesus! This is a true story! I can't change the damn ending!

Need from the store: Printer toner and Kit Kats.

To do: Take Hedda to Shampooch. Advertise on Craigslist for a new web person to replace Jeanne Morgan.

◆

Love You to Death

PART THREE

ADRENALINE AND CAFFEINE PROVIDED THE RUSH to keep the sleep-deprived Martin Raines and his fellow officers awake as they made their way to the Parker residence in search of a big dumb kid named Danny. It was 3:30 a.m. when four cars-two marked, two sneaker-cut their headlights and pulled up the road fronting the Parker's address. November gusts off the ocean had knocked several large limbs on to the driveway.

No one knew what kind of reception the law would get in the backwoods part of a county so rural its largest city was a paltry 14,000. Most who lived in the woods were folks who had something to hide, didn't like people, or couldn't afford better. None particularly cared for the police. The cops, they figured, meant bad news was coming their way.

A couple of officers stepped out of their cars to pull the impeding Douglas fir branches aside. The wind howled through the foothills and rain pelted their faces with needle-sharp pricks.

Raines dialed the Parker phone number from his cell phone. A moment later a light came on, illuminating the figure of a man lumbering toward the incessant ringing of a telephone.

"Hullo?" a groggy young man said.

"This is the county sheriff," Raines announced with firm, practiced authority. "We have surrounded your residence and we want everyone outside now. Hands in the air. We want you to come out and lay down on the grass, face down."

"Huh? This is a joke?" the young man said.

"This is no joke. We want you and everyone outside right now." Raines flashed his headlights as proof that there was somebody out there to make good on his implied threat.

The man on the line mumbled something about getting dressed and hung up. A few seconds later, more lights went on.

Raines didn't ask if the man was Danny. He figured it had to be.

Three minutes after the call, the front door swung open and the group of officers tightened their grip on their guns, now pointed at the house. Three figures emerged from the flood of light: The man who had answered the phone, presumably, along with an older woman in her nightgown, and an old man in a wheelchair. The woman was crying.

"Don't shoot! We done nothing wrong!" the younger man called out.

The woman pushed the wheelchair onto the grass, cutting parallel slices through what in the spring had likely been a lovely flower garden. Dogs circled the three and barked in the direction of the intruders.

116

"My husband can't walk! He can't get onto the grass!"

Jesus! Raines thought. *The woman was trying to pull the man out of his chair.*

The lady in the nightgown was frantic. The investigator wanted to tell her that she didn't have to put the invalid on the wet, cold lawn. It was too late. It was all happening so fast.

"Don't shoot!" she cried out again, yanking on the old man's arm as he tumbled onto the lawn without making a sound.

"Danny Parker?" Raines called from his car.

"Danny ain't here. I'm Davy. Danny's my big brother," the younger man said.

"My boy's been gone all night long!" the woman sobbed. "My husband and I are worried. Is he all right?"

"That's what we want to know. Where is he?"

"We don't know."

In the dark, the light from the house and flashlights and headlights converged on three members of the Parker family as they huddled, shivering in the wet of November. The woman, identified as June Parker, was fiftyish. She had patches of dried-on Noxzema on her face and her hair was a medium-length mess that made her thin frame resemble a Joshua tree. She wore an ecru-colored flannel nightgown with a thin, white chenille robe-now stained from mud, grass and the indignity of what was occurring on her property.

Raines was awash in empathy. She had probably never done anything wrong in her entire life and yet there she was suffering the humiliation of wearing nightclothes while

117

uninvited company pointed guns and high-beamed flashlights in her direction.

The man in-and out of-the wheelchair, Dwight Parker, never said a thing. He apparently *never* did. Mr. Parker had been falling apart piece by piece for better than twenty years. He had lost both feet in a terrible logging accident. His larynx was removed when cancer stole his voice at forty-seven. At a hard-living sixty-five, his hearing was lousy and his eyesight was failing by the month. Mrs. Parker used to tell friends that if her husband lost the use of one more part of his body, she'd strap him in his chair and wheel him into the Pacific Ocean to put him out of his misery.

"It would be an act of love," she said.

There wasn't much left for Dwight Parker.

Raines looked on as a pair of young cops hoisted Mr. Parker back into his chair and pushed him in the direction of the house.

Davy Parker wore a red auto supply company T-shirt and jeans that fell so low that the top third of his butt hung like two loaves of unbaked bread. He was in his late twenties, with thin, oily brown hair and a tattoo of an anchor on his right forearm. He had the tattoo made when he was seventeen in anticipation of going into the Navy after graduating from high school. Instead, he got a girl pregnant and took a job at the Wendy's stocking the Garden Spot salad bar in the mornings before the lunch crowd arrived. The girl had the baby, but refused to marry Davy. By that time, Davy had spent so much on household items getting ready for a family that didn't want him that he owed Visa and MasterCard more than four thousand dollars.

The anchor tattoo was an indelible reminder of what might have been.

Fifteen minutes after the phone call that rocked their neat little house, when it was clear there was no Danny around, the Parkers and the cops went inside to the living room. Bowling trophies gleamed from a corner cabinet, the *TV Guide* was spread open to the programming log for ESPN, and motor oil had stained the carpet where one of the Parker sons had worked on his mini-bike. It was the house of men; the kind whose interests had stayed frozen in the seventh grade.

"I knew something bad was going to happen," June Parker stammered as she fought for composure. She pulled her robe tight against her chest and absentmindedly re-stacked the newspapers on the coffee table. "I had a bad feeling about tonight."

"Ma'am, tell me what you know," Raines said, softly, leaning closer.

Mrs. Parker put her fingertips to her thin lips and tapped. For a few seconds she said nothing. She was reviewing the night before she spoke.

"It started around ten tonight," she said. "My son's fiance Janet called every fifteen minutes. Her old boyfriend was hitting her... beating her up again. Danny was fit to be tied. He had it in his mind that he'd go beat up Deke to give him a taste of his own medicine."

"Janet Lee Kerr and your son were going to get married?" Raines asked, trying to hide his surprise.

"Yes, in Vegas. Before Christmas. For Thanksgiving dinner, we had Janet and our daughter over and she and Danny got online to pick out wedding rings from the Sears web site."

Raines asked Mrs. Parker to fast forward to the events of the night.

"Danny was pacing the floor after every call. Goodness, the girl called every twenty minutes. He wanted gas money to go see her, but I refused to give it to him. He makes good money driving a truck. He just doesn't know how to hang on to it. I didn't want him to go beat up anyone."

"When did he leave?"

"About midnight, I guess. My husband and I had gone to bed. Danny's okay, isn't he?" She asked once more.

The detective felt sorry for her. "We don't know. We don't know where he is."

When asked to see if any of the Parker family's guns were missing, son Davy led the officers to the closet. A sixteen-gauge shotgun was propped up against the back corner. A quick sniff of its barrel suggested it had not been fired recently.

"What was Danny driving when he left?"

"His '84 Escort," Davy answered.

"Hatchback wagon?"

The brother and mother nodded in unison.

"Blue and white?"

"Uh-huh," June Parker answered. "The 'New Wave' package with a splattered interior and a row of distressed stars etched on the back window. There aren't many like them left on the road. Danny is real proud of his car."

Mr. Parker tugged at his wife's arm.

"Potty?" she asked sweetly.

The man in the wheelchair nodded and said "yes." It was the only thing he said during the interview. Mr. Parker was a man of few words.

Note from Val: *The description of June Parker needs a fix. The dried-on Noxzema on her face is good (mom used to wake up with that caked on, cracked mask every morning), but a Joshua tree? Jeesh, honey, no one outside of Arizona will know what that looks like. I'm not even sure and I've been there. The line: "Raines was awash in empathy?" Is that meant to be ironic? A pun? Last thought... I feel sorry for these people. I'm not sure if you want me to. But I'm just saying. —V*

Chapter Fifteen

Monday, August 19

ONE DROP FALLS, THEN ANOTHER. It starts the same way every time. Rain again. Being a native Northwesterner, I knew that as well as anyone. I only wished I had new tires as I drove off the interchange and felt the road slip beneath the old white Chevy LUV. I was on my way to more interviews, and while it was more of the same, it's what I loved more than anything. First up was June Parker, Danny's mother. I also made plans to get together with Jett for a tour of Timberlake, after hours.

"Wait 'til you see the Poodle Dog Inn!" she had said the night before. "I'll meet you there after you're done with Mrs. Parker."

"I can hardly wait," I said in a jokey, sarcastic manner.

"What time are you going out there?"

"About five-thirty... I asked her what time she ate and I'd show up afterwards. Her husband has physical therapy on Mondays and Wednesdays."

I told Jett that I had written what I called "update notes" to her sister and mother, letting them know that I was busy on the book and would see them at Riverstone soon—possibly as early as the following week. Provided, of course, the prison media flack wasn't too busy and could accommodate a special visit into her schedule. Jett seemed so happy that someone was writing to Janet and their mother. No one else did, and mother and daughter were very lonely.

"They don't even share a cell anymore," she said wistfully.

I didn't tell her that I knew that Janet had moved in with her lover Angela, and Connie was stuck with some new gal, refusing to "go lesbian" because it was too late in life to do so.

I checked my recorder, two new AA batteries and a small yellow pad. Those were the tools of the trade. I was ready for anything.

Or so I thought.

♦

EVEN IN DAYLIGHT, OLD STUMP ROAD could use a succession of streetlights. With all the accidents that took place as a result of its steep curves and blind driveways, it had become the kind of place tow truck drivers knew by rote. With nearly drill-press precision, the road had been bored through a forest as a tunnel of dark green that let in only the skimpiest of light. Most of the vegetation on the ground was leggy, straining for the glow of the sun. By now I found a peculiar irony about the road. It was the site of the shooting and it was the address of two victims. Paul Kerr lived at one end and at the other lived the Parker family. I had finally convinced a Parker family member to see me for the book. June Parker at first resisted, but with her son facing all those years in prison, she "had some things she wanted to get off her chest."

We had brief conversations over the phone and she had reluctantly provided a few details that I knew would enrich the story by making Danny Parker a kind of victim of his love for Janet Lee Kerr. Mrs. Parker cautioned me several times that I was dead wrong if I thought I knew the whole story.

"I hate being teased," I kidded her when she once again became evasive.

"I can tell you more when you see me."

And so I drove south.

The rain splattered onto the sodden roadway, falling impatiently from a heavy gray sky interrupted by the smallest flecks of blue. In deliberate strokes, the LUV's windshield wipers sloughed the moisture off and the act was repeated, matching the beat of the music on the car radio. The wetness from the sky slathered the road.

◆

THE HOUSE AT 2121 OLD STUMP ROAD, Timberlake, was a simple white and turquoise-trimmed two-story. A patchwork flower garden of daisies and Cosmos in the front, and an acre of compost-topped land in the back, made perfect beds for the annual vegetable garden. It had been the Parker home since 1977, when Dwight Parker had the old mobile towed away and the little house built. Some thought it was funny that June Parker chose the same color for the stick-built house as the old aluminum doublewide, but she didn't give a hoot. She always wanted a white and blue house and she was going to live her dream.

I parked the LUV in front of what I assumed had once been a chicken house, though it had been a long time since anything but spiders laid eggs in it. A larger enclosure, about twenty-five yards away, was the rickety remnants of a hog pen.

I knocked on the front door, but there was no answer.

Through the front window, I could see the sliding glass door on the other side of the house had been left partly ajar. *Maybe Mrs. Parker was in the backyard?* I walked around the house and let myself in through the door fronting a small dining area.

"Mrs. Parker?" I stuck my head inside. "It's Kevin Ryan. I'm here for the interview. Forget I was coming?"

I hated it when people changed their minds and didn't bother to call to let me know. It wasn't as if I was in the area and just stopping by for a little chat. I had courted this woman and had done all I could to let her know that I would be writing a true story and her input was needed to ensure proper balance. Whereas Anna Cameron had screamed at me, June Parker seemed more open to the idea of an interview for the book I was writing.

124

"Hello?" I said as I followed a noise coming from the kitchen. It was the sound of the tap water gushing from the sink. It was the only noise breaking the stillness of the tiny house. Though they had little money and the decor was truly from the *Brady Bunch* and *Partridge Family* era—muddy earth tones, Naugahyde recliners, "mushroom" wall art for their sons. It was also obvious that this was the home of a couple not feeling well. Three of the familiar red and white cans of soup, sore throat spray, chicken bouillon cubes and cold pills were pushed to the end of the cluttered counter.

I called out again, but there was no reply.

While shutting off the running faucet, I noticed one of the four high-backed dinette chairs encircling the table had been overturned. It was glaringly out of place in what seemed fairly neat and organized. I wondered if June Parker had left in a hurry, perhaps to go to the doctor? Maybe she had knocked over the chair as she ran for her car. A trip to the hospital? A family member in need? A dog hit by a car? Something made her rush out.

I turned to leave when curiosity or impulse got the best of me and I went further into the house. Something felt peculiar.

I pushed the hallway door open and I saw her.

The horror began in a series of images that I instantly knew would play repeatedly in my mind over the next few years— indeed, the rest of my life. Red seemed everywhere. Spattering the walls, the baseboard, the floor. I was drawn to the color. The red was a light at the end of a long tunnel. I felt the air leave my lungs in a quick rush. I commanded my eyes to move over the figure slumped next to my feet.

June Parker lay on the floor in the front of the door leading to a bedroom. Thick red blood had painted the dark flooring beneath her limp body. Her throat had been slashed so deeply that it altered her facial muscles, making the woman's face strangely distorted, like a deflated rubber balloon with a human likeness hastily painted on it. In shock, I knelt beside her and

125

touched her neck. I was not a doctor, but I knew there were no signs of life. Her round-framed glasses cracked beneath my knee.

I ran to the kitchen and dialed 9-1-1 on the white wall phone, gave the operator the address and did what the dispatcher told me to do.

"Go outside and wait."

I stood shivering outside in the driveway and waited for the strobing lights and whining sirens of aid cars, the Pierce County Sheriff, the fire department. The image played again. *Red.* The distortion of her face. *Red.* Her hands frozen and contorted... reaching and clawing for protection... the screams that no one heard.

No one except her killer.

I shuddered in the cool, damp air. The direction of the wind had shifted and for the first time in my visits to Timberlake, I smelled the salty air of the Pacific Ocean instead of the wet sneaker smell of the mill. A few minutes later, I watched without word as the Timberlake Adult Daycare blue van ferrying Dwight Parker was surrounded by several of Pierce County's finest. An officer leaned inside the vehicle and spoke quietly to one of the passengers. I couldn't see the man's face, but I could imagine his irrevocable shock. His world was changed forever at that moment. June Parker's husband was just coming home from a day of "passive activity" to learn the unthinkable had taken place inside the walls of his little house. Mr. Parker, understandably and tragically, would never be the same.

The van driver pushed the button activating the wheelchair lift, and the man who couldn't speak was lowered to the driveway.

Detective Raines arrived, looking frazzled, as though he had been yanked once again from his family and his home. His sandy hair hung like a bunched-up curtain over his forehead and his necktie hung limply and askew over the outside of his jacket. He had left in a hurry. How the job ruled his life, his wife, their

126

children. Time and time again, it had been proven in the Raines household: Homicide was not an eight-to-five job.

There was no smile for me, only the grim nod of recognition as Raines took a statement about my discovery. It took all of five or ten minutes. I hadn't seen anything other than the body, and I hadn't touched anything.

"Wait," I remembered, "the tap was running when I came inside and I turned it off."

"Kitchen? Bathroom?" he asked

"Kitchen. And that's all I touched. Besides her. I touched Mrs. Parker to see if she was alive."

Raines made some additional notes and walked back toward the house.

Wet from my own perspiration as much as the subsiding rain, and exhausted from the relentless questioning, I called over to Raines that I was going to go home. I couldn't think of anything else to say. Even those words fell flat, but the detective didn't seem to notice. He nodded over his shoulder and told me he'd be in touch. He had work to do. There would be photographs, witness interviews, blood samples, autopsy, media inquiries.

My brain was mush as I drove north on the freeway. I ground the gears of my truck twice. My mind was gone. I couldn't shake what I had seen. I had seen crime scene photos before, terrible photos. Children murdered. Women mutilated. The cruel and lethal handiwork of knives, razors, guns, and various ligatures. I would never forget the image of a dead teenage boy who had strangled himself with his father's necktie during autoerotic play. Or the woman whose face had been horribly disfigured with a hot waffle iron—before her husband stabbed her on top of their Sunday morning breakfast table.

I had seen what the ocean did to the human body after it sank, then floated to the surface as the gassy ballooned remains of what had been the mother of three. I had seen what carbon monoxide poisoning did to a father and his two daughters after he strapped them snugly into their car seats and drove them to hell. I had pored over color photographs of a maggot-infested corpse that had been dumped in a ditch. I meticulously counted and measured each rice-sized larvae to see if the coroner had correctly determined the age by the size and number of tiny white flesh-eaters.

I knew from my work what murder looked like in all of its hideous faces.

I had seen everything that juries were required to see and what the curious friends of a medical examiner showed to impress them.

It was true that I had never seen the real thing and while the photographs were always graphic, the shock value was mitigated by the horrible fact that you know you are going to see something horrible before you look upon it.

With Mrs. Parker, I had expected coffee and cookies. Maybe I was in fantasyland? Maybe she would have thrown me out and told me never to come back again? *That* I could live with. I had not expected anything like this. Not a murder.

Not in a million years.

Chapter Sixteen
Tuesday, August 20

THE DAY AFTER JUNE PARKER'S MURDER, I WAS IN AN EERIE, impenetrable fog. I tried to write. I tried to talk it out with Val and the girls, but the words did not come easily. Each phrase choked in my throat. Each flash of what I had seen made the shock of it all hit deeper. I couldn't purge from my memory the images that haunted me. Valerie canceled appointments and stayed home with me and the girls. I watched television. I talked with a reporter, and though I had always prided myself on being quotable, I could not think of anything to say.

When the phone rang just before lunch, I told Valerie to tell the caller—a reporter, I was sure—that I was taking Hedda for a walk.

"It's Jett," she said quietly, her hand muffling the mouthpiece. "Better talk to her. This is the second time she's called for you today."

I got on the line and said hello. Jett took it from there.

"Now I know why you stood me up," she said. Her voice was somber. "I was mad as could be at you last night... but I saw the *news* this morning. It must have been awful finding her. Right on the front page there's a photo of Mrs. Parker."

She read the headline and a few lines:

MURDER ON OLD STUMP ROAD: CRIME AUTHOR FINDS BODY

In a page out of one of his pulp crime books, Port Gamble author Kevin Ryan was in the right place at the wrong time... a

129

source close to the Sheriff's Department stated that the author had been "badgering" the dead woman for an interview...

Pulp crime book? Badgering the deceased? I had enough. Valerie and the girls formed a circle around me as I set down the receiver. I was shaking slightly. I felt sick to my stomach. I was so sorry that I had even come out to see Mrs. Parker. I was so sorry that I had been the one to find her. My wife put her arms around my shoulders. Like blonde-headed dominos, Hayley and Taylor fell into us with reassuring hugs of sympathy. We were a family and we had made it through bad times before. Lots of bad times. The ups and downs of plain old living. If anything, by the nature of my career path we had seen much of the worst as it affected others. But we were removed from it; it was just fodder for a book. Whenever a book was finished, the pain and horror of what someone else had endured would fade somewhat. It had to. I had to move on. I had to get on with another story; another murder.

Nothing had tested us like we all knew this would. It was one thing to be late on a power bill and cook over a wood stove and tell your daughters that you were "indoor camping."It was completely different to have your lives shattered by a gruesome discovery and the steady invasion of the purveyors of publicity that accompanied it.

◆

THREE DAYS AFTER THE GRISLY DISCOVERY on Old Stump Road, a producer named Ashlee Something-hyphen-Something from *Rita Adams* called to book me on a show they were putting together called "Unbelievable Ironies."

"Rita loves your work and when we saw the piece on the wire —"

I was startled by the revelation. I hadn't Googled myself in days. "It was on the wire?"

"Uh-huh. When we saw the piece we thought your story would be just the right touch for the Ironies show."

A week earlier, I couldn't have imagined that I would ever give up the chance for publicity, but considering what happened, it didn't feel right. Even so, I was torn. I struggled with the idea of going on television to blab about finding June Parker and the fact that I was there to interview her for a true crime book. It seemed distasteful. It was, I knew, deep down, too soon.

"Who else is on?" I asked, halfheartedly.

The young woman—probably some underpaid intern from a Midwest university trying to make it in show business—gushed about the potential guests.

"Get this! A Kansas man who had the wrong leg amputated! A woman who's allergic to chocolate but won the Pillsbury Bake-off with a brownie recipe. They are so *good*! She sent Rita a batch. Oh, and there's a guy from Boise, Iowa who was a confirmed bachelor until he married his sister."

"That last one sounds like *Jerry Springer* to me," I said, not bothering to correct her geography. People living on the East Coast rarely comprehended a difference between Iowa and Idaho. They incorrectly assumed the world stopped at Chicago.

The producer laughed at the *Springer* comment. "He didn't know she was his sister at the time. He found out *after* they were married. He didn't know he had any siblings whatsoever."

"You know, Ashlee, it sounds like a great show and you know how much I appreciate Rita inviting me on in the past, but I think I have to pass this time. It doesn't feel right to me."

Ashlee wasn't about to give up. Not easily, anyway. She appealed to my sense of personal greed. My need for viewers to buy my books.

"Could be a sweeps show if it goes well," she said trying to up the ante to make me change my mind.

I really didn't care about sweeps; it was the nadir of talk show programming, anyway. I detested going on against aliens on another show.

131

"How about another time? Maybe when the book comes out I can come promote it?"

The associate producer burbled a snotty "you'll be sorry to miss this opportunity," and we both hung up.

The hell with Ashlee. My editor had liked what he'd seen of *Love You to Death* so far, and wanted another chapter. Valerie and our girls wanted to go out for dinner. I was hungry, too. Stress always made me hungry. I planned on working after we ate. I put Hedda on her chain outside the door and off we went to Round Table Pizza in Silverdale for the "Guinevere," a veggie pizza my girls ate with gusto. Val and I liked it, too, though we pretended we wanted the "Lancelot"—more meat than a butcher's display case piled on top of a chewy crust. Sometimes kids have to be tricked.

But as it turned out, I wasn't that hungry, after all. I kept seeing Mrs. Parker's body in her hallway.

Even as I sat in the sticky vinyl booth at the pizza place, the volume of blood at the crime scene continued to bother me. At first when I found Mrs. Parker, I had seen nothing but red. Red everywhere. But the red was somewhat swirled, a kind of chiaroscuro effect. It hadn't been flat, elongated pools of blood, like I had seen in crime scene photographs. Blood almost always pools into a glistening mass near the wound on a butchered or bullet-riddled body. It oxidizes to a deep chestnut color within an hour. The blood at the Parker residence was red and thin. And streaky.

"I'm not going to eat," I said when Taylor offered me a slice of pizza topped with a plasma-red tomato slice. "Just don't feel that hungry, honey."

My daughter swung her golden ponytail and grinned as she set the piece on her plate.

"You want to leave?" Valerie asked me.

I faked a smile. "Oh, no. You guys finish."

♦

Monday, August 26

I WAS BACK ON *Love You to Death*, but not because I was really up to it. God knew I wasn't. It was because I had no choice. It was seven days after the murder and I still had a deadline with my editor. If I didn't produce, I figured they'd find someone who could.

Jett Carter asked me to meet her after work if I had time during my trip to Timberlake. She worked at Ho!, a juniors store specializing in what parents hated and what young girls apparently loved. Or it could have been the girls loved the stuff simply because their parents hated it? In some ways, at least at first blush, it wasn't too far off from what girls wore in early-Britney: cropped tops, low-riding jeans, chunky-heeled shoes and the like. But after looking around, it was clear that the envelope had been pushed. I shuddered at the prospect of a not-too-distant future when Taylor and Hayley would go to a place like Ho! for back-to-school shopping.

"I'll be done in a minute," Jett called from the cash register. "As soon as these girls decide on the perfect bathing suit."

I nodded and watched two teens wave a thong bikini bottom at each other. It was light pink with an opalescent sheen to the fabric. It was also very tiny. I winced at the thought of it.

A fat dumpy friend kept urging the more slender, yet still thick-thighed, girl to buy the suit, telling her it would make her look like Selena Gomez.

"It looks so hot on you," the friend said. "It makes me so jealous."

The girl was unsure. "You think?"

"Yeah. Everyone'll be looking at you and ignoring me, as usual."

The thick-thighed girl finally succumbed to her friend's pressure and assurance. Jett rang up the sale and packed the suit in a single sheet of tissue paper.

133

I figured it was the role of the Fat Dumpy Friend, aka FDF, as my daughters explained it to me. It was the FDF's job to make sure her friend looked as ridiculous as possible. That way she spared herself scrutiny and could gossip about her best friend's folly behind her back. I hoped for two things when the time my girls would mature enough to end up in a place like Ho!: one-piece bathing suits and no FDFs. An FDF could be as lethal as a spree killer.

"She's going to try to bring that thong back," Jett predicted as we walked to the Food Circus for lattes. "So sorry. But no returns on bathing suits—intimate apparel, you know."

We talked for about an hour, mostly about Connie and Janet and, of course, Mrs. Parker's murder. I told her that I had learned from Detective Raines that Mr. Parker had been released after questioning when the obvious was proved. Besides his physical limitations, there was no way he could have killed his wife. He had been, in fact, at adult daycare when June was murdered. Davy Parker was working at Wendy's.

Jett looked down at her coffee and shook her head sadly. "It sucks. She was a real nice lady. Her son is a jerk and a liar, but she was nice."

I agreed. It *did* suck. I wiped the foam from the edge of my mustache. Lattes always left their foamy milk mark on me.

"No matter what you think of Danny, that family has been through a lot of personal tragedy," I said.

Jett nodded. "Yeah, brought on most of it themselves."

Though I was in a hurry, I offered a ride back to her apartment. I had to get over to Detective Raines' house and couldn't stay to chat. We walked across the parking lot to the LUV.

"I've been meaning to ask you about your license plate," she said when we stood by my truck.

"Yeah?"

"What in the world does *Truck Rim* mean?"

I started to laugh and when I saw her look of curiosity turn to embarrassment I stopped short. I stood in front of the back plate. In dark blue letters against a graphic image of Mount Rainier, it read: TRUCRYM.

"True crime," I explained. "It's supposed to read *True crime.*"

I could see she still felt a little foolish, so I lied.

"People are always asking what *Truck Rim* is. I guess I need additional letters to make it more obvious."

Jett grinned and I knew she understood that I had lied to make her feel better.

When I dropped her off outside her building, I felt sorry for her and glad that I knew her at the same time. I hoped my daughters would be as resilient as Jett Carter when the inevitable occurred and life dealt them the occasional bad hand. This girl—this young *woman*—was a fighter.

I watched her turn and wave to me from her front door. The girl was not only a fighter, she was also a sight. Dressed in a red lace back crop tee and cut-off denim shorts, Jett was a walking promo for the store she in which she worked.

God, how I hoped my girls never worked at Ho!

Chapter Seventeen
Late Monday, August 26

Frazzled and Tired as I was, I somehow found the energy to write the next chapter. Needing the dough had a way of doing that.

◆

Love You to Death

PART FOUR

HIS PLACE WAS AN OLD LOGGER'S ramshackle house pitched on five muddy acres outside of Big Slag, Washington, just fifteen circuitous miles from Timberlake. Brian Jackson was no Mr. Fixit and he hated what the old man had done to put his place together. Wires like a kettle full of spaghetti ran willy-nilly underneath the floors and between the walls. Nothing seemed to go anywhere. Nothing made sense. The man who built the two-bedroom place boasted as he pointed to his temple while telling prospective buyers that he had "everything, right upstairs. " He'd write it all down.

"Yup, that I'll do for ya," the old guy promised as he spat out the brown goo from his chew. "I'll write it up like a fuckin' Christmas list."

The old logger had lied. The day after the sale cleared escrow, he took his money and skedaddled out of Big Slag. Brian Jackson was left without either rhyme or reason. To turn on the lights in the living room meant going into the second bedroom. The hot water faucet turned on the cold and so on. Even so, it was all Jackson could afford. His mortgage payment was $143 a month, which included a reserve for property taxes.

Living in Big Slag, if anything, was cheap.

At 1:20 in the morning on November 28, Brian rolled out of bed to answer a loud banging on his front door. He threw on a shirt, stepped into a pair of work jeans and took a rifle from behind the bedroom door. Always be prepared, he told himself.

Brian found jittery pal Danny Parker sweating and pacing on his front steps. Behind the one-eyed dyslexic behemoth was Janet Lee Kerr. Janet also appeared somewhat agitated, though Brian did not know her well.

Danny spoke. "We need a place to crash. Can we stay here tonight?"

Brian didn't hesitate. Danny had stayed over before whenever he had a little too much to drink; the fact Janet Kerr was standing in his doorway at that ungodly hour was of no concern one way or another. Janet had probably downed her share, too. As far as Brian knew, she was the type of girl who'd sleep it off anywhere.

"Come on in," he said, shaking the sleep from his eyes and managing a foggy smile for Janet. "You can crash on the couch. Danny, you take the La-Z-Boy."

Later that morning, while Janet continued to snooze under a thick layering of Army-surplus blankets, Brian and Danny went to the mall. Not only was Christmas stuff needed-

After Thanksgiving Sales were in full gear-Danny said he wanted to talk. At noon, they picked up a baker's dozen at Dunkin' Donuts, and disposed of a pair of women's LA Gear running shoes in a Dumpster behind the Wards store. Danny spilled his considerable guts over the events of the night before. He admitted he had been the shooter and the shoes belonged to Janet, who had been there when it happened.

"Janet told me to get rid of 'em," he said.

"You have to turn yourself in," Brian urged as they drove around Timberlake. "Don't you know how much trouble you're in?"

"I messed up," was all the big guy could say. "I messed up bad."

"You bet your ass you did."

"My ass, I sure did."

"You know where you gotta go, don't you?"

Danny blinked back tears. "Yeah, take me to the sheriff."

"Good."

"Brian, do me a favor?"

"Yeah?"

"Call my mom. She's probably worried about me, not coming home and all. With my dad the way he is, my mom depends on me."

Brian Jackson crossed the River Bridge to the Justice Center, a tomblike building of aggregate cement that engineers elevated from the earth to allow parking under its stilts. It was ugly as road kill, but it was convenient-a kind of one-stop shopping approach for all local law enforcement needs. The sheriff's department, the prosecutor's office, judge's chambers, the jail-everything was there. Everything he needed.

Danny ate another doughnut and went inside to give himself up.

138

WHEN THE LAW WENT LOOKING FOR JANET Lee Kerr, they didn't have to look far. She wasn't at her little second-floor apartment on Beverly Street. She had taken her old yellow pickup to the grocery store when police pulled her over in front of the Quick Stop gas station on Ocean Boulevard.

"I'm going to pick up my daughter. She's at my mother's," she said as tears fell from her brown eyes.

"We just want to get a statement from you about the shooting of your boyfriend this morning."

"Can I get Lindy first?" Janet said, not really responding to what the deputy was saying. It didn't seem as if she were even concerned that Deke Cameron had been shot.

"Later," the officer said firmly. "Come on with us now."

She stepped from the cab of her pickup. The smell of stale beer clung to her sweatshirt. She looked weary, beat. Her long brown hair hung limply. Her makeup had rubbed off in patches. She wore no shoes. She looked like the late Anna Nicole Smith's backwater cousin after the hardest, longest night of the century.

"Where are your shoes, Miss?" the cop asked.

"I don't know," she answered without the slightest hesitation. "I have no idea."

-

THE PIERCE COUNTY SHERIFF'S interrogation room was one of those functional, spartan rooms with a big rectangle table and four plastic chairs that give it the uncluttered look of a classroom study hall. The blank expanse of one cinder block wall was interrupted with a four-foot-wide mirror. Most knew it was two-way glass. Even so, every once in a while a subject would turn to their reflection to pick their teeth or nose.

Detective Martin Raines had conducted hundreds of interviews in the little room in his dozen years at Pierce County, which neighbored my own Kitsap County. He had interviewed suspects from all walks and all *crawls* of life. He remembered them all. The teenage girl with the heavy-mascara raccoon eyes who had stabbed her mother because she wouldn't let her go on an overnight beach campout with her boyfriend. The old man who had backed his Pontiac Fiero over a little boy in a grocery parking lot. The neighbor who poisoned another's dogs because the damn animals barked all hours of the night.

Raines had played host and antagonist to many in that little room. In the first minutes after the door closed, he calculated an approach that would net him the best results. Good cop? Bad cop? Father Confessor? Skeptic?

With Danny Parker, it was easy.

Danny was thirty-two, a hundred pounds overweight, legally blind in one eye and slower than a stopped clock. He had the manner of an apologetic, big, stupid kid. He always said "sir" and "thank you." He took every breath through a gaping mouth that could have benefited from orthodontics. Yet as disconcerting as his appearance was, Danny seemed a nice enough fellow-for an attempted murderer. He listened intently to each question Raines posed over the course of the two hours he would spend facing him across the table.

Ten minutes into the interview, Danny volunteered that he was hungry.

"Haven't eaten since a couple of doughnuts for breakfast," he said, his good eye staring at the investigator.

Raines nodded.

"How 'bout a Big Mac when we're done here?"

Danny smiled broadly. He sat straight up with his hands folded on the table in front of him like a first-grader. "Yeah. Thank you. Sounds good."

While Danny admitted to a great deal, he didn't give up Janet Lee Kerr. Every time her name was broached, he shook his heavy frame with firm denial. *He* had shot Deke. It was his idea. He fled the scene. He ditched the weapon. He tossed Janet's shoes in the Dumpster. Everything was his doing. His alone.

Raines knew better. He had been this route before many times in his career.

"Come on, Danny, we know Janet put it all together."

"Did not."

"Did too."

"Janet's not like that," the young fat man said. "You don't even know her."

♦

Note from Val: *I feel sorry for Danny. Your description of him seems a little harsh —"the young fat man said." Hasn't the guy been used and abused enough? Maybe you could say he had an engaging smile? Straight teeth? A dog? Or nice eyes? As written he seems like a lovelorn Quasimodo without a hump. Besides, a lot of your readers are on the heavy side of thin. In fact, YOU get a little chunky before you finish a book. Stress eater! —V*

Chapter Eighteen
Tuesday, August 27

MARTY RAINES DIRECTED ME TO WAIT in his den. Something had come up and he would take care of it on the phone in the kitchen. I drank tepid coffee and looked around. April Raines had decorated her husband's lair in a lodge and fishing theme. Antique fishing gear, lures and floats mostly, lined a shelf that went from one corner of a wall to the other. A finial on top of a dark green paper lamp shade was a tiny salmon breaching the surface of a river. It was the kind of decorating an interior designer would dismiss as hopelessly kitschy. But I thought it was wonderful. It was more about what April Raines had wanted to do for her cop husband than it was about making the pages of *House Beautiful*. She had wanted to create a sanctuary where the spectre of murder and violence was remote. Plus, I loved salmon.

Raines breezed into his den and swung the door shut. He wore a yellow and black striped shirt and jeans. He looked like an overstuffed bumblebee.

"Off the record, okay?"

He had uttered my least favorite words.

"It's too late for that," I answered, somewhat defensively. "We've taped hours of interviews, and what you've said has already been incorporated into my book. You know that, Marty."

Martin sat behind his desk and regarded me with a nod. He was serious. Stone cold. "That's fine," he said. "I'm talking about what I'm going to tell you *now*. Do you want to hear it?"

I didn't blink. "Am I stupid? Of course."

"Nothing leaves this room."

"Right. Agreed." I didn't like it, but I wanted to hear what the man had to say.

Raines paused for dramatic effect and cleared his throat.

"June Parker was already dead or about dead when the killer slit her throat. *Slit,* that's almost a joke when you think what was done to her. The knife cut clean into her vertebrae. Cut the bone. An OJ slice. Whoever did that was strong, very strong. But that's not the freakiest part."

"What is then?" I asked. I reached for my neck, a reflex, a reaction, to his description of the slashing. I did not want to shave ever again.

He paused again. "The tox screens came back, cyanide."

"Cyanide?" I was dumbfounded. It didn't make sense.

Raines studied me and my reaction. "That's what the medical examiner says. Lethal amounts of the stuff."

"But what about the cuts? The blood?"

"Maybe done to cover up the identity of the killer. To confuse us? In reality, there wasn't much blood. What there was had been carefully spread around."

I thought about the smearing of the blood, how oddly it showed paint through the baseboard. How thin it had been, how much coverage it had commanded in the hallway.

"Then who?" I asked.

"Well, if it isn't you and it isn't Mr. Parker—"

"Thanks for the vote of confidence."

"—then it's someone June Parker knew. Someone who wanted us to see a brutal act that could have been committed by a husband."

144

"Or a lover," I said, feeling foolish that I had suggested such a thing about a woman who, by all accounts, was a saint and completely devoted to her husband on wheels.

Raines shot an icy stare. "Didn't have any."

"Sure?" I gulped.

"Positive."

Beads of sweat started to collect under my mustache. "Why are you telling me this?" I asked.

"Two reasons. Because you know these characters better than just about anyone."

"So? The two I know who are capable of anything remotely as evil as murder are in prison already. What's the second reason?"

Martin Raines waited a good five seconds before he answered. I couldn't tell if it was because he was going to tell me something highly confidential or if it was because he was trying to think of a second reason when there really hadn't been one.

"Because your name was on a note found inside the dead woman's hands."

My heartbeat quickened. "I was coming to see her."

"We know. But, Kevin, isn't it possible that someone didn't want you to talk with Mrs. Parker?"

"For God's sake, Marty, she was just the mother of the shooter. She isn't—*wasn't*—even important to the book. She was someone's mother, that's all. I only wanted to speak with her for background on her son."

We went around and around for another half hour. I looked at the crime scene photos and felt nausea wash over me all over again. It wasn't what I was seeing that made me sick, it was the recollection of being there and finding her. I could remember the smell of her blood, the running of the tap water, the dimness of the hallway. I was there again. Photos never made me sick. It was true that they often brought a reaction of shock, but I covered

145

that up well. I could act. I could pretend to cough to deflect my facial response to what I had seen.

The photos were haunting because they were from my own reality. I had seen what had happened in that photo. I had been there. For the first time in my career, I felt truly ashamed. I was ashamed at how I had so callously interviewed the husband who discovered his wife shot to death or the teenage girl who had discovered the body of her raped and murdered sister. The words they used were from pictures in their minds. Of course I knew that. But I never knew the depth of the emotion, the haunting of the soul that comes from such a discovery. I had not known Mrs. Parker, but I would never forget her. Bloody. Lifeless. The image of her killer recorded in the spongy folds of her dead brain tissue.

I left the Raines charming home on its tree-lined street in the good part of Timberlake, thinking about the note with my name on it. Wondering what else it said? Wondering why Raines said I couldn't see it.

"It's in the lab," he had intoned. "There are some forensic possibilities we're looking into."

Chapter Nineteen

Late Tuesday, August 27

When I got home I picked up the file folder of my next *Love You to Death* chapter for Valerie to read and slid it onto her lap. She began, turning the pages upside down on to each other in a neat stack. I resisted asking what she thought as she read.

She glared at me whenever I did that.

♦

Love You to Death

PART FIVE

GIRLS LIKE JANET LEE KERR were a grimy dime a dozen in Pierce County. Martin Raines had seen more than his share of their ilk, from appearance to attitude. Their propensity for big hair and form-fitting attire was in direct relation to the distance away from Seattle or Portland. With Timberlake stuck equally between the Northwest's two major metropolitan areas, it was surely VO-5 and spandex's last stand.

Janet Kerr was neither a beauty, nor unattractive. She had a young woman's figure, despite the fact that she had a baby and done nothing in particular to see herself back into good shape. She smoked menthol 100s because she liked the buzz and thought they freshened her breath. She had no real job, no career, no ambition beyond a good time on Friday night. When it came right down to it, Janet had one thing going for her. And that was the downfall of the men who fell for her. What she had was between her thighs.

She could also cry like a February rainstorm. Her shoulders heaved in agonized spasms as she made her way to the conference room adjacent to the one occupied by Danny Parker and an officer. She tried to pull her matted hair out from under her sweatshirt collar.

"I never believed in my life that something could go this wrong... this far," she told Raines as he led her into one of the four hard-as-steel aqua fiberglass chairs. A strip of cloth fluttered from the heating duct. Despite the incoming cool air, the room was hot. Stiflingly so.

"Janet, we need to know what happened." Raines was gentle in his approach. He always was at first, though deep down it never left him that a girl like Janet would brandish a box cutter for a six-pack.

Janet nodded, but said nothing.

"You know, Deke might not live. Whatever happened out by Ruston is either a tragic shooting or, if he dies, murder," he said.

The switch went back on. Instantly. Janet started to cry again.

"Oh," she wailed. "My daughter... Lindy needs me. Let me go to her. Please."

"We need to know what happened, Janet. If you want to see your daughter any time soon, you need to tell us everything."

And so over the next fifty minutes, Janet blabbed. She told her inquisitor that Danny Parker was obsessed with her. Head over heels. He had it so bad that he'd do anything to be with her. *Anything.* She didn't know how far he'd go.

"Who would have thought he'd *shoot* Deke?" she said, tears once again flowing down her cheeks. "I thought they were going to fight. That's all. Fight. I didn't know he thought he was Jacob from *Twilight*, or whatever. We were just friends."

Raines asked Janet for an official statement. She was told to recount, step-by-step, the hours leading up to the shooting. As they talked, he'd write down what she said and she'd have a chance to go over it to make corrections. Janet agreed to it. She had one question, however.

"Can I ask you something?" she asked, her tears dried and her attitude much improved.

"About your daughter?" Raines asked.

"Well, that, too. After we're done, can I get something to eat?"

Raines would have rolled his eyes if Janet hadn't fixed her eyes on his with crosshair preciseness. *Unbelievable.* Danny was in the next room dreaming of a burger and his girlfriend had food on her mind, too.

"I'm not making any promises," he said casually as he fiddled with his wedding band as it choked the puffy girth of his ring finger, "but we'll see."

Janet Lee Kerr indicated that Danny Parker had been obsessed with her for seven or eight years. Deke Cameron was also in love with her. And what happened up on the logging road was a battle over who would marry her.

She said the day had started with several altercations between Deke and Danny and

149

herself. Deke had even hit her in the side of the head during one row.

"He called me a bitch and pulled my hair!"

She had been afraid and tried to calm him down. They bought a bottle of Potter's Fine Whiskey and a half rack of Bud and drove to a parking spot under the River Bridge. Deke drank the Potter's and Janet consumed a couple of beers. After that, they went driving, though Deke was so drunk he had to pull over to throw up. Janet took over the wheel.

She said she made several calls to Danny that evening, telling him Deke had threatened her. She was afraid for her life-and Danny's.

"Danny said something about how he could shoot Deke, take care of him. I told him how Deke threatened me and him both," she said.

The detective could see where it was going, but kept his expression flat, steady. He didn't let on. Full and complete control. He simply wrote down what the young woman with the menthol breath said.

Danny had told her during a telephone call to go up the logging road near the Ruston Tavern. It was interesting, she admitted, because it just so happened that she had been there earlier in the evening drinking with Deke.

Been there before, scoping the scene. Plotting the murder....

"Knowing Danny was waiting for Deke, I drove the car going up the hill and all of a sudden I needed to pee. I got out. I heard someone coming to the car, I recognized Danny. Danny told me to move. I moved back and fell down the hill. I didn't see Danny shoot Deke, but I heard two or three shots. I think

150

Deke was in the passenger seat when Danny shot him."

"Then what?" Raines asked when she stopped talking to draw in a big breath into her menthol-fresh lungs.

She thinks that this is it. She thinks she's ready to go get the burger.

With some prompting and the promise of a Big Mac, Janet continued. Deke was calling her name, saying he was bleeding. But she couldn't get to him. In the commotion of the shooting, she had fallen down the cliff that bordered the road. She had tried to claw her way up, only to hear the car start and drive away. Danny, she said, helped her up and the two drove down the hill.

She seemed shocked all of a sudden.

"I had no idea Danny would try to kill Deke," she said. "I thought they were just gonna fight."

Raines asked her to review and sign the statement.

"Can I go now?" she asked.

"'Fraid not," he said. "You're under arrest for the attempted murder of Deke Cameron. Janet, you're going to jail."

"But I didn't do anything. Danny did it. Ask Danny!"

The officers down the hall would never forget the sound coming from the interview room. It burst through the heating ducts like a twister.

"Thought those rooms were soundproof," one commented to the other.

"Haven't had a screamer this good in years. Wonder who Raines has in there."

"The girlfriend of the shooting victim at Pac-O. And, get this, she's also the girlfriend

151

of the fat guy in room number two. The shooter."

"OH, GOD, NO..."

The officer had seen and heard it all.

"Ain't love grand?"

-

WITHIN HOURS OF THE SHOOTING, the shotgun used to pump Deke Cameron full of birdshot was recovered. Danny Parker beat Janet Kerr in the race for the burger and led investigators to a weedy ditch along the highway. The weapon was hauled off from underneath a sodden covering of fast food wrappers and fall leaves. There was no way that it could have been hurled there to land in the position as Janet and Danny had both maintained when they made their initial statements. While their stories matched on most key points, it was clear to many in the sheriff's office that the suspects' statements were a little too closely aligned to be regarded as gospel. Everyone thought Danny had been duped by Janet.

One officer working outside the case scribbled across the local daily's account of the shooting: *Somebody's not telling the whole story here.*

Martin Raines was at home snacking on a tuna sandwich and thinking about catching up on his sleep when word came from the Com Center by way of a doctor on rounds at Pac-O: Deke Cameron was agitated and wanted to talk as soon as possible.

"Be there in ten," he said. He hung up the phone, and grabbed the sandwich.

On the way to the hospital, Raines learned that two county deputies went fishing in the

Dumpster at the mall. Inside five minutes, through the confetti of stale popcorn and dead bedding plants, the men pulled a pair of ladies' green and white *LA Gear* running shoes from the depths of the Dumpster. The laces were hot pink. They were Janet Lee Kerr's shoes.

And there was blood on them.

◆

Valerie underlined the word "burger" and wrote in the margin: *Reminder! We're out of buns. Get some more veggie burgers, too. Maybe some sprouts or something green and crunchy that we can pile on those oatmeal discs. —V*

◆

DEKE CAMERON WAS A REMARKABLE young man. Not in the way any parent would be particularly proud. He had barely held down a job in an industry that only cared if the worker was strong enough to lift sixty pounds, breathe on his own and get to work every day. Deke had worked in the mill off and on since he dropped out of high school. What made him remarkable was not his looks, his brains or his personality. None of that. It was the very fact that by all reasonable accounts, he should be laid out in a coffin and not a hospital bed. But he wasn't. Deke was sitting up, propped with a pillow, tubes in his nose and his forearm. A Mylar balloon picturing a Band-Aid labeled with *SORRY ABOUT YOUR OWEE* fluttered from a ribbon tied on the steel tube of the bed rail.

"Detective Raines," he said, shifting his bulk in the bed and popping an IV line.

Raines acknowledged him with a concerned nod.

"Second time this hour," an impatient nurse complained. She reinserted the needle and triple-taped the line.

"Don't wiggle around so much, okay?" she admonished the patient before shutting the door.

"Heard you arrested Janet and Danny."

"That's right, Deke."

"Set me up, didn't they?"

"Looks like it."

"Well, I want to talk to you... I don't think you know what kind of people you're dealing with."

"We have an idea. A pretty good one."

"No. There's more. I'm afraid."

"What about?"

"I'm a little embarrassed to say it, but considering what happened... I'm afraid of Janet and her mother. They know people...."

Deke Cameron's voice trailed off as he attempted to wipe some spittle from his chin.

"What *people*?'

"People... who hurt people."

The detective could see that the victim zonked out in the hospital bed was trying to frame his words carefully. He was so slow. He was pausing so often that the homicide cop wondered if it was the painkillers the man was on-or if it was that he was plain dumb and had a hard time thinking about whatever was on his mind.

"What are you getting at?" he asked. "Tell me so we can take care of this."

Deke's eyes drooped and he coughed up a wad of mucus.

"Those women," he said, "will stop at nothing to get what they want... they wanted to

154

kill Janet's ex-husband so they can get custody of Lindy."

"How do you know?"

"Cuz I was gonna do it."

Raines was unsure he heard right. "Kill him?"

Deke breathed his words in. "Yeah. But I didn't. I chickened out and they told me they'd get someone else. God, they were mad at me."

"Mad enough to kill you?"

"You don't know them."

I looked over my wife's edits. Very clean. I was on the right track. She'd gone through the material quickly—always a good "I-read-this-book-until-I-almost-dropped-dead" indicator. I didn't have to nudge, harangue or even pretend to be hurt that she wasn't plowing through the material at a fast enough clip. Good. She even added a couple of "smiley" faces on some lines she liked. I added buns and oatmeal burgers to the list.

BOOK II
THE FINGER OF GUILT

"I lived with the Ryans for six weeks...
six of the most frightening weeks of my life."
—WANDA-LOU WEBSTER

Chapter Twenty
Wednesday, August 28

I HAD AN AUTHOR BOOK SIGNING scheduled for the afternoon in Seattle and there was no way out of it. It was during a "soft" grand opening for a discount variety market that had just been converted into a food store called Bag 'n Save. It was in one of the worst, reader-less parts of the city: the kind of place where food stamps are the currency of choice. A "soft" opening meant there would be no publicity, no promotion.

No book buyers.

The sales representative from my publisher had set it up through the distributor.

"It'll be fun, Kevin," Susan, the sales rep, persisted. "And it'll be good for your career."

I highly doubted either. I considered a signing anywhere but a bookstore to be the ultimate in humiliation.

"I think I'm busy, Susan. Research, you understand. Gotta write that next book."

"Please," she begged, her whiny voice coming across the phone in what I was sure was an abuse of fiber-optics. "I've got C.J. Cunningham and Misty Dawn scheduled with you. It will be so much fun."

C.J. Cunningham was a Seattle writer who was always on the verge of great success. Her books were funny, well-plotted and under-published. I liked her just fine. Misty Dawn was a romance-queen wannabe from Vashon Island. Her real name did not approach the Live-Nude-Girls! name her publisher had bestowed upon her when they signed her for a two-book contract. She was born Diane Hornung. I didn't know her and I figured she wasn't much of a threat at a signing table. She had only written one book.

"Okay, Susan, I'll be there," I begrudgingly told the sales rep.

As I drove across the Narrows Bridge, then north on I-5 to Seattle's melancholy south end, I could not help but recall the miserable signings I had suffered through in the past. I had been humiliated in malls, airports, school libraries. I had endured some of the most incongruous of book-signing venues. The coup de grâce had been the time I was skunked at a friend's bed-and-bath shop. My friend put my table and chair next to a Granny Smith potpourri display and I smelled of the stuff for days. Worst of all, my own mother showed up, but got so enamored with the soaps of the world display that she forgot why she had come there in the first place. She bought everything but a book.

[Valerie got a quadruple-pack gift set of Lavender of Kew Gardens soaps for Christmas that year. The scent reminded me of the miserable day when I sold no books and reeked of Granny Smith. I used to run hot tap water over the bars to make the damn things shrink faster. FYI, triple-milled lasts forever.]

I was the last to arrive at the Bag 'n Save. Misty was not exactly the image I had seen on the inside back cover of her book, *Neptune's Daughter*. With the exception of her hair, which was auburn and wavy, she looked nothing like a Misty Dawn. Her lips were thin. Her face sallow. Her eyes drooped. The woman was more in need of a Photoshop *and* Glamour Shots makeover than anyone I saw hovering around the photography/lingerie studio at the mall in Timberlake.

C.J. Cunningham, with whom I had endured other signings, pulled me aside and gave me a nudge.

"Check out her giveaway."

"Giveaway?" I asked, somewhat puzzled.

C.J. pointed at the display table. "In the basket."

I couldn't make out what the glittering golden shapes heaped

160

inside a large, tulle-trimmed white wicker basket were supposed to be. "What are they?" I finally asked.

"Seahorse angels! She made a bunch of seahorse angel pins to commemorate the release of her book."

"Oh. God," I whispered, shaking my head. "What am I supposed to give away? Crime scene refrigerator magnets?"

Two hours later, I felt sorry for C.J. and myself. Misty Dawn had given away all her stupid pins and sold about sixty books. Maybe more. I sold two; C.J, four. At one point it was so slow at our end of the table that a store checker asked me to help an elderly lady out with her groceries. I did. C.J. gave store patrons tips on recycling. During one of the few times she was able to put her pen down, Misty Dawn told us that Nicole Kidman's people called her agent to say the actress was interested in playing the title role in the feature film adaptation of *Neptune's Daughter*.

"I'm so happy for you," I lied, as I forked over the money for a copy of the book my sister-in-law would devour in a sitting. She was one of those romance addicts who read three or four a week and never threw one away. She had a spare bedroom lined from floor to ceiling with books. On the back of the door was an autographed poster of Fabio (pre-margarine commercials and his goose-whacking on the roller coaster) that I got for her at a writers' expo in Portland. She gushed when she got it. There were millions of readers like her.

Nicole or not, I figured Misty Dawn ought to do all right. There was no justice in the world.

♦

I WAS HOME BY 3:15 THAT AFTERNOON. Despite the dismal book signing, the time by myself in the LUV gave me the opportunity to think about the Parker murder and how it related to *Love You to Death*. Of course, there had to be a connection. But what? Who would kill Danny's mother and try to suck me into the bloody crime by having me find her?

It came to me as I pulled up my driveway, Hedda barking

161

from her dog run. The answer had to be somewhere within the book I was writing. Within the cast of characters in *Love You to Death*. As inane as the story was, somewhere it was real and undeniably evil. Somewhere within the bunch of low-rent losers I was interviewing was the killer of an innocent woman.

In writing *Love You to Death*, I knew that I just might solve June Rose Parker's murder.

Valerie left a note that took the girls to an early movie. They wouldn't be back for at least a couple of hours. Good. I gave Hedda a Milkbone and sat down at my desk. Valerie and I had a pact that I wouldn't work evenings and never on Saturday.

"Saturday is a family day," she said.

And while I pledged to keep evenings free, it was a difficult promise to keep. When sources agreed to an interview, I had to go. When a phone call came, I had to take it. When a book rep called to get me to a soft grand opening... well, I knew I would say no to that next time. The fact was that I was not in the position to put anyone off. I needed them far more than they needed me. They had the story. I took the notes.

I made a couple of calls. Anna Cameron's daughter told me that her mother was out shopping.

"You that novelist writin' the book about my big brother?" she asked.

I didn't see any sense in explaining the difference between nonfiction and fiction.

"Yes, I am," I said.

"I'm not supposed to talk to you. My mom says you're trying to write bad things about my brother."

"I'm sorry she feels that way. Will you at least tell her that I phoned? I really want to talk to her about Danny. I don't want to make any mistakes."

The girl told me she'd pass along the message.

I tried to get Jett on the phone, but all I got was her voicemail.

162

Finally, I tried Paul Kerr's number. Paul was Janet's ex-husband. Though he was outside of the main action of the story I was writing, he was very much a player.

"I'm trying to reach Mr. Kerr," I said. "Is he home?"

"This is his wife, Liz. Who's calling, please?" The woman's voice had a kind of southern sound to it. Her words were somewhat stretched.

"Hi! I hope I'm not catching you at a bad time. My name is Kevin Ryan and I'm writing a book about what happened with Janet, Deke and Danny. Do you think your husband would talk to me?"

There was a slight hesitation. "Well, I don't rightly know," she said. "Let me ask him."

Though she pressed her palm to the mouthpiece, I heard her call out: "Some reporter writin' a book wants to talk to you about Janet Lee!"

A voice came through loud and clear: "Tell 'em I'll talk with him! I want the whole world to know what kind of woman that bitch is! Tell him to come right on over."

When she got back on the line and repeated what I had already heard, I explained that I was a couple hours away, and if I left immediately I could be there around dinner time. I was not fishing for an invitation by any means—far from it—but that's what I got.

"Then you can have supper with us. Makin' cabbage-stuffed buns tonight," she said cheerfully.

I scrawled a message for Valerie, begging for forgiveness and pledging undying love. I was doing this for us. For the kids. For that dream house with hardwood floors we would build one day. On Sunday we'd take a drive to the Olympic Peninsula and let Hedda and girls run around on the gray sands of some desolate stretch of the Washington coast.

It will be fun, I wrote.

163

Chapter Twenty-one
Thursday, August 29

I HAD DRIVEN PAST THE KERR RESIDENCE several times on previous visits to Timberlake. The last time was that terrible evening when I found Danny Parker's mother dead in the hallway of her tidy little home. As I understood it, the investigation was making some progress. What I had learned from Martin Raines, however, troubled me greatly. The cyanide that killed June Parker was a component of a mix used by gardeners to rid their vegetable patches of rodents. Weasel-Die was ninety-nine percent filler and one percent sodium cyanide. One little taste, however, was the last thing a weasel or mole would ever get. I knew the product quite well. The killer in my book *Over the Counter Murders* had killed her husband when she refilled headache capsules with the deadly poison ten years before. The crime lab in Olympia had sent a sample on to a chemist at the University of Washington for additional analysis. Another sample was earmarked for the FBI—though it was such a low-priority case that it was doubtful chemists there would process it any time soon.

A pack of dogs barked from a rusty chain link kennel enclosure next to the metal gleam of the brand new double-wide trailer that Paul and Liz Kerr shared with Paul and Janet's daughter, Lindy. The dogs riveted my attention, the way large, threatening animals always did. They were a Siberian Husky and Gray Wolf cross, and they seemed hungry. They were also scary, but I knew they came with the territory. Breeding with wolves was popular out in Nowheresville. One man even raised a pit-bull/wolf cross and advertised them as great pets for kids. I preferred droopy-eared Hedda.

The pungent smell of dog urine pierced the cool air. On a hot day in summertime, I was certain the place would stink to high heaven.

A three-year-old girl ran down the front lawn and crossed the road.

"That was Lindy," Liz Kerr said as she emerged from the other side of the yelping kennel. "Sent her to the neighbors. She's heard plenty about her mother and I guess we just don't want her to hear any more of this garbage."

"I can imagine," I said. "It must be very hard on such a little girl."

Liz nodded and motioned me around to the front door of the mobile.

"She really doesn't remember her mom much, which I guess is a good thing." Liz tossed a hunk of meat over the kennel wall, sending the dogs into a slobbering and yelping frenzy.

"Come on in," she said, smiling. "Paul's watching the tube."

Liz Kerr looked to be in her forties, though she could be younger. She had deep brown hair with a skunk-tail streak, a thin face, and under her eyes, circles as dark and clear as lines left by thick-tipped Magic Markers. Her features were small and pleasant. She might even have been pretty before hard knocks keeled her over. She was cautious, but friendly, and despite the fact that she had stirred her dogs into a bloody riot, I thought she was pretty nice.

The stinky smell of cooking cabbage seeped unpleasantly from inside as she pushed the aluminum front door open. I wasn't hungry in the least.

"Dinner will be ready in five minutes," she announced.

"Great. Smells great," I lied. "I'm starved."

"Paul!" she called out, her voice loud and clear. "That reporter is here!"

"Get him a beer and send him in here," the voice I had heard over the phone shot back from another room.

"Better take one for him, too." Liz handed me a couple of cold cans and pointed me in the direction of the living room.

Paul Kerr was stretched out on a brown and tan plaid sofa. The back of his head had left a slightly greasy transfer on the armrest furthest from the television. His big toe poked through a hole in his thick, white work socks at the other end. He was no more than a worn-out thirty-year-old. He was a logger, like his father and grandfather before him. He had such rough, callused

166

hands I doubted it was possible for him to leave a fingerprint. His forearms were massive and the skin hammock of his stomach slipped over his Peterbilt belt buckle. Pockmarks on his face from teenage acne were the only reminders that he, like his wife, Liz, he had once been very young.

"So you want to know about Janet and her mother, huh?" he said after I introduced myself and gave him a beer. Spray from his flip-top hit my face.

"You caught me," I said, jokingly as I searched for something to wipe the sudsy spray off my mustache and eyebrows, both of which were in need of a good trim.

"Well, I'll tell you, you haven't got a clue about those evil bitches. Hell, if I were you, I'd sleep with one eye open. Heard you've been talking with those she-devils up at the prison."

"Yeah," I said. "Just a couple of times."

"Ever say anything about me?"

"Not really. Nothing comes to mind, anyway."

I didn't feel that it was the best time for me to tell him that Janet had told me Paul had only one testicle and had once considered an operation to have a ping pong ball inserted into his scrotum to give him the bulge he was sorely lacking. At least he thought so. Janet had not done much to assuage her husband's manhood. Whenever they got into a screaming match, Janet's heart-stabbing nickname for him was "One-Ball Paul."

Better not bring that up.

Or the story Connie Carter had confided about how Paul had molested Lindy and attempted to sell her into white slavery off the loading dock at the Timberlake Lumber Mill, where he delivered trucks of logs each week.

No, it wouldn't be how I would start the interview. Just not a good idea.

Liz Kerr served cabbage rolls as we chatted and watched *Wheel of Fortune*. The rolls were actually pretty good and I ate three. Paul had at least seven and Liz consumed two. I washed the food down with another beer and suggested that after *Wheel* was done spinning we could turn off the television and talk about the case that landed his ex-wife and former mother-in-law in prison.

"After *Jeopardy*," Liz insisted.

And so we watched, and after it was over, Liz turned off the TV on the intro to *Dancing With the Stars* and we talked. Liz brought out a Tupperware container of Snickerdoodles and matching Snap-on Tool mugs of coffee. Paul, however, stuck with his beers. Lindy stayed down at the neighbor's. Though I only saw her that moment when I first arrived, evidence that a little girl lived in that house was everywhere: a painting of a turkey taped on the front of the refrigerator, a Barbie with butchered hair on the floor by the TV and a stack of little girl's laundry on the redwood burl coffee table. Lindy Kerr was a sweet little thing. And from what everyone was telling me, she was without question at the center of the mess.

About three and a half hours with the Kerrs, I was on my way home in the LUV with the goods to write the next chapter of *Love You to Death*. In fact, all I had to do was transcribe it from the thoughts in my head.

Chapter Twenty-two

◆

Love You to Death

PART SIX

MEMORIAL DAY WEEKEND ALWAYS guaranteed long lines at the supermarket and fried chicken buckets full of rain. It had been that way ever since Paul Kerr could remember. He got off work from the mill in time to run home, shower, change to a clean T-shirt and jeans and get to the store to pick up supplies for a weekend camping trip with his buddies. They planned to meet in the parking lot at the Fred Meyer discount store at seven before driving to the ocean for three days of camping, beer and good times. Paul packed a little bag of pot into the zippered compartment of his backpack. Others would carry more illegal goodies, though that wasn't all they were bringing. One buddy found a couple of girls with nothing better to do. One was a honey blonde teenage checker from the discount store named Michelle McMahon. She was a nice enough girl. Made it to work on time. Lived with her parents. And when the opportunity came up to do some thing a little different, a little dangerous, she jumped at it with trampoline-like abandon. She told her folks she was camping with her best friend and her family.

"We're going to Seaside," she said. "They have a cabin just one block from the beach."

Seaside was a rinky-dink resort town of bumper cars and saltwater taffy stands on the northern edge of the Oregon coast. It was the kind of place the middle class swarmed to with the first sign of the elusive warmth of summer weather; a place that was still within the means of the folks of Timberlake.

Michelle's best friend, however, didn't have a cabin there. In fact, she had never been there before in her life. She didn't even have parents, not really. Michelle's best friend was a sixteen-year-old Timberlake High School dropout named Janet Lee Carter.

Paul Kerr was young and horny, and Janet looked pretty good. By the end of the first night on the beach, Janet was inside his sleeping bag, acting every bit the consensual adult she insisted she was. It was only the next morning when his buddy told him that she was jail bait and that he'd better watch his step.

"Her mom's a real bitch and already sent one guy to jail for molesting her. I'll tell you one thing, Janet was *not* molested. She's been screwing since she was twelve."

Paul Kerr ignored the warnings. He liked Janet. He also liked the idea of having a girlfriend. He'd been alone for a year.

Janet was also between boyfriends. She had recently dumped a drummer from a Timberlake bar band. She wanted a baby and he was unable to get her pregnant. She left him five days before the camping trip. In many ways, she was a girl on a mission.

Friends later recalled that Janet had told them repeatedly that she wanted a baby.

170

"She wanted someone to love," Michelle McMahon said several years later. "She was out of control, and I think she knew it. She thought if she had a baby, she'd not only get a man, she'd have someone she could love."

Janet and Paul spent the long weekend bombed. Janet told him that he was the best lover she ever had; Paul told her that he saw something special in her the minute he laid eyes on her. Others, of course, had told such stories to their one-night stands. Others had made the promises of phone calls and movie dates. Most of those were lies, of course. But not with Paul and Janet. Theirs wasn't true love. It was true convenience.

-

TWO WEEKS AFTER THE CAMPING TRIP, Janet moved into Paul's rented basement apartment at 44 Klipsun Avenue. She brought her waterbed and spent the first morning patching a leak after setting it up. She even cooked dinner that evening for Paul's arrival after work-hamburgers and crinkle-cut fries. If the first day was an indication, Paul Kerr would have thought that his life with Janet Lee Carter was pretty good.

Of course, it wasn't going to turn out that way.

Janet Lee was a drug user.

"The funny thing was," Paul Kerr said years after, "I could never tell when Janet was drunk or high. It never showed on the girl. No matter how much she drank. I could watch her drink and smoke pot for two days straight and no sleep... Hell, I drank plenty myself,

171

smoked some, but never to the extent that Janet did. She even did needle drugs. She had a mole or something on her arm and she always shot right into that."

Janet also ran around like some kind of sex-starved decathlete.

"Good God. I should have known when she put out within three hours of meeting me on the camping trip to Seaside," Paul Kerr remembered. "What an idiot I was! Sometimes I figured she thought sex was the same as shaking hands with someone. 'Nice to meet ya, wanna blowjob?' Who knows? I caught her screwing a half dozen guys during the early days. One was an old boyfriend, a drummer. Another was some guy she met at the car wash-and she didn't even have a car at the time. When it came to opening her mouth or dropping her pants, there was no stopping Janet."

And there was her mother. If Janet was bad, Paul had seen the scary future-Connie Carter.

"Connie, even before Jan and I got hitched, was the mother-in-law from hell. She was a bigger drunk than her daughter. She was more of a slut. Once I met Janet's mom, I knew where Janet got all of her worst ideas. Sometimes I wondered if Connie was involved in some kind of sick competition with Janet. *First one to screw a dozen different men in a night wins the grand whore prize!* Connie was one of those women who hated men and I think she raised her daughter in the same way. Whenever Connie was around, I thought of an excuse to get lost for a few hours. Worked on my truck, went to the store, anywhere just to get away and stay clear."

172

When Janet became pregnant two months after they met, she told Paul that if he didn't marry her, she would do something drastic and make him sorry for the rest of his life.

"I'll take a coat hanger and kill your baby and flush it down the fuckin' toilet if you don't do right by me like a real man!"

Connie Carter was equally persuasive.

"I'll fix your other nut with a pair of pliers!" she threatened.

When Paul Kerr agreed to make the drive to Las Vegas for a wedding at the Little Chapel of Flowers, he did so with the idea that he was saving two lives. His own and that of his unborn child.

"Oh, honey, I'm gonna be a grandma," Connie cooed to her daughter as they drove southeast through the wooded northern reaches of Oregon before heading east toward the Nevada desert and Las Vegas.

"Gonna be a grandma! The youngest and prettiest grandma in Timberlake," Janet sang to her mother.

"Maybe not the youngest," Connie laughed back.

-

THE PREGNANT BRIDE WORE A CREAMY white faux pearl-accented Gunne Sax dress that her mother had picked up at a thrift store for twelve dollars. Heavy bleaching to remove a big red stain from the bodice left the dress quite fragile and frayed. The groom wore new blue jeans and a clean button-up long-sleeved shirt. The witnesses who signed the marriage certificate were Connie Carter and Ron Something or other. The signature made out by an old man who worked for the chapel was so illegible, no one could make it out.

In the end, that wouldn't matter. Neither the bride, the groom, nor the ever-present mother-in-law, held much hope for a long-lasting union. They all hoped that for a "first marriage," it would turn out all right.

Connie won more than one hundred dollars on a gas station slot machine just after the ceremony. She jumped for joy and bought a big bag of nacho cheese-flavored Doritos and a six-pack of beer for the long ride home to Timberlake. Despite the windfall, there would be no wedding night in a fancy bridal suite. Of course, there wasn't enough cash for that. After giving half of her winnings to her daughter, Connie told the newlyweds the money was a good omen for the future.

Paul Kerr wanted to believe it was true.

"Big dummy me," Paul confided to a friend several years later, "for awhile, I thought we were going to be happy. I *wanted* us to be happy. Really, I honestly did. I thought having a baby would settle us both down. I know Janet was young. I was young, too. And I was stupid. I thought caring for our baby would make Janet grow up some."

-

JANET LEE KERR NEVER LEFT 44 Klipsun Avenue without leaving a love note for her new husband. It didn't matter that she was headed off drinking, sleeping around, or scrounging for money for drugs. She told him she had a hard time showing her feelings, that putting them on paper was easier. Paul Kerr found letters taped to the front of their empty refrigerator. He found his wife's missives at work in the bottom of his lunch box, in the bathroom next to his toothbrush, under his pillow. Once, he even found a note pinned to his Jockey shorts.

Janet left note after note, each beginning with the same salutation (though when she was in a hurry she wrote the initials SB instead of Sugarbutt; and one time she called Paul "Sweet Ass"-which he nearly considered an affront because it too closely resembled "Candy Ass.") One note written less than a full week after their wedding was saved by the bridegroom. He tucked it into the pages of a car magazine and put it in the closet. Paul treasured it because it seemed so genuine. Janet's love, her deep devotion, touched him. In the beginning, he felt lucky to have a wife who loved him... and soon, a baby, too.

Dear Sugarbutt:
You know you are my one and only. My big man. No woman could ask for a bigger man. You are my Sugarbutt and I love you. Oh, we will have the best life together. You and me. I want you right now! I'll be out late. Going with a girlfriend to get her hair cut and then over to the mall for a little shopping (she's doing the shopping, not me!) Don't wait up for me.

Love you!
Janet

Note from Val: *OK, two thoughts here. Sugarbutt and Sweet Ass are the worst nicknames or so-called "terms of endearment" I've ever heard. I'd leave you without looking back if you called me either of those. Secondly, when Paul says "Big dummy me," I thought, that's the smartest thing he—or anyone in this story said thus far. I almost wrote "twisted tale" instead of "story" because I know how much your last editor was in love with the term. :)*

Chapter Twenty-three
Thursday, August 29

"TOMORROW," she said once more.

I was floored.

"Tomorrow," I repeated slowly, allowing myself the extra time for it to sink in. I was glad Jett had made the invitation over the phone. I doubted my face could conceal my shock and doubt. "I guess I can be there," I said before hanging up.

Jett Carter had extended the most unexpected of invitations. She had to work a big Labor Day Weekend sale at Ho! and would not be able to make Janet and Deke's wedding at the prison chapel. The happy couple-to-be thought it would be nice if I stepped in to take her place. There were good reasons for it. I was already cleared to visit at the prison. I lived only a couple of miles away. And, just maybe they might have thought, my presence would put them in a more favorable light when I wrote *Love You to Death*.

"Are you going to bring a gift?" Valerie asked with a laugh when I told her the news of the prison nuptials. "How about a set of His and Her hacksaws? Maybe a file for the wedding cake? Bride's registered at the hardware store, I'll bet."

"Probably Walmart, too."

Both of us knew that nothing could be brought directly into prison—at least not by the honesty-inclined. Everything had to be mailed in. Even so, on the wall behind the prison visitors' desk was a huge display, maybe three by ten feet that had been mounted to the wall. It was labeled with perfect laser-printed letters: LOOK WHAT WE FOUND WHERE THE SUN DON'T SHINE. Amid the items on the contraband collage, among other

177

things, was enough cutlery to outfit a gourmet kitchen store, albeit a filthy and disgusting one.

Valerie crossed her legs tightly together when I told her how the flatware had been smuggled in.

"In there?" she said, wincing and pulling her thighs together.

"Yeah. In *there.*"

"Doesn't that hurt?"

"God, Val, of course it hurts, but sometimes mothers will do anything for their daughters."

Mothers, I explained, were the worst offenders of smuggling contraband. Sisters were less inclined to smuggle something in their vaginas. Daughters almost never did. Daughters, for the most part, were glad to finally have their wayward moms right where they knew they'd be—for the next ten years.

The display behind the desk also featured paper clips, the metal clips from ballpoint pens, disposable lighters, even a pair of handcuffs.

Valerie was incredulous when I told her about the cuffs.

"Why in the world would anyone smuggle handcuffs, of all things, into a prison?"

I shrugged my shoulders. "Who knows? I never said these people were bright."

Lastly, there were at least a dozen photographs of drugs and drug paraphernalia on the display. The real stuff had been hot-glued onto the board in the past, until the pills started to disappear.

Val again was appalled. "How'd the prisoners get to them?"

"Not the *prisoners*, Val."

"Visitors?" She shook her head in disgust.

"Nope. The *staff.* Seems the guards helped themselves to what was up there on the board. One guard who had been at the

178

prison for ten years—was even Corrections Officer of the Month on three different occasions—was fired when it was discovered she was replacing some of the pills with aspirin from her purse and red and yellow Skittles from the employee vending machine."

That night, I ironed the front of a shirt and the cuffs and tried to choose a tie. It had been several years since I held a "real job," and my ties were beginning to look as though they might be out of fashion. Too wide. Or too narrow. I wasn't sure which. I chose a blue-and-yellow striped tie to go with a navy blazer and slacks.

"Stripes are classic," I announced to Val as she shifted on her side of the bed while reading the paper.

"Uh-huh. 'Classic,'" she said without looking up from the business section, "is another word for old."

♦

I WAS SURE MURIEL-THE-PRISON-FLACK regarded me as an annoyance by now. She had seen more of me than the lifers that would never leave the razor wire-crested walls of Riverstone. She wore her bright red hair bunched up in a bouquet with one of those plastic clips that looked like a shark's jaw. It was fitting. The woman *was* a shark. She wore a green suit that would have cost a month's worth of groceries at my house.

"Are you in the wedding?" I said as she led me down a polished cement corridor to the chapel.

"You've got to be kidding. I'm not in it. I'm not going to it."

"You seem kind of dressed up," I remarked.

She looked satisfied with herself and smiled. "The *Nancy Grace* people are back."

"Satan's brother again?" I asked.

"Yeah. This time the inmate is going to tell all—supposedly the flip side to those touchy-feely books by Sylvia Browne."

Sylvia Browne was a chain-smoking psychic who, through her vague connections to God and the afterlife, had become a rich woman. It was good to have connections. Sylvia proved it.

"What are you doing here on a Saturday? I thought someone with your seniority wouldn't have to work on the weekends, let alone a holiday," I asked, knowing the jab would eat at her.

She made a face, a sneer.

"Cross-training. We all have to work one holiday a year. This is my time, plus *Nancy Grace* is in town, too."

Muriel stopped and pointed to an open doorway. "The chapel."

I scanned the confines of the small room. It was hardly a chapel. It was more of a craft room than anything. A weaver's loom occupied one corner. A trio of easels, another. In back of the room were a cabinet and a kiln for ceramics. Pottery, evidently, was very popular at Riverstone. Rows and rows of cups and bowls stood ready for glazing and firing.

"New inmate income project," Muriel explained when she noticed my stare. "With the garment profits fading, the girls are looking for something new to make some canteen money. Calling their venture 'Hoosegow Pottery.' Supposed to sound kind of country, I guess."

The chapel portion of the room was up front. Taped to the wall was an enormous "stained glass" made from torn bits of colored tissue and black construction paper. It portrayed a shepherd and his flock of lambs on one panel and the Virgin Mary on the other. It wasn't bad, as far as prison art went. It would have been enhanced, of course, with some light illuminating it from behind. But in prison, real light is always in short supply. Light fixtures buzzed from the ceiling like a horde of fireflies.

A guard with slicked back hair and a skimpy brown moustache sat under the Virgin Mary. A prison ID badge indicated her name: Darlene Fulton.

Muriel introduced us and indicated the officer was in charge.

"Not the minister. Darlene is in full control of this wedding."

She left us to wait for the bride, groom and chaplain.

The chaplain arrived first. His name was Vernon Hess. He had been ministering to the ladies of Riverstone for nearly twenty years. It was, he said, his calling from God. He was in his late forties, with black hair and skin as pasty as the rack of unfired greenware adjacent to the makeshift altar. Weddings were a rarity at Riverstone. Few women could hang on to their men once they were incarcerated, let alone snag a new one. The concept of prison groupie had never made it over to the women's prisons as it had at the men's institutions. Male criminals could frequently find several women to "save" them from loneliness and a corrupt, unfair system. Few women could pull it off.

"Call me Father Vern," he said while we waited.

I doubted I would call him anything.

Deke Cameron was ushered in next. His tie was far worse than anything I could have dredged up out of the dankest recesses of my closet. He wore one of those godawful "salmon" neckties that, until that very moment, I had mistakenly assumed only Midwestern tourists purchased when they came to Seattle. It was a full-length airbrushed fish, its head pointing to Deke's protruding belly. He had no jacket on and his corduroy pants made a swishing noise when he walked across the room to stand by the chaplain and Officer Darlene.

Father Vern smiled and pushed the button on a CD player for the music.

It was at that moment that I realized Connie Carter had not been asked to witness the supposed joyous event of her daughter's wedding. I guessed that Officer Darlene and I would be the names on the license when conspirator and victim were joined as one and it was all over.

181

From the boom box came the strains of Nazareth's "Love Hurts." I knew Deke Cameron had felt the song was about him and Janet and the predicament of their love.

Yes, love hurts. Yes, love wounds. But love doesn't take a shotgun and point it at your gut to kill you.

As I waited for the song to run its longwinded course, I watched Deke sway slightly to the music. Father Vern cleared his throat for the vows. Officer Darlene held the second CD, poised to put it in the minute the singing stopped.

"...Love is like a flame...it burns you when it's hot. Ooooh, Love hurrrts... ."

Janet Kerr was led to her second wedding in shackles. She mouthed a "glad you are here" to me and stood next to the man that would be her husband. She wore the same outfit I had seen in the photos of her Pierce County trial. It was a wine-colored skirt and a white blouse. Her weight increase since the trial was more than evident. A safety pin had been used to bolster the button and zipper at the back of the skirt. Janet's hair was in a tiny ponytail and for the first time, I noticed she was wearing makeup.

It was over in a flash, surely the shortest wedding ceremony I'd have been party to—besides my own, which lasted all of two minutes. Father Vern admonished the bride and groom that while there would be no touching during the vows, a brief kiss would be allowed at its conclusion.

After it was over, I approached the happy couple to wish them well. Cokes from the vending machine were distributed and Officer Darlene offered to buy a package of Ding Dongs for an improvised wedding cake. Everyone declined.

"I'm sorry your sister couldn't be here," I said.

"Yeah, me too. I've missed most of her life, too," Janet said.

"Congratulations, Deke." I extended my hand, and his salami fingers took it and shook.

"Thanks, Mr. Ryan. Glad that you could come."

As Deke spoke, he dribbled Coke down his double chin onto his fish tie. I futilely searched for a napkin to wipe it, and finally grabbed a Kleenex from a dispenser on a craft table and gave it to him.

"I thought your mother might be here," I said to Janet.

Her face went from vacant to sad. "Me and Mom aren't talking now."

"How come?"

"Mom don't approve of Deke. Says Deke is the reason we're in prison."

Deke's bulbous cheeks were crimson. "Hey, I'm a *victim*," he said, puffing himself up as if being a victim was some kind of badge of honor; the greatest excuse. "I just did what the detective wanted me to do. I was tricked."

I had heard that before, so I withheld comment. I wished the couple well and two minutes after the vows were exchanged, I was escorted out by Muriel, who had just returned.

"How was it?" she asked without looking at me as we walked to the gate.

"Fast."

"They always are."

"You have many like this?"

"About two or three a year. But none like this."

"Like this?"

"Come on, a woman in prison for attempted murder marrying the man whose testimony put her here?"

"*National Enquirer* material, isn't it?" I said.

A funny little half-smile cracked her frozen face. "Yes, as a matter of fact, they've already called."

Muriel-the-flack turned around and clacked her way down the corridor. Now, I knew how it was that she could afford that beautiful suit. Muriel was a stringer for the *Enquirer.*

I'd never get a break.

♦

I TOOK THE LONG WAY BACK HOME, which amounted to an extra five minutes. The sun had snipped a slit through the clouds, lighting the tops of the evergreens like fire on a Christmas tree. When I had turned into our driveway, my thoughts remained on the prison wedding. I was glad there had been no reception. I couldn't dance and hated to make excuses to my wife, who I saw running toward the LUV as I pulled in to park.

"Kevin, I'm glad you came right home," she said, nearly out of breath.

"Jett has been calling the house phone. You turned off your cell. There's something bothering her and she has to talk with you. She's very upset, crying, almost hysterical."

"Where is she?"

"First she was at work, then she called from home. That's where she said she'd be until she heard from you."

Valerie was shaken and angry. Her hair was clipped back in one of Taylor's tortoise-shell barrettes. Very tight to her head. It was a severe look and it matched her mood.

"Are you all right?" I asked, reaching for her hand.

She pulled away.

"I'm not all right. Kevin, enough is enough. This book is turning into another Wanda-Lou fiasco. Jett is frightened and I can't help her. Let's see, when I asked her if I could help with whatever was upsetting her, she said, 'It doesn't concern you, Val. Not directly. I've got to talk to Kevin right away.'"

Val took a deep breath, her face was flushed. I knew it was because she was both frustrated and worried.

184

I let her talk.

"Those books aren't worth it, Kevin," she said. "Just get it over with. Don't get me wrong, I like Jett fine. I like her very much, you know that. I wish her well. But I can't make her life better. Finish the book."

I followed my wife into the house.

"Val, I'll see what the matter is. It's probably nothing. Probably someone at Ho! was rude to her at the sales counter."

Val had blown off the steam that had collected through the series of frantic phone calls.

"I don't know," she said, "I'm worried about Jett. She seems so..."She searched for the words. "*Distraught.*"

I went to my desk and pushed the speed dial button for Jett's number. She picked up before the first ring was completed.

"Kevin! God, I'm glad you called me."

"Val says something is up. Are you okay?"

"I'm fine. I'm worried about *you*."

"What for? I only attended your sister's wedding. I wasn't the groom, for God's sake."

Usually Jett would laugh at such a remark, but her voice grew hushed. I prodded her to talk.

"What is it?"

"Oh, Kevin, Detective Raines was here this morning."

"What for? Are you in some kind of trouble?" I looked around for my coffee cup and waited for her reply. "Jett, what is it?"

Finally she spoke. "I'm not the one in trouble. I think *you* are."

"Me?" I asked, my voice full of surprise.

"I think so. Detective Raines was here and he asked me about you and Mrs. Parker."

My heart dipped below my waist.

185

"June Parker?"

"Yeah. He kept asking me about what kind of person you are and if you had ever said anything to me about Mrs. Parker."

"He doesn't think—"

"I think he does. Kevin, I think Raines thinks you might be behind her murder."

I was reeling now. The very idea someone could suggest that I could have done anything like murder shook me hard. I wrote about murder. I didn't commit murder.

"Kevin? Are you still there?"

I pulled it together.

"Jett, I'm here. I just can't believe it. Martin Raines is my friend. How could he even think, let alone *say*, such a thing to you?"

"He said they have evidence against you."

"Evidence? What evidence?"

"He didn't say."

I thanked her for calling, though I had been the one who called her.

"I'll talk to you soon."

"Kevin? How was Janet's wedding?"

The question caught me off-guard and for a second, in spite of everything, I was embarrassed that I hadn't told her right away that the wedding went off just fine.

"The wedding? Oh, it was lovely. Janet looked terrific. Very pretty. Everyone missed you being there. I'll tell you more when I see you. I'm going to Timberlake tomorrow morning, first thing."

I hung up and looked for Valerie. I nearly cried when I told her what Jett had said. In the instant her words passed through my eardrums, I was already, in my mind, on death row. Another

186

statistic, that was me. Another man falsely accused, convicted, forgotten. I could see it all, because I had *written* it all before. I had done a piece for one of the women's magazines about a Denver man who had been convicted for the murder of his neighbor. The evidence was weak, almost nonexistent. The man had been involved in a dispute over a tree that had hung over the property line. The dead man was found with a hatchet in the back of his head in his workshop. The prints matched the neighbor's. The hapless con was denied a new trial, even when previously undisclosed fingerprints were matched with a drifter from Colorado Springs who had been passing through the area around the time of the killing. The man hung in legal limbo for three years, waiting for a new trial.

His wife left him for his defense lawyer.

His house was auctioned for legal bills.

His kids claimed he had abused them, too.

He was eventually freed, but for what? He had nothing.

"It'll be all right," Valerie said as my mind drifted back to reality. She held me in her arms and squeezed. I felt better.

"You'll get through this. Martin Raines knows you."

"That's what *I* thought."

"You'll see."

Chapter Twenty-four
Friday, August 30

I HADN'T SLEPT A MINUTE AND THE OVERPACKED BAGS under my eyes were proof. My face was eclipsed by the stubble of a brown beard that I had often wished could be transplanted to my thinning pate. At 2 a.m., I tapped out the last few paragraphs of my fourth chapter of *Love You to Death* and put it in a folder for Val to read later. Anxiety was such a good motivator.

That morning, haggard, tired and beat, I stood in the shower letting the spray rush over me like a waterfall until I could feel the chilly result of a hot water tank depleted of its reserves. I caught my reflection in a shaving mirror that hung from the nozzle. I was thirty-eight and the aging process was accelerating. The fine wrinkles around my eyes were deepening. My blue eyes were set in a field of red. My hair... *What hair?* I looked terrible. I had always hoped that I would age as my father had, which as the years went by, seemed not at all.

But Dad had never been accused of murder.

I grabbed a towel and dried off, apologizing to Valerie for taking so long.

"Might want to wait a half hour before showering. Hot water's on the fritz."

"No wonder," Val said, handing me a cup of uncharacteristically weak coffee. "Kevin, I'm sure Marty was only doing his job. You're over the top on this. You shouldn't be so worried. Beyond the fact that you're not a killer, you have no motive and no opportunity."

"Yeah, I know that... it's just the idea that he'd even *think* it."

188

"You don't know what he thinks."

"I know that he's asking questions about me that are turning my stomach."

I dressed, scratched Hedda behind the ears and kissed my girls goodbye. Taylor and Hayley were cuddled up into little balls in their beds. Taylor was uncovered and Hayley was buried beneath the thick folds of a comforter and two blankets. Hedda jumped on Hayley's bed and snuggled next to her. Valerie read the paper at the kitchen table and waited for the water to heat to a tolerable level.

I pointed the LUV toward Timberlake and drove the freeway south. Every so often, I looked beyond the road in front of me to scope out where it was that I was driving. My mind was not on anything other than what I had seen at Mrs. Parker's home. *Her blood. Her hands.* The slip of paper she clutched barely registered, yet I knew that it was there. I knew from talking to Raines that my name was on it. I knew that the poison ingested by Danny's mother had been the same kind used by the killer in one of my books. I turned off her kitchen tap. I had touched nothing else.

That was all I knew.

♦

I HAD KNOWN MARTIN RAINES FOR MORE than three years. He was one of those instantly likeable law enforcement officers who could joke about being addicted to Dunkin' Donuts honey-dipped doughnuts one minute, and make an appearance at a local junior high school to talk about what drugs can do to young minds the next. He could just as easily grind on a suspect with the force of a man who knew exactly where the internal affairs cops drew the line. Just to the edge. No further.

The Raines I knew was not my best friend, but I felt as comfortable with him as one does with a trusted colleague. He respected my work. I respected his. I had never betrayed a cop in any of my books. Cops were heroes. Editors uniformly considered them the "natural rooting interest." Cops, quite

189

naturally, liked being cast in the glow of heroism. Even though my books were merely paperbacks, to most cops they were as close to immortality as a set of Britannicas in the local library.

Raines had been thrilled when I told him I was going to do the *Love You to Death* book.

"Don't make me fat, all right?" he had half-joked.

"You fat? You've got the build of a teenager."

"Smart, too?"

I grinned. "You're Mensa material."

He laughed and so did I. As I remembered it, that particular moment shared between us seemed a million years ago.

I parked under the first floor overhang of the Pierce County Justice Center and went inside. Raines was in the front office and the look on his face said more than any words. His face was ashen. His eyes were bloodshot. He looked around the room—and right through me—before he conjured any recognition.

"Kevin," he said with irritated surprise, "you're here."

"Of course I'm here. I want to talk."

He looked at the clerk typing some ridiculous legal paper. She sat behind a government relic, a *manual* typewriter. White-out was splashed on its keys like seagull droppings.

"Ginny," he reminded her, "you need to type the middle initial on each page. Every page."

The girl, who looked to be about twenty and weary beyond her years, agreed.

"The L key sticks, detective."

"When are you guys going to get a laptop and get rid of this junk?" I asked.

Raines didn't look back at me. I had the feeling it was that he didn't want to. He was avoiding me.

I stiffened. "Martin, what's going on?"

When he looked up, he didn't have the face of a friend anymore. He didn't look like anyone I knew. If I hadn't known the man, I wouldn't have liked him.

"We need to talk," he finally said. "Come in to the back room."

The back room. What he meant was the *interrogation room.* One of the very rooms in which Janet and Danny had been questioned. I had been in them. I had written about the cool air blowing from the ventilation ducts. I had noted the mirror that was obviously a window to some faceless observer.

"Kevin," he said, pointing me to a chair. "I guess it's good that you came down. It'll make this a lot easier in the long run."

My stomach jumped. "What easier? What the hell is going on?"

"We have some questions about the Parker murder."

For a second, an instant and welcome calmness washed over me. I hoped what he wanted was my expert opinion on the crime scene. *Yes,* I thought, *that had to be it.* I sat up and forced a smile. My face was frozen to the pint of phoniness that I knew I must have looked stupid.

"What can I tell you? I don't know any more than I told you."

"But you do, don't you?"

My eyes bulged. "What are you suggesting?"

"Coffee?"

"Hell, I don't want coffee. I want to know why Jett Carter says that you suspect I was involved."

I could hardly even say the words.

"I couldn't believe it at first," he said, his tone turning a little combative. "Couldn't believe it. Now I wonder."

I stood up and slammed my notebook on the table.

"Could you tell me what you're talking about?"

"Yes, but you tell me something first."

I was losing my patience. I was tired. I hadn't slept. I wanted that coffee after all. I was also scared.

"What?"

"Did you kill Mrs. Parker, Kevin?"

"No! How could you even say that?"

"Kevin, it's not me—"

For a moment I thought he was going to be the affable Martin Raines that I knew. I was wrong, for the concern in his voice evaporated.

"—not *you*?"

"I better call Davidson in here. Just a second."

Davidson was a young deputy and I knew why Raines was calling him into the interrogation room. He needed a witness to back up what he said and what procedures he followed. Davidson was a skinny guy, dumber than pea gravel. He had sucked up to me the last time I came to interview Raines. He offered me a soda while I waited and hung around within earshot of the interview so that he could "figure out what this book writing is all about."As if I cared, he spilled the beans on a romance he had with another officer.

When Davidson lumbered in, he nodded in my direction and slumped into a chair next to Raines.

"Kevin Ryan?" Raines said.

I stared hard. My eyes were bullets.

"Is that your name?"

"You know damn well it is."

And then he went on... my rights were read and I could barely hear them. If someone had quizzed me about them for a grand prize of one million dollars, I would have been as poor as always. I sat there stunned. I only saw his mouth. Not his eyes. Not the rest of his body. Just the movements made by a coffee-stained mouth spewing out words I could never have imagined in my wildest nightmares would have been meant for me.

"...for the capital murder of June Rose Parker..."

From what I gathered, as Raines began to question me, there had been an informant. An anonymous informant that had placed me at the scene of the murder an hour before I had said I was there. Okay, maybe a mistake. Big deal. But there was more. The cyanide, it turned out, was, in fact, an exact match to the poison used by the killer in my *Over the Counter Murders* book. A little damaging, but still hardly incriminating.

"Neighbor says he saw you throw some Weasel-Die out after Mrs. Parker's death."

"That's right. I did. I threw out what I had purchased when I did a demonstration on how easy it was to buy the lethal stuff. I did it and wrote about it in an article for *Redbook*."

"But you threw it out *after* the Parker murder."

"So? For God's sake, I was reminded I had the stuff when I talked to you at your house. I have kids," I said.

In your stupid fishing lodge office!

Raines shrugged his shoulders. "Too bad we'll never be able to pull a match on the batch you had."

"Too bad," I echoed. I was terrified now. "Come on, what is the motive here?"

Raines refused to look me in the eye. "We don't need a motive," he said.

"Yeah, but come on, tell me why you think I would do such a thing. You owe me an explanation."

"Kevin, your career is going nowhere. Your latest book flopped. You're up to your neck in credit card debt. You need a winner. You said so yourself. Mrs. Parker didn't want to play your game. We know that you are broke and desperate and to our way of thinking around here, that adds up to a pretty good motive."

193

I was astonished by his ludicrous reasoning.

"Yeah, I'm going to kill so I can have a best seller! Some peripheral character doesn't agree to an interview, so I killed her. That makes a lot of sense. Let's see, why don't I just go into a classroom and gun down a kindergarten class if I'm so desperate to be a best-selling author? I could call it *The Death-Selling Author.*"

Raines shot an annoyed and impatient look in my direction.

"You're sick," he said.

"No, you're sick and you know better."

"We have more."

"What *more*?"

"Your fingerprints in the house."

"I know. I told you. I touched the faucet. I turned off the running water."

"Not just there."

"Where else?" I wondered what I had touched that I had forgotten to mention. I told them about the phone, the door, the faucet. I recalled her eyeglasses crushing under my knee, but I didn't think I had touched them with my hands. There was nothing else.

Raines stared me in the eye. "We pulled your prints off the scrap of paper in her hand. The slip with your name written on it... it has your prints all over it."

I didn't believe him. "You're lying," I said.

"'Fraid not."

"'Fraid so. I didn't touch that note. Are you trying to trick me? God, Martin. I don't know a thing about any of this. Nothing at all."

My accuser's face was frozen. "Your prints came up on Edgar."

194

Edgar was the nickname of the computer system that had millions upon millions of Americans' prints held within its vast memory bank. The fact that Edgar turned up my prints surprised me for a moment. I had not served in the military, the basis for most of the data. Nor had I worked for the government or in civil service. I never had been arrested for anything, though when I was eleven, my brother and I were questioned for shoplifting a U2 cassette tape at Kmart. We hadn't of course, and the fact that the tape was a U2 release was our saving grace. No true fan would shoplift Bono's stuff.

Then it came to me. I had been printed at my girls' elementary school when I became a volunteer there. It was such a fluke. I was flabbergasted. I was being named in a possible murder indictment because I brought granola bars and helped out in the classroom once a month.

"Marty, I never touched that paper."

My friend looked me in the eye. "Edgar doesn't lie."

"Why would I—*just what if*—why would I put my name and number in her hand and call the police?"

Raines remained unmoved by my pleas, my desperation. "I thought about that for a long time. Why would Kevin do that? It was a piece that didn't really fit. Not until you added in the other factors, like the poison, for example. And the answer came to me overnight. It woke me up out of a sound sleep. You wanted the press attention of finding the body and playing the hero. With your name in the dead woman's hand, you become *part* of the story."

My jaw hit the grimy floor.

"You're nuts," I said, finally raising my voice. I could feel my composure slipping away, retreating like small waves on the shore of Puget Sound. "I want to call my wife and lawyer."

"One call's all you get."

"Marty, I've known you for years. You *know* I didn't do this. You know I couldn't do this."

"I thought I knew you, Kevin," he said, crushing a Styrofoam cup and tossing it over his shoulder to the trash can without hitting the rim. It was a nice shot, but I didn't say so.

"And don't you know, more than anything, I hope I'm wrong," he said.

I didn't even want to look at him then.

"Just take me to the phone," I said.

♦

THE REST OF MY ORDEAL SEEMED as close as I would come to an out-of-body experience. I told Val to sit tight and everything would be fine. She said she'd call my lawyer. *My lawyer*? I didn't even have one. She was upset, but she reassured me that everything was all right. It was a terrible mistake.

An officer named Mona—"Moan-a-lot," Deputy Davidson had called her, as he bragged about a patrol-car liaison they'd shared—took down some information and rolled my fingers in an ink that I had always assumed was sticky. It was smooth and creamy. Almost like lotion. My fingertips were placed onto a card. Though it hadn't been in the cramped little room at Pierce County, others had been there before me. Erik, Lyle, Scott, Ted, O.J.... all of them and more. All had felt the ink, and the indignity of a hot, rubber-gloved hand as it pressed their fingers onto the little white card. The experience was as far as humanly possible from the fun I'd had pressing my fingers into the Silly Putty-like material Jett had brought over to our house that night. A night that now seemed impossibly distant.

Officer Moan-a-lot gave me a paper towel and a blob of a greasy gray concoction called Goop.

"This'll get that icky ink off your wittle fingers."

I wanted to slap her in her condescending wittle mouth. Her Elmer Fudd impression was over the line. Cutesy-poo was not needed, not appreciated. I felt my face grow hot. And as I rubbed the ink off and rinsed in a home wet bar-sized stainless steel sink, I spoke.

196

"Deputy Davidson says you're a real screamer."

"Huh?" She looked clueless.

"Screamer," I stupidly repeated.

Recognition hit her hard. She flashed a hateful look. Her eyes were fastened to mine.

I pushed harder. "Does your husband call you Moan-a-lot, too?"

Another hateful look.

"Get on the tape," she said, indicating a pair of gummy pieces of masking tape affixed on a floor so dirty I could not make out what color the linoleum had been.

Two blinding flashes emanating from behind a scuffed camera decorated with a dancing row of Mr. Yuk stickers from the poison control unit down the hall and I was done. *God, was I done.*

As in finished.

Chapter Twenty-five
Late Friday, August 30

Not really *finished*, but a little obsessive, that's for sure. I'd left Val with the latest chapter of *Love You to Death* and even though circumstances had sent the random images of my lackluster life flashing before me like a roller rink strobe light, I wondered what my wife thought about the next chapter left for her to read. I know that's sick. But that's how writers are.

As we're lowered into the grave, we yearn to call out, "What did you *really* think of the scene on page 88?"

◆

Love You to Death

PART SEVEN

IT HAD BEEN FEWER THAN TWENTY-FOUR HOURS since Janet and Danny had been picked up for questioning in the Cameron shooting. Both were settled behind bars in the impossibly tiny Pierce County Jail. With no separate provisions for female prisoners, a pair of deputies stretched a blue plastic tarp between the two cells that made up the jail. The tarps were a ubiquitous commodity among the folks of Pierce County. Often the water-resistant sheets were used to keep a cord of alder firewood dry, or a leaky shake roof from rotting everything in the attic. The backwoods of the county was dubbed Blue Tarp Country

198

for the proliferation of the plastic coverings found there.

Danny Parker huddled his heavy, hulking frame in the corner furthest away from the love of his life's cell. The blue plastic shield, of course, did not stave off words from Janet.

"Danny, how could you do this to me?" she seethed as she held her face against the cold, black grate of her cell.

She waited, but when there was no response, she called out again. This time her voice was more plaintive than angry.

"Danny, how come?"

"Didn't do nothing," he finally answered.

"Danny, how could you? We're gonna be married. You know that. You know I love you, Sugarbutt."

"Don't know much of anything," he said.

Bitterness rose in Janet's throat. "You stupid son of a bitch! You ruined everything. You didn't stick with what I told you, did you?"

Danny started to cry. It was the blubbering sniveling of a big kid. Fits and starts. His was a herky-jerky cry that reverberated through the jail.

"Grow up," Janet demanded. Her eyes were cold steel buttons.

"I need you to grow up and get us out of this mess. Think of Lindy! Lindy's in trouble. She needs her mama and her new daddy! Buck up, dipshit! Think of Lindy!"

Years after it was all over, Danny Parker searched for the words that would convey how he felt that first day in jail, as a victim of love.

"She kept telling me over and over that if I didn't stick to the story, Lindy would end up as a ward of the state. She could end up with that asshole Paul Kerr. Janet never let up, never stopped," he recalled. "It was 'do this, say that, or else.' I was mixed up. Mixed up more than I ever had been. Never been book-smart, but I know I was in a world of hurt. I was worried about that little girl. She was gonna be *my* little girl."

-

MARTIN RAINES GUIDED HIS FORD TAURUS up to the little window of a drive-thru espresso stand called Turning Javanese. He ordered a double, tall non-fat latte with one packet of Equal-and a blueberry muffin. He knew that the nonfat milk and fake sugar only offered a slight reprieve from the advancing circumference of his waistline. The muffin was more than a thousand calories. But he didn't care that morning. He was irritable and tired. Only a jolt of sugar and caffeine could boost his flagging energy level.

He gave a fifty-cent tip to the dog-collared slacker who dispensed the hot drinks and drove toward the hospital.

The nurses at Pac-O had flipped a coin to determine who would watch the patient in Room 113. The combination of medication and the birdshot in his gut had left Deke Cameron with bowels looser than a six-year-old's front teeth. Every fifteen minutes someone had to mop him up. None of the nurses wanted to do it.

"Maybe we can just leave him until the girls from the high school class come tomorrow?" one suggested with false hope.

"You wish," her co-worker replied. She handed over the clean-up gear, which consisted of a stainless steel dish, warm water, and a solution called Orange-Fresh. It was a citrus-scented product that cleansed, disinfected, and left the room smelling of "Citrus Groves in Florida."

No one who used the product ever bought an Orange Crush soda again.

Martin Raines arrived in Deke Cameron's room just as the nurse had cleaned him for the umpteenth time. The room smelled of oranges and feces. Raines could feel his blueberry muffin battling to stay in his stomach. He had been around decomposing bodies that smelled better.

"How you feeling today?" the detective asked.

The smelly, beached whale of a young man managed a fleeting smile.

"Better, I guess. Thanks. At least I'm alive."

"You up to talking?"

"Yeah. I've been laying here thinking about a lot of things... lots I wanna tell you guys. Wanna sit?" Deke indicated a chair next to his bedside.

The blueberry muffin inched upward through the detective's esophagus. He didn't need it to be any closer.

"Nah. Thanks, anyway. I'll stand. Been sitting on my butt all morning."

Deke Cameron understood. "Got a feeling I'll be lying on my ass for quite awhile."

Raines shrugged. "Maybe not. It took a lot of fortitude to drive down that hill after being shot. You might be the kind of guy who gets better fast. It's mental, you know."

Later when Raines recounted what was told to him in that room at Pacific Ocean Medical Center, he would joke that the patient "spilled his guts for a second time."

It started about a year and a half before the shooting....

-

CONNIE CARTER INVITED JANET AND DEKE for Easter dinner. It was the first time she had actually accepted the two of them as a couple. Though he never heard her say it out loud, Deke always felt that Janet's mother had considered him the lesser of the two evils. If it was a choice between her daughter's ex-husband and the mill worker, it seemed that Connie had decided in favor of the mill worker. Only by default. The luck of the draw. Better than nothing.

Connie Carter lived at 394 Seastack Avenue South. It was a forty-year-old, three-bedroom lemon yellow house trimmed in white. Outside of a pair of faded plastic gnomes under a dead rose bush, the landscaping was nothing more than a flat expanse of lawn that irregularly overlapped the edges of the sidewalk. The spring afternoon still held the bite of winter when Janet, Deke and little Lindy arrived.

Connie grabbed the baby the instant they came inside. The smell of booze wafted from her lungs.

"Baby should have a coat on! And shoes! For crying out loud, Janet, what on God's freakin' earth were you thinking?"

Janet made a face at Deke.

"Mama, it was just a five-minute drive! It's not gonna kill her!"

Connie shook her head in contempt. "I've told you fifteen times that a baby needs to be warm."

Janet said nothing more. She had learned long ago never to argue with her mother. It didn't matter that she would be left alone for days at the Seahorse Motor Inn when her mother was out partying. It didn't matter that she had crawled into a Dumpster to get Jett something to eat because the little girl wouldn't stop crying. It didn't matter that she had called more men "daddy" or "uncle" than any child had a right to endure. It didn't matter because Connie Carter had vanquished all of that from her memory. Booze had been an eraser. She could remember what she wanted to and what she chose to remember was a sanitized version of motherhood that held no basis in reality.

Arguing with Connie meant denial and anger. It was Easter. No need for that.

"Does Lindy want her Easter basket? The Easter Bunny hip-hopped to grandma's house early this morning."

The little girl smiled and giggled, showing off two perfect, tiny white teeth.

Connie went into the back bedroom and retrieved an enormous store-bought basket festooned with curled ribbon and yellow cellophane. Through the plastic, a chocolate bunny could be seen nestled next to a tin beach bucket, a small sand shovel and a plastic sandcastle mold.

Deke Cameron was quiet for most of the meal of rolled and tied turkey roast, a cylinder of jellied cranberry sauce, and mashed

203

potatoes made from the real thing. Janet and Connie took turns holding the baby and lamenting the fact that Paul Kerr's family wouldn't ease up on their claims to Lindy.

"But the Kerrs are the other grandparents," Deke said between big, mouth-stretching bites.

"They have other grandchildren. They don't need Lindy, too," Janet said bitterly.

Connie put her fork down and deeply inhaled on her cigarette before extinguishing it in a swirl of potatoes on her plate.

"Does he know what's going on with those people?" Connie asked.

"Not everything," Janet said.

"Time he did. If he's gonna be Lindy's new daddy, he'd better know in a hurry."

Connie Carter proceeded to outline a litany of the Kerrs' minor and severe transgressions. They were low class, though they thought they were better than everyone else. Old man Kerr ran a five-and-dime and his missus was the volunteer coordinator at Pac-O.

"*Volunteer supervisor*! Big fuckin' deal," Janet chimed. "They gave that to her so she could stay on her fat ass and be happy making six bucks an hour for the rest of her life."

"You got that right, honey." Connie twisted off the top of another Bud.

Worst of all, the reason for the Carter women's ire was the family's insistence at keeping tabs on Lindy. As mother and daughter saw it, the Kerrs had tried to hog Lindy. They had wanted her for Easter dinner.

The thought of it made the older woman bristle.

"I told them hell no! The baby is staying with her Nanna and her mommy."

204

"Pissed off my ex-mother-in-law real much," Janet said.

Deke leaned back from the table and loosened his bulldog belt buckle. He saw the anger. He understood it was genuine. Still, he just could not grasp the reason for the hatred; the depth of it puzzled him.

"Well, Lindy's his daughter, too," Deke said.

Mrs. Carter slammed her fist on the tabletop, jiggling the tube-shaped cranberry sauce nearly out of its dish. She shot a bitter look at Deke. Janet dropped her jaw, as her mother unleashed a verbal assault on her boyfriend.

"Don't you get it?" Connie asked, punctuating each word with a pounding of her fists. "Are you dense? Paul wants to take Lindy from Janet. He wants to take her away from me. His stupid parents want that. They are out to get us and if we don't do something we'll lose Lindy. We'll fuckin' lose her forever!"

"How do you know that?" Deke asked.

"Do I look stupid or are you looking in a mirror? They have said they want custody. Full custody of our beautiful Lindy. But they're not gonna get it. Not at all. She's not safe there! He'll try to sell her for a fishing pole and a sleeping bag!"

"He's scum. Fuckin' scum!" Janet yelled as she held her now-wailing daughter. "Your daddy's fuckin' scum!"

"We've got to find a way to stop him," Deke finally said.

Connie sucked on a toothpick. "Only one way I know."

Janet spoke up. "For good, Momma, for good."

205

"Yeah. We've got to kill him."

Deke didn't know what to say.

"Sugarbutt," Janet said, her tone jarringly sweet after the tirade, "you gotta help us. You got to."

"I'm not killing nobody."

"If he's gone, we can be a family. Get married in Vegas. Have kids of our own."

Deke blanched at the idea of murder. He wasn't that kind of a guy. He didn't want to get caught and didn't want to go to prison.

"Ain't gonna kill nobody," he finally said.

Janet got up and put her hands on Deke's shoulders.

"We have to... for Lindy," she said.

-

THE FOLLOWING MONDAY, THE MILL was going full blast when Deke Cameron pulled his buddy Jim Winston aside near the veneer manufacturing platform. The noise was too loud to allow for a private conversation. Deke worried that the machinery would shut down as his secrets were yelled over a nonexistent din. Jim was one of those men on the fringe of the survivalist movement that had brought undue attention on the Northwest. During the day, the compliant forty-year-old fellow wore dungarees and flannel, but at night, he donned army fatigues and an attitude. His hair had receded since he was a junior in high school and for the last few years he had shaved his head, leaving a gleaming pate that shined up on the sides where the leather inside his hard hat rubbed against it. The fingers on his right hand had been sliced off at the first joint during a work accident, making them appear as short as a bunch of Vienna sausages.

Deke leaned over to speak.

"My fiancé's ex gonna take the baby away from us. We've got to stop him."

"How can I help?"

"You got to help me get rid of him. Once and for all."

Jim Winston leaned close enough to kiss.

"What do you mean?" he asked quietly, nearly in whisper.

Deke calmly gave the answer.

"Got to waste him, I guess."

Inside—that's the term the incarcerated call *their digs*. Slammer. Big House. Hoosegow. The Pen. I sat in my cell, thankfully alone and therefore without the prospect of being someone's soap-dropped-in-the-shower bitch until I got bailed. The cell had the vibe of a really bad high school detention room. There was no tin cup. No porn splattered with ejaculate from the lonely men spanking away the hours. Not really much of anything. Three cinderblock walls marred with graffiti of varying skill and merit, and an old-school steel-barred gate that ran the length of the cell fronting the corridor to the jail and police offices.

I wanted to cry. Not because there wasn't any porn, of course, but because I'd done nothing to deserve this gloomily austere guest room. I'd always been on the side of law and order. My whole middling career had been about that. In my books, the good guys always triumphed over evil. To think that I would hurt someone for any reason made me want to hurl. It wasn't who I was.

Marty Raines, damn you for doing this to me!

But as I sat there, head spinning, stomach turning, wondering what had happened at 2121 Old Stump Road, I knew I couldn't argue two things. June Parker was dead. And someone killed her just as I was about to interview her for my new book. It wasn't a big leap to think that there was a connection between me and the victim. Who would have done this? And why?

As I sat there waiting for Val to get me out of there, I played that scene at the Parker place over and over. I could see no clue written in her blood. No finger pointing to anyone who would want to do her harm. I put my head on the pillow and looked at the wall, my eyes immediately locking on an equation written by an unsteady hand.

$$DP + JC = Luv$$

It hit me then, I was in Danny Parker's jail cell. JC was Janet Carter, of course. They'd stripped me of every sharp object that I'd had in my pockets when they processed me, of course. No pen. No pencil. I looked around the cell for something I could use to leave my mark, too. A broken toothbrush caught my eye. It was in the corner, by the stainless steel sink and toilet fixture. I picked it up and started scratching on the wall.

$$KR + VR = Love$$

I put my head back down on the thin pillow. I wanted to die. I wanted to stage a prison break. I wanted, really, more than anything, for Valerie to get me the F out of there.

"Ryan!" the gravelly voice of a jailor came from down the corridor.

I looked up. The man had squinty eyes and, apparently, a department-issue moustache that swept under his nose with a quarter-inch dip below the corners of his mouth.

"Yeah?"

"No choice on the entree for your meal. Swiss steak and mashed potatoes. You want Jell-O or a slice of pie for dessert?"

I wanted freedom!

"What kind of pie?"I asked.

208

"Apple. Jell-O is lime made with Sprite instead of water."

"Pie, then."

I never got the slice of county jail apple pie. An hour later, the same corrections officer came back with a key jangling and a smile on his face.

"You're out of here. Go home."

Chapter Twenty-six
Saturday, August 31

Home. Where the dirty dishes were stacked until five minutes before Valerie and her un-air-conditioned car pulled up to the driveway. *Home.* Where Hedda stretched out on my clean carpet to dig for fleas at the base of her tail. *Home.* Where Taylor and Hayley threatened each other over who was more powerful on Nickelodeon's Nick at Nite TV lineup—Samantha on *Bewitched* or Jeannie on *I Dream of Jeannie. Home,* where I was free. Sort of free. Martin Raines ate crow when the prosecution abruptly backed down on the case against me in the murder of Mrs. Parker. I was home. The anonymous tip was rescinded by whoever it was that had said I had been there earlier. A receipt for my two dollars' worth of gas at the Flying J was time/date stamped. I was exactly where I said I had been. The girl in the gas station's glass booth identified me. She had read *Murder Cruise.*

But she wasn't a fan. She thought my books victimized the victims.

"I'd rather pump gas than do what he does for a living," she reportedly told investigators. "At the end of the day, I can wash off my stink."

By then I was a cocktail of emotions: Bitter, relieved, mad, tired. I thanked God I didn't need the attorney I didn't have.

My wife and daughters put their arms around me so tightly that if I had wanted to breathe in, it would have been impossible. I didn't want to. I just wanted to stand there frozen in time with Valerie, Hayley and Taylor. Valerie had been crying and I let her face brush against my chest, leaving a swipe of mascara. We had talked on the phone from the jail and she had called an attorney for a criminal referral. Thankfully it was not needed. Not then, anyway. Valerie had alternated between tearful and stoic.

"Better take a look at this," she said, releasing me from her arms. In her hand she held a copy of a Seattle daily newspaper.

I studied her eyes for a clue about the content of the paper.

"Not good, huh?" I said.

"Not good."

She unfurled the front page. The headline was below the fold.

MURDER, HE WROTE
CRIME WRITER HELD IN SLAYING

Beneath it was a publicity photo I had sent in for the "Library Chats" series held for children at the Seattle Public Library. The editors had published it the size of a postage stamp back then. This time it was larger than a playing card. I smiled my authorly smile from the page. I was thankful that Moan-a-lot's mug shot had not been used. Even so, I was sure that someone would characterize my photo as "the picture of evil... Those eyes... they are almost otherworldly."

"Val, I'm so sorry. I'm so sorry for this mess."

"Honey, don't be sorry. You have nothing to be sorry about. This is not your fault." She drew closer and squeezed my hand. "In a day or two it will all pass. You'll see. Life will be normal again."

"I know," I lied. "All normal again."

There were seven phone calls winking at me on my telephone answering machine. Jett three times. My agent. My mother. My editor. A hangup.

"...hope you're okay..."

"...can't believe what they've done."

"...didn't know if I could see you in jail..."

211

"...I know its been hard on your family, but your sales should really pick up..."

"...Honey, now that you're out of jail, dinner's still on?"

"...This little setback won't delay your manuscript delivery?"

I returned no calls. I was still too numb to speak to anyone. I just wanted something to eat, a shower, and bed. Valerie and I had homemade lasagna. We had wine from a box with a spigot in our refrigerator. The girls picked at their food in front of the television, pulling apart layers of pasta as if participating in an archaeological dig. Both were certain that the noticeable lumps in the pasta sauce were hamburger meat, which they now called "Dead Animal Matter" or "DAM."

Four disturbing little eyes, two blue, two green, stared at us.

"Mom, is this meat?" Hayley asked.

"Soy, honey. *Soy* protein," Valerie convincingly insisted from the kitchen table. "It only *tastes* like hamburger."

A few minutes later, a shout came from the family room where they flopped in the glow of the TV.

"Dad! Wanda-Lou's on!"

"What?" I hadn't thought of Wanda-Lou Webster in a long time. Maybe months. She had ditched the true crime writer I sicced her on and wrote her own account of her sister's case for Toe Tag Books. They paid her $7,500 and sent her on a tour of six major cities. I saw her on a *Rita Adams Show* called "Triumph Through Adversity."

I thought a far better title would have been: "Making Money Off a Family Tragedy."

"She's plugging that book again?" Valerie slid over on the white sofa next to me.

Taylor's eyes widened. "No, Mom. She's on *Inside Edition* talking about Daddy!"

The Botoxed host faced the camera with some kind of unexplainable demeanor while graphics came up proclaiming a "WORLD EXCLUSIVE."

"...she lived to tell..."

I grabbed a pillow and held it against my stomach. I was going to get sick.

"Could it be true? Is the true crime author's story...written in blood?"

The words spun around before stopping on the screen to drip a red goo that was supposed to be blood. I hadn't killed anyone yet, but I wondered if I could knock off the idiot who devised the graphics and title for the piece.

I barely recognized Wanda-Lou when the camera followed her along a stretch of beach. In her hand, she held a copy of her book and a lighted cigarette. Her hair was very blonde. She had lost twenty pounds. At least. Her outfit was tasteful and flattering. Expensive. Wanda-Lou Webster had traded up since I saw her get into her car and drive away from Port Gamble.

"I lived with the Ryans for six weeks... six of the most frightening weeks in my life!"

"Six weeks?" Val whispered with great disdain. "Seemed like six years to me."

"...There was a desperation about Mr. Ryan. He seemed so driven to make a success out of my cousin's story that it scared me. All he cared about was making the story bigger than it was...."

The camera zoomed in for a close up. A tear spilled down Wanda-Lou's cheek. I never knew the woman had cheekbones. I never knew her eyes were so blue. I guess when it got right down to it, I flat-out didn't *know* the woman.

Her lip trembled as she choked back tears.

"I feel so lucky. So lucky to be alive."

"Alive? What is she trying to do to me?" I screamed at the television as my face went from white to red. Sweat condensed along my brow.

Valerie didn't answer and the girls stayed transfixed by our unwelcome houseguest's image on the screen.

The answer came when she held up a copy of *A Cousin's Loss.*

The new look of horror on my wife's face betrayed her as she attempted to dismiss Wanda-Lou and calm me.

"Kevin, she's only trying to sell copies of her book," she said.

I clinched a fist and hammered on my own thigh. "She's trying to kill me with bad publicity."

Val turned off the TV just after the show's announcer revealed I had been released from jail and promised viewers a look at the next show's "Studs of the Outback."

I had enough. I was going to bed. I was devoid of feeling. A shell.

Valerie tried to soothe my battered psyche once more after turning off her bedside reading light.

"If it is any consolation, Kevin," she said softly as our eyes adjusted to the darkness of our bedroom, "the last chapter of *Love You to Death* was the best of the bunch so far."

Even Valerie's comment of praise fell flat. She cuddled closer to me. But I resisted her. I was too upset. Nothing, *nothing*, could make me feel better. Not then, anyway. I turned over and tried to sleep. When slumber eluded me, I did what I thought I did best. I went to my computer and got to work.

♦

PART EIGHT

THE BARS HAD CLOSED WITH A SLIPSHOD clang that could be heard from Timberlake to the ocean. Taverns, too. It was two o'clock in the morning and the drunk and disorderly got into their dented Trans Ams and their pickups with sound systems that would rival a movie theater's. The lingering done by the lonely, looking for a ride home or a bed to sleep in, was over. That night, two women from the outskirts of Timberlake had made good on threats to their no-good husbands: They went home with a man who promised a good time, some more booze. The gal who ran the checkout counter at the AM/PM mini market on Ocean Boulevard sold most of her beer just after two a.m.

Deke Cameron and Janet Lee Kerr followed Jim Winston to his place on G Street. Deke was too drunk to drive so Janet took the wheel for the last three blocks after he got out to relieve himself on some lady's rose bushes.

"The last thing we need is to get pulled over when we're on our way to get rid of One-Ball Paul."

"Yeah," Deke agreed. They parked on the street and Deke staggered up the driveway. Janet steadied her boyfriend as they followed Jim inside.

"Can't hold his liquor, huh?"

"He's okay. He just had a little beyond his limit."

Deke slumped into a papa-san chair.

215

The front room of Winston's little house was impeccably ordered. A floor-to-ceiling cinder block and one-by-six bookshelf held practically every spy thriller paperback that had ever been published. Some were vintage, from the thirties or earlier. All were filed by author's name. The magazines on the wood burl coffee table had been fanned out like a card dealer's deck. The one on the top was the latest issue of *Soldier of Fortune*. A Boston fern thrived in a corner window. Jim Winston, a lifelong bachelor, was as good a housekeeper as any. The fact that his interest fell along military, or survivalist, lines spoke to that. Though the man never served in the Army, the Navy, or the Marines, he carried the legacy of a military discipline as if he had actually earned it.

Janet Lee Kerr pushed the button on her own emotions. She trembled her lip and held her beer can with such vigor it crunched slightly, but she didn't seem to notice. Or she didn't care. She just wanted to make a point.

"Jim, we've got a terrible problem. My ex-husband is trying to get custody of my daughter." She turned to Deke, who was half asleep, and patted his knee in a gesture of affection. "*Our* daughter."

Jim appeared to understand. "Deke told me. He told me everything. I'd like to help, but I don't think so."

"He hasn't told you everything."

"He has, Janet. I know what you want done."

"Lindy-that's my-*our*-daughter-is in trouble. Bigger trouble than you know."

Jim Winston furrowed his caterpillar brow and drained a beer.

"What do you mean?'

"A few days ago I found some blood."

"Son-of-a-bitch beating up his little girl?"

"Worse."

Deke raised his eyelids. He wanted to hear what Janet was saying. It was something he hadn't yet heard.

Janet put her hands in her face and started to cry.

"I found blood! I found blood in her underpants! I can't prove it, but I'm pretty sure he's been messing with Lindy."

Deke sat up like a shooting gallery duck. Fast and straight. Adrenalin pumped straight into his brain. He had never been so alert in his life.

"That piece of shit! Why didn't you tell me, Janet! That fucker has to die!" he raged.

Jim Winston was also appalled. "Call the police," he said. "It's better for them to handle it."

"The police won't do shit," Janet said. "They didn't do a thing to stop him from beating the crap out of me. Yeah, I've called the police for help. Some help!"

"Yeah," Deke said, "the police will probably want to make Paul Kerr one of his dumbshit deputies."

Janet started to pace. "We got to get rid of Paul before Lindy is abused again. It has to be tonight."

The urgency startled Jim Winston.

"Tonight? Not tonight. We've got to plan this thing, unless you all want to spend the best years of your lives in prison."

"If not tonight, tomorrow," Janet said. "We can't wait. Think of what that monster will do to Lindy on his next visit."

217

"When is that?"

"Saturday."

The three of them piled into the front seat of Jim Winston's white Cavalier and drove out to Old Stump Road to Paul and Liz Kerr's place. Jim wanted to cool everyone down and get a better feel for Paul Kerr before they developed any plan. He called out landmarks and numbers off his odometer to Janet, who logged the information down on the backside of his car registration.

"Two-tenths."

"Half mile."

"One mile."

Deke Cameron cracked the window and blew a jet of gray cigarette smoke out into the darkness of the early morning. Jim Winston's last name was the same as a smoker's favorite brand, but this Winston allowed no one to smoke in his vehicle. His ashtray was a virgin, holding only loose coins from the drive-in window he stopped at when he went out to eat on his own. As he was at home, Jim was fastidious when it came to his car: The change was organized by denomination. The maps in his glove box were folded back in the same manner as they had been when he bought them.

"Slow down," Janet said. "It's up there on the right. That's his truck out front."

Jim pulled over and cut his headlights, stiff beams of light brushed over a front yard of brambles, bicycles and a blue Chevy half-ton truck. A tire swing moved in the wind. The only illumination coming from the Kerr's mildew-ravaged mobile home was coming from a porch light. An enormous rectangular hole was carved in the hillside, barely visible

218

from the truck. A dog barked off in the distance.

"Swimming pool?" Jim asked about the hole.

Janet shook her head.

"No, a new mobile. I heard they were getting a brand fucking new mobile home." Her face tightened. "Seems like he gets everything he wants. I get nothing."

"You have me," Deke said.

"Right. I have *you*. I am losing my daughter. I have no money. I have basically nothing going for me."

"What about the money?" Jim asked.

"I'm broke, what do you mean?"

"The money. Who's going to pay for this job?"

"My mother. My mother's going to come up with it."

"I want half up front."

"No problem. Half of what?"

"Five thousand dollars."

Janet gasped. She bounced her elbow into Deke Cameron's gut.

"Five grand? We want to kill him, not give him a freakin' funeral! Jesus, five grand! I don't believe this!"

Jim Winston stared straight ahead.

"Half up front."

"We were thinking more like a thousand for the whole thing."

"Better rethink that. Anyone who'll do the job for a thousand is an idiot."

"Can you meet us halfway?" Deke asked.

"This isn't a flea-market bargaining table, guys. Five grand is what I need for the job."

The three sat in silence. Deke could feel Janet tense up, but she said nothing.

219

"Five thousand bucks, I don't know," Janet finally said.

Jim Winston remained firm. He seemed to enjoy the power, the control. "That's the price."

"It's a lot of money," Deke said.

Jim shrugged. "It's a big job, dude."

"Yeah, but how do I know that you can pull it off?"

"Because I say so."

Janet narrowed her steely eyes. "Done it before?"

"Lots of times," Jim lied. "Lots."

-

MARTIN RAINES WAS RIVETED. He couldn't even smell the stink and the orange grove used to mask it. All he could think about was the ramifications of what the young man with the bandages around his middle and arms was telling him.

"Funny thing," Deke Cameron murmured as he let out a groan while trying to shift his weight within the tight confines of his hospital bed. "Funny thing, they were talking about Paul Kerr thinking of selling Lindy on the black market so he could get a new camper for his truck. Boy, them two were hot about that. Connie ripped Paul a new asshole. But what she didn't know was it was Janet's idea. Janet had been the one who asked a guy at the Hammer 'n Nail if he knew someone who'd buy Lindy. It was Janet who done it. Not Paul."

Raines made a hasty call back to the sheriff's department for a video recorder. He told the deputy that the allegations made by Deke Cameron not only implicated himself in a murder-for-hire scheme, but fiancé Janet Kerr and future mother-in-law Connie Carter.

"Better get down here. This guy's singing like an American Idol on meth."

"Why the video gear?"

Raines didn't doubt the care at Pac-O, but lowered his voice so as not offend anyone.

"Who's to say he's gonna make it? We're not talking Jason with a hockey mask. We're talking about a young guy with a stomach full of lead that'll stay there for the rest of his life-if he lives. We need his deposition on video and we need it posthaste. We need someone from the county attorney's office, too. We're talking immunity in exchange for testimony."

Raines drove back to the office. Janet Lee Kerr and her mother Connie Carter were the perfect example of the old axiom that the fruit doesn't fall far from the tree. Poisoned fruit, though it was in this case. Both women had it in mind that they'd have whatever they wanted. No matter what. No matter the cost.

They had seen too much TV.

Yet, they were smart enough to realize that if they found the right lovesick men, they'd never have to get their hands dirty. Not really, anyway.

All they had to do was promise a wedding in Vegas.

Paul, Deke, Danny... Raines figured if someone added up their cumulative IQ scores, maybe they'd break triple digits.

Maybe not.

Chapter Twenty-seven
Sunday, September 1

TODAY'S LIST

Google: Being arrested in a homicide case skyrockets an author's Google hits. More than 14,000 articles mentioned me. I should get arrested for murder more often.

Crime case in the news with the most hits: Me. It's all about *me*.

Possible book title: *Shocking True Story*.

Amazon ranking for backlist: Huge gains! I'm in the top 100 for the first time. Call Mom.

Need from the store: Photo paper for more publicity shots.

◆

I DOUBTED I'D EVER TALK TO MARTIN Raines again. I had a good mind to rewrite what I had written in *Love You to Death* and turn him into a really fat cop with zits the size and color of plum pits. He was a little overweight and his face sometime possessed a kind of ruddiness that easily could have been mistaken for a skin condition associated with alcoholism. I'd think it over. Maybe I'd cool down later. In the meantime, I ran a search for his name in the chapters I had written to see how much time it would take to tweak his part.

When the phone rang, the detective who'd been on my mind was the last person I'd ever expected or *wanted* to hear from.

"Kevin?"

I recognized his voice immediately.

"Who is this?" I asked.

"Kevin, it's Marty." The cop paused. "I don't blame you for hating me. In all fairness, you know I was only doing my job. I knew you didn't have anything to do with June Parker's death. God, I'm sorry for putting you and Val and the kids through all that."

I thought of slamming the phone down on his Dumbo-sized ears. Yeah. I thought, I'd write a passage that indicated *Detective Raines' ears were the size of an African elephant...*

"You have no idea what you did to me."

"I saw the papers."

"See the TV last night?"

"Yeah, saw that, too. Like I said, I'm really sorry, Kevin."

Then the reason for the call.

"You still gonna write that book?" he asked.

"What's it to you?"

"Am I still going to be in it?"

"Oh, yeah, Marty, you'll be in it, all right. Don't you worry."

By the time we finished our conversation, I had softened my stance somewhat. It wasn't that I *forgave* him. I doubted I could ever do that. At least, not completely. I was stuck. I needed Martin Raines's full cooperation if I was going to finish *Love You to Death*. While I had him on the phone, I asked him a few questions to see if I could keep the lines of communication open—even though I would have preferred never to speak to him again.

"What color was the interior of Deke's Escort hatchback?"

"Not sure. Let me call you back on that one."

I switched gears. "Do you remember when it was that you first wanted to be a cop?"

Silence on the other end.

223

"Martin?"

"I guess it was when I found my mother. I wanted to do something good for people. I wanted to put some good back into the world."

I rolled my eyes and exaggerated a pause to pretend to make a note of it. "That'll be all. I guess I'll still talk to you, provided you keep Moan-a-lot and her sticky little ink pad away from me."

"Fair enough," he said.

I went to the kitchen for a snack before heading to my Mac and resuming my shattered career. Work would save me, I told myself. The house was quiet. Val left to run an errand and the girls were playing over at Cecile's on a trampoline I was certain would end our friendship with her family when one of my daughters broke her neck or leg. If only they stuck to something safe like Scrabble. Hedda was asleep under the kitchen table, wiggling her front legs in throes of what Valerie always insisted was a "puppy dream."

I planned on a toasted cheese sandwich, but I couldn't get the plastic shrink-wrapping off the baby loaf of cheddar. I fumbled in the knife drawer for one of the Ginsus—my one impulse purchase from QVC. Taylor and Hayley called them "Knife Chinese Brothers," though the brand name seemed more Japanese than Chinese to me. There were five of them in a simulated rosewood case. When I opened it, I noticed "Hop Sing," the littlest of the brothers, was missing. I took "Kung Fu," the next largest of the blades. The bottom of the drawer was littered with half pennies. The girls had been slicing coins again. I made a mental note to tell them for the umpteenth time it was a crime against our country to cut Lincoln's head in two.

When my sandwich was just short of scorching, I took it from the pan and went back to my work. Again, my message machine was flashing a red light; it was a light I now considered a warning more than the promise of anything positive.

"Kevin, Fred Ross here! How's it going, buddy? Sorry to read about the mixup with the cops down in Timberlake. How are you

224

doing now that you're back home? Hey, did I tell you I have one more book for Toe Tag? God, I'll be glad when I'm done with that slimeball outfit! Hey, I got an idea. Why don't I write a book about you, you're probably too close to the case... Let me know! Let's talk! Hey, loved the cover on Murder Cruise! *Call me."*

I pushed the delete button. If anyone wrote a book about my miserable life it would be me.

♦

Monday, September 2

THE MORNING AIR HAD BEEN SLOWLY cooling over the last days before school approached. I knew the feeling that accompanied the change in seasons very well. I had lived my whole life in the Pacific Northwest, but now, in my thirty-eighth year, I had begun to wonder if I had been cheated out of something, like summer. It was so brief, so hurry-up and enjoy, that from June to the beginning of September was a blur of gotta do's. The rocky beach, the country arts fair, Port Gamble's annual Old Mill Days festival—everything had to be done before the gray lid of winter slammed down. I even considered moving to the Midwest, the place no one moved to, but everyone was from. Sure, while it was a lot colder during the winter there, at least the skies were blue most of the time. You could look outside your window and see the sun.

Valerie and I had talked of moving in the past, though the time was never right. The girls were entrenched at Breidablik Elementary, both involved in the basketball program and both excelling in their schoolwork. To move them could be damaging. Valerie had moved four times after her parents divorced and she knew firsthand that the advantages of being the "new girl" were good only for about a week.

We had resigned ourselves to the idea that we'd live and die in the Northwest.

Now there was a new incentive to leave. Though I loved Port Gamble, I knew everyone there. Until the incident with Mrs.

225

Parker, I *loved* knowing everyone. Now it wasn't such a good feeling to see the smiles of recognition at the store or the post office. Behind the smiles I knew what they were thinking.

"Arrested him....thinks he might have killed that woman down in Timberlake. Just couldn't prove it."

Valerie told me I was paranoid, but I had better hearing than she did. I knew that though I hadn't done anything wrong, I'd have to live with Mrs. Parker's blood on me until the real killer was brought to justice.

I thought about what Raines had told me at his house about the tox screens for the cyanide and the brutality of the slaying.

"June Parker was already dead or about dead when the killer slit her throat," he had said. "*Slit,* that's almost a joke when you think what was done to her. The knife cut clean into her vertebrae. Cut the bone. Whoever did that was strong. Very strong."

Strength appeared to be a key. Who could he be? While Pierce County was undoubtedly populated with more guys in flannel shirts than Seattle in its grunge music heyday, the killer was also someone that was quite clever, quite devious. It was clear the murderer had meant for a connection to be made with the Parker murder and myself. The poison used was almost certainly Weasel-Die, which had been the source of the cyanide poisoning used by product tamperer Marnie Shaw in *Over the Counter Murder*. One aspect of the similarity worried me more than anything. I wondered when Raines and the crime lab would come up with what I already knew.

After the Shaw killings, the makers of Weasel-Die changed their formula. They switched to a potassium cyanide additive because they were able to chemically infuse it with a strong, unpleasant odor. It was a kind of rank scent that they hoped would sound a warning that the stuff was not meant for human consumption. A skull and crossbones on the box had not been enough of an admonition. If the product were put anywhere other than in a weasel burrow, folks would know it in a sniff.

226

Though not near as intense, the smell was worse than limburger on a newly married bride and groom's car radiator.

I hadn't smelled anything like that at Mrs. Parker's. I wondered if that meant the poison used had been from a box before Weasel-Die revised its chemistry. The box had to be a decade old. That would make it impossible for a storekeeper to finger the killer as had happened in Marnie Shaw's case. Too much time had passed.

I let the phone ring and the machine pick up. There was no one I wanted to talk to.

"Hi Kevin! Monica here! I've been talking with Doralee Samuels at HBO and—I hope you're sitting down when you get this—she's interested in your story."

It was Monica Maleng, so I found myself breaking down and answering. In doing so, I considered that there was no one outside of Valerie whom I'd pick up the phone for at this, the most miserable part of my life. Not my mother, not my agent.

"Monica? I just came in. I was outside raking leaves. I missed what you were saying about HBO."

"God, I'm glad you're there. Doralee wants the story for an original."

Original, as in original movie. I loved it when she talked that way. Besides, this was HBO. Not Lifetime! No Suzanne Somers, Kate Jackson, Markie Post or some other escapee from TV Land's last stop for aging actresses.

"What is it with those people down there? First they want it, and then they don't. They do again. Why can't they just make up their minds?"

"Because they have all of America to suck up to," she said.

"I guess you've been following the mess up here."

"Of course," she said. "When can you get me some pages on it?"

227

"I'm nowhere near ready. The book's not even fully researched, let alone written."

There was no answer.

"Monica? What is it?"

"I don't think we are singing the same song here," she said.

"What do you mean? You know *Love You* isn't going to be done until after Christmas."

"I don't care about *Love You*. I mean, I do, of course." She backtracked and a long silence followed. "Kevin, I'm talking about *your* story, not *Love You to Death*."

"What do you mean *my* story? *Love You to Death* is my story."

"Doralee Samuels wants to develop an original film on your involvement in the Parker murder. They are in love with the idea at the network. In-absolute-love-with-it. You know, true crime writer yadda yadda yadda."

My heart began to race and I drank a mouthful of coffee I was sure had been on my desk long enough to grow green hairs. A lump went down my throat and I did my best to stop myself from gagging.

"Yadda nothing," I finally answered. "Are you telling me that they want to do a movie about *me*? They want the rights to *my* story?"

"Actually not."

"Good," I snapped.

"Actually, not your rights. They want Valerie's and the girl's...in case, you know."

"No, I don't know."

"In *case*. In case you're convicted."

My voice rose with my blood pressure. "Convicted? I've been released. It's over! I didn't do it and they know it. I can't believe *you*, of all people, would suggest such a thing."

228

"Listen, Kevin, this is your chance. I know it isn't as you imagined, but if you hold on and play along a little, we can get some decent option money. That'll help you with your defense."

The hairs on the back of my neck were a hedgehog's spine.

"Defense? There won't be a defense. I didn't *do* anything," I snapped bitterly.

"Of course. I know. But you've got to work with me here. I don't want Doralee to know that. If you're found innocent, it will be a dealbreaker."

I had reached my limit.

"You know, Monica, I'm going to pretend we didn't have this conversation, all right? I want to remember you as a friend and not some huckster looking to capitalize on my misfortune."

"Gee, Kevin, you just described yourself."

I slammed down the phone. I did not know this person. My hands were shaking.

Immediately it rang again.

I let the machine take the message. It was Monica.

"You know, Kevin, I know you're there. Pick up, pick up! Either you work with me or I'll do this thing public domain. I hate to do that to you and Val, but I've got a cracked pool to repair. Call me. Still friends, okay?"

I didn't think so.

Adena King, the producer who had screwed me over by stealing a copy of *Murder Cruise* before publication, had a soul mate in Monica Maleng.

I was just too blind to have seen it before.

♦

But not too blind to type. In fact, I'd been the only guy in a high school classroom of girls in Typing III, and a bonafide member of the Flying Fingers group that could type 120 words per minute without looking at the keys. I tried to calm down as I shook the fading toner cartridge and waited for the printer to spit out the next pages of *Love You to Death*. I handwrote a note to Val: *I promise you, baby, everything will work out. Tomorrow is Labor Day—I'm calling it Hard Labor Day now—and I promise not to work. But for now, read on:*

Chapter Twenty-eight

◆

Love You to Death

PART NINE

DETECTIVE RAINES STOOD ON THE FRONT STEP of Jim Winston's G Street address, pulled open the screen door, and knocked. While it was clear that survivalist and mill hand Jim Winston had not killed anybody, the fact that he had been offered a sum of money by Timberlake's mother/daughter would-be murder team was sufficient to get him in deep enough to squirm. If Deke Cameron was to be believed, then Janet and Connie had only let their budget get into the way of their plans to use Jim as a hit man to kill Paul Kerr.

Timberlake was a small enough place that when Jim opened his door, the recognition of the cop was instantaneous.

"Jim Winston, I'm Martin Raines with the Pierce County Sheriff's office."

He nodded.

"Can I come in and talk?"

"About?"

"Deke Cameron's over at Pac-O and he's given us a statement," the detective said, fixing an intimidating stare.

Jim shifted his weight. Nervousness was setting in. Trouble was, quite literally,

231

knocking on his door. "He, I had nothing to do with that. Nothing to do with any of it."

Five minutes later, magazines still in place, room still spit polished, Jim Winston told the cop what he knew. He had not wanted to kill anyone.

"Hey, I was just having fun," he said.

"Plotting a murder's a good time for you?"

Jim's eyes wandered over the wall behind the detective. His face flushed. "You know what I mean. I was just playing with those two. They had a problem and I wanted to see how far they'd go. I didn't do anything wrong. I didn't mean anything."

"Playing spy? Soldier boy?"

"Something like that."

Then he told his story...

-

FORTY-EIGHT HOURS AFTER Janet, Deke, and Jim conspired to kill Paul Kerr, Mrs. Carter called them over to her home in Seastack when their shift concluded at the mill. It was two in the afternoon and she had been drinking since ten that morning. The garbage can in the kitchen overflowed with paper cups. Connie Carter never used the same cup twice, never a cup that could be washed. She told herself she wasn't drinking that much if the cups were small and disposable. A cloud of cigarette smoke hovered over the living room sofa like the grey belly of a UFO.

Connie Carter was not a happy drunk. She was never lampshade-on-the-head kind of fun. It wasn't her nature. Drinking only made her mean. Janet and Jett had felt their mother's

232

drunken wrath: first, the sting and squeal of a rubber Old Mother Hubbard spoon; later, when they were older, the buckle end of a leather belt.

"We are running out of time," Connie barked from the sofa when the trio arrived. "Do you know that Lindy is in danger of being raped again by that monster?"

Everyone knew it. They all felt the sense of impending doom. A clock was ticking. Louder and louder. If something wasn't done in time, there would be hell to pay. A little girl, a sweet and innocent little girl, was in danger.

Janet introduced Jim Winston and seated him next to her mother.

"You must think you're really something," Connie said, stubbing out another cigarette in a black plastic ashtray that resembled a hedgehog from the proliferation of butts that overflowed from it.

Jim's eyes widened. "Come again?"

"Big shot. Mister-I-want-five-thousand-dollars-for-a-rat's-ass-hit."

He sprang up. He was a marionette. "I don't need this. I don't want any trouble."

"Sit down and shut up," Connie instructed.

Jim ignored her and remained on his feet.

"I said, sit down. I have a compromise."

Deke nodded at his pal from the mill. "Better listen to her."

Jim slid back into his place on the sofa.

"I'm a little short on the down payment. I almost have it and I've been thinking that if you'd wait this out until after the job, I'd pay you ten grand when it's over."

Jim Winston refused and he backed off. His little game had gone too far and he was desperate for a way out of that smoky living

233

room and away from that bleached blonde with red chipped fingernails and murder on her mind.

"How much have you got?"

"I'll give you $420 now and the rest later; when I can get my hands on it. And, trust me, I can get it. Lindy is a beneficiary on a policy I bought for her and I'll use her money to pay you off."

Jim said he'd think it over. He wanted out of there. He made up an excuse about calling his brother who was working offshore in Australia.

"Got to call him before it gets too late their time."

Jim Winston, of course, had no brother."

-

"I LIED TO THEM TO GET THE HELL out of there. I had never seen such stupid people in my life. Speaking of stupid, God, was I dumb," Jim Winston told Martin Raines when they talked that first time in his living room.

The detective agreed. "I won't argue with you there. You know, you're going to have to come in to make a statement down at the Justice Center."

"But I didn't take any money. Not one dime. I didn't even really consider it. Connie tried to hand me $420, but I left it on the coffee table. Like I said, I just wanted to get out of there."

An enormous tortoise shell brown tabby leapt up onto the investigator's lap and Jim jumped up to shoo his pet away.

"Soldier! Get down!"

The cat hit the floor and Raines stood up to indicate it was time for the two of them to leave.

"Am I going to be arrested?"

Raines didn't think so.

"I can't promise anything, understand? But I think it's fair to say I don't think you'll be in too much trouble if you cooperate with us," he said.

Jim Winston fed Soldier and grabbed a navy pea coat before locking the door.

"Hey, I thought of something that'll back up some of what I told you."

Raines stopped in his tracks. "What?"

"Are you sure you're not gonna arrest me?"

"I told you it isn't likely, but I can't promise."

"I guess I'll go with that. I won't need a lawyer, right?"

"Not if you're not going to be arrested. Remember, cooperation is key here."

Jim Winston went to his Cavalier and retrieved a State of Washington vehicle registration.

"We're not impounding your car, either," Raines said, offering a laugh to break a little tension. He was an expert at putting people to ease. It was a skill that served him well and probably kept him younger than his colleagues who couldn't make-and certainly never take-a joke.

Jim grinned slightly. "I know. Look at the back of it."

The detective flipped over the green and white sheet.

"So?"

"Look right here." He pointed to some pencil marks along the right hand edge of the document.

"Yeah?"

"It's Janet's handwriting... it's from the night when she and Deke came over and they wanted me to kill Paul Kerr. We-*they*-were mapping out how far things were from each other... making a plan for the hit."

The detective could distinctly make out words tied to local landmarks. If the handwriting checked out, the hot water Janet Lee Kerr was sitting in was about to rise to a boil.

Two-tenths.

Half mile.

One mile.

"You know something, officer?" Jim confided during the short ride to the Justice Center. "I hate to admit it, because by doing so might make you think less of me than you probably already do, but I'm not surprised Danny Parker is mixed up in the Cameron shooting."

Raines hated when people called him *officer*, but he had grown weary of explaining the difference over and over. At least by using the term officer, it was a measure of respect.

"Why is that?" he asked.

"I saw Janet not long after I turned her and her mother down. She was at the Hammer 'n Nails. She was playing pool for beers and had a couple of empty schooners balanced on the side table. She wasn't sloppy drunk, just real mouthy."

Raines was beginning to put together a picture of the young woman he sent kicking

236

and screaming to a jail cell. It was an ugly picture.

"I hear she gets that way," he said. "What'd she say?"

"She flat out told me that I was a coward-her exact words were 'Jim Winston, you're as fuckin' big a weenie as Deke Cameron.' I asked her what she meant and she told me-and I'll never forget her words-'Boys like you and Deke pale next to a real man. You need a *big* man to do a man's job'."

"Did she say if she found a *big* man to do the job?"

Jim shook his head up and down. He had been talking so fast that spittle formed at the corners of his mouth and the force of his movement sent a bubbly spray into the air and landed white against the near black of his coat. He was dying to point the finger at someone else.

"Sure did. As bold and ballsy as could be, she said Danny Parker was going to do the deed for her. And she said she didn't have to pay him one red cent. I remember she even laughed at that. She said Danny Parker was going to do it for love."

-

THE JUSTICE CENTER HAD NEVER been more convenient, which of course, was the very reason it had been designed as it had been. Raines handed off Jim Winston like a Frisbee to another deputy, whom he briefed, to make the veneer maker-cum-misbegotten hit man's written statement. It was time to see if Danny Parker was ready to talk some more.

237

♦

Note from Val: *Two things. Your toner is about dead. I heard you shaking it like a maraca last night and I'd say you've squeezed every last bit of black out of the thing. Get a new one. You're a professional, Kevin. Act like it. Look like it. Toner is the answer here. OK, that was item no. 1. Number 2, Connie is scary! She's actually got the nerve to bitch slap a hit man and then dicker him down to a $420 down payment? She's treating him like a sales clerk at Loehman's. Poor Jett. I even feel sorry for Janet. Make that everyone who's ever met Connie Carter.*

Chapter Twenty-nine
Tuesday, September 3

THE FIRST DAY OF SCHOOL CAME just in time, as it always did. I was so thankful for its arrival and the relief it would provide. From morning to afternoon, I'd be back to a routine that would allow me to get my work done. Valerie had Taylor and Hayley line up in front of our weather-beaten rose arbor with Hedda as she photographed the event for posterity. Our girls were lovely. Low teased fishtail braid on Taylor and swept bangs on Hayley. New jeans and tank, one covered with hearts, the other peace signs. The festival style from Coachella had traveled up the coast and had finally reached Port Gamble preteens—a sure sign the look was officially over. They looked like high-schoolers, more so to me, than sixth-graders beginning their final year at Breidablik Elementary. Valerie had taken photos of their first day since preschool. Only fourth grade was a battle. By sixth, both girls knew that the First Day photo was something they'd have to accept until they graduated from college.

"At least mom doesn't make us stand beside the bus anymore," Hayley said as she squinted into the morning sun and smiled for five more shots.

"Don't even say it, or she might try," Taylor warned her sister.

After big hugs and near tears, Valerie loaded the Honda for a client presentation in the city and the girls and I took the LUV to school. Hedda was left with a new rawhide bone to occupy her day in the backyard. I was so glad for things to be returning to normal. I was so happy that the days of blue raspberry Mr. Freezes were over for another year. This summer, more than any I could think of, had been a frighteningly wild ride. It had been rough on all of us, especially Valerie. Her temper had flared at the slighted provocation. I took it for what it was: the stress over her job and mine. The worry about money. School clothes had tapped out the bank account and we were back on charge cards until my publisher sent the money for signing the contract on *Love You to Death*. Valerie's business was picking up, however. She had several new artists to rep and a strong shot at an online catalog for an outdoor gear-maker in Seattle.

"The client wants no photos, only computer-generated illustrations. We're talking about eighty to ninety images," she said that morning.

"Maybe we'll have Christmas after all," I said.

Valerie looked a little doubtful. "Christmas? I'm worried that we'll be able to pull off Thanksgiving."

"Should have the advance money by then," I said.

"Don't those people in New York understand that writers actually live on their advances?"

We both knew from experience that they hadn't a clue. They had no idea that their writers were actually trying to make a living out there.

I dropped off the girls into a living and breathing sea of brand-new clothing and fresh-scrubbed hair and skin for their first day of class. Neither was crazy about the teachers they had, but both were relieved that Renny Ann Quinn was not in either's classes. Renny Ann Quinn was a booger-eating ditz who had latched onto the Ryan girls like a barnacle on a rock. This year was the first year one of my girls didn't have to deal with her. They could not have been happier.

The girls would take the bus home after school. Taylor had a house key she kept on the zipper pull of her black canvas backpack.

I had arranged for a couple of appointments in Timberlake. At lunch time, I was going to see Martin Raines. After that, Jett Carter and I were going to meet at the kiosk in front of the Hotdog on a Stick stand at the Food Circus in the Columbia Mall.

◆

APRIL RAINES WAS ROLLING BEESWAX candles when she invited me in, the air heavy with the sweet scent of the honeycombed wax. She explained she was making candles for a Christmas wedding for one of the mothers in their church. She led me inside, past her kitchen work table, and pointed down the hallway.

"Marty's in his den. He's expecting you."

I found my way to the faux fishing lodge. It was exactly as it had been last time I was there. Not a single new wooden pole or lure had been added. The detective was sitting behind his desk watching CNN. An electric hotpot on his credenza steamed.

"Your home inside your home," I said, surveying the room. "Seems like you've settled in here for the fall."

A wary smile slightly broke across his face. "Sometimes I wish I could. Make that, most of the time, I wish I could."

His ears didn't seem as large as they had nor did he seem as fat. I was glad at that instant that I hadn't written him as some kind of human gargoyle.

"Marty, I'm glad we're still talking."

"Since the incident, you mean," he said.

"The arrest," I said. "The fucking *false* arrest."

He didn't blink. "Yeah, that."

We talked a few minutes more, sizing up each other, wondering if the author/source relationship was still within our reach. I was still bitter. He was still doing his job.

"Kevin, I'm talking out of school here, but I have no choice."

He had my interest. "Go on," I said.

"What I tell you can never, never, never leave these walls."

"Is this another *I'd love to tell you something, but it has to be off the record* speeches?"

241

"It is."

I stood up. "I thought we were beyond this. Marty, you owe me. I hate to use those words, but it's a fact. Your arrest could have cost me everything."

"Could have," he said. "Those are truly the operative words."

"It *still* can. I don't know what kind of long-term damage this has done. Monica Maleng of Green Light Pictures wants to make a goddamn movie out of this."

"No shit?"

"No way. She wants the movie only if I'm rearrested and charged with Mrs. Parker's murder."

He pretended to brighten. "Wonder what kind of percentage I could get?"

"It isn't funny. My family has been through hell... God, my own mother called me and said she'd still love me even if I killed the woman. My own mother!"

Raines told me to sit down. "What I'm about to tell you has to be off the record because there are people in the office who think you still might be guilty. I know you didn't do it. I have another idea about what's going on. It's an idea that I stand alone on."

I sat on the edge of the chair. "What? "What is it?"

Raines got up and poured hot water into his cup and tugged on a used-up tea bag. The water barely registered a light amber hue.

"How many times do you reuse those damn things?" I asked.

"Too many. I'm trying to give up caffeine. Gave up lattes two weeks ago. April tells me I was getting too fat and too jittery. Want some tea?"

"No. I just want one thing. The truth. I want to know what it is that you're going to tell me."

Raines shut the door and sat on the edge of his desk facing me.

242

"We thought the technicians made a mistake when they ran your fingerprints through Edgar's system."

"What kind of mistake?"

"They were backwards."

I was puzzled. "What do you mean, backwards?"

"The prints came back a perfect match for yours, with one exception: they were a mirror image of yours."

"A mirror image? I don't follow you."

Raines set his anemic teabag on a napkin. Liquid bloomed from the teabag, a slightly brown-edged circle formed on the white paper. It was time for a new bag.

"Want some? I can get another cup of this."

I declined his offer for the second time. "What do you mean, a *mirror* image?"

My mind raced as Raines explained how the Edgar system worked. I wanted to tell him to get on with it—I had been to the same damn seminar he had. He said Edgar mapped out the prints off the paper, fed it into its mammoth brain, and spit out a match. My prints had the exact same configuration.

"You mean that someone out there has the same prints as I do, just in reverse?"

He shook his head with great adamancy. "At first we wondered about it, but then we figured the lab guys reversed the laminate that held the prints. It was a mistake, pure and simple. We went back and found that there had been no mistake. The prints had been made on the paper in reverse in the first place.

It still didn't set in. My mind continued to speed. *What did it mean?*

"Kevin, the fact is, your prints were put on the paper found in Mrs. Parker's hand. Do you get it? Someone meant for us to, excuse the pun, *finger* you for the crime."

243

I thought my head was going to explode. The room seemed small and claustrophobic. "How? I don't see how someone could put a person's prints on another object?"

"We didn't either. I mean one guy in the lab said he read of a case where a dead man's prints were put on a gun by a killer to fake a murder/suicide. But you weren't dead."

"My career is on its last legs, but, no, I'm not dead. Not yet, anyway. Besides, in that scenario they would be right-reading, not reverse."

Raines nodded. "So we finally figured."

Reeling, I got up to leave.

"One more thing," he said, putting his cup down.

"Yeah, is this a *CSI* move?"

"Sort of. The paper found in June Parker's hand was manufactured in Japan. The company that produces it is Kubuta International Paper."

I looked blank. "Huh?"

"Yeah, it isn't even available in the U.S. It is a high-grade cotton rag with an eight percent silk content. It's a paper admired by calligraphers because ink imbeds itself onto a surface unparalleled for its durability—or some marketing-type jargon like that."

He had my interest. I asked if he knew where the paper could be purchased.

He didn't.

"Nowhere that we can find. We're still looking... and while the paper is important, it is not as important as what was on it."

I was caught off guard. *What more?*

"But you know my prints were put there," I said.

Raines drew in a deep breath and then wheezed a little. I wondered for a second if he was hesitating or if he had started smoking again.

"Not just the prints—and I'm risking my pension if this leaks—there is an adhesive residue on the paper, too. We're still checking on it. There are about a zillion formulas from 3M alone."

I was left to wonder who would want to frame me? And why? And when did they have the opportunity to do so? Why kill Mrs. Parker? I had plenty to think about and very little time.

A killer who wanted to frame me and do me irreparable harm was on the loose.

Chapter Thirty

Wednesday, September 4

I HAD SO MUCH ON MY MIND THAT at first I didn't see her. I tried to bolster my shattered emotions after the meeting with Martin Raines with some overbearing self-talk. *I am fine. I am going to get to the bottom of this. I'm a survivor!* But no matter what I told myself, I felt sick inside. I could not imagine that someone would want to set me up for some woman's murder. My hands shook on the wheel of the LUV as I turned into the Columbia Mall parking lot. I knew it wasn't because of the lack of caffeine. It went deeper than that. The part I kept trying to stop myself from thinking was that Mrs. Parker had been killed to frame me. So that meant, in some way, I was responsible for her death. It had not been a crime of passion. It had been planned. It had been cleverly planned. I held my face in my hands. I would not cry.

Jett Carter stood in front of the kiosk as if she was waiting for a bus, her clear plastic purse over her shoulder. Her gaze was steady toward the mall's west entrance. She was a small figure with short, dark hair and pale skin even as the summer came to a close. She wore a lime and pink retro dress that I assumed was the spoils of an employee discount from her job at Ho!

She smiled and waved when I came into view.

"Your shoes are great," I said desperately, observing her thick-soled black stompers.

"Doc Martens?"

"*Mock* Martens, $28.95 at—"

"Ho!?"

"Yeah, how'd ya guess?"

"Just a hunch."

We chatted about Janet and Connie. Both remained miserable and frustrated that as the months passed since their appearance on *Rita Adams* no one seemed to care about them. *Inside Edition* sent Janet a letter, saying that her story simply wasn't for them.

"We're getting away from your sort of thing...."

Jett was shocked. She felt the story deserved to be on television. She was certain it was better than half the stuff the networks put on every day.

"I guess I'm a little surprised, too," I said. "The other night they had a story about a woman who gave birth to triplets, each with a different father—two white and one black."

"I didn't see that," Jett said. "What's really eating at Janet is that she was promised a trailer visit with Deke, but the prison won't let her have one. They say she needs to be in the system for two years before she can be a trailer trustee."

"Two years? That's a long time." I changed the subject. "How's your mom?"

"I'm not talking to her—"

Just then, a familiar face moved toward us. It belonged to a hulking woman, with heavy foundation and bubble hair. The gold bus and #1 earrings jogged my memory of the failed interview at Dairy Queen. She recognized me long before it registered in my mind that she was Anna Cameron, Deke's mother.

"Too bad they let you out of jail," she spat at me.

"Excuse me?"

Jett took a few steps back. I tried to ignore the vitriolic remark. After the meeting with Raines, I needed no more trouble that day.

"Hello, Mrs. Cameron. How are you?" I asked.

"Fine, until you came into my life."

"I've hardly *come* into your life. I've stayed away, respected your wishes."

"My boy told me you stood up for him and Janet at their little prison wedding. What kind of idiot are you? Apparently you have no regard for anyone. Everything you do is colored by your own ambitions."

"That's not fair. I went because they asked me," I said. "They had been counseled. Your son knew what he was doing."

"My son's a victim." She leaned so close I could smell her hazelnut latte breath. "Do you get that? He's a victim of that woman and he can't see straight. He loves her... it's like a victim of abuse who keeps coming back for more."

"She's not an abuser!" Jett cut in.

"Who are you?" Anna Cameron grimaced at the girl she apparently believed was some mall-shopping bystander.

"I'm Janet's sister. Connie's *my* mother. If you think either one of them is capable of murder, or attempted murder—"

Anna Cameron laughed. "I didn't know there were any more at home like Janet and Connie Carter. Good Lord, Timberlake's not safe."

"Mrs. Cameron, please. Leave her alone." I lowered my voice after noticing a small group of shoppers congregating nearby to listen to the school district's top bus driver read me the riot act.

"You make me sick!" Anna Cameron said loudly as she turned around to leave. Her Kohl's bag clipped my side. I didn't react. I chose to believe that she hadn't meant to hit me. It was an accident.

"You people will do anything to make a dollar," she went on. "I'm smarter than June Parker, because I'll have nothing to do with you...and you know what? I'll live longer."

I was sure she sneered as she walked away. The small crowd shook their heads in horrified unison. I wanted to crawl behind the kiosk. I wanted to give back the money my publisher was advancing. I wanted to work at McDonalds.

You'll do anything to make a dollar.

♦

IF I THOUGHT THE DAY MY FRIEND Marty Raines had questioned me for murder was bad, the day officer Moan-a-lot inked my fingers and took my mug shot, I hadn't been able to compare it to the day Raines told me someone had attempted to frame me for murder—the day the world's greatest bus driver told me to kiss off. I drove north on the interstate until I found a gas station with a grocery. I bought two rolls of Rolaids and a bottle of diet peach tea Snapple. I had wanted Tums, but that was the way the day was going. By the time I approached Port Gamble, I was ready to throw up the chalk I was certain was the main ingredient of the antacid remedy.

Taylor ran out to the LUV beaming when I arrived home. I slapped a smile on my face and took a deep breath and told myself to relax, to set aside Timberlake.

"Daddy," she said, nearly jumping with enthusiasm. "Guess what?"

I climbed out of the truck and hugged her. "I can't. How was your first day?"

"Mine couldn't have been better... Hayley's, I don't think, was quite so good."

"What happened?" I asked.

"Renny Ann Quinn transferred into Hayley's class! Mrs. Alexander seats her kids alphabetically. Alphabetical order for the whole year!"

I knew where she was going with it, but as long as Hayley wasn't around I could prolong the joy her sister was so obviously reveling in.

"Any kids with B last names?" I asked.

Taylor let out a surprisingly wicked little laugh. "Nope...Ryan falls right after Quinn. Right *after*! Booger-eater is sitting next to Hayley!"

We went inside. On anyone's scale of reality, I knew that my day had been far worse than Hayley's. Yet when I saw her sullen little face, framed by an unraveling ponytail, I set aside my own troubles. If there were any justice on God's green earth, the murder frame-up that had sent my heart pounding and stomach turning would be sorted out soon enough. I had faith that Raines would figure it out and put it all to rest. There would be an end.

Hayley's sentence, however, was nine grueling months. Renny Ann Quinn was going nowhere until June.

♦

I CALLED MARTIN RAINES AT HIS HOUSE every night for a week. I wanted to know if any more information had come in that might provide a clue to the identity of the killer. The first conversations brought the usual response: They were "working" on it. The only good news was that the lab tech that had botched the fingerprints and nearly sent me to prison was on unpaid leave pending an internal investigation on negligence. I hadn't even considered a lawsuit, but in the event that *Love You to Death* tanked, I was relieved that there was something to fall back on.

By the last conversation, the investigation had sputtered once more. It was time to rehash what we knew.

Raines, I learned, was good at rehashing.

"We know that whoever tried to set you up is someone who knows you well. He's aware of your schedule," he said. "He's read your books. I talked to the boys at the university and they are going to profile the perp. It is possible he is a fan. He's strong, too. Think about it? Any weirdos write to you? Hang out at your book signings?"

I laughed into the phone and waved to Valerie as she came into the room carrying a bouquet of yellow roses.

"I'm beginning to think it's only weirdos who go to my signings, period," I said. "And, Martin, let's face it...if it was a fan, you won't have to go through too many names to talk to them all. I don't exactly have a huge following."

"Yeah, I guess," he said.

"And why do you keep saying it was a man? The woman was poisoned first and poisonings are almost the exclusive domain of female killers. The killer could have cut Mrs. Parker up when she was half-dead."

We talked a bit longer, and I made an excuse to hang up. I promised to call him back later.

Valerie cleared a spot on the mantel by shoving aside a clay figure that Hayley had made in first grade. It was an animal of some sort; she told us it was an elephant, but if indeed that was true, it was the first elephant without a trunk. Val fanned out the dozen long-stems while I wrapped up the conversation with Raines.

"Secret admirer?" I asked, finally hanging up the phone.

"Actually," she said, handing me a small white envelope, "they're for *you*."

"Me?" I was amazed. I had never received flowers before. I expected that the only time I ever would was when they were sent to my own funeral. Of course, I wouldn't know about them, for certain, but I was sure someone would send something. I ripped open the little flap and read the message written by some clerk at the florist.

Sorry for the misunderstanding! My best to you, Valerie, and those pretty Ryan girls.

It was signed with Monica Maleng's name.

"God, Val, they're from Monica!"

Valerie laughed out loud. A good hearty laugh, like one I hadn't heard come from her in weeks. It brought an instant smile to my face.

251

"Green Light must need your rights, after all, honey. No public domain for your story!" she said.

"I'll let her stew for a day or two, and then I'll check in."

"Good idea. Say we were out of town and found the wilted roses on our doorstep. We're sure they were absolutely lovely. Monica, it's the thought that counts, you know."

I gave Valerie a hug and we held each other for a long time. She seemed so happy. Mid-September's cooler weather brought an end to the need for an air conditioning unit in the Honda and it obviously agreed with her. As I held her close it was abundantly clear that she still deserved those highlights for her hair.

Chapter Thirty-one
Friday, September 13

AFTER DROPPING THE GIRLS OFF at school, I drove down to the library in West Bremerton on Sylvan Way (which might have been sylvan at one time, but was now a dreary stretch of former fast food franchise restaurants that had been converted into restaurants that looked like a Taco Bell but weren't). I had called ahead to make sure Kate O'Brien would be working. Kate worked in the reference section and had been a friend since the day I walked in to the research the product tampering killings for *Over the Counter Murder*. I wanted to know everything I could about Weasel-Die and cyanide and Google could only do so much. Wikipedia was even worse. In the quiet of the library, Kate, a woman with a lean figure and gorgeous dark eyes that screamed "sexy librarian," piled up one reference after another. By the end of my work there, I felt I easily could have called the company and hired out my services to write Weasel-Die's annual report. And for my knowledge of cyanide? I could have killed anyone and gotten away with it.

"What can we find out about Kubuta International Paper?" I asked when she looked up from her work.

Kate gave me her "I won't be Googled out of a job" grin. She knew that when I arrived for help, it was usually more interesting than the run-of-the-mill requests she endured on a daily basis. Even if it sounded like a run-of-the-mill request.

"Plenty. What exactly are you after?" she asked.

"Product lines mostly. Availability of products in this country, that sort of stuff."

"It will be more available. I can tell you that."

"How so?"

Kate tapped out some characters on her paid-database-rich library computer terminal and started reading.

"Kubuta bought the old Western Paper Company plant on the bay six months ago. The EPA has been fiddling around with their land use application. Because it was an existing plant, there seems no doubt they will get approval."

Noticing the blank look on my face, she stopped.

"There's been nothing much about it in the papers, so don't feel so in the dark. Kubuta's filing indicated they had no plans for the site in several years. They are just increasing their presence in the U.S."

I asked if she could find anything about their product line, especially papers with a silk content.

"That's an interesting request," she said, once more playing the keys on her terminal's keyboard. "Let's see. *Artist Today* has a fairly comprehensive review on silk impregnated papers, in its 50th anniversary issue. Kubuta is mentioned." Another ten seconds or so passed as she scanned the dark surface of her computer screen. "We have it. I'll go to the stacks in the back and find the issue."

I devoured the article in less than five minutes. Several products were featured in a photo layout and I considered it a major folly for an art director to show the papers and rave about their textures when the photo was on the surface of a 60-lb. enamel web stock. Kubuta's label, featured on the layout, was a bright orange sun against a midnight blue rectangle.

Kubuta's eight percent silk paper was called Shantung Rag. It was, in fact, used by graphic artists that preferred a traditional inking process over spewing something computer-generated from their laser printers. A reader response card offered free samples of each of the papers shown in the magazine.

On the second half of the card, the company solicited the occupation of the reader for its database. It listed the following as options: professional fine artist; graphic arts manager; paper supplier; graphic artist; designer; retailer; educator.

Chapter Thirty-two
Monday, September 16

JETT CARTER STOPPED BY after another marathon visit with her mother and sister at the Riverstone prison. It was obvious that the encounter had not gone particularly well. She was pale as chalk and the short hair on the nape of her neck stuck in patches against her skin. Even the skin on her toes through her open sandals seem to give off a ghostly glow. Our hearts went out to her. Jett had been dragged down into a mire that seemed to be swallowing her up. She was reaching out from the quicksand for Connie and Janet and they—or at least their circumstances—were pulling her under.

"Not so good at Riverstone?" I asked, sensing the answer. I led her into the house, to the kitchen, where Valerie and I had been spending a few quiet moments before dinner. Taylor and Hayley were in their respective rooms finishing up their homework.

Jett said nothing and sat at the table. Valerie poured her a cup of licorice tea, which we now purchased solely for her visits. Licorice was her favorite and no one in the family could stand the stuff. Everyone in the Ryan household hoped that the friendship with Jett Carter lasted beyond the publication of *Love You to Death*. There was no way that we'd be able to consume the mega box of Elegant Herbals we bought at Costco.

Jett looked as though she was going to cry. She told us that she didn't think she could bear coming to Riverstone much more. It hurt too much.

"I'm not worried about Janet, she's a fighter," she began. "But Mom... I keep thinking that my mother is going to die in prison. She's weak and she can't sleep and her heart is bad...."

Her voice trailed off and the tears came.

"She hasn't put up a single picture I sent her because she says she doesn't want any reminders of what she's missing. She stopped wearing makeup. She cries almost the whole time when I talk to her. And I cried all the way driving straight here. I'm surprised I didn't crash."

Something about what she said twigged a nerve in the back of my brain, but whatever it was, was lost as I watched Valerie put her hand on Jett's shoulder. The young woman tilted her head to embrace my wife's gesture.

"You know," she continued, "I understand that she did something wrong, at least *probably* did, but I don't think she would have really paid someone to kill anybody. My mom isn't that way. If she wanted someone dead, she'd have shot him herself. My mom isn't as bad as they say."

"Maybe she just got caught up in something," Val said.

"I guess so. I guess that's what I think now."

"And Janet?" I asked.

"Jan is a different story. Jan has always considered herself first. She always got her way."

I leaned a bit closer. "So now you are believing she did set up Danny and plot to kill Paul and Deke?"

Jett wiped her red eyes on her arm. "She never was a saint. She tried once in a while to do nice things for me as a kid, but she was always more concerned about herself and what she wanted."

"Most big sisters are," Val offered.

"Yeah, but I bet yours never dumped you the minute you got into trouble. I was only eleven. The second I was in that foster home, my sister never called. *Never wrote.* When she had her baby, I didn't even know about it. Lindy's my niece and I didn't even get a baby picture."

257

Taylor and Hayley lingered by the kitchen entry. I knew that they were as mesmerized by Jett's life as they could be. She was not Wanda-Lou. She was not any of the other goofballs that had passed through their lives because of my work. She was more like them than the others.

"Hayley, you ask her," Taylor said, pushing her sister into the room.

Hayley stepped forward and waited in silence for everyone to turn her way.

"Jett, my mom and dad want to know if you want to go Trick or Treating with us this year."

A smile immediately eclipsed the sadness of her face. "Sounds like fun. Do I have to dress up?"

The girls laughed and looked at each other.

"You don't have to go to the doors," Taylor interjected. "You just have to drive us around from neighborhood to neighborhood."

"I see," she said. "Sounds okay to me, but on one condition. I get every Baby Ruth you guys collect."

"Fair enough," Hayley said.

Val and I knew that Hayley hated anything with nuts in it. Taylor, however, was none too happy about the arrangement.

"How 'bout every box of Good 'n Plenty?" she suggested.

Jett looked serious. "Nope. Baby Ruths. Nothing else. You should be glad I don't want the Hershey bars and Butterfingers, too."

Taylor put her hand out. "Deal."

"Planning early," I said, "just like their mother. Valerie shops for Christmas in August."

"July," Val corrected.

Jett ate dinner with us and kidded the girls that she was going to make sure they went to Renny Ann Quinn's house first.

"Maybe she's giving out something with raisins in it."

"You're gross!" Hayley said, as milk threatened to come out her nose.

Jett laughed. We all did. We needed a little laughter around the house.

After Jett left, Valerie cornered me at my Mac. I thought she was going to tell me to come to bed. At least I hoped that she was. Instead, I got a compliment. Sort of.

"*Love You to Death* is really good," she said.

Her words were fine, of course, but there was something in the delivery that seemed flat, like an e-mail, devoid of true emotion.

"But what?"

"Since you ask, you need more about Jett. She's a better rooting interest than Raines, really. She's troubled. She has a sense of humor. She's young. What do her friends say about her? Her mom? Her sister?"

I took my hands off my keyboard and cradled my chin against my knuckles.

"She doesn't have any friends. I never talk about her to her sister or her mother, unless they bring her up, which they seldom do. I told her I wouldn't say much because she's afraid they'll think she's cashing in."

"You need more about her, Kevin. When it comes to making this book stand out in the true crime market, she's the one to do it. She's the one."

Val had good instincts, and I knew she was right. I had to learn more about all of these women. Deeper, below the surface. Connie, Jett, Janet. The mother/daughter connection was appealing to true crime readers, most of whom were women.

259

But even as I considered the Carter ladies and sifted through my *Love You to Death* notes and timelines, I couldn't help but think of another woman, another mother. June Parker and her grisly murder never faded from my thoughts. Just who killed her? *And why?* Finally, because it's all about publicity, anyway, was my stalker involved?

Chapter Thirty-three
Monday, September 23

It had been awhile since I'd felt compelled to Google anything on the internet. Googling had started to make me feel bad about myself, my life, even my potential stalker situation. I felt shame for feeling celebratory about having a stalker when I read several magazine articles (almost always titled with snips of the Police classic creep-along classic song, "Every Breath You Take"). Sure, there was some kind of ego boost in having a stalker, but some of the objects of idolatry ended up in the worst possible way.

Like dead. Famous. But still dead.

I shook the toner cartridge again—hoping Val wouldn't get all over me for not having a dark enough font that would indicate I hadn't heeded her advice about being professional—and printed out the latest chapter of *Love You to Death*.

I wrote on the faint first page: *Will buy new toner cartridge tomorrow. Promise. —K*

♦

Love You to Death

PART TEN

DANNY PARKER WAS LED DOWN the back corridor to the same interview room in which he had been questioned when first arrested. He wore bright orange coveralls and plastic sandals with dingy white socks, standard issue at Pierce County. On his back was silk-screened *Property of CCJ*. Danny's wrists were cuffed but his legs were not shackled. Jailers could not find the extenders that would allow leg clamps to fit humanely on the inmate's hefty ankles. Raines waived their use.

"Janet's been crying real hard," the prisoner said as soon as he sat down. "Isn't she gonna get to go home to see Lindy soon?"

Raines shook his head. The young fat man was as dense as he was wide.

"Don't you get it? She's going down. You're going down. You both conspired to kill Cameron."

Danny Parker's good eye was downcast. He fidgeted nervously in his seat and intermittently licked his lips. "That's what you say," he finally muttered.

"Son, I want you to listen very carefully. We want to help you. We want you to help us. We know that you are...dyslexic and, you know...disadvantaged...we know that you were tricked."

Danny's face brightened. "I was just gonna fight him. It was my idea. I wanted to."

"Was it your idea to kill Paul Kerr, too?"

A worried look edged his soft, doughy features. "Paul's dead?"

Raines shook his head emphatically. "No. No. He's not dead. But we know that you were behind a plot to kill him, too. Deke Cameron's buddy from the veneer plant, Jim Winston, told us everything."

His eyes went dull and Danny once more stared at the tabletop. Sweat surged from his temples and he reached up with his cuffed hands to brush the annoying wetness from his

262

cheeks. He asked for something to drink. Nervousness had dried his lips to nearly cracking. Raines motioned the two-way mirror for the observing officer to retrieve a soda.

When the Sprite came, the prisoner spoke.

"I guess I can tell you what you want to know. See no harm in it. It wasn't Janet. It was her mother that was behind all that stuff with Kerr. And she had a good reason for it. Janet would never do anything like that. I swear she wouldn't. She wouldn't harm a spider."

And as he told his story, Raines pondered the same question over and over: *How dumb can these guys be?*

-

CONNIE CARTER HAD NO BETTER LUCK in coming up with the money for a hit man. She was growing exceedingly desperate, even looking through her sofa cushions for spare change. She begged her boss at the bar for extra hours, but times were slow and he could barely afford to keep her on as it was. She even had a garage sale one Saturday afternoon.

Her white-blonde hair disheveled like a used Q-tip, Connie was a mess. Bitterness had consumed her. She hated the entire Kerr clan. She hated Deke for letting them down. Jim Winston was a loser. *They all were.* Nothing was going her way.

She was pacing on the floor of her living room when Janet and Danny returned from dinner at McDonalds.

"Shit. Shit. Shit," Mrs. Carter said, her booze-soaked Dixie cup bouncing off the fireplace screen and rolling off the hearth. "We have got to do something. We have got to stop Paul from abusing Lindy."

"How'd the garage sale go, Mom?" Janet asked.

"I got forty-three bucks and a sore back from sitting in a goddamn lawn chair while Timberlake's idiot-poor tried to get everything I put out for free. I priced the terracotta pots at a quarter apiece and one woman said she'd seen them at another sale for five for a dollar. Mine were too high. A nickel too high!"

Janet popped open a beer and handed it to Danny.

"I told Danny what was going on."

Connie sighed. "As if he could do something to help us!"

Janet smiled warmly at Danny. She stood and put her arms around his thickset shoulders and buried her face into his chest.

"As my future husband," she cooed, "I think he's willing to help put our new family back together."

Danny nodded like a spring-necked car toy in a rear window.

Connie poured another drink and held up her paper cup.

"Welcome to the family, Danny."

"Thanks, Mrs. Carter," he said, beaming.

"Please call me *Mom*."

"Okay, Mom."

Connie Carter put her feet up on her dusty coffee table and alternated her cigarette drags and sips from her cup. She smiled sweetly and spoke as she inhaled, holding in the smoke from her Camels as though she were smoking a joint.

264

"I'll tell you what I'll do," she said, nodding at her eldest daughter. "If you pull this off, Danny Boy, I'll pay for your wedding in Las Vegas. I'll pay for everything, including champagne and the honeymoon suite."

Janet jumped up and hugged her mother. "Oh, Mom, I knew that you would accept Danny. I just knew it."

"Mrs.-" He snipped his words and corrected himself. "*Mom*, I will be a good father to Lindy. I will take good care of Janet."

Connie nodded. "I know. Now, we've got a wedding to plan and a problem with the ex-husband to take care of, right?"

-

THE WORDS THAT CAME TO MARTIN RAINES'S mind would not be uttered by the detective. *What a dumbshit. What a sucker.* The scenario of hard-drinking Connie and her no-good daughter pulling the wool over the behemoth with an IQ of a slow-witted fourth-grader was more than appalling. It was heartrending. Raines also wondered about the fascination the Carter women had with Las Vegas. It was their glitzy dream. The end-all. Danny Parker was the third husband or potential husband to be pointed in the direction of a Las Vegas wedding. Before getting into what, if anything, Danny had done to try to kill Paul Kerr, Raines just had to ask something.

He slid a second Sprite across the table.

"Did it ever occur to you that Lindy might not be abused by Paul?"

265

Danny took a moment to collect his thoughts, then a look of satisfaction came over him. It was as if he had just come up with the cure for the common cold. He had the answer.

"Of course she was abused," he said. "I saw the bloody panties, myself. With my own two eyes, I did. Janet had them in a Ziploc bag and kept them in the freezer. She said she was going to use 'em as evidence at her custody hearing."

"But there are no records, Danny. There are no records of *any* kind of abuse of the Kerr girl."

Danny looked vacant again.

"What do you mean? I heard Janet talking to you guys on the phone. She told you everything. I even dropped her off here when she had to give you the statement about the stuff he was doing to their daughter."

Detective Raines threw his hands up in the air. He could not hide his escalating skepticism.

"Danny, no one here has any record of abuse on Lindy Kerr. No one. Janet never came here. She never called. Danny, *think*. Danny, don't you think it was odd that if a report was made that Paul Kerr would still have unsupervised visits with his daughter?"

"No," he said flatly. "Janet and Connie told me that Lindy went to see doctors at Pac-O after every visit. You all were looking for more stuff, evidence, I guess. You just didn't do your job, that's all. You just couldn't find it after the first time.

Raines let out a big sigh of exasperation. "We would never let a child remain in a dangerous environment when there was physical evidence to back it up."

266

"But the panties. Wouldn't they be evidence?" he asked.

Raines nodded reassuringly. The young man across the table was stupid and in love. In the annals of crime, there had never been a more dangerous combination. Raines urged Danny to continue with his story.

-

THE NIGHT AFTER THE CARTER WOMEN welcomed Danny into their family, the young couple drove out to Paul Kerr's house and parked the Escort hatchback off the road in the same spot Jim Winston had parked. They smoked and watched while Paul and Liz went inside after feeding their dogs.

"That bitch will never be a mom to Lindy," Janet said.

Danny let his arm slide around Janet's shoulders. "Right. Never."

"None of that," she said, disentangling herself. "None of that until after we do the job...and after we're married."

Danny was embarrassed. He had never had a girlfriend before. He had gone too far and he was sorry. He put his hand in his lap and told Janet that he was willing to wait.

"I've been kind of saving myself, too," he said softly.

Janet turned away and watched the lights go out. "We need to sit tight and wait. Then you'll need to go inside and shoot Paul in bed."

She drew a sketch of the mobile's layout. It had two bedrooms. Lindy's room was in the far back end by the bathroom, and the master was up front, off the kitchen.

"What about Liz?" he asked.

"Shoot her if you have to, but she's no threat to us. She hasn't adopted Lindy and she'd never get custody of her. If she gives you the slightest reason, I give you permission to waste her too-"

Janet stopped talking and reached over to Danny's hand. She parted her legs slightly and set his hand in her crotch.

"I want you so bad," she said. "I can hardly wait to make love with you. I'm so horny."

"Me, too," he said.

Janet snapped her legs together like a clamshell and Danny yelped. "After we're married in Vegas," she said. "We'll love each other. We'll have this special bond, knowing what we did for Lindy."

Two hours passed. Janet slept while Danny watched the numbers change on his wristwatch. She told him to wake her at two a.m. Two a.m. was the magic hour. Two a.m. and he and Janet would be bound forever, headed toward the altar and the honeymoon suite. *Maybe a heart-shaped bed.* Two a.m. and he knew what he had to do. He nudged her and her eyes opened like they were spring-loaded.

"Now?" he asked.

Janet patted his knee, slowly swung the door open and pulled back the seat. The pistol's barrel gleamed in the creamy yellow light of a half moon. The gun had been her father's. It had a mother-of-pearl handle and, as gorgeous as it was, surely deadly. She pressed her lips against the handle, her long, stringy hair enveloping it, and kissed it almost salaciously so before handing it to Danny.

"This is for Lindy. And for us," she said. "Now get 'er done."

Danny lumbered up the road as quiet as his heavy frame would allow. Every snap of a stick or movement of gravel caused his heart to skip. The dogs were asleep in their kennel on the opposite side of the mobile. If they barked a little it would be all right. Dogs barked at raccoons all the time and residents that far out of Timberlake learned to sleep through the racket such encounters produced. Danny looked over his shoulder only once to see Janet, by then sitting in the driver's seat. She blew him a kiss and started the engine.

Paul and Liz Kerr were country people and as such they never locked their doors at night. Danny knew there would be no problem getting inside and finding the right bedroom. He hoped that in the darkness he wouldn't botch the job and kill Liz by mistake. He was there to kill Paul, set Lindy free from the bastard sex abuser, and cement the bond with his betrothed. Still, as ready as he thought he was, his heart rate escalated with each step toward the door.

As he crept onto the porch, a floodlight switched on and turned everything white. It was such a blast of light it almost made a noise.

The Kerrs had installed a motion-sensitive security light.

Danny nearly jumped out of his skin, discharging the pistol and turning to run back to the car. He fell on his face and scrambled for the gun as he got up to make it back. The dogs were howling and barking as if the place was being overrun with intruders. A light in the bedroom snapped on.

269

Janet stared stony-faced at Danny as he jumped into the running vehicle and they burned rubber to get away.

"The gun? Have you got it?"

"Yeah," he said gasping for air.

"Did you shoot yourself? Are you all right? I swear I didn't know about that stupid light. It must be new."

"I'm fine... I let Lindy down. I let you down."

Janet was fuming. She held the steering wheel with all her strength. Her knuckles were white. Her face, red.

"We'll have to think of some other way," she said, pressing the pedal to the floorboard as they drove back to Timberlake.

"Can't we let the police take care of the abuse stuff?"

She shook her head. "The police don't care about people like us. We have to handle things on our own. And, you know what, we can."

♦

Note from Val: *I got you a new toner cartridge, btw. In the backseat of my car. Sometimes, as you know, a wife has to take matters in her own hands. Good work, honey.* —*V*

BOOK III

JUMPING TO
CONCLUSIONS

*Jaan Uhelszki for the Morton Report: Is there a song that's most
you? Maybe "Bad Reputation"?*
*Singer Joan Jett: Well, "Bad Reputation" would certainly be right
up there.*
*JU: Do you feel you deserve your bad reputation? Why do you think
people consider you have one?*
*JJ: Well, I think the reason I have a bad reputation is because I'm a
girl and dare to do these things that, you know, boys do.*

Chapter Thirty-four
Tuesday, September 24

IT WAS AGAINST MY BETTER JUDGMENT, though I knew many doubted I had any reserve of that mental property within any of the confines of my weary brain. My agent and editor, who seldom worked in tandem, had convinced me it would be good for my career. *Good for my career.* I had heard that before and I knew better. At various times appearing on *Nancy Grace*, signing books at the bath shop, giving an interview to an insufferable radio show in the middle of a mall—all had supposedly been for the good of my career. But here we were heading to New York for a taping of the *Rita Adams Show*.

The producer/twit named Ashlee had struck again. This time the show was about what I was calling the *Love You to Death* case and the murder that ensued after the principals were jailed.

"This will be your chance to tell your side of the story, Kevin. Your fans want to hear from you," Ash had said over the phone.

"I guess," I answered. I wanted to tell her that my fans were all related to me and had heard my side ad nauseam.

I had agreed to participate, in part, because *Murder Cruise* was actually showing a little renewed life in the chain bookstores. The chains were always primed for the television effect. *Oprah*, of course, moved thousands of hardcovers whenever she welcomed an author and endorsed him or her on the show. Sales for *Murder Cruise* were up. Better, in fact, then they had been when the book was first launched. A third printing had been ordered. For the true crime genre, where books have a shelf life shorter than a gallon of milk, that was good news. Renewed life in a book on death was nearly unheard of.

I also blamed my editor for encouraging me to do the show. He had raved about the *Love You to Death* material he had seen and I wallowed in his overblown praise.

"This is another *In Cold Blood*. Another *Fatal Vision*. It is the true crime book for the new millennium, full of folly, slackers going nowhere...driven to murder over the love of a child."

"Don't start writing the back cover copy yet," I said.

"If you go on *Rita* and play it right you'll come out a best-selling author. Remember, Rita's people have signed a deal that says they'll put a shot of your book on a single card."

"Single card?"

"All by itself. Single frame, you know, movie talk."

"Right, movie talk."

"Kevin, this may be your big chance. This may put you on top!"

"Right over the top," I said. "Or over the edge."

After he told me how much he loved what I was writing— "this is your fucking classic"—I thanked him and hung up.

My agent had been no better.

"Kevin," she told me, "this is your time. The whole disaster was meant to be, meant to take you out of the midlist and give you the best seller you have always deserved."

"Are you sure?" I asked.

"I have never been surer—excuse me, I've got another call."

I listened to a treacly version of Katy Perry's "Firework" while I waited for her to come back on the line. When one minute turned to two, then three, I hung up.

Everyone was so sure that I should go on, that I wouldn't appear to be on the program for some self-serving reason, that I felt I had no choice.

Valerie even wanted to go, though she was somewhat reserved in her enthusiasm. She had never seen Ground Zero, the Empire State Building or the Statue of Liberty. Rita's producers promised us an extra day in New York. My mother would watch Taylor and Hayley while we were away.

Just before the plane touched down at LaGuardia, I turned to Val and lied to her. "I am so glad we're here. I have a really good feeling about this."

She barely smiled. "I'm glad that at least one of us does."

"What do you mean by that?" I asked.

Valerie slid her magazine into her carry-on and fumbled for her shoes.

"I'm glad we're coming to New York," she said. "It's just that I have a bad feeling about the *Rita Adams Show.* So soon after Mrs. Parker's murder, you know."

I did. I had turned down *Inside Edition* for the same reason. But much had changed. For one, in the space of the weeks following June Parker's murder I had been arrested, released, and confided in by the police that the murder was motivated at least in part by someone who wanted to frame me. Above all, among the guests on the show was the person I thought could be responsible. I had it in my mind that I would force the issue on national television.

I would unmask the killer. Or I would look like the biggest fool to ever write a sleazy paperback.

We picked up our things from baggage claim and found an old man holding a sign that read *Ryan Limo.* It was not a limo, of course. Talk shows always promise a limousine as if the wife abuser from Mississippi or the pregnant cheerleader from Wisconsin wouldn't buckle and agree to go if a limo was not waiting curbside. The mantra of the talk show industry was "pick them up in a limo, send them home on a bus."

Valerie and I climbed into a Dodge Caravan with a back window decal for the "Cozy Spirit Cab Company." Our driver

275

didn't know English and we didn't care. It was dark and we couldn't see any sights anyway. The flight from Sea-Tac had been long; a two-hour delay in Minneapolis had left us wandering from gift shop to gift shop. We were tired. He dropped us off in midtown Manhattan at the Park Royale ("How Suite It Is To Be Serving You") and we went to our tiny quasi-suite to sleep. The show taping was in the morning and we planned to pick up day-of-the-show tickets to see Disney's latest princess-with-a-dead-mother-discovering-empowerment-and-true-love musical. Rest was in order.

◆

Monday, September 30

THERE I WAS. READY FOR RITA'S make-up people to gloss, fluff, cream, matte, blush. Whatever it took. The green room was neither green, nor much of a room. A tray of fruit and white powdered Hostess donuts were spread out on a small, black lacquered buffet table. A trail of powdered sugar pointed to the person who had consumed most of the donuts—Davy Parker, Danny's brother. I smiled at him. He turned away and I returned my gaze to the platter. I ate a donut and asked the woman powdering my forehead to make it look shorter.

"Don't follow you, babe," she said, slapping a puff on my cranium.

"I don't want to look so—you know—receding on the hairline," I said softly.

"Honey," she said, pausing to look directly in my eyes through the mirror in front of us, "You are what you are and we gotta go with what you got."

I nodded and slipped lower in the chair.

Ashlee, the producer, tapped on my shoulder. I had never met her in person. She didn't look like an Ashlee at all. She was short, round, and dark. Her black hair was held high on top of her head by a butterfly clip, cinched tightly and overflowing like an oil gusher on the top. Her eyes were sharp and unfriendly. She was one of those people who was better on the phone than in person.

"We've got to go upstairs to talk about the new show," she said.

I pulled the plastic drape off my neck and followed her down the hall past a photo gallery of the talk show elite: Tom and Katie before her divorce from him and Scientology; Taylor Swift looking surprised after winning an umpteenth award; Kirstie Alley after her reality-show blitz; two shots of Lindsay Lohan (one happy, the other happier); and a photograph of the entire cast of an ABC show starring a Sally Field as a sexy grandma.

"Rita guested on Sally's show two years ago," Ashlee said.

"Sorry, I missed it. Does she plan to act again?"

"Kevin," Ashlee deadpanned. "She *acts* every day."

At the end of the hall, in a black velvet-draped case with a halogen light shining on it as though it was one of the crown jewels was Rita Adams's Emmy for best talk show host. The winged gold creature stretched her arms outward and spun slowly on a turntable. It reminded me of a music box of a ballerina Hayley had when she was a preschooler...the tune mechanism had long since given up the ghost, though the ballerina pirouetted forever.

I followed Ash upstairs to a little room even colder-feeling than the green room.

"Strategy time," she said. "Let's run through the show. We want to see fireworks! We're taking a chance on this story and we're relying on you to give us the fireworks."

"How so?" I asked.

"You've got to confront these people! You've got to flush out Mrs. Parker's killer! Only you can do that. Coffee?"

"No coffee, but how about some Tums?" My stomach started somersaulting and I knew that I was about to feel worse.

277

"Let's run down the list of guests and you tell me how you're going to back up Rita and give us the fireworks we simply have to have. *Have to have.* Got it? First we'll have you and Anna Cameron and Davy Parker on the set. Rita will use you to frame the story of *Love You Forever*—"

"To Death," I corrected.

Ash looked confused. "Huh?"

"No. *Love You to Death* is the name of the book I'm writing."

"Whatever. You are Rita's safety net. This is very important for you. It is your job to see that Rita doesn't flounder. She has to look like she's totally in charge of the show. You have to jump in and keep things rolling. Now, what are you going to say to Davy?"

"Well, seeing that I was arrested for his mother's murder, I guess I'll tell him that I didn't do it and how very sorry I am for his loss."

Ash made a face and looked ticked. "Can't you say something with a little more sizzle than that? Come on, Kevin, you're a writer. You've got to be creative. Spontaneous, in a planned way, of course."

If I had the coffee she had offered I would have dumped it in Ash's lap. Instead, I went on with it. I had read the fine print on the show contract. If I walked out, if I wasn't cooperative, I would have to pay for my way back to Seattle. Valerie and I would have to beg Visa to raise our credit limit for that.

"It'll come to me when I'm there. I'm good at this. I've done this before. This show, I mean."

Ashlee tried a smile on for size. She meant it to be reassuring, comforting. "We know. That's why we've put this together. It's riding on you." She looked down at her clipboard. "Anna. Anna Cameron. How will you handle her?"

"Don't worry. I know how to handle her. Can we skip this session? It's making me nervous."

278

I didn't tell her that I considered Anna Cameron at the top of my short list of possible murderers of June Parker. I hadn't told anyone outside of Valerie. But when I considered hostility as a proponent of murder, I thought of Deke's mother. She was utterly consumed by bitterness and hatred. She hated the Parkers. She hated me. She had told me so in no uncertain terms. She thought my book would portray Danny Parker as a victim. And though I hadn't yet come to that conclusion, as a writer, I knew that it was a reasonable route to go. And while I couldn't fathom how she would have retrieved the Weasel-Die, or the note with my supposed name on it, she did have the opportunity to take my fingerprints.

At Dairy Queen, that first meeting, she took my Styrofoam coffee cup by mistake. Or had it been on purpose?

Ash shook her head at my faltering cooperation. "Don't you know what they are saying about you? You know, I'm not supposed to say anything. We have a talk show code of ethics here at *Rita*. But, listen, you're gonna be ambushed by these yokels."

My heart picked up its already rapid pace. Sweat rolled down the insides of my shirt sleeves in monsoon-heavy droplets.

"Who?" I asked.

"Anna and Davy...all of them...they all think you're the killer but your cop friend is covering up for you."

I was stunned. And I was sick. I stood up and sat back down like a yo-yo. I couldn't believe that anyone would do that to me.

"Martin Raines? They are going to drag Marty through the mud, too?"

Ash nodded. "If you let them. It's up to you."

I pondered my Visa balance once more and wondered if I begged, *pleaded* with the service rep in Omaha or Pakistan answering their 800 number, if he'd give my credit line a little breathing room.

A voice came from the hallway. *"Four minutes!"*

279

My editor had said this show would be good for my career. My agent, too. I wondered what in the hell they knew. They hadn't even bothered to come to sit in the audience. I hoped that I was wrong, that they were just lazy and not a part of the sham of a show.

The voice called again.

"Ash! Where's Cameron and the Parkers?"

"Marlene's prepping them. Can you take Kevin to the set? I've got a couple of incest survivors in the other room to prep."

Anna Cameron and the Parkers were being prepped. I had been prepped. Even the incest folks were being prepped. Prepping, I guessed, was something like pouring gas on a campfire and inviting all of America to come over for S'mores.

I would never be prepped again.

Chapter Thirty-five
Still Monday, September 30

RITA ADAMS WAS AS THIN as an alley cat, with unnaturally black hair, feral eyes and fingers as long as Freddy Krueger's. She had a smile as rubbery as a bicycle tire. When she sauntered up to the stage, she did so in such a low walking stride, it seemed as though she was going to squat and mark her territory. The lady owned the stage. She owned the chairs we sat on and for a moment I was certain that because we had taken her free trip to New York City, she owned *us*. For the hour at least. A silver charm bracelet dangled from a wrist so thin I was glad for the viewers' sake that the camera added ten pounds to a person's weight. Rita could use it. She smelled of cigarette smoke and a mocha.

I was in the middle. On my left was Anna Cameron, on the right was Davy Parker. I saw Val in the audience smiling at me. She didn't know. She hadn't a clue.

The music came up and Rita spun around to the camera, her bracelet jangling against the cord of her microphone.

"We've got some old friends here today. Old friends tied together by the bloody ropes of a terrible murder. Meet Anna Cameron. She was with us not too long ago. Anna is the mother of a man who married the woman who had him shot. Say hello to Davy Parker. Davy is the brother of the man who shot Anna's son....do you all follow me?

Most of a tour group from a Connecticut senior center nodded.

"Davy's also the son of June Parker. June was murdered on August 19 of this year, after she agreed to an interview with our next guest...or did she?"

The red light pointed at me and I felt sweat collect under the layer of foundation and powder the makeup woman had puffed on me. Perspiration beaded under my TV-trimmed mustache.

"Meet Kevin Ryan. Kevin has been on our show before, too. Kevin is a true crime writer and some say he killed June Parker because she wouldn't give him an interview."

I saw Valerie. Her brown eyes were popping out of her head, but she pretended to smile. She tried to send me a word of encouragement. I thought she mouthed: *You're flocked.*

The music rose again and the announcer boomed: *"True Crime Writer or True Crime Killer? Today's Rita."*

The show was a nightmare. My defenders were Janet Kerr and Connie Carter once more via satellite from Riverstone prison. Jett, who had planned to come on the show but didn't feel well and canceled at the last minute, spoke over the telephone to support me.

"Can you be certain he didn't kill Mrs. Parker?" Rita asked her.

"I am positive. Kevin is not a killer. I know he wanted to interview Mrs. Parker real bad, but he would never kill her."

The cameraman zoomed in on the talk show host.

"And your sister and mother—are you certain they are innocent, too?"

"Yes. Yes, I am."

"No one is to blame for the shooting of Deke Cameron and the plot to kill Paul Kerr? Look where they are, Miss Carter. They aren't in prison for nothing," Rita said.

The audience laughed a little. There was no doubt that the poor girl was blind to the truth. She was the type that figured there was good in everybody. One of the old women from a New

282

Jersey retirement home popped a Certs and shook her head in sympathy for the poor girl on the phone.

I looked up at the monitor at one point to see my face and I almost bolted from the stage.

Visa. Visa. Visa. It rang over and over. No money on Visa.

The producers made a split screen image of me: a front view and a side view. Underneath were the words: *Having the crime of his life?*

Amid audience gasps of sympathy, Dwight Parker was wheeled out during the final segment. I thanked God he didn't have anything to say. I thanked God—and his surgeon—that his larynx had been removed. No one wants to be derided on national television by a man in a wheelchair. He had continued the long slide to become even more of a shadow of his former self. Mr. Parker's left hand had been amputated the month before and part of his nose had been removed, the result of melanoma.

At the end of the show that bitch Rita got up and spouted something about how I had been released and a phone call to Martin Raines had verified that I was absolutely no longer a suspect, but the victim of an unfortunate incident. What good would that announcement do then? By that point in any Rita show all of America was going to the bathroom. Two old ladies in the audience were thinking of shopping at Abercrombie & Fitch for their grandkids followed by drinks in the Rainbow Room.

"It got better at the end, honey," Valerie said as we walked out to the taxi.

I was numb, Novocain from head to toe. I couldn't think of anything to say. It was almost like a nightmare that had been described it to me in such vivid detail that I could imagine it. A single thought came into focus as we rode a cab back to the hotel.

"Did they show the *Murder Cruise* cover?" I asked.

Valerie griped my hand and faked a hopeful smile. "Twice, Kevin. Two very long times."

That afternoon I numbly took Valerie to see the Empire State Building. *Big building.* After that we saw the Statue of Liberty. *Big statue.* I tried to be enthusiastic for my wife's sake. I tried very hard. We skipped Ground Zero. I was already as low as I needed to go.

As evening came, we dressed, ate an overpriced meal at the hotel, and saw that Disney musical. It was such a perfect choice, given the *Rita* debacle that morning. I had never seen a more "uplifting" production in my life. When it got down to it, the heroine's mother was dead. Her dad was an oblivious dork. Her only friends were animals. No wonder she hooked up with the first guy she'd ever kissed. She wanted out of that damn castle. Her misery made me happy.

There was hope yet for someone with a made-for-TV miserable career like mine.

♦

Tuesday, October 1

THERE WAS A GOD AND IT TOOK only twenty-four hours for Him to answer my prayers. Ashlee from the *Rita Adams Show* called to tell me that the show we taped would not be airing during sweeps. In fact, it would not be airing at all. The producer who had left *Oprah* for the top spot at Rita's show had a new direction mapped out that no longer included what that newly anointed guru of gab called the ABCs of daytime talk: Assholes, Bimbos, Cretins.

I didn't ask Ashlee where I had fit into that list. I hoped that the new senior producer had deemed someone else on the show with one of those names. It couldn't have been me.

"Kevin, if you have anything softer that might work for a show, call me. We're switching to relationship and inspirational shows. Triumph through adversity, that sort of crap."

I pretended to write down her new direct-dial phone number. I was free of Ashlee and Rita and the nightmare in Manhattan. I

284

even asked her to repeat it as I disregarded each digit she uttered. It had been for nothing. All of it. I wasn't going to get a bump from the exposure for *Murder Cruise*. As much as I wanted a bestseller, I knew it was better to be midlist than trashed in front of millions of jobless TV watchers.

I had been grilled like a Whopper, but now I was free. I printed out a chapter and looked for another Kit Kat. Things were good.

◆

NOTE TO VAL: If ever you were going to make Mexican food again after that enchilada reference back in Part Two, I'm feeling pretty sure that's off the menu for good after you read this one L. Sorry, Babe, I write like I see 'em.—K

◆

Love You to Death

PART ELEVEN

DANNY PARKER SHIFTED IN THE HARD plastic chair that could scarcely contain his bulk. He had three empty cans of Sprite, all turned on their sides, in front of him. He wanted something to eat and he had to go to the bathroom. Raines told him that their interview was over. Though the detective didn't say so, he would try his best to see that Parker's sentence was tempered with mercy.

The man deserved compassion. He had been used.

Raines went to Moan-a-lot's desk and took another piece of saltwater taffy. He just couldn't shake the stupidity of it all.

"No mother would delay contacting the police if she suspected child abuse," he said. "Danny's too dumb to see that."

285

"Too in love," Mona offered, slapping her colleague's candy-stealing hands.

Raines ignored her and continued. "We need those panties. We can't run another search warrant on Janet's place."

"We can make a report to CPS."

A sly smile broke out on Raines' face. "Let's do it. Get the panties out of the woman's freezer and get them to the lab. Let's see whose blood is on them."

Later that day, frozen Wizards of Waverly Place panties were taken from a mostly empty freezer in Janet Kerr's apartment and sent by legal courier to the state crime lab in Olympia for semen and blood analysis. DNA swabs from Paul Kerr were tagged and bagged and sent along. Paul Kerr had cooperated fully. He insisted he had never touched his daughter in any inappropriate manner. Never in a million years. He didn't need an attorney to advise him.

"I'm on the side of right," he said.

Three days later, Raines got a call from the lab.

"Big surprise on the Wizards of Waverly Place panties you sent to us," the lab tech said, almost with a sense of glee.

"Whose blood did you come up with?"

"No one's."

"Not enough to type?"

"No blood at all."

"What about semen?"

"None."

The lab tech started to laugh.

"What's so funny, buddy?" Raines tone shifted from interested to annoyed.

"Picante sauce, dude. The panties were stained with, you know, *taco* sauce. Someone

286

might be trying to pull a fast one, but who would fall for taco sauce?"

-

WORD CAME DOWN FROM THE county attorney's office an hour after the picante sauce news hit the Justice Center: Danny Parker would be offered a deal in exchange for testifying against Janet Lee Kerr and her mother, Connie Carter. He had been manipulated and misled. He was mentally impaired. Danny would still serve time in prison for shooting Deke Cameron, but the sentence would be light as a Twinkie. He would have five years to think about the next time he fell in love.

Danny was glum when Raines and a junior prosecuting attorney told him and his public defender the offer. The public defender who smelled of breath mints and hair oil assured his client that it was a good deal. All of it, of course, hinged on Parker's testimony.

"You shot Cameron, correct?" said the prosecutor, a recent law school graduate who wore the same Macy's suit every day.

"Yeah."

"Was it planned?"

Danny nodded.

"We need to hear you say the words, Danny," Raines said quietly.

Tears came from the lovelorn's deep-set eyes and he began to sob. "Yeah, I did," he answered.

"Who planned it?"

Amidst his tears and delayed by a slight hesitation that had more to do with his brainpower than anything, the answer finally came. "Janet did. Janet did. She told me that he was beating on her. She even showed me bruises. She said we'd never get him out of our lives. The only way to save Janet was to kill Deke. The only way to save Lindy was to kill Paul Kerr. She promised she'd marry me in Las Vegas. She did."

Danny Parker pulled himself together and wiped his eyes. "Mr. Raines, I'm scared. Can I have a hug?"

-

MONTHS LATER, WHEN ALL THAT HAD HAPPENED in Timberlake was a vague memory for most, a jailer found a note rolled into a tube and shoved behind the plastic molding of the county jail cell. It was written in pencil on the back of a napkin. The handwriting was pitiful, letters in search of a baseline on which to anchor themselves. It had been written by Danny Parker.

Dear Janet,
Forgive me. They made me lie about you. They told me terrible things about you. I love you. When I told them about you and your mom they made it sound like you had tried to trick me. I know now that it was a big fat lie. I hope that when I get out of Walla Walla you and Lindy will be waiting for me. Hoping that you will be there for me is all that keeps me from killing myself. Mom tells me to forget you, but I can't. She tells me that you are no good, but I know better. I'm your man. You and Lindy are my family.

Love Danny,
Your Sugarbutt

NOTE TO KEV: You're right, honey. We're now officially a taco-free zone. Thanks for that. Why on earth doesn't Danny get off his sugarbutt and get some kind of reality check? His note to Janet is about the most pathetic thing I've read so far. No one will be waiting for him when he gets out of prison. —V

Chapter Thirty-six
Wednesday, October 9

IT RAINED EVERY DAY THE WEEK after we returned from New York. I had not cleaned out the overflowing gutters which were hopelessly clogged with fir needles, badminton birdies, tennis balls and leaves. It was one of those late summer projects that was so easy to put off. I had waited too long. I put on an old sweatshirt and a pair of jeans and took a stepladder outside. The three steps that I allowed myself to climb did not give me sufficient height to see what I was fishing out of the gutters, even though I was over six feet tall. Black, stinky debris fell in sticky bunches onto the front step. The ladder teetered on the aggregate walkway and I held tight as I scooped out the mess with my bare hands. Two hours later, I showered, shaved and left for Riverstone.

If I hadn't made such a big deal about it with those snippy Community Relations toads at the prison, I would have postponed my interview with Connie Carter. I was not up to it and I was certain it would show in both my questions and my attitude. I decided to abandon going over the story—I knew she would say she was innocent—in favor of discussing her relationships with her daughters. Valerie had raised a good point during her last reading: Jett was on the outside, innocent; a victim of her mother and sister.

Muriel Constantine escorted me into the now-familiar conference room. This time the red-haired flack wore a powder blue suit that I thought was a Chanel knockoff. I allowed myself to believe that it was another quasi-benefit of her job. She probably sold another piece to the *National Enquirer.*

Seated at the interview table, Connie looked thrashed. She didn't have a speck of makeup on, and her hair was either wet or oily. Her lower lip was swollen and as I leaned over the table to shake her hand I noticed that her wrist had been taped.

"What happened to you? Are you all right?"

"I'm okay," she answered.

"What happened?"

She picked at the adhesive tape. Its gummy edges had collected dirt and sweatshirt fuzz. "Got in a fight with Janet and her lover, and it looks like I'm just a little worse for the wear."

"Looks like you were beat up," I said, shaking the picture of what she was describing from my mind.

Connie Carter asked the guard stationed at the end of our table if she could get a glass of water. The Buddha in the polyester uniform looked up from his Lee Child paperback and cocked his square head toward the water dispenser. He told her to be quick. I understood it wasn't because he thought she was going to make a run for it. It was simply that the prisoner was getting in the way of his reading. As long as she was sitting down talking to me, he didn't have to look at her. Warily, and impatiently, he watched while Connie drank two cones of water, returned to her chair and resumed her story. The guard and Jack Reacher were reunited in fourteen seconds.

"Those girls make me sick and I told them so," she said. "That was it. It made 'em mad enough to attack me in the shower. Sometimes I wonder about Janet. I wonder if I even know her. She's selfish. She's stubborn. She'll let nothing stand in her way. She'd sell her mother up the river if she thought it'd do her some good."

I turned on my recorder.

"She sounds a lot like Marnie Shaw's daughter in *The Over the Counter Murders*," I said.

Connie looked completely blank. "Not familiar with it."

291

"My book," I said with a smile, though I wondered why she hadn't read it. I considered it one of my best. A minor true crime classic, at the least.

She shrugged and pulled a piece of red licorice from her pocket and tore off little bits and ate them one at a time. "Sorry. Haven't read any of your books. I'm going to as soon as the prison's library orders them."

"That's okay," I said. "What I'm getting at—now, don't blast me for doing my job—is after talking with Paul and Liz Kerr, I get the distinct impression that the sexual abuse allegations made by your daughter were the sole catalyst for your hatred for your former son-in-law. I mean, before that you thought he was an okay dad, right?"

"Okay would be a fair assessment, I guess. Not great." Connie picked at a piece of red candy that stuck to her upper molars. I watched her fight with the licorice until she liberated her teeth from the gooey bondage.

"Are you convinced that there was sexual abuse involving Lindy?" I asked.

Connie Carter did a slow burn. "What are you hinting at, Mr. Ryan?"

"Kevin, please."

"What are you suggesting, Kevin? There is no doubt in my mind that there was abuse of my granddaughter. I saw the evidence with my own eyes."

I said nothing. I let her fill the silence. Connie's posture stiffened and her eyes flashed a bitterness that I had not detected before.

"I saw it," she said.

"Saw what?"

"The panties... that's what. I saw the baby's bloodstained panties. I never needed any backup beyond that. Would you?"

292

I didn't know what to say. She was in such denial. The panties were picante-stained! It wasn't blood from Lindy. Connie flatly ignored the lab reports and trial evidence. It left me with only one sad conclusion: Danny and Connie had been set up by Janet Lee.

Connie started to weep when I prodded her for information about Jett. She bit down on her lower lip, causing it to bleed anew. Her train of thought was scattered. I wondered where she was going when she began to ramble.

"I can't talk about Jett. I miss her. When God judges me—and God is the only one who can—he'll know that I loved her. She was gone so long and now she's back. During the times when life was better and I sobered up, I thought of my baby girl coming home again. I counted the days, I'll tell you. And now look at where I am? Just look at me. I'm in prison and she's out there. She's almost as much a victim as I am."

♦

MY OFFICE LANDLINE PHONE WAS RINGING when I returned from the women's prison.

"I hate to sound like some CNN finance-babe reporter," Martin Raines said without so much as a hello, "but to solve the Parker murder we've got to follow the paper...the *paper* trail."

Of course, I knew he was referring to the Shantung Rag found in Mrs. Parker's hand. I wanted to tell him what I learned at the library, but something told me not to say anything about it. Instead, I turned it around, to seek information—not *give* any.

"What more do you know about the paper?" I asked.

"What more is there to know? It was never sold in the U.S. The only active market is the only place that ever had it—Japan. From what we know, this so-called Shantung Rag hasn't done all that well there. It is still made, but in very rare quantities. We figure that whoever killed her had access to it from a trip to the Orient."

293

I didn't mention the reader response card from *Artist Today*. Instead, I changed the subject. I was worried.

"Any more on the signature?"

Raines didn't skip a beat. Maybe there was nothing to say about Shantung Rag.

"Yes and no," he answered. "Yes, the signature shows similarities to yours, but it more than likely was made by someone else."

"More than likely?" I wondered what he was getting at. Of course, I hadn't signed that stupid piece of paper.

"Yeah. It's an odd forgery, though. It is only *similar* to yours. If someone really wanted to screw you over and point the finger of accusation at you, the killer could have made it more of a ringer to how you normally sign...."

I felt my heart erupt through my T-shirt. My mind wandered over a number of scenarios. None were particularly pleasant. I sank so low into my chair that I had become part of the cushion, its loosely woven mesh fabric imprinted the back of my legs. I needed air.

"Kever?" Marty was the only one who called me that. I kind of liked it.

"Yeah?"

"I was asking you how the *Rita Adams Show* went? When's it going to be on the tube? I want to Tivo it."

I snapped myself back to the conversation. "I don't feel so good," I said. "I'll call you back later."

I let the handset fall softly into its cradle. The clock face on the phone showed that I had been on the line for seven minutes. Seven minutes and my whole world had changed forever. I looked down at my hands as if they belonged to someone else. They were trembling. I clasped them tightly together to stop the shaking.

It could not be true. What had crossed my mind was so ugly, so gruesome, it could not be true. The laser printer with an output now as crisp and black as a priest's collar had stopped humming and I reached for the perfect little pages of *Love You to Death.* I doubted that I'd ever finish the book.

I doubted that I could live with myself if I did.

Chapter Thirty-seven

♦

Love You to Death

PART TWELVE

CONNIE CARTER WAS NO LONGER a barmaid, those Good Time Gal years far behind her. She now cleaned up flatware and glasses behind the bar at the Rusty Anchor and mopped the floors of the restrooms marked: BUOYS and GULLS. Her hands smelled of Pine-Sol and the big white cakes of deodorizers wedged at the bottom of rust-stained urinals. Martin Raines parked in front of her little yellow house at 394 Seastack Ave. S. the morning after Danny Parker had implicated her in the murder conspiracy scheme.

He saw a woman sitting near the front window, a television on in front of her, a bank of cigarette smoke moored against the yellowed ceiling.

She answered the door right away. She had flinty eyes, roto-tilled hair, and a crinkled-bag mouth from a three-pack-a-day smoking habit. Connie Carter was exactly as Deke had described her.

Rode hard and put away wet.

"Mrs. Carter? Connie Carter? I'm Martin Raines. I'm the investigator handling the Cameron shooting case."

Connie, of course, knew that, but he was required to identify himself. Proper procedure always meant repetition and stating and restating the obvious.

"Yeah? And it's about time you got your butt in gear and came to see me. I want to know when my daughter's getting out of your goddamn jail! You have some nerve in taking so long. I want my Lindy away from that pervert of a father of hers," she said.

Such a pleasant greeting. Such a lovely woman.

"Mrs. Carter, I'd like to ask you a few questions."

"Not without a lawyer, mister. My daughter told me what you've been up to and I'm not going to put up with your bullshit. You know why?"

Raines said nothing. He wanted her to keep going on her own. She had probably been sitting in her chair all morning, maybe all night, judging by her disheveled appearance, thinking it over. She had hours to come up with the words that would sting cops, but set her daughter free.

"I fuckin' don't have to talk to you at all. You can't make me say anything. You can't. You know it and I know it. And you know what? We've got an attorney for Janet and he's gonna get your badge for how you treated us. Civil rights. We got rights."

-

OUT OF THE HOSPITAL AND BACK on his feet, Deke Cameron was waiting for Martin Raines. His recovery had been remarkable. So was his attitude. He was eating one of Moan-a-

297

lot's candies and showing his grotesque wounds to everyone who passed by her desk.

"Look-ee here," the young man said, pulling up his dirty sweatshirt to reveal a spare-tire stomach white-walled with ten yards of gauze. "Janet did this to me."

When he saw the sheriff's detective, Deke pulled down his shirt and lumbered over.

"Detective Raines! I brought some proof for you."

Raines, surprised to see Deke out of the hospital, ignored his remark at first. His face showed genuine concern. "Deke, what are you doing out of Pac-O?"

"They said I could go. I'm gonna be fine. Won't be looking good on the beach, but I guess I never really did. But I'll be all right."

"You sure?"

He reached into his pocket and held out a letter written on pale lavender stationery. "Yeah, and like I said, I brought proof about Janet's plan to kill Paul."

"What's this?" Raines asked, unfolding what appeared to be a letter written by a woman, a very young woman, judging by the handwriting. Raines recognized the penmanship instantly. It was the scrawl made by Janet Lee Kerr. A smattering of the i's had been dotted with hearts.

Deke urged him to read. "It's from Janet. You be the judge."

The letter was dated more than a year ago.

Dear Sugarbutt,
I miss you when you aren't around. Every time a sad song comes on the radio, I think of

you...I'm missing you and I can't wait for the day when we are a family. You, me and Lindy.

We gotta do what we've been talking about. Court is coming up soon and mom says that if we don't take care of our problem, we're in deep shit. Sugarbutt, you know that I'm depending on you. Lindy, too. Even mom thinks you are a real man (she doesn't think that about too many guys!)

I want him dead (bang! bang! and its over). We can make it look like a robbery or something. God, he'll probably be drunk anyhow. Better burn this little note! If you don't, could give us some trouble later.

Love you,

Janet

P.S. There's a monster truck show in Seattle on Saturday. I really, really wanna go!

Underneath the postscript, in another's handwriting were the words: *Don't disappoint me or my Janet. I want this done right!*

Raines asked the obvious, to be one hundred percent certain. This would be filed under the too-good-to-be-true category.

"Janet sent this to you?"

"Yeah, she did. But I didn't burn it. I saved it. I saved all of 'em."

"I'm glad that you did, but why?"

"Because I loved her. God, no woman ever wrote me a love note before. I guess...I guess I still love her a little bit. I just wanted you to see that I wasn't lying about nothing." His voice caught a little and it seemed for a moment that he might cry.

"You all right?"

299

Deke fought for composure. "Yeah, when I think about all that Janet and I could have had...our own trailer...our wedding in Vegas...taking Lindy to the beach to dig in the sand and shit."

"I'm sorry," Raines said, as the two walked back toward his office, out of view of the others.

"I guess even though she tried to kill me, I just now realized how much I still love her."

Those were dangerous words. Raines had heard them before. A woman whose second husband had beaten her with more black bruises than a garbage can full of spoiled bananas came immediately to mind. She had made a complaint from her hospital bed while her teenage daughter stood in loving support.

Never again, Mother, never again.

Forty-eight hours after her release, the woman called Raines to announce that she would not be pressing charges. It had been her fault. The medication at Pac-O had clouded her judgment.

"I realize how much I still love him," she said.

Six months later, on Christmas Eve, the daughter reported her mother was missing. The husband said she went shopping and never returned. The girl put up posters. She ran ads. She even called TruTV. Her mother was never heard from again.

Probably dead, Raines thought. Probably buried in a shallow grave somewhere off a logging road in Pierce County. Probably because she realized how much she still loved him.

Raines changed the subject. He didn't want Deke Cameron to labor over the love of his girlfriend. He wanted to nail Janet and her mother to the wall. Again, the question was an obvious one.

"Do you know who wrote the last line?"

Deke looked surprised. "Of course, Mr. Raines. It was Connie. Connie wrote that."

The detective knew handwriting analysis would bear it out. Welcome Wagon reject Mrs. Carter was up to her neck in a conspiracy to commit murder.

The detective scooted papers off an office chair and motioned for Deke to have a seat. He wanted a better handle on the relationship between mother and daughter.

Deke Cameron was only too glad to oblige. "Like I said, it was a love-hate, really hate-hate relationship, half the time, anyway. It was like they were there for each other and against each other at the same time. Weird. One minute it was I love you, the next I wanna kill her. Janet thought her mother fucked up her life, her sister's, too."

"What's with the sister?" Raines asked. No one knew much, if anything, about Connie's youngest daughter.

Deke shifted his weight and grimaced. The pain pills were wearing off and he needed more.

"What's to say? I never met Jett. She was in and out of foster homes and when they didn't work out, they shipped her to her aunt's east of the mountains. It was like they didn't want her around. Connie used to say that Jett reminded her of the bad old days."

-

301

THREE HOURS AFTER WAITING AROUND for a judge to sign an arrest warrant, Martin Raines returned to Seastack Avenue. Connie was still in her bathrobe when she opened the door and peered through the mesh of a torn aluminum screen. Alcohol vapors strong enough to be a fire hazard came from her heavy, smoky breath.

"Connie Carter?" the detective asked.

"You again?" she snarled. "Yeah, you know who I am. I guess you're here to apologize, but I'm not accepting it. Not on your fat butt will I accept it. I'm gonna sue."

Raines smiled.

"You're under arrest for the conspiracy to commit murder and solicitation of first-degree murder," he said.

Connie's cigarette fell from her lips.

"You have the right to remain silent..."

-

THE NEXT MORNING, APRIL RAINES brought the paper to her husband as he toweled off from his shower.

"Look at the front page," she said. "Your two favorite gals."

Raines shook his head. Two photographs, one of Connie and one of Janet stared at him. Both were mug shots, blank-eyed, messy-haired.

The headline read:

LIKE MOTHER, LIKE DAUGHTER?
DID TWO TIMBERLAKE WOMEN PLOT TO
KILL TWO MEN?

Raines gave the newspaper back to his wife.

"The public defender's going to have to run these two through a car wash to clean them up for a jury," he said, dropping his towel and stepping naked onto the bathroom scale.

Good, he thought. He was down four pounds.

Skipping those breakfast muffins had been a fine idea.

♦

I looked over Val's markup. There were no encouraging words. No telling me what to put on my list. She caught a couple of typos that Spellcheck missed. Nothing else. I inputted her changes and stared out the window. I was sure of only one thing: None of this had been worth it. None of this would have happened if I'd only written romance or Westerns.

Chapter Thirty-eight
Saturday, October 19

MY DAUGHTERS WERE GETTING A LITTLE OLD for the annual romp in the pumpkin patch, but they were pretty good sports about going—or at least getting into the Honda to head in that direction. Whining was at a tolerably low level. I was very grateful. I had more to contend with than I could handle. About ten miles outside of Port Gamble a farmer grew some of the best pumpkins north of Half Moon Bay. We had been going there for four years in search of the pumpkin with the most character. We were not a family that aspired to carve the most beautiful pumpkin. Not at all. We sought the pumpkin that had a little personality that we could play up when we carved it. Our first year we carved Angelina Jolie out of a freakish pumpkin that had sizeable lumps on its sides. We thought they'd make perfect cheekbones.

We had yet to top our Jolie-o-lantern.

Last year we found one with an elongated oval shape and we tried to make Jay Leno of *Tonight Show*, but most people thought it was a "terrific Frankenstein."

This year we'd outdo ourselves. Because, this year, I'd leave it up to the girls to do their own carvings. I wasn't going to compete. Valerie wasn't going to offer design tips. We were going to let them find their own and do their own thing.

It was the only way to get them to go to the patch this year.

"Kind of round," I said to Taylor, as she gripped a five-pounder.

"Round is what I want."

"A little smooth... a little perfect," I added.

She put her hand on her hip, a gesture she had copied from her mother and sighed. "Dad, you said it was our turn."

I gave in. "Right."

I looked over at Hayley and Valerie. Hayley's selection appeared to be equally, well, perfect.

"Ready for the hay ride?" I asked.

The girls shook their heads.

"Dad, we're almost twelve. We were beyond hay rides last year," Hayley said.

Valerie put her arm around me. "The best pumpkin patch trip ever," she said. "I hate that damn hay ride, too."

I shrugged. I wanted the outing to last longer than five minutes. If I had known they were going to pick out globe-shaped pumpkins the size of perfect basketballs, I'd have taken them to the mountain of orange piled in front of Safeway.

"Cider?" I asked, a little hopefully.

Three quick affirmative responses told me that I had found something on which all four of us could agree. The cider tradition would remain intact. As we sipped the sweet, cinnamon-scented drink, I knew that the next time my girls would likely go on a hay ride was when they had children of their own. Then, again, I thought, maybe they'd just send grandpa.

When we got home, we spread out a layer of newspaper and got out the carving tools, the knives, and big spoons. Val and I drank coffee, and once the girls removed the pumpkin's cold, slippery guts, we rinsed and seasoned the seeds for roasting. I resisted offering advice to the girls on how to make their pumpkins look more original.

In the end, they were wonderful. They looked just like... *jack-o-lanterns.*

Taylor asked me to cut in some eyebrows to overhang her triangle-eye cutouts. I rooted around the kitchen for the littlest Ginsu knife.

"Valerie, have you seen Hop Sing?" I asked. I hated to ask because I had the feeling that it was probably my fault that it wasn't in the case. I had failed at consistency when it came to putting things back where they belonged.

She looked up from the oven where she was turning the pumpkin seeds with a wooden spoon. A sweet and savory scent drifted through the kitchen. "The *Bonanza* character or the Ginsu knife?

"The knife," I said, annoyed.

"Top drawer. In the case."

I shrugged. "I looked. Couldn't find it."

She shut the oven door. "Probably in the dishwasher. I hate it when our kids play with knives."

"Yeah, me too. Those knives aren't dishwasher safe."

"That's not what I meant," she said, smiling at me.

"I know, just joking, just trying to put a little humor back into our lives."

◆

THAT NIGHT I COULDN'T SLEEP. I dragged a pillow to the white sofa and pulled an afghan that Val had casually draped over one side to conceal a few of the most notable stains. I wondered about our missing knife. It dawned on me that I hadn't seen Hop Sing in weeks. *Nobody had.* I thought of the pennies my daughters had sliced in two. I thought of the infomercial on QVC that had induced me to dial the 800 number to order the set of knives.

The host, a Papa Smurf-coiffed guy in an expensive sweater, spoke over a video clip showing a little Asian girl as she sliced and diced everything from pennies to a sorry-looking chicken carcass.

306

"Easy as can be! The knife that can cut through coins and loins...we make no bones about how good these knives are! No bones? In fact, this knife cuts through bones like butter."

The little girl whacked a rib bone in two and smiled.

"Dear God," I said to myself. My heart almost stopped beating.

Mrs. Parker had been slashed with such force that the lab geeks assumed it had been a man who had done so because the knife used had cut into her bone. They assumed only a man could have wielded such fury. But as I sat up on the couch, clutching the afghan, I knew it might not have been a man. It easily could have been a woman accompanied by Hop Sing.

Tears welled up in my eyes and I buried my face into the crochet webbing of the afghan. I didn't want to think the thoughts that were spinning in my head. I fought it. I wanted to think of anything—*anyone*—else. If the murder weapon was our missing Ginsu knife and I hadn't been the killer, the only other person in our household who could have done it was—Valerie.

My wife's words came back to haunt me.

Tell me what to do, Kevin. Tell me how I can help you make this book a success. I'll do anything.

And...

Sometimes a wife has to take matters into her own hands.

I tried to sleep. I tried to *forget*. I wanted to put it out of my mind. I could do none of that. I was awake with worry until the pink light of dawn filled the gaps in the blinds.

The next morning Valerie, her hair piled up in a faded yellow towel that had been a wedding gift thirteen years before, came into the kitchen while I was putting the rosewood case holding the four knives into a plastic bag. She pushed the button on the coffee maker she had filled with coffee and water the night before. The water burped, the machine sputtered, and steam puffed from its top.

307

"Where are you taking those?" she asked, getting the milk out for her coffee.

"They're getting a little dull. I think the pumpkin carving was a little hard on them. I'm taking them in for sharpening."

"Oh, I thought they came with a guarantee they'd never need sharpening."

I played dumb and folded the bag over and used a strip of masking tape to seal it.

"Really?" I said. "Guess I didn't know that. Besides, after the *Rita* experience, nothing on TV should be taken for gospel."

I hoped that I was wrong about everything.

♦

Monday, October 21

THERE WAS FIFTEEN MINUTES BEFORE the bus dropped the girls off at the corner, and though it had been my practice to wait in the LUV for them when they were younger, I felt secure enough to let my sixth-graders walk the block home. Valerie and I had argued about that decision a bit. She reminded me of recent news stories of young girls from New Mexico and Oregon who were snatched a few steps from their front doors.

"We cannot be with them every second of the day, Val. Sometimes we've got to stand back a little. They have to grow up."

After I had said that, I agonized through every second after 3:45 when the bus screeched down the hill and stopped. I often timed the pickup of the daily newspaper for 3:45 p.m., though the *Kitsap Sun* was a morning edition. I was certain the girls saw through my ulterior motive, but I didn't care. Nothing was going to happen to my children on my watch.

I had fifteen minutes.

308

Among Valerie's graphic design magazines, I recovered a copy of the 50th anniversary edition of *Artist Today*. It was stacked neatly in the bookcase, as neat as a librarian would, I thought. I flipped to the article on silk-content papers. Kubuta's bright orange sun logo with the blue background stabbed at my eyes. I found the article. There was no mistaking it. I turned to the back of the magazine, hoping to find a reader service card still bound to its spine.

God, let me be wrong about this.

But the card was missing. The slim edge, the remnant of the perforated card, taunted me. It was gone. Valerie had indeed ordered the samples from the magazine. It could not be true. I ran the scenario over and over. Yes, she had access to the Weasel-Die; yes she ordered Shantung Rag, yes she wanted me to be successful...all of that checked out. But murder? Valerie, the woman I loved above all, could not have done the unthinkable. I stopped thinking and let my sense of self-preservation, or rather the preservation of my family, take over. I felt like some kind of animal as I lunged toward the woodstove and stuffed a bunch of newspapers into the firebox.

Matches! I needed matches! Where in the hell are the matches?

I ran to the kitchen and pulled open drawer after drawer. Summer had ended. We had no fires. Our goddamn barbecue was gas and its ignition was a flip switch. No one smoked in the house. God, I had wished I smoked. I turned on a burner and watched it slowly grow from black to red.

The girls will be home...five more minutes!

I took a wooden shish kebab skewer and pressed it against the hot coil.

Dear God, why, Valerie, why?

Of course I knew the answer. It had been for me. *For us.* For Taylor and Hayley and even Hedda. I put the thought from my mind and took the burning bamboo stick to the open black jaws of the woodstove and lit the mass of crumpled papers. Fire burst from the door and I tore off pages of *Artist Today* and threw them into the flames.

Two minutes and the girls would be home. I was never good at math, but I knew I only had one hundred and twenty seconds.

Better burn all the issues. Better to leave nothing for anyone to find. Not now. Not ever.

If I was destroying evidence, I didn't care. I didn't care if I went to prison. It would serve me right. It was my fault that this happened. It was my fault for everything. I would say nothing to Valerie. I could never let her know that I knew.

I loved Val too much for that.

Chapter Thirty-nine

Monday, October 28

TAYLOR AND HAYLEY'S JACK-O-LANTERNS GLOWED their firefly eyes and Hedda barked as if she were a mad canine when I got up from the dinner table to answer a persistent knock on the door. I was met by the shock of my life. Standing on the front step was the last person I expected to see. It was Wanda-Lou Webster, looking like a seven-figure book advance. Her hair was blonder than it had been when she was on *Inside Edition* trashing me. She was thinner, too. Her eyes weren't so sapphire blue after all. I could see where her contacts had shifted slightly, revealing a so-so blue hue. Around her neck she wore a *Cousin's Loss* pendant. Pewter, I thought. She looked good. *Damn, she looked successful.*

She noticed my eyes on her jewelry.

"Like it? My publisher gave it to me. It's one-of-a-kind. White gold and platinum. I don't even want to tell you what its worth."

Platinum. White gold. I cringed. My publisher only sent me a Christmas card, and that invariably arrived in mid-January. What was it with her book, anyway?

"You're not staying here," I said harshly, though I tempered my words with a smile. In case she was the Next Big Thing, I'd want to send her a copy of my next book for a blurb for the cover. I detested her, but I might need her.

"Kevin, I'm so sorry for the piece on *Inside Edition.* Don't hate me. It's those damn producers. You know they cut here and cut there until they get the words they want out of your mouth."

I kept my foot planted firmly against the inside of the door.

"Gee, Wanda-Lou, I recall you saying something about there being a 'desperation about Mr. Ryan.' Kind of hard to put those words in someone's mouth—unless you say them, of course," I said.

"Val home?" she asked, craning her neck to see past me. "Love to see her and the girls, too."

"We're eating dinner now."

"Great, I haven't eaten." She pushed on the door hard enough to make me wince, and I let her inside. "Besides, you kind of owe me, anyway."

"How's that?" I asked, irritated that I hadn't slammed the door in her face when I had the chance. New dental veneers or not.

"Your *Love You to Death* story. I sent the girl to you."

I didn't know what she was talking about.

"Come again?"

"The daughter and sister of those two Timberlake women at Riverstone. I met her at a book signing at the Tacoma Barnes & Noble. I met a lot of the lost and weird at the signing—sold almost one hundred books, though. Ninety-four, to be exact. I did the signing after I did that noon news spot," she said as I followed her through the living room. "Still haven't got our couch recovered, huh?"

"My couch. Not *ours*." I was about to ask her more about her encounter with Jett, but Wanda-Lou plowed right into the kitchen and put her arms around my startled wife. I could see Valerie recoil like a frightened snake.

"Val! Oh, Val! I hope we're still friends. Sorry for the nasty, nasty way *Inside Edition* turned out. Not my fault. I plead not guilty!"

"I'm sure," Valerie said, gently pushing away the new and improved Wanda-Lou.

312

Wanda-Lou spun around to face Taylor and Hayley, looking them up and down. "Girls, you've grown! Lots of little changes happening, I see."

My daughters blushed and barely acknowledged our mealtime intruder. I could see the look in their eyes that I knew meant: *Please Dad, don't let Wanda-Lou live with us again. We'll be good.*

"Wanda-Lou was telling me all about her friend, Jett Carter," I said.

"Her friend?" Val looked as surprised as I had been.

Wanda-Lou slid a chair over and plucked a tomato wedge from Taylor's salad.

"She's not a friend. She just wanted to meet you. Didn't she tell you?"

I knew she hadn't. "Probably," I said. "Guess it just slipped my mind."

"She's read all of your books, her mother was in prison, her sister, too." Wanda-Lou stopped to regard Taylor's icy stare which meant: *Keep off my plate!* "She wanted to have you sign the books and hoped you'd be interested in hearing her story."

"I was," I admitted reluctantly.

"So it was all right that I gave her your address?"

I shrugged. I remembered how Wanda-Lou had tricked me when she asked for our address and ended up using it as a road map for free lodging.

"It's okay," I mumbled.

"Cute girl. She'd been wanting to meet you for some time."

"We like her. Just don't give out the address again, Wanda-Lou."

Valerie fixed another plate and set it in front of Wanda-Lou.

"This reminds me of old times," she gushed. "Here I am with the Ryans sitting at the table of my old place."

Over the next half hour, Wanda-Lou blabbed about her success. She was doing seminars for survivors of incest and those who lost cousins ("losing a cousin is like losing a limb off the family tree of your life"). Her second book was due out in five months. She dropped the word *hardcover* like an anvil on my foot. Her appearance on *Inside Edition* boosted *A Cousin's Loss* to the top fifty on the *USA Today* list.

"Did any of your titles get a bounce?" she asked. "Any publicity is good publicity, you know."

I knew the theory. I knew it all too well. I had been besieged by bad publicity since the day Mrs. Parker was poisoned and stabbed.

"Big bounce," I lied. "*Murder Cruise* sold out at the chains."

"Oh, Kevin, that's fabulous! You just might make it in hardcover yet. I'm so proud of you. I've always hoped that you'd enjoy the same kind of success I have. I owe all of mine to you."

Her words stung. *She was proud of me?* I wanted to stab her with my fork, but I knew that she'd just use it as another example of my violent temper that caused her to be in fear for her safety during the ten years she would say she lived with us as a prisoner in our basement.

"Thanks, Wanda-Lou, for the vote of confidence. It really means a lot to all of us. Speaking of which, I almost forgot tonight is curriculum night at the school. We have to get out of here. Sorry."

Wanda-Lou picked a piece of lettuce out of her appliance-white, bonded teeth.

"Gee. I guess I better go...to a motel or somewhere. My seminar's in Traverston tomorrow...."

"Try the Blue Water Inn in Kingston," Val said, turning off lights and ushering us all out the front door. "Rooms are clean. Rates reasonable."

Wanda-Lou fished in her purse as I locked the door. "I brought your key back," she said. She placed a single house key into the palm of my hand.

I regarded her with skepticism. "Didn't know you had one."

"Val had it made for me. She was so sweet to me."

As we drove off for ice cream and not for the fictitious curriculum night, we all hoped that was the last we'd seen of Wanda-Lou Webster. Deep down I knew fate would continue to be cruel in that regard. Wanda-Lou Webster was probably going to make millions. She was the one on the *USA Today* list! Not me. I could have killed her.

"Val, you'll be glad to know Wanda-Lou returned her house key."

Valerie looked puzzled.

"The one you had made for her."

"I did no such thing. I couldn't stand the woman and you know it. I wouldn't give her a key to our out house if we had one."

◆

ICE CREAM EATEN AND CAVITIES INCUBATING, the girls were in bed and Val and I were getting ready for the end of yet another day that had somehow evolved into something beyond our control. Wanda-Lou had that peculiar effect on all of us. I drew my wife a hot bath until the water ran cold. I shook in some Calgon and nearly gagged at the cloying lilac scent that drifted through the hot moist air.

"God, how much did you put in?" Val said as she stared at water so purple it almost looked indigo.

"Too much, huh?"

"A lighter touch on the lilac, Kevin, and Calgon will still take me away."

315

She slipped into the water and she was right where I wanted her—trapped. I sat on the floor.

"I've been thinking about what Wanda-Lou said about Jett."

"Me, too. Don't tell me you think she's one of those crime groupies?"

I didn't think that at all. I had grown fond of Jett. We all had. She had that horrible mother and rotten sister, and as far as I knew, she had no one but us.

"No. But, you know, as much as I know about her family, seems like I should know more about her."

"Like what?" Val eyed a legal thriller she had been reading and I knew I was losing her interest.

I slid the paperback out of reach. "After we talk, you can read."

Val slumped lower into the purple water. "I know she's just twenty-one, but it seems like there should be more going on in her life. More I could learn about."

"Maybe there is. Maybe she has a boyfriend? Maybe she's been divorced?"

I shook my head. I didn't think so.

"I feel bad that she didn't tell me she got our address from Wanda-Lou Webster."

"You're the investigative crime reporter. Do a little digging on her. See what you come up with."

I picked up a washcloth and dipped it into the water.

"Want me to wash your back?"

Val shook her head. "No. I want you to give me my book."

◆

I CALLED MY FRIEND AT THE DEPARTMENT OF Motor Vehicles in Olympia. Brandon and I had gone to college together and whenever I needed a name checked through the system, he did so over the phone. There was nothing illegal about it; it only expedited a process available to anyone with five dollars and a name. We chatted about old times while he waited for access into the state's database. A couple of minutes later he had a hit.

Jett L. Carter, 1771 Beverly Street, Apt. 2-E, Timberlake, Washington.

I already knew that, of course.

"Brand, you got a previous for her?"

"Just a second...Yeah. Here it is: 21 Maplewood, Winters, Washington."

"Anything else you can tell me?"

"Yeah, the driver's license was issued in June of this year."

The date was odd. "She told me her birthday was in January."

"It is in January. January 4. The weird thing is this is the state's *first* issuance to her as a driver. The previous issuance was only a state ID card."

I verified the address once more.

"It makes sense, I guess," I said. "She'd been in and out of foster homes since she was eleven."

Brandon put me on hold. I listened to a commercial for the state's tourism board extolling the "Wonders of Washington" until he came back on the line.

"Hey, Kevin, foster care ends at the age of eighteen. The address in Winters isn't a foster home."

317

Chapter Forty
Thursday, October 31

WINTERS, WASHINGTON, WAS EAST of the Cascade Range, the rugged spine of mountains that cuts the Evergreen State in two like a giant, inverted saw blade. On the west side of the mountains was rain and a bulging population of millions. On the east side was irrigated land and a vast community primarily consisting of wheat and apple growers. Winters was a tiny town known for beer gardens in the summer and alpine skiing in the winter. Winters had tried to make a go of it as Bavarian-themed town ala Solvang in California, but the idea never caught fire. A bank, a restaurant and a garage were the only buildings to convert to gingerbread and tole. Even so, on busy weekends beer-gutted men in lederhosen mingled with tourists and oompa bands.

Val took the day off and agreed to go along—if we "didn't have to rush and could enjoy the drive." She brought her digital Nikon along and a camera bag full of no-longer-useful lens filters, relics from days when special effects were taken with the camera and not through the magic of Photoshop. The seasons moved more quickly in the Cascade foothills than they did in the Puget Sound lowlands. Vine maples had already burnished their green with bronze and red. Alders had turned yellow and dropped most of their leaves. More people packed cameras than guns when they went hunting this time of year.

We told the girls we were going on a photo safari for one of Val's clients and that we'd be home later that evening. Cecile would come over to keep them company after school. She was not, by any stretch of the imagination, *babysitting*. Cecile was our girls' friend. She could never be their sitter.

We always paid Cecile in private.

♦

WE ARRIVED IN WINTERS JUST AFTER NOON and pulled into a spot in front of Der Edelweiss, which outside of its name was no more Bavarian than a Taco Bell. It had rained all morning of the drive and we had seen nothing but windshield wipers sloughing off the spray. Every pothole was filled with nougat-colored water. Val and I scurried in, dodging raindrops and puddles, and seated ourselves in a booth along the creek side of the restaurant. I ordered a grilled cheese sandwich and Val asked for a German Caesar. A woman of about fifty wearing a sunny yellow pinafore and clogs took our order.

"What makes it a German Caesar?" I asked.

"There's a wurst tucked inside."

"I didn't realize that," Val piped up. "I'll have the German Caesar without the sausage, okay?"

"We aim to please," she said without a trace of sincerity before disappearing into the kitchen.

After the food arrived, I asked the waitress if she could tell us how to get to 21 Maplewood.

"Maplewood? You want Maplewood Road?" She impatiently shifted her weight from one clog to another and put away her order pad. We wanted directions. Not a strudel.

"I think so," I said, ignoring her attitude. "The address didn't specify road or avenue or anything. Just 21 Maplewood."

"Are you going to visit someone?"

"Not really."

The waitress tilted her head sadly. It was very slight, the kind of movement a person makes in empathy. I could see that her blue eyes, full of compassion, had rested in bags deep and weathered like single robin's eggs in twin nests. I imagined it was a practiced emotion for the woman.

319

"We get a lot of you folks in here, it's all right. Our hearts go out to you."

I wondered if she was referring to their food as I looked down at my congealing sandwich.

"Turn right out of the parking lot go three miles out of town and turn left on Maplewood," she explained. "You won't miss it."

Another rain-drenched couple came inside and the waitress left us to eat.

"Now I'm intrigued," Val said.

"Now, I'm still hungry," I said. The sandwich was cold and I pulled it apart with my hands, eating it in tolerable bits. The German Caesar, sans wurst, looked much better. It was hard for anyone to mess up Romaine and croutons. Val scooted it in the middle of the table and invited me to have at it.

We drove the three miles out of town, leaving Winters and its oompa band, behind. A small green highway marker pointed the left turn to MAPLEWOOD HOME.

"Maplewood Home?" Valerie read the sign.

"As in Maplewood Looney Bin," I said.

We drove up a small hill past rows of half-dead cottonwoods. If there was a maple anywhere within the expanse of the property, it was a seedling. Four small buildings erupted from a lawn-covered plateau. A flock of crows picked at the remnants of someone's picnic lunch, their stark, inky blackness peppering the green of the lawn. We parked and followed the signs to the office.

A young man with a badge that indicated his name was *David R.* looked up from a spotless, white Formica counter.

"Can I help you?" he asked.

"I hope so. We're trying to verify some information about a former resident of Maplewood."

"I can't tell you anything about residents. Sorry."

"Can't you confirm if a person lived here?"

"Nope."

"Can't you tell us anything?" I asked, frustration building in my voice as it grew a little too loud for the office.

David R. shrugged. "Maplewood is a private home for the troubled and less fortunate. We are funded by private donations and have had a long tradition of providing excellent long- and short-term care to many children of Washington State."

His delivery was flat and disinterested, like a kind of rehearsed speech given because he was required to do so.

I took a deep breath. *Relax. Be smart.* "Can you tell us if a person was an employee here?"

The look on David R's face made it clear he was no dummy. He knew we were attempting to get around the rules. A slight smile formed on his lips.

"Only yes or no," he said.

"Great, now we're getting somewhere. The name is Jett L. Carter."

Oddly, the clerk didn't have to look up her name. He seemed to know instantly. He picked at his niblet teeth.

"Never an employee," he said.

"How long have you been here?" I asked.

"What's it to you?"

"Just want to find out a little information, that's all."

Valerie smiled at the clerk.

"Miss Carter has applied to be our nanny and we're just running a check on her," she said. "Can't be too careful."

The man remained stony. If my wife's warm smile couldn't melt his reserve, then I doubted anything could. "I can't say anything about her. State law, you know."

Val tried once more. "Let's put it this way, would you hire her to take care of your children? Do you have children, sir?"

321

"Any other applicants?" he finally asked, giving an answer the only way he could. The guy was by-the-book.

"None we're considering," she said.

The clerk stared at his computer terminal. "You're not hearing it from me. But I'd run an ad or something. Would be wise."

♦

A WOMAN IN A WHITE SMOCK with almost blue hair ran out to the car just as we started to pull away. We had seen her in the office, lurking among the file cabinets behind David R., so Val instinctively reached for her purse, in case she had left it on the counter. It was next to her feet on the car floor.

"Folks, I hope I'm not intruding," the elderly woman said. Light rain fell on her starched, white uniform.

"Can we help you?" I asked.

"I think I could help you." Her face was lined with years and worry. Her hands were gnarled and grey like the driftwood limbs Taylor and Hayley liked to gather and decorate with wiggly eyes.

"I'm probably out of line talking to you folks about your potential nanny, but no one has ever asked about Jett Carter."

"Do you know her?" Val asked.

"Can I sit in your car? I'll tell you where to drive."

Lynette Watson was a semi-retired nurse's aide who had worked at Maplewood since it opened in the mid-1960s. The brick and stucco buildings had been a Catholic girls school in the years before the state purchased it as a foundling home. Mrs. Watson was hired on to work with the babies, many of whom were Hispanic, orphaned when an apple processing plant blew up in an explosion caused by fermenting applesauce in 1968.

"I worked on the floor with those little kids for ten years before some idiot in Olympia decided to turn the facility into a home for troubled kids—*throwaway kids,* they called 'em. I hated the very idea of it... special needs didn't sound much better, it set them apart. These kids, at least most of them, could have done a lot better if they weren't set apart from the rest of the world."

She directed us behind a building that had once been the school's steam plant.

"Park here," she instructed.

I pulled the Honda into a space and turned off the ignition.

"Sad to think of anyone as a *throwaway* anything," Valerie said as she turned in her seat to face the old lady.

Nurse Watson nodded. "I always thought so. I always saw good and value in every kid that came in through those double doors. From the beginning with all those babies, to the end to those mixed up kids from the other side of the mountains. Even after they sent us the fire starters and the stomach carvers."

Nurse Watson explained that in the early 1990s, Maplewood dropped another notch lower. For a two-year period, the doors were swung open to offer supervised shelter to children with severe emotional issues. Some of the kids had been abused in the worst ways a human being could conjure; some had been neglected by the cruelly indifferent. All had been through the hellish system called family court and had been sentenced to serve time—a prison sentence—really, at Maplewood.

I didn't know it had been a reformatory and I said so to the blue cotton candy-haired nurse's aide.

"It was only a *corrections institution*—that's what we were supposed to call it—for eighteen months. Jett came to us during that time. She came and stayed. She was lonely. God knew she had some issues. Her mother and sister came a few times. And her father... the poor mixed-up girl never came to terms with what happened to him."

Mrs. Watson told us that after the state's trial run of using Maplewood as a kid's jail ran its course, most of the kids were shipped off to the boys' and girls' institutions on the west side of the mountains. The move made sense, in many ways. Most of the kids came from the cities and towns along the coast.

"A few petitioned to the state for their kids to stay here at Maplewood. Mrs. Carter was one of those who wanted her daughter to stay right where she was. Jett took it hard, but she told me she understood. I always thought it was because Connie didn't want to see her daughter that often."

"A mountain range between the two of them suited her just fine, right?"

"Exactly. I had great hope for the girl. When she turned twenty-one and was eligible for release, I was optimistic. For me, the greatest hope came from the fact that her mother and sister were in prison at that time. Hooray! I hate to say it and I'm glad that they didn't kill anyone. I don't wish anyone ill will. But Jett needed to start over. Completely over. You understand? A fresh start. She needed to get out of here. She had a boyfriend at the institution and involvement with him wasn't doing her any good. He was released six months before she was and I was glad. She was a nice kid. As far as a nanny for your kids, you couldn't ask for a better one. There's a gentle heart in that girl."

Valerie and I could have asked a million questions, but we were too shocked to think of any. The reason there had been so little about Jett in the book I was writing was because no one knew her. No one had seen her since she was eleven. I wondered if Raines knew about her incarceration at Maplewood. What had the girl done to deserve a decade of court-ordered supervision?

I tried to call Raines from my cell phone but we were out of range. It was almost 4 p.m. I knew our girls would be home from school and getting ready for Halloween. God, I almost forgot it was Halloween! I imagined the girls running around the house in the last minute Trick or Treating frenzy. Taylor was going as an *American Idol* contestant, all messed hair and attitude, and Hayley was dressing in a bright green leotard and sweatshirt, a dill pickle—free range, I presumed.

It was Hayley who answered after I went back inside and dialed from the Maplewood office phone.

"Hi, Dad!"

"Hayley, don't tell anyone where we are. I mean *anyone* where we are. Okay?"

I didn't want to alarm Jett. She had kept the secret of her incarceration at Maplewood for a reason, embarrassment probably. I would leave it out of the book.

"Is Jett there?" I asked as casually as I could.

"Yeah, right here. You want to talk to her?"

"No. Just let her know we'll be home soon. Been out taking pictures of the fall foliage."

"I'm not a tattletale, but Taylor is hogging all of Mom's makeup."

"You girls share, all right?"

I didn't tell them to stay out of Val's stuff. I didn't want to fight a losing battle over the phone. I promised we'd be home in time to go Trick or Treating that evening. I was certain that after Hayley hung up she trotted down the hall to tell her sister that I said it was her turn with the makeup. I could hear it all the way from Maplewood

"Dad says you're in trouble. Big trouble."

THE DAY-LONG RAIN HAD SENT FIFTEEN cubic yards of mud and rock over the westbound lanes of the highway across the mountains. It was not a major slide and the traffic inched past it. It did cost us time. At five-thirty, the cell phone once more within range, I called Martin Raines at home. I knew that unless he was at the gym, he'd be there. He was. April put him on the line. I told him what Valerie and I had learned at Maplewood.

"No shit?" he said. "I had no idea."

I asked if he'd look into Jett's file—if one existed—to see what he could scare up.

"I don't feel good about relying on a source so heavily when they aren't one hundred percent truthful. She's the book's hero, for crying out loud."

"I thought I was the hero," he shot back.

I had dug myself in a bad spot. "You are. You are the cop hero. There's always got to be a family hero, too. Like the big brother in *Deadly Score*."

Raines bought it. "Yeah, I know what you mean. Hey, I'm going in to get my racquetball gear. I'm off tomorrow. I'll look into it."

I thanked him and told him that if he turned up anything to sit tight. Val and I would detour a bit to get to Timberlake.

Valerie and I stopped at a McDonalds drive-thru where the mountain highway met the interstate. It was six p.m. We'd be home around nine. Thankfully, we had missed the bulk of commuter traffic. I had Chicken McNuggets and put the sauce between my legs, so that I could continue to drive and eat at the same time. Valerie dipped the chicken into the hot mustard.

"Hey, I could learn to like this," I joked as her hand brushed against me.

"Bet you could. Should have ordered the twelve-piece."

We laughed. And I drove on to the Edmonds ferry, and on to Port Gamble, wondering how I could have ever doubted her. How I could have ever thought she could have killed anyone. I was a lucky man.

Chapter Forty-one
Late Thursday, October 31

OUR HOUSE WAS DARK AND STILL. A single light glowed from the porch as I went to the front door. The happy faces of my daughters' oh-so-perfectly-bland jack-o-lanterns had burned out. Val went around the house to the backyard to get Hedda, who was barking intermittently. I went to the front door where I found a Tupperware bowl filled with a dozen full-sized Hershey bars. *Please take one only! Happy Halloween!* read a card taped to the front of the brimming plastic container. I knew instantly it was Taylor who had made out the card. All of the o's had been fashioned with smiley faces. Taylor had been going through that phase for the past few weeks.

"They should be home by ten. I doubt Jett knows as many of the good neighborhoods as I do. Besides, tomorrow is a school day," I said when I met Val inside.

A flashing red light indicated two messages on the machine. The first was from Gina, our neighbor.

"Girls, pick up! Pick up. Cecile's still in makeup and is running a few minutes late. I'm going to give her a hot dog and we'll be right down. See you soon!"

In the background I could hear Cecile's chirp, *"My mom wants all of the candy corn we get!"*

The second was from Martin Raines.

"Kever, call me when you get in. I can't find your cell phone number."

I dialed his home phone and April told me that he was out with their kids Trick or Treating.

"Marty swears it'll be his last year," she said, though it was clear she doubted it. "I'll have him call you when he gets back."

"You want me to drive around and look for them?" Val asked when I got off the phone.

I shook my head and lied. "I'm sure they're having a good time, getting the basis for tomorrow's dental expenses. They'll be home soon. Let's sit tight. Jett is all right. Her problems are in the past. She's a friend."

Gina and Cecile showed up about a half hour later. Cecile was dressed as a witch. She tinted her skin with lime Jell-O and she smelled of it.

"Where are Taylor and Hayley?" Gina asked.

"And Jett?" Cecile added.

"I thought they were with you, Gina." I said.

Valerie pricked up her ears. She knew something was wrong and I knew that worried look on my wife's face all too well. I was usually the source of it.

Gina made a face. "We were running a little late so I guess they left without us. I thought they'd be back by now."

I could feel my heart freefall.

"But Cecile *always* goes with the girls," Val said. "They wouldn't have it any other way. They were looking forward to going with her—and Jett."

Gina went to the kitchen to fix herself a cup of licorice tea in the microwave. "Yeah, that's what we thought, too. But when we got down here they were already gone."

Neither Gina nor her daughter seemed alarmed. Cecile turned her pillowcase upside down and dumped its contents. A rainbow of candies spread over the floor.

"I got more than last year!"

Where are our girls? Be calm. Be calm. They are out with a friend.

Val and I said nothing more about our worries, nothing about what we had learned at Maplewood. Gina drank her tea and Val and I took turns answering the door and dispensing the candy from the Tupperware bowl. Each time the bell rang, we hoped our girls would be outside, tricking us by pressing the doorbell instead of coming right in. Every kid in America did that as they came home to the parent that had been stuck at the house passing out treats.

And just before ten, as Cecile and Gina were packing up to leave, the phone rang. It was Martin Raines. I waved goodbye to our neighbors and motioned Val to the phone.

"I got something," he said. "I don't know how interesting it'll be to you, but it's all I could find. I found it in an incident report under Jett's father's name."

"Did you know Buzz Carter supposedly jumped off the River Bridge?"

"Yeah. She told me about it. So did Connie."

"Did you know she was there?"

"Connie?"

"No, Jett."

My eyes met Valerie's. It was the instant of recognition that something terrible, far worse than I had imagined was happening.

"Go on," was all I said.

"The man was drunk. God, his blood alcohol was through the roof. A guy—let's see—some mill-head reported that he saw a little girl lead him to the middle of the bridge...and push."

I was flabbergasted. "What? I'm not sure I heard you right."

"You heard me. The witness said he thought he saw the little girl push her father off the bridge. She ran off to a waiting car. The witness had been drinking and wasn't sure what he saw. The guy disappeared before investigators could get to him a second time. There were a few other notations that backed up the wife's

329

theory that her husband had been a no-good drunk and her daughter was asleep at the Seahorse Motor Inn where they kept a room. So it was dropped."

Valerie was practically on top of me, straining to hear what Raines was saying.

"The girl went nuts and her mom turned her over to the state and they sent her to Maplewood. Committed her...until she turned twenty-one."

"How could that be?"

"Ten years ago it wasn't so hard. Lots of folks with a bone to pick got rid of their kids. Connie got a court order to protect her and Janet from Jett. She said she was afraid for their lives. She had wounds to prove her case. That's what got her from foster care, then to Maplewood, at least I'm guessing. I'm filling in the gaps, because there are an awful lot of them."

"Martin, she's out Trick or Treating with my kids," I said.

There was a long silence on the phone.

"As long as she doesn't know you know anything, there's probably nothing to be concerned about. Up until you knew this, you didn't view her as a threat, did you?"

I had not. I hated the fact that because of her past, I now considered her less than what I knew to be true. I liked her. We all liked her. People change. I tried to convince myself Jett Carter was not a danger to Taylor and Hayley.

I could feel my composure slipping. I fought hard. I didn't want my voice to break. I had to be strong, but I was afraid.

"Martin, I hate to admit it, but I'm worried." I tried to stay as calm as I could. "I'm *very* concerned."

He told me to call back if the girls weren't home soon. He'd put out the word as soon as he could—officially, twenty-four hours after they were last seen. He consoled me that the girls would probably be home with stories to tell about Trick or Treating in every subdivision on the peninsula.

As I told Valerie what he said, I absentmindedly fiddled with the Caller ID button on the cordless phone. Val did her best to remain calm. Jett's lies were a protection for herself. She was not a danger to our girls. She *loved* them. Jett had lied for no other reason than to give herself a better chance at being judged for who she was now. She didn't know we had uncovered something from her past; she was entitled to keep it secret. She had been treated, and by God, she was well now. I fibbed to myself again and again.

"It just makes me wonder if she could have lied about other things as well," Val said.

"I know—" I stopped talking. A name popped up on the Caller ID and it sent a chill down my spine.

"MPLWD INST" stared at me like the dead eyes of a snake. It took me a second to decipher it, like some goofy vanity plate that made no sense to anyone but the vehicle's driver.

Dear God, I had called from Maplewood.

I turned to my wife.

"Val, I think Jett knows what we know."

Chapter Forty-two
Later Thursday, October 31

I HAD NEVER THOUGHT I WOULD BE one of those people on television pleading with the public for information about his missing child or children. I had told my girls from day one the rules of safety when it came to strangers. Our favorite show from the time they could watch TV from behind a baby bottle was *America's Most Wanted*. My mother thought her grandchildren had no business watching that "trash." But I disagreed. I saw no harm in letting my daughters know that there were dangers in the world. *Real danger.* I told Hayley and Taylor that most of the mysteries involving missing kids would never have happened if their parents taught their children to stay away from neighborhood weirdoes.

"We'll have no milk carton kids in this family," I had often remarked.

I had even gone to the elementary school and talked about safety. I was the goddamn Block Watch captain for our neighborhood. And yet, I had screwed up. I had screwed up bigtime. I had let my guard down and my girls were gone in the night.

I could not wait for Raines and the county sheriff's office to help me. I could not wait for anyone. It had been six hours, maybe more, since Taylor and Hayley went off Trick or Treating with Jett Carter. Val stayed home to be near the phone and I drove the LUV to Timberlake. I had not slept; I had not even tried. My eyes were drawn apart like slits, like off-brand Kmart mini blinds jammed open forever. Vomit had burned my throat and my stomach heaved as if something more could come up. I knew there was nothing left inside of me. I was empty. I had never felt emptier in my entire life.

I drove as fast as I could. I didn't care if I got another ticket. I almost hoped a cop would pull me over. I needed help. I needed a police escort. My girls were gone.

I punched the buttons on the radio desperately seeking a news account of our plight. But there was none. Radio, usually the first to jump on an abduction case because the medium needed no visuals, had been cool. One reporter, a supposed friend I had called for help, had the cruel audacity to ask if my story was a publicity stunt for a book I was working on. I wished I were that clever.

"Tell me the truth. I'll still play with you on it, but I gotta know."

If the interview had been face-to-face rather than over the phone, I would be fleeing from a murder scene instead of searching for my missing daughters.

I turned down the street to Jett's apartment and parked in the back. I carried a flashlight and a screwdriver from my glove box. It flashed through my mind that Ted Bundy had kept the same tools in his famous VW. If I couldn't get inside with a screwdriver shoved into the doorjamb, I planned on breaking a window. A Pierce County Sheriff's business card fluttered from the door frame and fell into the remains of a smashed pumpkin.

MARTIN RAINES, CHIEF INVESTIGATOR

Marty had been over to see Jett, but she hadn't been home. Or, she hadn't answered the door.

I turned the knob to the right and then left. It was locked. I stuck the flathead screwdriver into the thin space between the doorknob and the jamb and pushed. Harder. I twisted it. I could feel the wood crunch. I pried again. The knob became loose, but still I couldn't push it open. Another twist and I slammed my shoulder against it. The door creaked open and I slowly went inside. I could sense that I was alone, but the empty room still made me jumpy.

A floor lamp was switched on, bouncing light off the mostly empty room. My heart rate increased when I saw two bulging pillowcases on the floor. One was a mint green case with purple irises on it; the other was a faded scene from one of the *Shrek* movies. The last time I had seen them was at home, on my daughter's beds, with their sleeping faces pressed against them.

I bent over and looked inside each one.

Halloween candy.

"Hayley? Taylor?" I called as I walked to the apartment's only bedroom. I had never been more awake in my life. I didn't need any more light. I was a cat. I could see everything in the hall, everything in the room.

"It's Dad. Girls? Are you here?"

There was no sound, just the buzz of a radio not tuned in adequately. I saw a row of my books on the bed stand. A young woman's clothes were scattered from the bathroom to the bed; newspaper accounts of the Parker murder had been clipped and arranged on the pillow. It was a *display*. A vignette, I knew, meant for my eyes. The pace of my heartbeat quickened again as I moved around the small room, but I saw nothing more of my children. I held one of the pillow cases to my face and nose and breathed in the smell of my babies. I knew the smell of their hair, their breath, the sweet scent of my children.

Where were they?

My eyes frantically scanned the front room. There was no television, no table. The sole piece of furniture was a futon, its fabric a black and white Holstein cow print. Against the white and black were bright orange and fuchsia rectangles. The light played off the pieces and drew my eyes closer. Like a crow straining for a shiny bit of foil, I bent down. It was the Fantastic Plastic. I remembered how Jett had brought it over in her "kid's kit" to entertain the girls before dinner. They had made barrettes out of the shiny, malleable material. I had even been coaxed into playing with the stuff myself.

The fingerprints that had turned up in reverse on the Shantung Rag paper sample had been pulled off the Fantastic Plastic.

The reception on my cell too faint to make a call, I went to the kitchen telephone and punched in the numbers for our home. I had to talk to Valerie. I had not been to church since I was confirmed in high school, but I prayed to God right then like a television evangelist. Out loud I called for God to help me put my family back together.

The kitchen counter was immaculate in its neatness. It was the kitchen of a fastidious person; or a person who seldom cooked at home. A badly chipped almond-colored sink was devoid of all, but a few dirty dishes. Each dish was a black plastic divided dish. I had recognized them as microwavable TV dinner trays. Jett had never learned to cook. She had her meals at Maplewood for half of her young life. A pair of scissors, some butchered magazines, and a sheaf of familiar gray envelopes caught my eye.

And raised my pulse another notch.

A 1980s Laurel Burch cat purse on the floor also resonated in some strange way. I'd seen it before, but not with Jett.

Valerie answered my call on the third ring.

"They were here, Val. I found their candy bags."

My wife didn't say anything. I heard her cry, "I know. I know."

"I know, honey. I know," I answered back.

"Kevin, they're here. All—"

She was cut off. I called Val's name over and over. In a moment I heard a familiar voice on the line. It was Jett Carter soundly oddly robotic, cold. "Yes, we're here. We're all here. You should have left well enough alone. No police. Don't talk to Martin Raines."

The line went silent for a few seconds.

335

"Jett? Why?"

"I'll tell you. Meet us on the Narrows Bridge at midnight. Mid-span. Park TRUCRYM on the east side and walk across."

I wondered why the bridge, but I didn't ask her about it. Now, I knew fear. I knew it in a way that had been completely foreign to me. It was *my* fear. Not someone else's.

"Jett, I'll come now. I'll come right now. Please, are my girls... is Val all right?"

There was a deliberate pause.

"No, don't come here," she said. "We won't be here. So don't bother. Listen carefully, Kevin. I'm in charge now. Everyone is fine. You should worry about yourself. Think about yourself. You're good at that, Kevin. You've always been good at that."

Amidst the muffled cries of my family, the phone went dead. I held my arms around my chest and squeezed. *What was happening? Why in the world was she doing this?*

As I debated whether I'd call the police or handle it on my own, a flash of steel caught my eye. It came from the sink. I moved closer and stretched my neck as if I were a kid looking into a box of snakes.

Among the plastic, divided plates was a Ginsu knife.

It was Hop Sing.

It had not been Valerie who killed anyone. God, I had been so dimwitted to even think it. It had not been Wanda-Lou; nor Anna Cameron. And God knew it had not been me. It had been Jett. She had been the one who poisoned Mrs. Parker and slashed her with the knife. Things were falling into place. Jett could have taken the knife anytime during one of the first visits to our home. She had found our house through Wanda-Lou. I dismissed the thought that Wanda-Lou had anything to do with it. She was ambitious, but she was not a killer.

Neither was Valerie.

Jett also had access to the Weasel-Die. She might have been the caller who pointed out to that police that I had thrown out the stuff. I had told her I did that. What of the piece of paper, the Shantung Rag, found in Mrs. Parker's hand? I couldn't make sense of that. It was true that she could have taken it from the house, but I never saw the paper. I was still certain that Val had in fact really ordered it. How could the fingerprints be in reverse and the signature "suggest" that it had been written by me?

I pulled myself together and called Martin from Val's commandeered cell phone.

"Any word about the kids?" he asked. His voice was deep, full of concern.

I told him that we had heard nothing. Though I knew what Jett was capable of, I felt that I knew her well enough to believe that she wouldn't harm the girls and Val. I had seen how she played with Hedda. How she had teased the girls like an older sister. How she had talked with Val about going back to school so she could get a better job than the one at Ho! We had been friends. We had taken her into our family. We consoled her after every visit to the prison when she saw her sister and mother. She wouldn't hurt us.

Finally, he answered. "They'll be fine, I know it. We're working on it."

"I know you are," I said.

I didn't tell him that I had been inside Jett Carter's apartment and I knew more than he did. "Martin, I've got to see that slip of paper. That Shantung Rag. Can you meet me at the Justice Center in five?"

"Where are you?" he asked.

"I'm here in Timberlake, but I have to leave right away. I've got to get home to be with Val by midnight. I promised."

Chapter Forty-three
Even Later, Thursday, October 31

THE JUSTICE CENTER WAS NOT AS UGLY IN THE LIGHT of the moon and street lamps as it was during the day. I had not been there since my arrest and the place did not hold fond memories for me. I waited in my truck until I saw Raines walk toward the front door. I called to him to wait and the two of us went inside together. He flashed his ID to the officer in the property room and introduced me as a "fiber expert" from out of town. He signed in his name and the night property clerk unlocked the evidence vault and returned with an envelope.

"We'll need to see it on the table."

The night cop nodded and pushed a release mechanism for the bottom half of the Dutch door that separated the outside world from the exhibits and evidence that would be used in court. It was a poor, insecure system, but I did not take the opportunity to criticize it. I looked at my watch; twenty minutes had passed since Jett had given her instructions. Part of me wanted to tell Marty, but I couldn't risk it. I couldn't risk my family.

We walked over to an ancient light table.

"Was used at the local newspaper during its cold type days," Raines said of the glass-topped oak relic.

The manila envelope marked with the case number assigned to Mrs. Parker's murder was opened. A pair of tweezers was used to pull the paper from its holder. It appeared blank. It was in the shape of a goose egg, about the same size.

Raines flipped it over. I saw the writing as clear as could be. It was *Kevin Ryan*. On top was the word *Ishes*.

The night cop lingered for a moment, so Raines spoke.

"The name is clear, an exact spelling and a modified approximation of Mr. Ryan's signature. We're not sure about the meaning of the source of the word on top."

"The man wrote that, too," I said. Without moving his head, Martin Raines turned his eyes to mine. "*Ishes* is part of *Best Wishes*," I added.

The Shantung Rag had been a piece of scrap paper on which Wanda-Lou and I had practiced signing our names on during the weeks she stayed with us. She had told me that my scrawl was not authorly enough. I needed to work on it. So, we played around on paper that Valerie had in a pile next to her graphic arts supplies.

"Can we call Wanda-Lou Webster from your office?" I asked. "I know it's late, but I think we'd better talk to her."

"Wanda-Lou Webster, the famous author?"

I cringed at his quick observation. "That's the one."

"April loved her book," he added.

♦

THE PHONE RANG SIX TIMES when Wanda-Lou's machine finally kicked in.

"*Hi, I'm either writing another blockbuster book or giving a seminar. Be sure to watch Maury on the fifteenth. I'll be on the panel. Leave a message and be sure to leave your address to get on my newsletter mailing list....*"

"Wanda-Lou, it's Kevin Ryan. Are you there? Pick up, dammit."

A groggy Wanda-Lou got on the phone. "Kevin, it's late...got a seminar to give in Las Vegas tomorrow evening...what is it?"

"Wanda-Lou, you know Jett Carter? The gal you sent out to my house? The big fan?"

Wanda-Lou hacked into the phone. She needed to quit smoking while she still had lung function.

"Are you still mad at me for that?" she asked.

I told her I wasn't, though she was another in the long line I would like to kill.

"Did you give her anything other than my address?"

"Don't think so."

"Think! Think again!"

Wanda-Lou took her time. So many seconds passed I was afraid she had fallen back to sleep.

"Well?"

"I gave her the address...."

"How did you give it to her?"

"I wrote it on that card we were messing with when we did our signatures. God, Kevin, who would have thought that my signature would be more important than yours?"

I hated that woman.

"Bye, Wanda-Lou."

I hung up. Jett Carter had planned it all from the beginning. She had gone after me and my family. She had done so for a reason. I just didn't know what it was.

"Martin, this whole thing with Mrs. Parker's murder was a total setup, everything from Hop Sing to Shantung Rag."

Raines stared at me as I turned to leave. His look of confusion was overwhelming.

"Who in the hell is Hop Sing?" he called out.

I disappeared into the hallway. My heart pounded harder with each step. Each beat was a terrible and unnecessary reminder: I had a date on a bridge.

Chapter Forty-four
Early Morning, Friday, November 1

THE TACOMA NARROWS BRIDGE knew no time of day when cars ceased crossing its mile-long span. But at midnight, that Friday night after Halloween, it was quiet. A bread truck lumbered across and a spotty stream of moviegoers drove home to the peninsula. The bar crowd would drive across at two. And during the week, the commuter traffic would pick up as early as four a.m. for the men and women who worked at Boeing plants in south King County.

I saw Val's tuna-can car and my heart sank lower as I pulled into the little park that commemorated the day when high winds rocked and rolled the first bridge into Puget Sound's treacherous Tacoma Narrows. A used condom stuck to my shoe and I scraped it off on the curb. For a second, my mind was diverted from the troubles that I was about to face.

I was terrified of heights. I could barely stand on a ladder without breaking out in a sweat. When Cecile and Gina invited Taylor and Hayley to walk across the bridge that summer, I had been horrified. I couldn't stand *driving* across it. I could not imagine *walking* across it.

Each vehicle gave the bridge a little bounce, an unnerving vibration that reminded me that I was one thousand feet above the chasm between the mainland and the peninsula. Water rushed below faster than anywhere in the world. Pity the boater without enough power to get out of its tremendous pull. Nobody went near the Narrows without an understanding of currents and the tides. At least, as far as I knew, nobody with half a brain ever did. The wind howled and flashing yellow lights warned motorists of excessive winds. An orange wind sock, full and erect, pointed to the north. I held onto the handrail. I looked only in front of me; never at my feet.

I saw them at mid-span. Four figures huddled against the rail. I knew who they were, of course, but if I had been a driver passing by I would have thought they were tourists with a bad sense of timing. The view from the bridge was more beautiful during the day, though nighttime lights off the bay and along the shore were charming. Tonight it only seemed sinister. No one called to me, though I was certain Valerie had turned her head to watch me approach. No one said a word. When I moved closer, I could see why.

Jett had taped my wife and daughters' mouths with wide patches of silvery duct tape. The glossy tape wrapped the circumference of their heads, like permanent hair bands hidden in the back of the hair. I could see the terror in their eyes. All had been crying. The salty residue of tears had dried in telling streaks on their faces. I could also see a knife in Jett's right hand.

She stood in front, the three members of my family in a row behind her. "You're right on time," she said.

I was nearly out of breath from the walk. I stood a few feet from her and I told myself to remain calm. *Being calm will make this turn out all right.* Steady. Calm. Steady. "What's going on? Jett, why are you doing this?"

She didn't respond at first. And she didn't speak to me. Instead, she turned away, and told Taylor and Hayley to stand next to their mother and hold onto the rail facing off the bridge.

"Don't move until I say so." Her words were sharp. Cold. Like a piece of steel stored in a freezer. "You too, Valerie!"

Jett stepped closer. She had a kind of bitter look that I would never have thought her capable. I had always believed, I had always told everyone, that Jett Carter was the rare success story. She had been through hell because of her upbringing, yet she had turned out normal. As I stood there, I revised the assessment.

"You don't care who your books hurt, do you? All you care about is your next advance, your next movie deal."

"I always care about the people I write about."

"Yeah, right. What you care about is that your next book is bigger than anyone else's. That's the bottom line."

I tried to remain calm. I reminded her that I hadn't even written *Love You to Death* yet.

"How can you judge it when it hasn't been written? Jett, you were a victim of the crimes of your sister and mother. You didn't have a hand in them. I would never hurt you."

She pulled the knife out in the open and flashed it down by her thigh. She wanted me to see it again. Not anyone else. Not the passing cars.

"I'm not talking about my mom's story. I'm talking about Austin's story."

I looked at her blankly. I didn't know who she was talking about. I hoped for a second that this had been some bad misunderstanding. She had the wrong true crime author. Maybe she wanted Ross or the other Ryan?

"Who's Austin?" I asked.

Jett looked to the sky and shook her head in exasperation. "It figures that you don't know. Some great researcher you are. What did you tell me? You might write like a hack but you research like a fiend? Something like that, right, Kevin? For your pathetic information, Austin was Melinda Moser's son. He's my boyfriend. At least he *was* my boyfriend."

Melinda Moser was the woman whose murder I had written about in *Murder Cruise*. I vaguely knew she had a son. He'd gone to the luau with his father and his murderous paramour that night they killed Melinda. But he was an infant, then, or so I recalled. Surely he wouldn't be more than twelve by now? I barely mentioned him in *Murder Cruise*.

Jett spat her words at me. "You made her sound like some kind of slut."

"I hadn't meant to do that," I said, inching slightly closer. I could see my wife and daughters shivering in the bitter combination of cold air and fear. I wanted to run to them and hug them, hold them against the wind and the terror from our supposed friend. I wanted to scoop them up to safety.

Jett was shuddering, too. She told me that she had met Austin at Maplewood when she lent him some of her books.

"He loved me. He loved me for *me*. When you wrote that book and said those nasty things about his mother...." Jett started to cry, though she didn't give up her tears easily. I knew she had fought those same tears all her life. She had told me she was strong. Stronger than her mother and sister. Strong as anyone could be. I knew then that it was a lie. She was still a little girl. She held the knife up higher.

"I didn't mean to hurt him," I said in my most soothing voice. "Jett, I'm so sorry."

She stared at me, then down at the water for a moment. She looked as young as ever. She was thin, pale and forlorn. She was a wasted life. She had come to the end of her rope and it had been my fault. Jett Carter was going to take no prisoners that night.

"Austin and I planned on teaching you a lesson, until it happened." She was fighting. She was trying to hold it in, but her tears came down in a torrent. She waved the knife around, her hand wavering like the wind sock atop the bridge.

I pleaded with her to tell me more. I hadn't a clue about what she was talking about. She seemed distant, oddly out of sync with the moment.

"Until what?" I asked. "Until what happened, Jett?"

She stiffened and stared hard at me. It was the first time in several minutes that I felt us connect. For a second, hope returned. I thought we'd be able to talk this out.

344

"Until you made him kill himself," she finally answered. "Think about it, Kevin. Think about writing some of those ugly things that you do and then going on television and telling the world trash about someone's mother. Melinda was Austin's mother. She was not a saint, but she wasn't trailer trash either."

I reached a hand out in compassion. "You're wrong. You need help," I said softly. "Let me help you."

The wild, tormented look returned to her brown peach pit eyes and she spun around and pressed the knife against Hayley's slender, pale throat. I heard a muffled scream from Valerie and I watched Hayley stiffen as she tried to pull her neck away. She couldn't move far enough. The bridge rail held her captive.

The knife glinted in the cold, faint light of the November night.

"You have been through so much," I said. "Let my girls, let Val go, please. It doesn't have to be this way. You don't have to end up like your mother and your sister. Think about it. Think about where they are and why they are there right now." I was begging Jett, but she was unresponsive. I implored. I urged. "Think of them."

"I hate them...." Her eyes met mine as she spoke.

I thought I saw a tear in her eyes. *Was it the cold air? Was it emotion?* If she were feeling something, it would be a start. It would mean that she could be reached.

"I know that's not true, Jett."

"You don't know anything. My mother sent me away after she made me—" She stopped and twisted the knife.

My adrenalin surged. I was so afraid for my daughter that I nearly panicked. *What to do?* If I jumped at her, Jett might drive the knife into Hayley's throat.

Jett hated me. I could see it in her eyes. She had the look of a person who had not one iota of time for me. I started talking. "Made you what?"

345

"It doesn't matter. You don't care. All you want is book material. Isn't that right, Val?" She turned to Val and studied her terrified eyes. "Isn't that what you told me? Let's see. Your exact words were something like, 'Kevin sees tragedy and murder the way others see new stock offerings.'"

Val made another muffled cry and shook her head. Her eyes were terror. But I knew that Jett was repeating her words with absolute accuracy. It was true that sometimes I had viewed the world that way.

"What did your mother make you do?" I asked.

"Do you see a TV movie here, Kevin? Do you see dollar signs again?"

I shook my head. "Please, tell me, Jett, what did your mother make you do?"

A tear fell from her eye. Then another. "My mother got my dad drunk the night he died...my mother made me go out on the bridge."

For an instant, sympathy mixed with fear. I knew what she as going to say. The other figure that the witness had seen that night in Timberlake *was* Jett's mother. A car was running. The exhaust sending a soft plume of white into the air. It was Connie, who had set up her husband. Jett had been used as a tool.

"I'm so sorry. You were so young, you were so abused." My words were meant to calm her, to win her over, though the effect was the opposite. "It wasn't your fault."

She wiped her eyes on her coat sleeve. The Jett who had planned to kill me was back. She had pulled herself together. She would not falter. I could see that she had been fighting for control. And if I had hoped that her confession would ease her mind, soften her heart, I was wrong.

"I want you to climb to the top of that tower, Kevin," she said. "You're gonna jump. You're sorry about your career. You're sorry that your shitty books aren't Number One."

346

I looked at the tower. A thin cable ladder dangled from the top. It seemed miles above us. It seemed to connect with the moon.

"But I can't," I said.

Jett moved the knife. It was a flickering motion, like an annoyed picnicker ridding herself of a fly. Hayley made an unintelligible cry and tried to move away. But there was nowhere to go. A smear of blood ran down the length of the blade and oozed along the edge of her green, now sliced, pickle leotard. Valerie screamed a muffled wail from behind her taped gag. Hayley's eyes were broken glass. Taylor's fingers were pink and white against the green railing; her eyes were glued to her sister and the bloody knife. Fear had contorted her face. It was the face of sheer terror.

"If I do, will you let them go?" I pleaded.

"Maybe. Maybe not."

I looked at my girls, my wife, trapped on the bridge with a young woman who I had befriended because I needed her help. I had used Jett, too. I had done so to make my story better, *easier* to write. I had invited a monster into our lives so that I could be Number One. I hated myself. It was that hate that propelled me up the first rung, then the second and third. I stopped and looked out at the water at a tugboat towing a log boom chugged in from the south, its yellow lights eyeing me like a cat in a wood pile. I wondered if I jumped—if she told me to jump—I wondered if I'd survive. Only a very few ever made the leap and lived. My face pressed against the inch-thick cable and my knuckles were frozen.

I heard a noise and dared to look.

Chapter Forty-five
Early Morning, Friday, November 1

A logging truck rolled onto the bridge, moving eastbound from the peninsula. Its silky-beamed headlights stretched the entire length of the span. I could see the truck was loaded with a full haul of Douglas fir logs, barreling down the right hand lane. Its weight vibrated the grilled surface and its weight-borne noise cut through the stillness of the night air.

"Hurry up," Jett yelled. "I've got places to go, things to do!"

"You won't hurt my family? You won't hurt them?"

"If you do what I say, I will let them go. If you don't, Val will watch me throw her precious twins over the side. Mrs. Parker wasn't the first time I've killed someone."

"What?"

"That idiot fan of yours, Jeanne Morgan. I poisoned her, too. No stroke there. Stupid medical examiner. I got all the information I could out of the cow."

I remembered the cat purse at Jett's. It was Jeanne's. She had five freaking cats!

"Now move it!" Jett screamed.

I was slow because I was scared. I could have used another pair of hands to pry my own off the cable.

"The truck's lost its steering!" I called out. In the instant Jett turned to look, I jumped down on top of her and she screamed. Val lunged for the young woman and kicked her in the back of the legs, knocking her down. As I tried for the knife, Jett sliced through my coat. I felt a sharp pinch, then the warmth of my own blood, wet against my skin. Val and I were in a frenzy. Jett was screaming at us and Taylor and Hayley were trying to break free from their silvery bondage.

Jett got back on her feet somehow and I lurched up higher on her, balancing our torsos against the iced railing. She leaned backwards, her butt on the rail. Again I reached, holding my body against hers for leverage. *I wanted that goddamn knife!* The water rushed through the channel. In a second, our eyes met. Hers were no longer the sweet innocence of youth, but a dark, empty stare. I could see her slipping backwards over the edge of the rail.

I hated that bridge. I would never take it again. I would ride the ferry or I would stay on the peninsula for the rest of my life.

"Jett, grab my hand," I said. The knife fell from her fingers, and I watched it disappear into the black below. Val, her hands now fully free, pushed me out of the way.

"Don't! Don't help her, Kev. We'll never be rid of her...She'll never go away and leave us alone."

Her words startled me. The tape was gone from her mouth. I stared. Val had never said a harsh word about anyone in the nearly twenty years that I had known and loved her. Never had she been pushed so far. Never had her children been threatened. My wife's eyes were cold. She pulled me away from the rail, away from the young woman who had been a friend the day before.

I stepped back.

"Fuck you!" Jett screamed. "Fuck all of you!"

I surged forward and pushed.

Then she was gone. It took almost ten seconds, though it seemed longer, before we heard her splash into the inky waters of the Narrows. Ten seconds and she was gone. Val and I went for our girls. They looked so tiny, so fragile. Neither cried; neither said much as we undid the tape and walked off the bridge. We were fine. We were going to be all right.

All of us.

349

No one said a word about Jett's fate. No one lamented her loss, least of all me. Serial killers, be dammed. I had finally met someone I didn't like. It was the girl who knocked on my door with a story that I was certain would bring me everything I had ever wanted. It almost took everything I had.

◆

TWO DAYS LATER life in PORT GAMBLE was normal again. At least everyone in the Ryan household pretended it was. When a body washed up on a beachfront neighborhood in West Seattle, I hoped it was Jett's and it would be ruled a suicide—like her father's had been so many years ago. I never said a word about that night. Not even to Martin Raines. And though, a week after it happened, the paper identified the victim as a transient from Tacoma, I still said nothing.

I was sure Jett Carter was dead, fish bait for the octopus that lived among the wreckage of Galloping Gertie, the first Narrows Bridge.

No one needed to know that my family had been out on the bridge the night Jett met her maker. Every family has its own little secret.

The Ryans would always have theirs.

◆

MY MESSAGE LIGHT WAS TWINKLING when I came inside to warm up from a frosty November morning raking up a bronze mountain of maple leaves. They had fallen in a heavy, wet heap from a neighbor's tree onto my driveway. *Die, tree, die*, I thought as I came in from the cold. My back ached and I cursed the fact that I had blisters on my fingers. Each stroke of my keyboard would smart. I slid into my chair and pushed the play button.

It was Raines's voice.

Kevin, Jett Carter was a wacko; a psycho! Goofier than her mother and her sister, if you can believe that. She was involved with a nut job at Maplewood who blamed one of your books for besmirching his mother's name. He told everybody that Melinda

350

Moser from Murder Cruise *was his mother. Funny thing, his real mother... let's see, her name is... Suzetta Jarvis... doesn't blame you for anything. You never wrote a word about her. She loves your books, by the way. Read every one of them. Her favorite was that one you wrote about the bank robber that fell in love with the teller and went cross country robbing banks. Sounds great. Get me the title on it. April wants to read it, too. Hey, how's* Love You to Death *coming along? Some gal from Hollywood called. Name's Monica Maleng. Wants the rights to my story. Doesn't that beat all? Call me.*

Unbelievable. I almost laughed out loud. Jett had been used. I had been set up. Everyone had screwed up. Up. Up. Up. What goes around, as they say, truly does come around. The worst of it was that I hadn't written a book about a bank robber in my life. Raines was referring to *The Cash Romance*...written by the *other* true crime writer with the Ryan surname. Jett's boyfriend had been a bigger nutcase than his girlfriend.

I organized the sheaf of papers that made up the book I had been writing. I was moving on. I didn't care one bit about Monica or *Love You to Death*. I'd given up the story.

I had an even better one to tell.

"Val," I said as I dumped the chapters for *Love You to Death: The Positively Shocking True Story of Murder, Obsession and a Wedding in Vegas* into a file-box tomb, "our ship's about to come in. This is the ticket, honey. I *feel* it. I really do. If this one doesn't work, swear to God, I'm giving this up."

I feel it.

Behind my back were crossed fingers and a half-melted blue Mr. Freeze, retrieved from behind a bag of year-old taquitos. I sat behind my computer screen and started to type.

Valerie put her hand on my shoulder and I stopped.

"Not now," she said. "I want you to look at this instead."

She retrieved her drugstore reading glasses, put them on, then handed me a copy of the classified ads.

351

"What's this?" I asked, knowing full well that she was putting me on hiatus.

"I circled some possibilities for you," she said, pointing to a page covered with red circles. "Let's give the writing thing a rest, all right?"

EPILOGUE

I LASTED AT THE HARDWARE STORE JOB until I could take it no more, until Valerie knew that whether or not I made it as a best-selling author, I was a better person at writing than I was at selling garden supplies. And so I wrote. Every word was true. Except the ending, of course. I left out the part about the little push, of course.

When my ship came in it was more of a dinghy than a yacht, but at least it did make it to port. Eight months after the Halloween that Jett Carter came to our home in Port Gamble, Trick or Treating with a Ginsu knife, *Shocking True Story* was completed for Toe Tag Books. *Shocking* was a slightly fictionalized "account of a true crime that brought unspeakable evil to a true crime writer's front door" (the back cover copywriter's words, not mine). Advance word was strong. The best of my career. It appears that Toe Tag is behind the book for once.

Just maybe I'll make someone's best-seller list this time.

With the advance dollars from *Shocking True Story*, Valerie finally had her lovely light brown hair highlighted with blonde and we had our sofa recovered with a charmingly bland fabric (stain-guarded, of course). Best of all, Val got a new car; one with air conditioning and cruise control. The girls got braces and a new cat.

When it came to hope for Big Money, I remained full of unbridled optimism. When my agent telephoned one afternoon to announce MTM Enterprises wanted to make a TV film offer for the rights to *Shocking True Story*, I could hardly contain my enthusiasm.

According to the agent, enthusiasm was definitely in order.

"We're talking Mary Tyler Fucking Moore's company," she said.

I flashed to Mary in the WJM newsroom, to Rhoda, to the whole gang. All of a sudden Joan Jett's guitar-fueled remake of

353

the sitcom's theme music percolated through my head, but the words were new.

Who can turn the world on with his books?

Who can take a nothing case, and suddenly make it all seem worthwhile?

It's you, man, and you should know it...

Crime is all around, don't need to waste it

You can have the List,

Why don't you take it?

You're gonna make it after all...

Things were looking up for everyone in the Ryan household. Taylor and Hayley finished sixth grade at the top of their classes and with a new best friend to fight over. It turned out that Renny Ann Quinn had stopped picking her nose over the summer and turned out to be surprisingly cool.

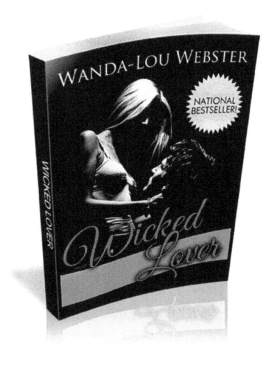

♦

OH, AND WANDA-LOU WEBSTER... as if I had somehow had a hand in creating a literary monster, kept reeling in the big bucks and calling me every now and then to thank me. *Thank me?* I could see right through her. She was only rubbing it in. When she switched genres to romance, I rejoiced. I was certain that Wanda-Lou who had no idea what romance was, would flop in the field. I was wrong, of course. Her first effort hit Number One. Wanda-Lou dedicated *Wicked Lover* to the "Ryan family for the love and support they showed during my darkest hour."

I also understood the concept of someone rubbing salt into a wound. Nobody did it better than Wanda-Lou.

After it was all over, the players in *Love You to Death* fell into three categories: dead, missing or stagnant.

Connie Carter and I traded Christmas cards and talked on the phone a few times. She had told me she had no idea Jett had been such a bad girl. *Really?* A killer, a veritable maniac, was more like it. Connie blamed the folks at Maplewood. I wondered why it was that she couldn't grasp the reality that she had played a role in sending her daughter on the downward spin that landed her in the institution in the first place. After all, she forced her kid to push her father off a bridge.

Connie remains at Riverstone with more than a decade left on her sentence. By the time of our last conversation, she had taken a lover, a black woman named Deelite. Apparently, she wasn't too old to "go lesbian." Her days are spent berating her daughter and washing dishes in the cafeteria. All of her appeals have been exhausted. When she called after New Year's to see if I could come see her, I told her I'd try as soon as I can. But there was no need to rush.

I have until 2023.

Janet Lee Kerr Cameron, of course, still resides in a prison cell, where she is expected to remain until she is fifty. Though she plans another appeal, she is without an attorney. She ballooned to almost two hundred pounds after she lost her zipper post. She took a new position with the grounds crew, but after she got caught having sexual relations with another inmate behind a beauty bark pile, she was sent to the Hole. She and Deke have petitioned the state for a trailer visit, but as of this writing, it had not been approved.

Deke Cameron still sets off metal detectors, as he most certainly will for the rest of his life. Pierce County Courthouse security guards have nicknamed him Leadbelly. Deke says he still loves his wife and will wait for her—even if the wait is a quarter of a century. He had her name tattooed on his chest under *Love Hurts*. The tattoo artist had a hard time doing Janet's name—it was not easy to tattoo a fleshy gunshot scar.

Others tainted by the *Love You to Death* saga have not fared as well.

Paul Kerr finally went under the knife and had an unsuccessful operation to have a ping pong ball inserted into his scrotum. His body rejected the foreign object and gangrene set in. Most of what he had in the first place was saved. He and his wife Liz separated when he went on a major drinking binge; Lindy, now in elementary school, is in foster care. The foster family has offered to adopt the girl, but Janet will not give her consent.

"She's mine," she told me the last time I saw her. "That's my baby they're trying to take away from me! What kind of mother would give up her baby?"

"Your baby will be thirty when you get out," I reminded her. "Maybe by letting her go, you'll be giving her more than if you kept her?"

Janet didn't agree. Deke had fixed up an old swing set he bought at a yard sale for Lindy. He didn't understand that the little girl wouldn't be swinging at his place anytime soon.

Neither one of them still got it.

Sadly, the dumbest of the bunch was the greatest victim. His life ruined over the promise of a Las Vegas wedding, his mother dead because of a disturbed young woman. Danny Parker went from bad to worse to tragic. Danny was killed two days before Christmas in a prison brawl over an extra serving of tater tots. Danny had wanted more than his share, and was too naive or stupid to know that the fellow with the plastic gloves dishing out the potatoes was a lifer in prison on a double murder conviction. Danny reached into the steel tray of the potatoes and grabbed an extra handful. The server swatted him with a spatula and the rest of the debacle made *NBC Nightly News* two nights in a row.

Danny's father Dwight Parker had his final limb amputated—his left arm. His depression over his wife's murder was unabated by a settlement with Weasel-Die, the source of the poison that weakened June Parker to the point of submission to the Ginsu knife-wielding Jett Carter. Now in a Timberlake nursing home that smells of Lysol and lavender sachets, Mr. Parker spends his days looking at the television. He does not understand that his son is dead. He thinks Danny's at summer camp.

Anna Cameron, who had hounded my family for months with hang up calls and threats, pleaded no contest to phone harassment and lost her job with the school district. Last I heard, she was working at the Green Grasshopper café, where she was named waitress of the month on two different occasions (February and March).

And finally, the others. The hangers-on. Those who were not involved in the action of the story, but who nevertheless were a part of it. At least, not in the way I had conceived *Shocking True Story*.

The administrator at Riverstone received an anonymous tip that their top PR person, Muriel Constantine, was selling access to the inmates to the *National Enquirer* and *Inside Edition*. Muriel denied it, but her new BMW was a dead giveaway. No one earning what she supposedly took from her job could afford that kind of a car—and eat, too.

Rita Adams's talk show was dropped by her syndicator when a wave of guest-and-audience-friendly shows swept on American television. After her show's cancellation, Rita ventured into talk radio with an ill-advised personal advice program, *Ask Rita*. It lasted fewer than two months. No one, it seemed, gave a hoot about asking Rita much of anything. The woman who gave me a double dose of my own medicine dropped out of sight for awhile only to resurface when she was tagged for a supporting role in *Where Everyone Knows Your Name—The Cheers Movie*.

Martin Raines is still plugging along in law enforcement at the Pierce County Sheriff's Department. He made sergeant six months after the Parker murder case was closed when it was determined that Jett Carter, in fact, had acted alone. We see each other every three weeks or so and he keeps telling me he's going to work on a book about his experiences. I hate to encourage him or dissuade him.

He'll end up like me or Wanda-Lou. I don't even know which would bother me more.

Hollywood producer Monica Maleng came crawling back after *Shocking True Story* was sold, but I had signed that production deal with Silver Screen.

"Too bad," she told me. "We were talking series at the network. I pitched the idea over lunch at The Ivy...a kind of *Murder, He Wrote* concept, but harder-edged and skewed a bit younger. They loved it enough to bat around the idea of a ten-show commitment. Ten freakin' shows is unheard of."

"Which network?" I asked.

Monica hedged. "Can't say, though it doesn't matter. I've got a deal there and they won't even look at your story without me."

Monica had always been such a good friend. I wished someone would kill her so that I could write a true crime tribute in her honor.

There was nothing to be done about Jeanne Morgan's murder (*Fatal Fan* or *Dedicated to Death*?). I couldn't very well tell the cops to dig up her remains and do a proper tox screen. They'd want to know how I knew. Specifically, they'd want to find the *source* of my information.

So finally, that brings me to Jett Carter herself. In the weeks after she went over the bridge, a few things fell into place. Things that had meant nothing before. A phone call to the new Community Relations specialist at Riverstone confirmed Jett had not visited her sister and mother in prison. She couldn't. Because of her stay—incarceration, really—at Maplewood, she was ineligible for prison visits. Those days when she showed up at our doorstep in Port Gamble, dressed inappropriately for a prison visit, should have been been a clue. The only contact between Jett and Connie and Janet had been over the phone. I remembered one time going to Riverstone for an interview and scanning the pages of the visitor log and not finding her name. I thought nothing of it at the time.

I also recalled how Connie said she was unfamiliar with one of the characters in one of my better books. She, in fact, hadn't read *anything* I had written. Jett had told me that her mom had read my entire list. Yet, it was Jett who had my books heaped at her bedside.

Jett's body was never recovered from the swift waters under the bridge. Never popped to the surface of Puget Sound like a cork, like some suicides do. Never washed ashore. Never caught in the net of a fisherman. Never. *Never found.*

In quiet tones, when we're alone, my family now talks about Jett and that cold night on the bridge, and I suppose we always will. Some things leave marks so indelible that time will never fade them from memory or remove them from the endless queue of discussion. Jett Carter, I am certain, is one of those topics.

Whenever I approach the moon-scraping span of the Narrows Bridge, my knuckles still turn white as blackboard chalk. I try to fight the impulse to clamp on the wheel, but I can't help it. I still keep my eyes focused straight in front of me, never looking to the side at the water below or the boats cutting through the choppy blue of the channel. I am an expert at averting my eyes. I never look at the spot where the young woman went over the green-painted railing, though I sense its presence like a dawdling dread deep in the pit of my stomach. And, always, as I drive

TRUCRYM across, a song runs through my mind like a clunky old, cassette tape player stuck on Play. It's an oldie by Jett Carter's namesake, the tough chick queen of black leather attitude herself.

Ladies and gentlemen, put your hands together for Miss Joan Jett! She doesn't give a damn about her bad reputation.

And that's just how I feel too. In fact, I kind of like it.

Joan Jett - Bad Reputation

(http://youtu.be/5RAQXg0IdfI)

— END —

ENVY

GREGG OLSEN

Chapter 1

WATER GUSHED OUT OF THE CORRODED FAUCET into the chipped, porcelain tub, pooling at the bottom with a few tangled strands of long, brown hair. The water was easily 120 degrees—so hot that Katelyn Berkley could hardly stand to dip her painted green toenails into it. The scalding water instantly turned her pale skin mottled shades of crimson. Perched on the edge of the tub with her right leg dangling in the water, Katelyn smiled. It was a hurt that felt good.

At fifteen, Katelyn knew something about hurt.

Promises had been made...and broken. Things change. People let you down—even those closest to you. Promises, she realized, were very, very hard to keep.

A blast of icy air blew in from her open bedroom window, the silver razor blade next to the half-empty bottle of Tea Tree shampoo glinted, beckoning her. Katelyn fantasized about taking control of the situation—of her pitiful excuse for a life—the only way she could.

She looked in the full-length mirror across the room. The glass was starting to fog as the steam billowed from the tub's rippling surface, but she could see that her eyes were red. There wasn't enough Smashbox on earth to cover the splotches that came with her tears.

"Merry Christmas, loser," she said.

She pulled inside of herself, into that place where there was only a little relief.

The bathtub was nearly full. Steaming. *Just waiting.*

Katelyn had no idea that, not far away, someone else was doing the exact same thing—just waiting for the right time to make a move.

As fresh tears rolled down her cheeks, Katelyn took off the rest of her clothes, threw them on the floor, and plunged herself into the tub

Downstairs, Her mother, Sandra, stood in the kitchen and poked at the congealing remains of a prime rib roast. She yanked at her blue sweater as she pulled it tighter on her shoulders and fumed. She was cold and mad. Mad and cold. She searched her kitchen counters for the espresso maker.

Where is it?

Sandra had a bottle of Bacardi spiced rum at the ready and a small pitcher of eggnog that she wanted to foam. It would be the last time she took a drink for the rest of the year. The promise was a feeble one, like many of Sandra's. There was only a week left until the New Year. All night Sandra had been watching the bottle's amber liquid drop like the thermometer outside the frost-etched window—single paned because the Berkleys' was a historic home and could not be altered.

Last drink. Promise. Where is that machine?

Her parents, Nancy and Paul, had finally left after their holiday visit, and Sandra needed the calming effect of the alcohol. They always dropped a bomb at every social occasion, and the one they had offered up that evening was a doozy, even by their standards. They'd rescinded their promise to fund Katelyn's college expenses, a promise made when their granddaughter was born. That night at dinner, Nancy had let it slip that they were no longer in the position to do so.

"Sandra, my kitchen counters were Corian for goodness sake. I deserved granite. And, well, one thing led to another. A $10,000 remodel, you know, kind of ballooned into that $100,000 new wing. I really do love it. I know you will too."

Katelyn, suddenly in need of better grades, stellar athleticism, or richer parents, had left the table in tears and mouthed to her mother behind her grandmother's back, "I hate her."

"Me too, Katie," Sandra had said.

"What?" Nancy asked.

"Just telling Katelyn I love her too."

Sandra had acted as though everything was fine, the way that moms sometimes do. But inside she seethed. Her husband, Harper, had left just after dinner to check on a faulty freezer at the Timberline restaurant they owned next door.

Every single day, even on Christmas, Harper has to find a reason to go to work.

"Katelyn?" she called up the narrow wooden staircase that led to the second-floor bedrooms. "Have you seen the espresso machine?"

There was no answer.

Sandra returned to her outdated, worn-out kitchen and downed two fingers of spiced rum from a Disneyland shot glass. She screwed on the bottle cap, pretending she hadn't had a drink. After all, it was almost like medicine.

To steady my nerves. Yes, that's it.

Katelyn had been taking the espresso machine upstairs to make Americanos the week before Christmas. Sandra had scolded her for that.

"It isn't sanitary, Katie. We don't bring food upstairs."

Katelyn had rolled her eyes at her mother. "Only a restaurant owner would call milk and sugar, 'food,' Mom."

"That isn't the point."

"Yeah. I get it," Katelyn said, feeling it unnecessary to point out that she'd been forced to have a food worker's permit since she was nine and could recite safe temperatures for meat, poultry, milk, and vegetables in her sleep.

The lights flickered and the breakers in the kitchen popped.

Another reason to hate this old house, even if it does have an extra upstairs bathroom.

Sandra started up the darkened stairs and made her way down the hallway. She could hear the sound of water running in the bathroom.

She called out to Katelyn and knocked on her bedroom door.

No answer.

Sandra twisted the knob and, at once, a wall of icy air blasted her face. Katelyn had left the window open. The lights were out, too. Sandra flipped the switch up and down more times than she needed to, to prove the obvious. The room stayed dark.

Lights from the neighbor's house next door spilled onto the wooden floor.

Sandra gripped the sill and pulled the window closed, shaking her head at her daughter's escalating carelessness. It had to be forty degrees in that room. It would take all night to warm it up. She wondered how any teenager managed to survive to adulthood.

"Katelyn Melissa, you're going to catch a cold!"

Sandra walked past the unmade bed—the one that looked good only on Sundays when she changed the sheets. Katelyn's jeans and black Penney's top—a Marc Jacobs knockoff—were heaped on the floor.

What a colossal mess.

The bathroom door was open a sliver and Sandra, still freezing, pushed it aside. Aromatherapy candles flickered.

"What are you thinking?" she asked, her tone harsh and demanding.

Katelyn wasn't thinking at all.

The fifteen-year-old was slumped over the edge of the old clawfoot tub, her eyes tiny shards of broken glass, her expression void of anything. Her long, wet hair dripped onto the floor.

Instinct took over and Sandra lunged in the direction of her daughter, slipping on the wet floor and falling. As she reached for the rim of the tub, she yelled, "I could have broken my neck! What's going on with you?"

No answer, to a very stupid question.

Sandra, her heart racing and the rum now gnawing at the walls of her stomach, tried to steady herself in the candlelight. She tasted blood. *Her own*. She'd cut her lip when she'd fallen, and several red drops trickled to the floor. She felt tears, fear, and panic as she looked at Katelyn in the faint candlelight. Her *lifeless* daughter. It was so very hard to see with the lights out. Katelyn's dark-brown hair, highlighted by a home kit, hung limp, curling over the edge of the tub. One arm was askew, as if flailing at something unseen.

The other was hidden in the sudsy water.

"Katie. Katie. Katie!" With each repetition of her daughter's name, Sandra's voice grew louder. By the third utterance, it was a scream that probably could be heard all over Port Gamble.

Katelyn Melissa Berkley, just fifteen, was dead.

"It can't be," Sandra said, tears now streaming down her face. She was woozy. Sick. Scared. She wanted to call for Harper, but she knew he was gone. She was alone in the house where the unthinkable had occurred. She slipped again as she pulled at Katelyn's shoulders, white where the cold air had cooled them, pinkish in the still hot bathwater. Two-tone. Like a strawberry dipped in white chocolate.

Katelyn had loved white chocolate. Even though Sandra had insisted it wasn't really chocolate at all.

"Baby, what happened?" Instinctively, Sandra turned off the slowly rising water. "Tell me you're going to be all right!"

At first, Sandra heard dead silence. Then the quiet drip, drip, drip of the tub's leaky faucet. There was no answer to her question. There never could be. Never again.

Sandra shook her daughter violently, a reflex that she hadn't had since Katelyn was a little girl and had lied about something so inconsequential that the terrified mother couldn't retrieve the full memory of what had made her so angry.

As she spun around to go for a phone, Sandra Berkley noticed there was something else in the tub. It was hard to see. It was so dark in that bathroom. Through her thickening veil of tears, she leaned over and scooted the suds away.

The mini espresso machine.

Her eyes followed the electrical cord. Like a cobra that had recoiled in to strike, the plug sat upright, still firmly snug in the wall outlet at the side of the tub.

In small towns like Port Gamble, Washington, news travels fast. 4G fast. Within moments of the reverberating echoes of Sandra Berkley's anguished screams, residents had begun to gather outside the tidy red house with white trim and pineapple shutters. Christmas lights of white, green, and red sparkled in the icy night air. A passerby might have mistaken the gathering for a large group of carolers.

Port Gamble was that kind of place. At least, it tried to be.

An ambulance siren wailed down the highway from Kingston, growing louder with each second.

That the teenager had died was known by everyone. What exactly happened, no one was certain.

Someone in the crowd whispered that Katelyn had fallen in the tub and split her head open. Another suggested that the girl had "issues" of some sort and taken her own life.

"Maybe she offed herself? Kids do that a lot these days. You know, one final grasp for attention."

"I dunno. She didn't seem the type."

368

"Kids are hard to read."

"True enough, but even so, I don't think she was the kind of girl who would hurt herself."

Scenes of sudden tragedy have their macabre pecking order when it comes to who stands where. Closest to the doorway were those who knew and loved the dead girl: her mother, father, a cousin or two. In the next wave were the friends, the church pastor, and a police deputy, who was there to make sure that the scene stayed orderly. Beyond that were casual acquaintances, neighbors, even the occasional lookie loo who was on the scene because it was better than a rerun of one of the various incarnations of *Real Housewives*.

There was a time when Hayley and Taylor Ryan might have been in the grouping closest to the Berkleys' front door. Though they were no longer *that* close, the twins had grown up with Katelyn. As it often seems to be, middle school became the great divider. What had once been a deep bond shared by three girls had been shattered by jealousy and the petty gossip that predictably turns friends into enemies.

What happened among the trio was nothing that couldn't have faded by the end of high school. The girls could have reclaimed the friendship they'd had back in the days when they used to joke about Colton James's stupid sports T-shirts, which he wore every single day in the fifth grade.

"Only a loser would support the Mariners," Katelyn had once said, looking over at Colton as he stood in defiance, his scrawny arms wrapped around his small chest, nodding as if he were defending his team.

But that was then. A million years ago, it seemed. Since then, Port Gamble's youths had grown into pubescent teenagers. Taylor and Hayley, still mirror images of each other, had blonde hair, blue eyes, and the occasional pimple. Colton had traded in sports T-shirts for '80s relic rock bands' insignias and was dating Hayley. And Katelyn was dead.

"When was the last time you actually talked to her?" Hayley asked, already trying to piece together what had happened.

Taylor brushed aside her annoying bangs, which she was growing out, and shook her head.

"Not sure." A puff of white vapor came with Taylor's warm breath. "Last month, I guess."

"Do you think she was depressed? I read somewhere that suicide rates are highest at Christmas."

Taylor shook her head. "Depressed? How should I know?"

"You have a better pulse on the social scene than I do," Hayley said matter-of-factly. "They're saying she killed herself because she was upset about something."

"Was Katelyn still cutting?"

Hayley looked surprised. "You knew about that too?"

"Duh," Taylor said, wishing that she'd brought gloves like her sister had. Taylor's fingertips were numb. "Everyone knew. Dylan, that sophomore with a shaved head and earlobes he's been gouging since Halloween, called her *Cut-lin* last week."

Hayley looked down at the icy pavement and said quietly, "Oh... I was under the impression she had stopped."

Taylor shook her head, then shrugged her shoulders. "I remember her telling people that she liked cutting. Liked how it made her feel in control."

"That doesn't make sense. Cutting made her feel in control of what?"

"She never said."

The crowd contracted to make room for a gurney. Covered from head to toe was the figure of the dead girl. Some people could scarcely bear the sight and they looked away. It felt invasive. Sad. Wrong to even look.

The ambulance, its lights rotating red flashes over the bystanders, pulled away. There was no real urgency in its departure. No sirens. Nothing. Just the quiet slinking away like the tide.

A few moments later, the crowd surged a little as the door opened and Port Gamble Police Chief Annie Garnett's imposing frame loomed in the doorway. She wore a dark wool skirt and jacket, with a knitted scarf around her thick neck. She had long, dark hair that was pulled back. In a voice that cracked a little, Chief Garnett told everyone they should go home.

"Tragedy here tonight," she said, her voice unable to entirely mask her emotions. Annie was a big woman, with baseball-mitt hands, a deep, resonant voice, and a soft spot for troubled young girls. Katelyn's death would be hard on her, especially if it turned out to be a suicide.

Hayley nudged her sister, who started to cry. "We probably should go home, Tay," she said gently.

In that instant, shock had turned to anguish. Hayley's eyes also welled up, and she ignored a text from her boyfriend, Colton, who was out of town and missing the biggest thing to happen in Port Gamble since the devastating bus crash. The twins looked over the crowd to see the faces of their friends and neighbors.

Hayley jammed her hands inside her coat pockets. No Kleenex. She dried her eyes with a soggy gloved fingertip. It could not have been colder just then. The air was ice. She hugged her sister.

"I feel sick," Taylor said.

"Me too," Hayley agreed. Curiosity piercing through their emotions, she added, "I want to know what happened to her and why."

"Why do you think she did it?" Taylor asked.

"Did what?" Hayley argued levelly. "We don't know what happened."

"I'm just saying what they're saying." Taylor indicated those in the outer ring of grief, just beyond their own.

371

"I'd rather know *how*. I mean, really, an espresso machine in the bathtub? That's got to be a first ever."

Taylor nodded, brushing away her tears. She could see the absurdity of it all. "Some snarky blogger is going to say this is proof that coffee isn't good for you."

"And write a headline like 'Port Gamble Girl Meets Bitter End,'" Hayley added.

The spaces in the crowd began to shrink as people pushed forward. All were completely unaware that someone was watching them. *All of them.* Someone in their midst was enjoying the tragic scene that had enveloped Port Gamble as its residents shivered in the frigid air off the bay.

Loving the sad moment to the very last drop.

BETRAYAL

GREGG OLSEN

Chapter 1

Olivia Grant wasn't exactly sure what she'd expected America to be like, but Port Gamble, Washington, most certainly wasn't it. As the sixteen-year-old foreign-exchange student had boarded the late summer flight from London Heathrow to Seattle-Tacoma International Airport and plunked herself down next to a smelly man and his chubby little boy, she daydreamed of palm trees and movie stars. The travel magazine in the seat pocket in front of her all but confirmed the glamour awaiting the redheaded teen in just a few short hours: the cover featured a big splashy photo of beautiful people living in sunny, USA splendor. She was almost giddy, but she held it inside. British reserve, of course.

Olivia immersed herself in American TV the entire way over the polar ice cap to Seattle and wondered if the little boy to her left was going to be a kid contestant on *The Biggest Loser.* His father definitely was destined for some kind of makeover show. He not only smelled vaguely bad—*garlic*—but his mustache hung over his lip like an inverted vacuum cleaner attachment. The stylist who cut his hair had apparently used a saucepan for the template. When he looked over, she simply smiled. Olivia Grant was always very, very polite.

As it had turned out, Port Gamble wasn't sunny Southern California. Not by a long shot. Instead, even in late August when she'd arrived, it was about as soggy and dismal as Dorchester was in the middle of winter. Gray. Wet. Windy. The people who lived there were average teachers, cooks, millworkers, nurses.

So *not* movie stars with golden hair and perfectly straight teeth.

OLIVIA PONDERED THIS WHILE SITTING in the living room of her first American party. Olivia conceded that her first American beer wasn't what she thought it would be either. Brianna Connors, her new best friend, had promised that her dad's favorite craft brew was no big deal, even at 11 percent alcohol content. Tonight at Brianna's Halloween party, Olivia—in full costume—had sucked down the amber liquid like water and at first felt great. Then all of a sudden, somewhere between fending off some geeky, eye-linered, pirate boy's cringe-worthy come-on ("Hey hot wench, you lookin' for a first mate?"), arguing with her host roommate Beth Lee, and trying to cozy up to Jason Deveraux, the hottest guy at Kingston High, a wave of nausea hit her like a mini-tsunami. With the party still in eardrum-splitting full swing, Olivia went upstairs and sought refuge in Brianna's acre-sized bed.

Olivia curled up for an hour, maybe two. If she'd been able to recount it later, it would have been hard to say exactly how long. Time came and went in the way that it does in a dream. Vapors. Mist. She wondered if she'd been drugged. She had only had one beer, two at most. She ran the scenario in her head. It was true that she had felt a little sick that morning. Maybe it was nerves? Maybe it was the onset of the bug that had been going around school? She hadn't really eaten a thing since breakfast. Could it be just the combination of really bad American beer and no food?

Where was Brianna? Olivia thought, feeling sicker by the minute as the room started to spin. *Was the party still going on?* She could hear loud music and some teen slasher DVD blasting from the TV downstairs. The bass from the two competing subwoofers pumped up through the gleaming, dark, walnut floorboards.

Slowly, slowly, and with great effort, Olivia sat up, pulled off the scratchy, sparkly costume, exposing her thin white Calvin Klein slip underneath, and looked at herself in the mirror across the room. Even in the dark and through her late-night drunken haze, she could see her red hair, her flawless pale skin, and her green eyes. Boasting was so tacky, but even then, sick as she was,

376

she thought she looked pretty good. It was ridiculous that she had worn not one, but two silly costumes during the party. Yet it was her first Halloween in America, a country that apparently reveled in the weird, macabre, and cheesy. She wondered why every boy's costume was that of a superhero and every girl was dressed up as a naughty or sexy something.

America, land of the puritan posers.

Slipping Brianna's bedazzled "Lights out!" eye mask on, Olivia wrapped herself in the slippery, satiny duvet—the same one on which she and Brianna had spilled nail polish the previous week when they were ragging on their absent mothers. She felt the circular dry spot that had stiffened the fabric. She picked at the spot with her long, slender fingers. It felt slick and smooth.

It wasn't the last thing she would feel that night.

Where Olivia's SLIP ended and the sheets of Brianna's bed began was impossible to pinpoint in the dark. Olivia tossed, turned, wriggled and, finally, had just started to get comfortable. As she drifted off to sleep, Olivia sensed movement in the far reaches of Brianna's expansive bedroom.

"Hello?" Olivia called out.

No response. Just the sound of a girl screaming on the TV downstairs.

Again, the air moved.

"Who's there?" she asked. Olivia unsuccessfully tried to lift her arms and head from the mummy-like yardage of sheets and the white fabric of her slip that had encircled her limbs and torso like a malevolent wisteria vine. She got one arm free and pulled off the eye mask. Olivia looked over. Silver glinted in the darkness as a shadowy figure moved toward her.

"Who are you?" she asked, still unable to see a face. Olivia was annoyed, but not unnerved. It was, after all, a party. Whoever it was might be looking for a place to crash just like she had when the beer hit her. Or maybe it was a Halloween prank? The living room and family room downstairs were full of kids looking to be the center of attention. Fighting to make an impression. Tweeted about. Facebooked.

"This isn't funny," she said, in her clipped accent.

It wasn't. Not at all.

It happened so fast, the way awful things almost always do. The mattress dipped under the weight of another person kneeling on the bed. The first cut wasn't the deepest. It was tentative, a slight jab through the snow white fabric just above her navel.

"Hey! Stop!" Olivia cried.

Her voice, loud as it was, was lost in the sounds of the music and laughter downstairs. If anyone had heard her muffled scream, they might have mistaken it for that terrified teen with the fake boobs on the enormous plasma TV in the family room where half the partygoers congregated.

Yet there was nothing fake about Olivia Grant or the fear that seized her. Her manicured fingertips found her abdomen. She pressed it lightly with the heel of her palm and cried out in pain. She barely had time to process the fact that her hand was wet.

All too quickly, someone was on top of her, holding her arms down. Everything conspired against her. Her flowing slip, Brianna's bedding, the eye mask, and even her long red hair entwined in her attacker's fist gave her little hope of escape.

Is this a sick joke? Did the geek pirate not understand NO means NO?

Pain shot through the sixteen-year-old's body and she started breathing hard. This was no trick-or-treat prank. Her mind reeled. Olivia thought back to the self-defense moves she had seen on American TV. The key was to have a survival plan, a strategy to save your life. She worked up a scenario to use her knee to shove off her attacker, freeing her arms and scooting to the edge of the bed where she could—just maybe—get away.

But that damn sheet. It was a magician's endless handkerchief. Olivia couldn't move her feet. It was like she'd been spun up in a

378

cocoon. The force of the continued onslaught pushed her, wrappings and all, crashing to the floor.

"Stop it! Stop!" she screamed. "That bloody hurts!"

Despite her beauty, Olivia Grant was no English rose. She was not frail, passive, or genteel. She was a fighter. Finally free, her arms and hands flailed into the darkness. Once, twice, she was hit by something sharp. Hard. It was hot and agonizing. Olivia realized what was happening was not a prank. She was fighting for her life and she knew it.

Was it a knife? Scissors? A box cutter? Something very sharp and deadly.

It passed through the teen's mind right then that she might never get to Hollywood. She'd never have a real boyfriend. She'd never get back to London. She'd never design that dress that every other girl in the world would covet. Her life and all her big dreams would be extinguished right there in her friend's bedroom.

With everything she had, Olivia lurched herself upright. She ran her bloody hands under her slip as she tried to extricate herself from the shroud, once white, now red.

Tears came as she thought of home. Her mind flashed to a memory. She and her mother were packing her suitcases for the trip in Olivia's bedroom back in London. Her mother implored her not to take her finest things to America, as she was all but certain that they'd be stolen.

"Everyone thinks that Aussies are descended from criminals, but I think there's a mix-up there. Take a look at America's crime rate," her mom had said. She sniffed in that superior-than-thou affect she used whenever the occasion called for it, which was always. "The U.S. is worse than Down Under by far."

She had been right. Her mother, with whom she'd battled about the smallest of things, had been absolutely right.

Just as the lightning bolt of memory passed, a pair of hands grabbed Olivia's shoulders and shoved her body backwards against the wooden floor. Hard and complete. So fast and so slow at the same time. She gasped.

I'm not going to die here. Am I?

Olivia filled her lungs and screamed once more—only to have a wad of fabric violently shoved into her mouth. She started to choke, but she refused to give up. She had come to America to snag a boyfriend, be discovered for the rocking talent that she was, and to import everything she had learned back to the UK. She, most assuredly, had not come to America to die.

Get. Off. Me.

The teenager felt hot breath against her face. It came at her in quick puffs and it smelled of beer. *Jason? Kurt? All the boys had been drinking. It could be any one of a dozen or more.* As Olivia tried to roll away from her attacker, the blade of a knife flew at her, burying itself in her throat. It came with speed and fury.

Just like that.

Over.

Out.

In a second, blood soaked the fabric gagging her, slipping over her tongue with a peculiar metallic taste as blood spilled from the corners of her mouth like candle wax.

In the final beats of her life, Olivia Grant caught a glimpse of her killer. Like a camera with a fading battery, her green eyes captured the image until they could no longer see.

Only her killer knew the irony of her last words.

That bloody hurts.

ALSO BY GREGG OLSEN

(Nonfiction)

1. Abandoned Prayers
2. Bitter Almonds
3. Mockingbird
4. Cruel Deception
5. Starvation Heights
6. The Confessions of an American Black Widow
7. Bitch on Wheels
8. If Loving You is Wrong
9. The Deep Dark
10. A Twisted Faith

(Fiction)

1. A Cold Dark Place
2. A Wicked Snow
3. Victim Six
4. The Bone Box
5. Heart of Ice
6. Closer Than Blood
7. Envy
8. Betrayal
9. The Fear Collector

Made in the USA
Monee, IL
30 November 2019